THE
ADVERSARY

THE
ADVERSARY

REECE HIRSCH

THOMAS & MERCER

Published by Thomas & Mercer, Seattle

www.apub.com

"Search And Destroy"
Written by Iggy Pop and James Williamson
©1973 (Renewed) BUG MUSIC (BMI) and EMI MUSIC PUBLISHING LTD.
All Rights for EMI PUBLISHING LTD. in the U.S. and Canada Controlled and Administered by SCREEN GEMS-EMI MUSIC INC.
All Rights Reserved. Used by Permission
Reprinted by Permission of Hal Leonard Corporation

ISBN-13: 9781477849026
ISBN-10: 1477849025
EISBN: 9781477899021

Library of Congress Control Number: 2013911781

Printed in the United States of America

Originally released as a Kindle Serial, August 2013

For Betty, Walt, and Brad

It's . . . clear that we're not as prepared as we should be, as a government or as a country. . . . Just as we failed in the past to invest in our physical infrastructure—our roads, our bridges, and rails—we've failed to invest in the security of our digital infrastructure. . . . We saw this in the disorganized response to [computer virus] Conficker. This status quo is no longer acceptable—not when there's so much at stake.

—President Barack Obama

Lookout, honey, 'cause I'm using technology.

—Iggy and the Stooges, "Search and Destroy"

CHAPTER 1

December 28

It was one of the heaviest air traffic nights of the year. Pete Egan was an hour into his 10:00 p.m. to 6:00 a.m. shift at Albuquerque airport's Terminal Radio Approach Control, known as TRACON. There was a scraggly Christmas tree in the corner straining to hold up a string of lights, but it was hard to make the cavernous air traffic control center look festive.

Jimmy Brindisi took a seat at the radarscope next to Pete, extra large coffee in hand.

"How's that coffee, Jimmy?" Pete asked, providing the traditional setup.

"It keeps me sharp, on the edge, *where I gotta be*," Jimmy said, reciting Al Pacino's line from *Heat*. Ever since Pete noted that his oddly overemphasized cadences resembled latter-period Pacino, Jimmy was always doing Pacino. Now Pete wished he'd never made the remark, but there was no putting that genie back in the bottle.

"You could have brought me one."

"I never bring you one."

"That's what I'm saying."

"You do look like you could use it. You sleeping okay?" It was the sort of question that controllers asked one another, looking for early warning signs of a flameout.

"Like a baby. A big, drunk baby."

In fact, Pete hadn't been sleeping well. He had been having nightmares all week. Or, to put it more accurately, he'd been having The Nightmare, the one that plagued all air traffic controllers, though few/none were willing to admit it. Most people's bad dreams are remarkably standard issue in comparison. Standing naked in front of a crowd of strangers. Taking a test that you haven't studied for. But air traffic controllers are not most people. When they descend into eyelid-twitching sleep, they are greeted by their own custom-fitted nightmare.

Pete was now standing in front of his radarscope, with his headset on. His eyes were locked on the green screen and the white flashing blips that represented passenger planes. His feet shifted slightly to keep the circulation going, but not enough to disturb his unwavering gaze.

When Pete was plugged in at TRACON, everything else receded into the background. In a weird way, this form of intense concentration was almost relaxing, because everything else was purged from his consciousness. When he was juggling planes, he had no available bandwidth to worry about his mortgage, his daughter's medical bills, or workplace politics.

Most airline passengers assume that their fate is in the hands of the occupants of the air traffic control tower that they see rising above the low-slung airport terminals. But the control tower only handles takeoffs, landings, and ground traffic. It is TRACON controllers like Pete who do the real work, from a bunker-like building at the edge of the airport. If a tower controller was a primary care physician, then Pete was a neurosurgeon.

"Two coming in heavy, Pete." It was Darnell Meacham, a controller at the Air Route Traffic Control Center in Phoenix known for his Zen-like calm. "Hotel Sierra Whiskey Two Five Zero and Tango Echo Oscar Nine Eight One."

These were the aircraft call signs for two 757s entering Pete's airspace en route from Phoenix. "Coming in heavy" meant they were big planes that required extra separation as they approached the airport due to the turbulence they trailed in their wake.

"Roger that," Pete said. Then, to the first approaching plane: "You're eight miles from outer marker. Maintain at two thousand feet till localizer."

"Packing a little tight there." It was unusual for Darnell to editorialize. Besides, Pete could see that the separation was perfect for the two new flights, as well as the two ahead of them that were almost ready to begin their descent.

"Looking good from where I'm sitting," Pete said.

Albuquerque International Sunport Airport handles more than five hundred flights per day. Pete took pride in the esoteric skill set that allowed him to bring them in safely. As veteran controllers put it, Pete could dance. For Pete, the radarscope screen was like a three-dimensional chessboard—and he was always at least two moves ahead. A good controller could see the planes converging on an airport and bring those little white blips in like a pearl necklace across the night sky. If weather, pilot error, or equipment failure threw him a curveball, Pete always left himself an out, a window in which he could make those little split-second adjustments and shimmies that a controller must have the ability to make. Because no matter what happened, you could not freeze. You had to keep it moving, keep it fluid.

Darnell's voice crackled over the headset, unusually urgent. "What are you doin' there, Pete?"

"What do you mean?"

"Hotel is nearly on top of Tango."

"No, no, that's not right," Pete said. "I'm good." His radarscope showed a safe distance between the two 757s. "I've got five miles' separation."

"Negative, Pete. I show three miles' separation and closing fast. Real fast."

Pete double-checked his scope, but it still indicated that there was a safe distance between the two planes. If they were as close together as Darnell said, an alarm would have sounded on his equipment. His boss would be tapping him on the shoulder by now like a baseball manager about to pull a shaky relief pitcher. Something was very wrong here, but he couldn't figure out what it was. He had never known Darnell to misread his instruments.

"Darnell, I don't know what's up, but my scope doesn't lie, I mean . . ."

Pete stopped in midsentence. His radarscope had just blinked off for a split-second in what looked like a short circuit. This had never happened before in twenty-five years on the job. Not once.

An instant later, the round green screen blinked on again, and Pete exhaled in momentary relief—until he saw what was now on his scope.

The two white blips, representing massive 757s full of holiday travelers, were on top of one another—he was looking at a midair collision.

There were no windows in TRACON, but in his mind's eye Pete saw the fireball in the sky, heard the explosion, and then the screaming descent as half a million pounds of aluminum alloy and hundreds of passengers plummeted to the desert floor.

Then Pete's radarscope went black, along with all of the other scopes in the control center.

Pete collapsed into his chair, his knees buckling underneath him. Now a cacophony of strident voices was coming through his headset. Darnell and several other controllers were shouting and cursing. At the next station, Jimmy was saying something to him that he couldn't make out.

Pete tore off the headset. He couldn't listen anymore. Without a working radarscope, he was helpless to stop the tragedy unfolding in the dark skies above. His breath was shallow and labored. The pressure in his chest felt like a heart attack.

If this was The Nightmare, Pete would be waking up right about—*now*.

But this was the nightmare that you don't wake up from.

CHAPTER 2

January 4

In Christopher Bruen's line of work, they called his assignment a "knock and talk." And that's all that was supposed to happen. No one was supposed to die.

Bleary from jet lag, Chris gazed out the window of the Mercedes at the green waters of Amsterdam's Prinsengracht canal. His flight from San Francisco had gotten in late the night before and his body clock was so out of whack that he'd barely been able to sleep. The cocktail of cancer drugs that he was taking didn't help matters. At least the morning sun was mercifully pale, smeared across low clouds. The car shot across a bridge and into the brick-paved streets of the Jordaan neighborhood.

Remko de Groot, a relentlessly amiable, relentlessly blond associate at the Amsterdam law firm Kunneman Blenheim, played tour guide as he drove, although Chris wished that he would stop talking.

"The Jordaan has always been a bit funky, with lots of artists and students. Even Rembrandt lived here when his career was

not going so well." Remko glanced over to see how his travel-
ogue was being received. He continued nonetheless.

"The neighborhood is on the upswing now. The great old
houses are getting renovated. Some of them date all the way
back to the sixteenth century."

Chris ran a hand through his shock of unruly black hair as
he watched the buildings blur past the window. He had a long,
pale face, a thin, pointed nose, and heavy-lidded eyes, giving
him the finely calibrated look of something bred for a particular
purpose.

"Are you okay, Chris?" Remko asked, his eyes thankfully on
the road. "You don't look so good."

"Thanks, I'm fine," Chris said. "I just don't travel so well
these days."

Chris was a partner in the San Francisco law firm Reynolds,
Fincher & McComb and an expert in data security law. Before
entering private practice, he had been a chief prosecutor in
the Department of Justice's computer crimes section. While
Chris was at the DOJ, it had been his job to convict hackers. At
Reynolds Fincher, he continued to battle cybercriminals, but
out of the public spotlight and for better pay.

For the past two weeks, Chris had been hunting down the
hacker known as Black Vector, whose real name turned out
to be Pietr Middendorf. Chris always found the pursuit more
interesting than the next step, which was inevitably anticli-
mactic. When he was uncovering the clues to the identity of
a hacker, he was playing to his analytical strengths. When he
reached the end of the trail, Chris inevitably found a misguided
young person, typically male, who reminded him a little too
much of himself when he was that age.

Remko's guided tour of Amsterdam was cut short as they
arrived at their destination, Middendorf's apartment building

at 5 Boomdwarsstraat. It was a nondescript, modern, four-story redbrick structure. Remko found a parking spot a block away so that they could make an inconspicuous approach. Chris didn't think that much stealth was necessary—their target was probably not going to be expecting them.

It was a bitterly cold January morning. Chris tensed like he had been slapped as he climbed out of the car. He unfolded himself to his full height of six foot three, then stretched and yawned on the sidewalk.

They were paying Middendorf a visit because he had stolen the source code of Aspira, the world's most popular computer operating system, which belonged to Chris's client BlueCloud, Inc. The source code for an operating system like Aspira consists of millions of lines of code supporting a host of applications. A sophisticated hacker with access to that code could identify system vulnerabilities that would keep cybercriminals in business for years.

Middendorf had boasted on an online message board that he would publicly post the source code in two days. The hacker thought that he was shielded by the anonymity of his handle and that no one could uncover his true identity. He was wrong.

Chris and Remko walked up the quiet street toward the apartment building. The rising sun wasn't lending any warmth to the day. A garbage truck was clanking and grinding on the next block. The gutters and sidewalks were still littered with exploded firecrackers and other detritus from the recent New Year's Eve celebrations.

The security door to the apartment building was ajar, so they would be able to walk right up to Middendorf's apartment on the top floor. They entered the vestibule. The bulletin board in the lobby was covered with posters for local rock bands appearing at the Melkweg club. Chris examined the mailboxes and saw the name "Middendorf" written in ballpoint and scotch-taped above the box for Apartment 4.

The objective of a knock and talk is to shut down a hacker and recover the stolen intellectual property as quickly and quietly as possible. The last thing BlueCloud needed was international press reports that its source code had been compromised, which would call into question the security and stability of its immensely popular operating system.

Remko looked at the name, then turned to Chris. "What if he climbs out the window onto the fire escape and runs?"

"If he runs, then he runs," Chris said. "I'm a lawyer, not a cop."

They walked up the narrow steps, with Chris taking the lead. Chris carried a leather folder with two documents. The first was a legal complaint charging Middendorf with violations of Dutch computer crime laws, which Remko's firm had helped prepare. Chris intended to flash the pleading at Middendorf to convince him that they were serious.

The second document was a settlement agreement that Middendorf would be asked to sign to avert the filing of the complaint. The agreement required the hacker to make no public statements, consent to a search of his computer, and return all copies of the stolen source code. There was no guarantee that Middendorf hadn't concealed a copy of the code on a cloud server or at some other location, but Chris would make it clear that if the source code turned up on the black market, he would return, but this time collaborating with a prosecutor in a criminal case.

When they reached Apartment 4, on the top landing, Chris felt a tightening in his stomach. In moments like these, Chris wished that he was the kind of lawyer who stayed behind a desk. He glanced back at Remko to make sure he was ready, then he rapped on the door.

Inside, Chris heard a muffled voice. Then a chair scraped and there was a sound that might have been papers falling to the floor. Whoever was inside wasn't approaching the door.

Chris hammered with his fist until the door rattled in its frame.

After about thirty seconds, they heard a man say something in Dutch. It had the intonation of a question. Chris assumed it was something to the effect of "Who's there?"

"Do you speak English?" Chris asked.

A pause. "Yeah, I speak English. Who's this?" The English was fluent, and the voice was high and adenoidal like a teenager's.

"Is this Pietr Middendorf?"

"You've got the wrong apartment, man. Fuck off."

"Open the door, Pietr. My name is Chris Bruen. I'm an attorney and I came all the way from the US just to speak with you. I'm here with a colleague of mine from a local law firm. We know you're Black Vector and we know about the theft of the Aspira source code. I'm here on behalf of my client BlueCloud."

"What part of 'fuck off' did you not understand?"

Chris exhaled slowly. This wasn't going to be one of the easy ones.

"If you open the door," Chris said, "we have a deal we'd like to offer you. If you don't open the door, I'm going to have a court bailiff come here and open it for us. If we do it that way, you're probably going to spend tonight in jail."

There was a long silence on the other side of the door, then, "I need a minute to put some clothes on. Is that okay with you?"

"No problem," Chris said. "In fact, we prefer it."

They heard the sound of footsteps shuffling around the apartment. Chris and Remko were both listening intently, their heads leaning in close to the wooden door.

And then they heard the gunshot.

In the thunderclap of the moment, Chris perceived it as more of a physical shock than a sound. He examined himself for a bullet wound.

"Are you okay?" Chris said to Remko, who had backpedaled down the hallway and was bouncing slightly on the balls of his feet, amped on adrenaline.

Remko looked down at the front of his shirt. "I think so. Are you?"

"Okay," Chris said, examining the door for a bullet hole and finding none. The shot didn't seem to have been directed at them.

From inside the apartment, they heard the groan of a window sash opening.

"Sounds like he's leaving by the fire escape," Chris said. "I'm going inside. Someone could be hurt in there." He wasn't going to admit it to Remko, but he had other motives as well. He tested the door, but it was locked.

Chris butted the door with his shoulder, but it was unyielding. Then he strode past Remko and headed down the stairs.

"Good," Remko said. "I'll call the police."

"No, not yet," Chris said. "I'm going to go up the fire escape and take a look."

"Are you insane?"

When Chris and Remko emerged from the lobby, the street was still empty except for a grocer turning a crank to raise the metal fence that guarded his shop. There was no sign of the shooter.

Chris walked around to the side of the building and saw that the ladder to the fire escape had been pulled down to the pavement. On the fourth-floor landing, the window was still open. From the corner, Chris surveyed the street and the alley but still saw no one who seemed like a candidate to have fired the shot.

Chris began climbing the iron fire escape toward the fourth floor. He was trying not to make too much noise, but the fire escape groaned and shuddered with every step. The iron railings were so cold in his grip that they burned. He looked down at the alley below and saw Remko vigorously shaking his head, trying to dissuade him.

He moved even more slowly as he neared the fourth-floor window. If the shooter was still in the room and looked out, he would be an easy target that even the poorest shot couldn't miss.

Finally, Chris stood outside the window of Middendorf's apartment. He saw his breath smoking in front of him in quick, chuffing bursts. But he wasn't as frightened as he knew he should be. Ever since his cancer diagnosis, a kind of numbness had settled over him—it was like being on beta-blockers.

Chris darted his head forward for a quick look into the room through the open window. He pulled back so quickly, though, that he wasn't really able to see anything. At least no one had fired a shot at him.

He tried again, this time allowing enough time to survey the room. There was only one figure inside, a man slumped at a desk, his face buried in the keyboard. The large iMac computer monitor in front of him was on and spattered with blood.

The figure did not move.

Chris climbed through the window, into a tiny flat with a bed to the right and the desk facing the wall to the left, next to a kitchenette. The room smelled of stale fried food and was littered with greasy, empty Styrofoam containers, and what appeared to be pirated copies of video games packaged with poorly reproduced artwork. A bicycle leaned against a wall in one corner.

Chris approached the body. The man's hands were bound in front of him using the type of nylon cord used to lash packages to a bicycle rack. There was a bullet hole in the back of his skull that was still oozing blood, matting his dark, curly hair.

Leaning down to examine the face, he saw that it was Pietr Middendorf, whom he barely recognized from a photo he'd gotten from his Facebook page. One of Middendorf's eyes was swollen shut. The other eye was open, but it was fixed and lifeless. There were lacerations all over the hacker's face and head from some blunt object.

"Pietr?" Chris said. There was no movement. Chris picked up Middendorf's wrist and checked for a pulse, but there was none. Chris's earlier knock at the door had apparently interrupted the fun and games, bringing the session to an abrupt close with a bullet to Middendorf's head.

Chris examined the room more closely now and saw signs that it had been tossed, but not very thoroughly. Every drawer in the apartment was open, from the desk to the kitchen to the nightstand. If Chris had to guess, he would say that Pietr's killer had been looking for something, searched the place a bit to see if it presented itself and, when it didn't, began working on Middendorf.

Chris figured that one of the neighbors would report the gunshot and he only had about five minutes before the Amsterdam police arrived. He looked under the bed, under the mattress, on the shelves of the small closet, places that didn't seem to have been examined by the killer. He moved on to the desk drawers, removing a pen from his pocket and using it to pull the drawers open, careful not to leave fingerprints on the hard surfaces. There was nothing of interest there, just some pens, paper clips, and envelopes. Then he stopped, realizing that he had just seen something that was slightly off.

There were two staplers on Middendorf's desk, one black and one gray. Judging by the disorder of the apartment, Middendorf didn't seem like the type to be so organized as to own one stapler, much less two. Not sure what he was looking for, Chris tested the black stapler, mashing down the upper arm. A staple ejected, tiny, silver, and crumpled like a swatted spider.

Chris tested the second, extra-large gray stapler, and nothing came out. He picked it up and opened the compartment that held the staples. There were no staples inside—there was no room because a flash drive had been wedged behind the spring mechanism. The silver plastic drive had a piece of paper taped around it bearing the image of a smiling red devil, with horns and a long, forked tongue. Chris was willing to bet that the flash drive contained the stolen source code.

He considered whether he should be removing possible evidence from a crime scene but only hesitated for a moment. His client had sent him to Amsterdam to do a job and he wasn't about to return empty-handed. He placed the flash drive in his pocket, then used a paper towel from the kitchen to wipe down the two staplers.

The baying of police sirens could be heard in the distance. He surveyed the cluttered room one last time to see if he had missed anything. It was then that he noticed that the green LED light of the computer's webcam was on. He was being observed.

His mind raced. The webcam must have been on the whole time, even through Middendorf's beating and murder. Perhaps the killer had been making an example of the hacker for the benefit of whoever was on the other end of the webcam. Chris leaned in and gazed into the lens as if he could see the person on the other end. He held up a finger to the camera as if to say *I know you're there.*

At that moment, the computer pinged—the sound of an incoming email. Middendorf's email inbox was open on the screen, but it took a moment to read the message, because the monitor was spattered with blood. The subject line read: "YOU HAVE SOMETHING THAT BELONGS TO US."

Chris looked into the webcam and said, "If you want it, why don't you tell me where I should send it?"

The computer pinged again. Another email. The message: "WE'LL FIND YOU."

CHAPTER 3

January 7

The long flight back from the Netherlands had taken its toll on Chris, so he decided to work from home after dropping off the flash drive in Reynolds Fincher's computer forensic lab for analysis. Home was a cavernous loft in a commercial district south of busy Market Street, within walking distance of the firm's offices. The one nonutilitarian object in the living room was the upright Steinway piano crouched in a corner, with a silver-framed photo of his late wife, Tana, perched on top. The place suited Chris because it was the right size for one person. A bunch of unused rooms would have seemed like a rebuke to his solitary life.

The light coming through the big windows was soft and gray, filtered through the marine layer that draped the city. The Bay Bridge loomed in the middle distance. The view had been even better before a phalanx of glass apartment towers had shot up south of Market—just in time for the real estate crash.

He put on a pot of coffee, made toast, and cued up a vinyl recording of Glenn Gould's 1981 performance of Bach's *Goldberg Variations*. Gould's playing was introspective, ruminative, the sound of an artist nearing the end of his life but still engaged. Chris admired Bach because his compositions were as mathematically precise as an elegant string of computer code.

Chris was still trying to make sense of what had happened in Amsterdam. The Dutch police had brought him and Remko down to the station and questioned them for nearly two days. They had been particularly interested in the email that read, "YOU HAVE SOMETHING THAT BELONGS TO US." Chris had fudged his timeline by a few minutes to suggest that the email came in before he was on the scene. Remko didn't contradict his story, because he had been too upset to note the time.

Eventually, the police seemed satisfied. Chris had feared that he would be detained in the Netherlands, but the detectives were reassured by the fact that he was associated with a major Amsterdam law firm, and they knew where to find Remko.

Chris had hidden the flash drive beneath a dumpster in the alley just before the patrol cars arrived. He returned to retrieve it after the police had finished their questioning. Chris never said a word to Remko about the flash drive. There was no need to implicate him in a possible obstruction-of-justice charge. And if it turned out that the drive did contain something material to the murder investigation, he would find a way to return it to Dutch law enforcement—once he was safely back in the US. Better to ask for forgiveness from a foreign jurisdiction than to ask for permission.

For the past two days, Chris had been trying to understand what Middendorf might have been thinking in his last hours. After taking such a beating, why would he still refuse to turn over the flash drive? It had to be either very valuable or very incriminating. Or maybe Middendorf knew he was a dead man and his refusal was a last act of defiance.

Chris brought his coffee mug and plate over to the desk and booted up the computer. The monitor screen immediately filled with a black-and-white photo of Darby Crash, the lead singer of the seventies LA punk band the Germs, all wild eyes and broken teeth. Chris had been hacked—again.

There was a cadre of hackers who took pride in their ability to take down Chris's computer. Chris's hacker adversaries usually couldn't get through the law firm's firewall, so they focused on his home computer. Chris had upgraded his security repeatedly, but clearly it still wasn't enough. At least he knew better than to store anything truly sensitive on his hard drive.

Chris knew instantly who the culprit was. Blanksy, a relatively harmless prankster, had a fondness for the late-seventies LA punk scene. The photo of Darby Crash was meant as a calling card. Chris respected Blanksy's skills and he had been a longtime source of information on hacks and hackers, but the disruptions were getting annoying. Blanksy had invited Chris to speak at DefCon, the annual hacker convention that was to be held in Brooklyn later that month, and had been pestering him ever since he refused.

Chris looked up Blanksy's number on his phone and dialed him up.

"Greetings, Chris." Chris had never met Blanksy in person, but they had developed a relationship of sorts over the years. He even knew that Blanksy's real name was Jay Hartigan. In conversation, Blanksy had the charmingly geeked-out enthusiasm of a comic shop clerk on Red Bull, which amused Chris on most days.

"You know, Jay, when most people want to talk to me, they just pick up a phone."

"Dude, you don't return my calls or texts. It's a little harder to ignore me when you've been pwned, isn't it? And please, call me Blanksy." "Pwned" was hacker slang for gaining complete "root kit" control over a computer.

"I have work to do, Blanksy."

"This is about your work—your little adventure in Amsterdam."

"So you've heard about that."

"You know how word travels. Some people are saying that you've gone rogue, that you've stopped arresting hackers and started assassinating them."

"And you believe that?"

"No, but you should watch your back just the same," Blanksy said. "When people start saying stuff like that, they can justify all kinds of bad behavior."

"Like hacking my home computer? How did you hijack my computer, anyway?"

"It's just a matter of knowing what sort of email you always open. Then I used Zeus." Zeus, also known as zbot, is a popular open-source malware toolkit for hackers. Zeus can be used to create a Trojan Horse, an email hiding malicious code, a practice sometimes referred to as "spear phishing."

Chris changed tack. "What is it that you want? I assume that there's a reason for this surprise visit."

Blanksy adopted the plummy tones of a monologuing super-villain. "You know, we are not so very different, you and I . . ."

"The main difference being that I'm an adult."

"You wound me," Blanksy said, only half kidding. "I am wounded."

"No offense intended."

"Okay," Blanksy said. "Apology accepted, but I want you to reconsider the invitation to DefCon. It would be massive if you could make it. You may be the enemy, but there's a lot of respect for you out there. If you stepped up to the podium at DefCon, it would be the biggest display of brass cojones ever."

"At this point in my life, I don't really need that."

"Say you'll consider it, if you want your computer back."

A long, grudging silence ensued. "I'll consider it," Chris said. "But that is not a commitment." Being heckled by an auditorium full of hackers was not Chris's idea of fun.

"That's all I ask, dude. You are released."

"Thank you. And please don't call me dude."

"I've just gotta say, though, that I think you're well on your way to being just a legendary badass."

"Good-bye, Blanksy." Chris hung up.

It distressed him that there were hackers saying that he had killed Pietr Middendorf, but there was nothing he could do about that sort of irresponsible chatter. Responding to the rumor on one of the hacker message boards would only serve to incite them further.

When his computer came back up, Chris saw that Eduardo "Ed" de Lamadrid, the director of the firm's computer forensic lab, had sent him an email: "Can you make it to the office? I found some very interesting stuff on that flash drive."

Chris tapped out a response. "Can't you just tell me?"

"This is something that you need to see. Trust me on this."

"I'll be there in fifteen minutes."

CHAPTER 4

The computer forensic laboratory, which was located in the firm's offices near the San Francisco waterfront on the thirty-eighth floor of Building Four of Embarcadero Center, didn't look like anything special. There were no technicians in white lab coats, oversize LCD monitors, or other crime lab trappings. Instead, there was just a whiteboard that ran around all four walls of the room, covered with scribbled passwords, cryptic decision trees, the names of hackers, and fragments of code. The counters were made of thick wood that did not conduct electricity. Most law firms did not have their own computer forensic lab, but it was an essential resource for Chris's unique practice.

As Chris entered, Ed was sitting alone in the center of the room in a black leather chair, staring at an array of three computer monitors. He was in his characteristic pose of intense concentration, pinching his lower lip and wispy black goatee between his thumb and index finger. Ed was in his early thirties, with short, black hair, a round face, and wire-framed glasses with round lenses. A copy of *A Scanner Darkly*, by Philip K. Dick, which he dipped into during downtime while a program was running, rested open and spine up next to his keyboard.

Chris met Ed three years earlier when he was investigating a hacker attack against a large accounting firm. Ed was working in the accounting firm's IT department, and he took an unusually keen interest in Chris's investigation. Eventually, Chris learned the reason for that interest. Ed's hobby was hunting down and decoding computer viruses, then sharing the information with a group of other professional and nonprofessional security experts who had appointed themselves unofficial guardians of the Internet. The accountants saw Ed as a pudgy and introverted Cuban kid from Miami. Chris recognized Ed for what he truly was—a geeky version of Batman who made up for his lack of superpowers with a vigilante's thirst for justice. Chris had immediately hired Ed away from the accounting firm to be the first director of his computer forensic lab.

"I hope this is worth bringing me into the office," Chris said.

Ed swung around in his chair. "Oh, it's worth it," he said. "First, you'll be happy to know that you got what you were after. The flash drive contained a copy of the Aspira source code."

"Great. If there was another copy on Middendorf's home computer, we can work with the Dutch police to retrieve that, too."

"But that, my friend, is only the beginning." Ed glided over to a monitor in his desk chair. "Check this out."

Chris sat down next to Ed and studied a string of computer code on the screen. Ed watched his face for the moment of recognition. About a minute later, Chris said, "It's a worm—a virus."

"You got it," Ed said.

"But it's not like anything I've seen before from a hacker. This coding is extraordinarily complex. And it's huge."

"Not your father's malware, right? It's about twenty times the size of most viruses."

"What does it do?"

"I can't tell yet. The adversary is pretty good at masking his intentions." Computer security experts commonly referred to a black hat hacker as "the adversary."

"What do you have so far?"

Ed leaned forward in his chair, bringing his face to within inches of the monitor screen. "I'm still working on unpacking it. It's heavily encrypted. What I do know is that the exploit is designed to hide itself once it's infected a computer. That's why I've given it a name—Lurker."

"How does it hide?"

"It's pretty cute, actually. Once Lurker invades a computer, it shuts down whatever security system is installed. But then it goes further. The virus blocks the computer from communicating with a list of top computer security websites and blocks all Aspira security updates."

"So it's targeting the Aspira operating system."

"It seems so, but I haven't found its way in yet."

Most computer viruses are designed to exploit a vulnerability in a computer system or program, which serves as their point of entry. Since Middendorf had obtained the source code for Aspira, it was likely that he had uncovered some chink in the program's digital defenses.

"And get a load of this," Ed said, pointing at a segment of coding. "It can use Bluesnarfing to spread itself wirelessly to any devices that are linked to an infected computer by Bluetooth. And it plants a beacon so that information on the infected system is beamed back to the hackers. They can monitor the infected computer and activate the virus remotely from a command-and-control server whenever they want."

Chris frowned. "Bad news for the client."

"Let's hope that Middendorf didn't share the source code with any of his hacker buddies," Ed said.

"Probably a safe assumption. He seems to have hidden the flash drive, because he was holding out on whoever killed him. And they clearly weren't done with him when I showed up."

"Now look at what else I found on the drive," he said, pushing off from the desk and rolling over to another monitor.

Chris leaned over the screen and saw strings of what appeared to be messages from an Internet Relay Chat network. IRC was a favorite mode of communication for hackers because it didn't require an account, and messages were nearly untraceable—unless one of the participants copied the thread.

The content seemed innocuous—boasts about firewalls breached and information pilfered. Hackers were even more self-aggrandizing than rappers.

"Looks like the typical hot air," Chris said.

"Keep reading."

Chris pointed to a line of text. "Here's Black Vector talking to two of his hacker buddies, named Enigma and Ripley."

Chris examined the message board postings more closely. "Look at what Enigma has to say here," Chris said, pointing at a line of text on the screen.

ENIGMA: We were beginning to worry about you.
RIPLEY: I came by your apartment twice yesterday and no
 one answered the door.

BLACK VECTOR: I've been around.

ENIGMA: We need that source code.

BLACK VECTOR: Not a problem. We can meet up on Friday. I'll text you with a place and time.

ENIGMA: That's three days. I can't wait that long. You know that there's no backing out at this point, don't you? Circle the date—January 14.

RIPLEY: He's right. We need you.

BLACK VECTOR: I still think you could make the same point with a smaller event. People are going to die. Maybe a lot of people. Wasn't Albuquerque enough for you? I didn't think this was what we did.

Chris stopped reading and sat up straight, remembering the news coverage a week ago of the midair collision in which twenty-one passengers were killed. "These are the people responsible for the virus that took out the Albuquerque airport."

Ed nodded grimly. "Keep reading. It gets worse."

ENIGMA: Every once in a while, there's a moment when the world changes, but it takes a while for people to catch up to it. It's like when the atomic bomb was invented. On January 14, we'll show the world what a cyber Hiroshima looks like. An act of war—but waged in code. Albuquerque was just a trial run. Fitting that it was in New Mexico— just like Los Alamos.

BLACK VECTOR: You know what's going to happen to us if they figure out that we're behind this?

ENIGMA: Don't worry, they'll never find us—as long as we stick together.

BLACK VECTOR: This is just a little heavier than I'm used
   to, you know?
ENIGMA: You're at home right now, aren't you?
BLACK VECTOR: Yeah. Why?
ENIGMA: I just happen to be in the neighborhood. I can
   be there in five minutes to pick up that flash drive.

"Now look at the date of the chat," Ed said.

"January 4, 7:00 a.m. This was only an hour or so before I
arrived at Middendorf's apartment. That means that this Enigma
person must have killed Middendorf."

"They were probably already watching his apartment building when they sent these messages," Ed said.

"And Middendorf knew that he didn't have time to escape,
so he made a copy of the IRC chat and hid it to identify his
killers."

"So what about all this talk about cyberwar?" Ed asked.
"Does this sound like a legitimate threat or just more hacker
delusions of grandeur?"

"Given the sophistication of the coding in that virus and
the connection to the Albuquerque airport event, I think it
would be a big mistake to ignore this," Chris said. "But that's
not our call, is it?"

"You're going to take this to the FBI?"

"Right. If they're really going to activate this virus on
January 14, that's only a week away." Of all the federal agencies, the FBI took the greatest interest in combating large-scale
computer viruses, but these types of threats were also within
the purview of the Department of Homeland Security and the
National Security Agency.

"But first, we need to share all of this with BlueCloud,"
Chris said. "After all, it was obtained on their behalf and belongs

to them. If they agree, we'll disclose to the feds. We don't want anyone thinking that we're holding out on them."

Chris knew that BlueCloud would have to produce the copy of the Lurker virus and the transcript of the message board chat to the FBI. If there was any truth to what the hackers were saying about the attack, then this was far too big to withhold.

But just because he shared the information with the FBI, didn't mean that he couldn't also conduct his own private investigation. If someone was going to track down the Lurker crew, Chris knew that his client BlueCloud would prefer that it be him so the matter could be handled discreetly. Like the hackers that he pursued, Chris thought highly of his own skills. He figured that he stood a better chance of locating Enigma and Ripley than law enforcement ever would.

"I've already begun running some Deep Web searches on the tags Enigma and Ripley," Ed said. "No hits yet." The so-called Deep Web consisted of more than one trillion Internet pages that cannot be indexed by search engines like Google.

Chris stared at a panel of whiteboard as if he were gazing through a window. "Enigma. That's the machine that the Nazis used to encrypt their transmissions during World War II. But what about Ripley?"

Ed smiled. "Ripley has to be a girl. Ripley? The movie *Alien*? She's the patron saint of badass chicks." He paused. "But why do you think it was so important to them to get the source code? They've apparently already found a vulnerability for the virus to exploit."

"They're in it for the long run," Chris said. "With the source code, they could find new ways to keep the virus evolving. They could probably stay one step ahead of us for years."

"It would have been nice if they'd mentioned which city they're targeting," Ed said. "Any guesses?"

"Well, they clearly want to make a statement. LA and Chicago are so sprawling it would be very difficult to take them down completely, no matter how sophisticated the virus. I'd guess they're targeting a place more geographically concentrated—maybe New York, or San Francisco."

Ed swiveled around in his chair. "I've never thought about it until now, but do you know if this building has a backup generator?"

★ ★ ★

After his meeting with Ed, Chris gave up on the notion of a peaceful morning of working from home. He sat down at his desk and started skimming the emails that had filled his inbox while he was out of the country.

As a matter of professional curiosity, Chris always made a point of checking to see what was in his spam filter. Usually, he'd find an assortment of solicitations for male enhancement products, a few attachments hiding a virus or spyware, and, occasionally, a classic like the Nigerian prince scam. Today, there were 542 emails in the spam filter, an unprecedented number. Checking the quarantined messages, Chris saw that they all had the same subject line—"WE OWN YOU." Each of the emails contained an attachment. Chris moved them to one of his forensic computers, then clicked the icon. He wasn't afraid of infecting the law firm's system with a virus, because the forensic computer was "air gapped," meaning that it was freestanding and not connected to the Internet.

The attachment opened haltingly to reveal a pdf of a document. It was a death certificate with the seal of the San Francisco Department of Public Health. The name on the certificate: Christopher Riley Bruen. It looked very authentic. Chris had received more than his share of threatening emails from hackers, but there was something about this one that stopped him cold. Maybe it was the lack of an explanation. Maybe it was the care that had been taken in replicating the death certificate. Most likely, though, it was the stark directness of the message—you're dead.

Then Chris noticed the realistically smudged date stamp in the corner of the certificate—January 14. This was not just a taunt from an angry hacker. It was a threat, apparently from Enigma and company. Or maybe it was a challenge.

He recalled the message from the person on the other end of the webcam in Amsterdam: "WE'LL FIND YOU." And apparently they had.

CHAPTER 5

The headquarters of BlueCloud, Inc., was a half-hour drive south of San Francisco in the suburban town of San Mateo and consisted of three black-glass office towers strikingly arrayed beside an inlet of the Bay. It was a cool, windy day, and fast-moving clouds scudded in reflection across the buildings' obsidian surfaces. Atop each of the towers was the company's logo—the blue outline of a wisp of cloud. Chris had been summoned to complete his debriefing with the client about his all-too-eventful trip to Amsterdam. He would have preferred to dedicate his time to the pursuit of Enigma and his crew, but there was no getting around the fact that he needed a client to fund that enterprise.

No cars were allowed on the campus, so Chris parked his car in the lot outside the security gate. After showing his credentials to a guard in a kiosk, he was escorted to the meeting by a guy in an electric golf cart. The street sign for the road that circled the campus read "Cirrus Drive."

They hummed across the immaculately landscaped corporate campus. Like a movie studio back lot, the place was a perfectly fabricated artificial environment, the work of a natural image maker who didn't stop at designing a product. Judging by the uniformly attractive twentysomethings that strode across the campus in business casual wear, Chris half suspected that BlueCloud might soon be announcing a new foray into genetic engineering.

After parking the golf cart out front, the driver escorted Chris into one of the towers and deposited him at the office of Scott Austin, the company's general counsel. Austin rose from behind his desk, a perfect specimen of his type—short, sandy brown hair graying at the temples, midforties, thickening in the middle, and a demeanor that transitioned easily from gruff command with outside counsel to dignified subservience with corporate management. But today he seemed unusually cordial.

"My wife always tells me that lawyers lead boring lives," Austin said, "but you're like some kind of freaking Navy Seal." He shook hands with more enthusiasm than Chris was accustomed to and motioned to the chair in front of his desk. "Did you really climb the fire escape and enter that apartment when you didn't know if the killer was still up there?"

Chris grimaced in acknowledgment.

Austin asked him to recount the full story of what had happened in Amsterdam. After two days with the Dutch police, Chris could run through most of the narrative on autopilot. When Chris got to the part about the faked death certificate, Austin asked, "You get many death threats in your line of work?"

"Not enough to be blasé about it," Chris said. He produced the flash drive containing the Lurker virus and slid it across the desk.

"Our security team can't wait to get their hands on this."

"It has strong encryption. They have their work cut out for them."

At last, Austin came to the real point of their meeting. "We have another assignment for you. We want you to continue to follow the trail of those hackers. This talk about a massive cyberattack has the C-suite types rattled. If a vulnerability in our operating system caused the shutdown of an entire city . . . or worse . . . well, I don't think this company could recover from a blow like that."

"Not to mention the city and its population," Chris said.

"Yes, of course," Austin hastily added.

"I'll need to share what we know with the FBI."

"Understood. We certainly don't want to impede their investigation. But we think you have a better chance of finding the hackers than they do."

"I won't disagree with you there."

"And if you happen to learn anything about the FBI's investigation of the Albuquerque event, we'd like to know about it. We're just praying that the virus used in Albuquerque wasn't exploiting a vulnerability in our system."

"So when do I start?"

"Immediately. You'll have a blank check when it comes to resources. This assignment could not be more important. Even the launch of our new smartphone next month has taken a backseat. To give you an idea of how big this is for us, Dave Silver wants to meet with you personally. You've been granted an audience with the great man himself."

Chris was surprised at Austin's tone of undisguised snark. "No one needs to tell me what's at stake for the company."

"But, you see, for Silver this is personal. He has nearly a billion dollars in stock value on the line. Given my current option situation, I can afford to have a bit more perspective."

Chris understood that he was supposed to be impressed by a meeting with Silver. Chris had been outside counsel to BlueCloud for ten years but had never met CEO Dave Silver in person. The closest he had come had been a primitive video-conference several years ago that had been so choppy that Silver might have been communicating with him from the Space Shuttle. Chris nodded in what he hoped was an appreciative manner. He knew that in the corporate culture of BlueCloud, proximity to Silver was the coin of the realm, the ultimate badge of acceptance. Out of BlueCloud's more than fifty thousand employees, Silver only dealt directly with The Hundred, an ever-changing group of anointed insiders who were invited to a supersecret annual corporate retreat hosted by Silver in Carmel.

As if on cue, and without a knock, the door to Austin's office opened and in stepped Dave Silver—the man, the legend, the brand. Austin stood and waited for Silver to speak, as if he were the president of a nation rather than merely a company. Silver didn't bother to make even a token apology for interrupting. He was accustomed to having everyone stop what they were doing when he entered a room.

Silver's physical appearance wasn't particularly striking. He was in his early fifties, thin, medium height, with a receding hairline. He was wearing gray slacks and a blindingly white button-down. But it was his blue eyes that commanded attention—Chris couldn't quite decide whether they gave the impression of seeing everything or seeing nothing. In the press, the name Dave Silver was often preceded by the word "visionary" but, in fact, what made people like him compelling was their ability to be willfully blind to everything but their own view of the world.

"I wanted to meet you personally," Silver said. "I was impressed with the way you handled that situation in Amsterdam. You kept your focus and got the source code."

"I was just doing what you paid me to do," Chris said.

"Everyone gets paid, but that doesn't mean that they would do what you did." Silver turned and said, "Why don't we take a walk."

Silver led him out of the building that housed the legal department and into another identical black-glass tower. Silver's passage through the lobby generated excited ripples among the employees, like a shark gliding through a school of guppies. Everyone moved a little faster in Silver's presence, heads swiveling, hoping to be noticed or not noticed.

They passed three increasingly forbidding security stations without so much as a word or the flash of an ID badge and entered a wing that bore a sign overhead that read simply "Lab."

By this point, Chris knew where he was—it was the super-high-security laboratory where BlueCloud kept the prototypes for new products. The room was spherical and everything was pristine white—the desks, the chairs, the sheets that were draped over the white tables. It was part showroom, part working lab, part impregnable vault. The tables arrayed around the large room held the fetish objects that geek dreams are made of—the next generation of the world's most popular smartphones and tablet computers, and maybe a new device or two that the world didn't yet know that it couldn't live without.

"Do you know what this place is?" Silver asked.

"Yes, I've heard about it, but I wonder why you brought me here."

Silver smiled slightly. "I know that Scott has already spoken with you about the assignment. We bring people here that we want to impress, major investors, visiting dignitaries, important media. Frankly, I always feel a little bit like a Bond villain when I'm in here."

"I'd say you're more like Q," Chris said.

"I like that." Silver smiled. "The point is that I want you to appreciate just how important you are to our team."

Silver refocused. "We've created something here at BlueCloud. Something that has changed the world in a lot of little ways—and maybe in a few big ones, too. If a flaw in our Aspira system leads to a major cyberattack, then all of that could be over in an instant. Then it won't matter how great our products are. And it's part of the BlueCloud mystique that our products are so well-designed that they're virtually bulletproof to viruses."

Chris nodded. He understood Silver perfectly. Most of Chris's clients came to him in situations in which they feared losing the trust of their customers.

"We won't be the only ones out there looking for the Lurker crew," he said, ready to move on to logistics. "There will be FBI, Homeland Security, Secret Service, FAA, and maybe other agencies in the hunt."

"Then you'll just have to get there first," Silver said, his frustration showing for a moment. "We're not going to let the feds make us a whipping boy. You're going to make this go away. This company was built on being faster and smarter than its competition. And we expect that from everyone here, including our lawyers. In your case, I don't think I'm expecting too much. I know a little bit about your story, you know. The arrest as a teenager."

Now it was Chris who was smoldering. "Those records were sealed."

Silver scoffed.

"If you think I understand hackers because I once was one, then you're operating on a false premise," Chris said. "That was a very long time ago."

"Say what you will, but I think I have a pretty good eye for talent. That thing you did when you were young convinced me that you had the right temperament for this assignment. Along with the way you handled things in Amsterdam."

"You should know that it's possible that sending me out there could make your situation worse. If the FBI or Homeland Security thinks that I'm in their way, they could arrest me and charge BlueCloud with obstructing a national security investigation."

"I know. Scott and I have already weighed the pros and cons and decided that you're our best bet. We've got your back." Silver locked on Chris with his best charismatic gaze. "*I've* got your back."

Chris hoped that was true, but he suspected that Silver viewed him like one of BlueCloud's smartphones—indispensable for a while, but with a very finite shelf life.

CHAPTER 6

Later that afternoon, Chris was called to the lobby of the law firm's offices to meet two FBI agents. When Chris arrived, they were standing at the floor-to-ceiling windows admiring the panoramic view of the Ferry Building clock tower and the Bay. On clear days like this one, the lobby was so brilliantly lit by the sun that it felt like you were outside.

The apparent leader of the pair stepped forward, wearing a serious expression that seemed intended to set a tone for the meeting. Chris had been expecting a dark suit and lantern jaw, but the agent was wearing a sport coat and khakis and looked more like an untenured college professor. Apparently, this was the FBI's geek squad. "Chris Bruen? I'm Michael Hazlitt, FBI."

"Nice to meet you," Chris said, shaking his hand. "You didn't waste any time getting over here."

"You don't remember me, do you?"

"I'm sorry, have we met?"

"When you were at DOJ, I worked on a couple of cases where we were collaborating with your office. I was a junior member of the team then, so there's no reason why you would remember me. I wasn't allowed to do much talking." Hazlitt pointed a thumb at his colleague. "Much like this guy here."

Hazlitt's partner, who looked to be only a few years younger, leaned forward and shook his hand. "Sam Falacci, silent partner." Falacci looked like a slightly down-market version of Hazlitt. If Hazlitt was Brooks Brothers, Falacci was Men's Wearhouse.

Chris smiled politely and led them into a small conference room off the lobby and closed the door.

"You had a great reputation back in the day," Hazlitt said. "Wish we still had you on our side."

"I thought we were on the same side."

"You represent your clients, which is not the same thing as the government's interest."

"My clients want to stop cybercriminals just like you do."

"Maybe, but we prefer to put them in jail when we can. For the FBI and your old buddies at DOJ, those settlement agreements that you use are . . . very unsatisfying."

"Maybe this will improve your impression of me." Chris handed over the flash drive containing the Lurker virus and the message board postings, along with a copy of the email containing the faked death certificate. He'd already briefed them by phone about the contents of the flash drive and the possible January 14 attack.

"You think this is for real?" Falacci asked.

"I don't know, but if I were you I'd treat it as if it were," Chris said. "Based on the complexity of the coding, that worm was designed by someone who knew what they were doing."

"We appreciate the cooperation," Hazlitt said. "I'm glad that you recognize that this isn't just about your client's operating system."

"That's why we called."

"But just in case you have any doubts about how seriously the government is taking this, I want you to know that Louis Vogel at NSA is involved."

"Vogel," Chris said, as if he was straining his memory. "He's pretty highly placed at NSA, isn't he?" Chris knew perfectly well who Louis Vogel was, at least to the extent that anyone who didn't have a top-level National Security Agency security clearance should know.

"Highly placed. Yeah, you could say that," Hazlitt said. "So highly placed he doesn't even have a title."

"So this is a joint investigation?"

"Sort of. We're doing the investigating, NSA, Homeland Security, and FAA are getting reports. I'm telling you this because I want to make sure you understand that full and complete cooperation is very much in the best interests of you and your client."

"National security matter. I get it."

"So, just for the record, I'm going to ask you again," Hazlitt said, slowing it down for emphasis, as he might for a suspect. "Is there anything else that you haven't told us?"

"You know what I know," Chris said and, at that point, it was true.

"We may be back in touch with you with some follow-up questions, so please stay available, particularly during the next week," Hazlitt said. "If the black hats send you any more emails or make contact in any way, we want to know about it immediately."

As they turned to leave, Chris said, "I'd appreciate it if you could give us back a copy of the flash drive with the coding for the worm. If there's a vulnerability in Aspira, BlueCloud wants to identify it so they can develop a security patch. No one knows their source code like they do, so it's in your interest to let them work with the virus."

"I'll ask my bosses and get back to you," Hazlitt responded. "I'm sure that your client will be provided with anything that they need to know."

Of course, Chris had made a copy of the flash drive, but he had to ask the question, anyway. Hazlitt's answer confirmed what he already knew—that the FBI and the other agencies would never collaborate with a private investigation. It made Chris feel more justified in proceeding with his own investigation for BlueCloud.

"What do you know so far about the virus that took down the Albuquerque air traffic control system?"

"That investigation is confidential."

"My client would, of course, like to know if the virus exploited its Aspira system."

"You'll know what we want you to know when we want you to know it." Chris took that as an implicit confirmation that the Albuquerque virus had targeted one of BlueCloud's products.

Hazlitt paused in the doorway of the conference room. "Oh, and I hope you're not planning to try to locate these characters Ripley and Enigma. If they're going to activate the virus on January 14, then we don't need any third parties mucking things up. If you get in our way, you're jeopardizing national security and that's exactly how it will be treated."

"Understood. Good luck, guys," Chris said as they headed for the elevators. For a moment, he missed the days when he could give orders to agents like Hazlitt and Falacci.

★ ★ ★

That night, after Ed had gone home, Chris entered the empty computer forensic lab and attempted to trace the threatening emails that he had received that morning. He was certain that the FBI would be doing the same thing.

Chris analyzed the email and traced the IP address that it had originated from. Chris's faked death certificate had been sent from an IP address registered in Barcelona, Spain. It was surprising that whoever had sent the emails had not bothered to cover their tracks better. Nevertheless, after a bit more digging, the IP address quickly led to a dead end.

Chris gazed out at the nighttime skyline of downtown San Francisco. As people returned home, the windows of the gleaming apartment towers lighted up and the office towers darkened. Beyond the towers was the Bay, a deeper black than the night sky.

Somewhere out there was a person, or a group of people, who were under the impression that they could steal his personal information and threaten him. They clearly knew plenty about him. For the moment, though, he knew next to nothing about them, except for the aliases Enigma and Ripley. Chris resolved to correct that imbalance.

CHAPTER 7

January 8

A computer virus is like a cancer—and Chris knew more than he cared to about both subjects. Without intervention, whether a security patch or chemotherapy, both grew without restraint. Both represented a kind of perverted life-force that propagated until growth became just another form of destruction.

Computer viruses and cancers were about a failure to follow norms. Why does a cell go haywire and begin dividing to form a cancer? Why does a component of a computer's operating system stop performing its designated function, creating an opening for a virus?

Chris sometimes wondered when he had stopped following norms himself. Maybe he and his wife, Tana, should have had kids. Maybe he should have gotten remarried after she died from breast cancer six years ago. Maybe he shouldn't have thrown himself into his work to suppress his grief during the years after her death. Maybe he should never have started an affair with Sarah Hotchner, a twenty-five-year-old paralegal at the firm who was fifteen years younger. Chris felt that after Tana's death he had begun to slowly, inexorably go haywire. In hindsight, he shouldn't have been surprised at all when he had been diagnosed with thyroid cancer. He'd been malfunctioning in so many ways for so long it seemed inevitable that the dysfunction would start manifesting itself at the cellular level.

His appointment with the oncologist was at 10:00 a.m. at California Pacific Medical Center, and Sarah had insisted on coming with him. He had not been angling for her to accompany him, at least not consciously. He didn't think they had that sort of relationship.

In fact, he didn't know what kind of relationship he had with Sarah. He wasn't her direct supervisor—at least there was that. She had been hired six months ago, and along with a battalion of junior associates and paralegals, they had worked together briefly on a due diligence project for a corporate merger, the entire team shut up in windowless rooms reviewing documents. Anyone who thought that drone warfare was confined to places like Afghanistan and Pakistan had never witnessed the corporate due diligence process.

Prior to the transaction's closing, they had pulled some late nights together at the office. One night, they'd left around 10:00 p.m. in separate elevators and both happened to show up several blocks away at the bar of the Four Seasons, both looking to unwind after a stressful day. When he saw her sitting across the room deciding whether or not to acknowledge him, what was he supposed to do, *not* have a drink with her? They'd shared one Maker's Mark, then another, then they'd walked back to his loft. They'd been together now for five months.

He knew it sounded tawdry, but he wasn't about to question it. Being with Sarah made him feel alive and, for a man in the middle of an experimental cancer treatment regimen, that was not to be discounted.

Dr. Alex Simon's office was in a medical complex next to the hospital. As Chris and Sarah sat in the waiting room, a pharmaceutical company sales rep in high heels and a shrink-wrapped dress emerged from the office. Chemotherapy and other cancer drugs were big-ticket items, and the pharma companies pulled out all the stops when it came to "detailing" the prescribing doctors. Detailing was the practice of learning about a physician's prescribing habits in order to better influence them, and it was performed by an army of gorgeous, impeccably dressed, well-educated young women who were employed as pharma sales reps. Dr. Simon had probably been detailed as often, and with as much loving care, as a vintage Lamborghini. Sarah said it all with the arch of an eyebrow directed at Chris as the sales rep clicked off down the hallway in her heels.

When the receptionist called his name, Sarah gave his hand a hard squeeze. "Would you like me to come in there with you?" she asked.

"No, it's fine." Chris stood up slowly and looked down at her. "You didn't have to do this, you know."

"I know," she said.

★ ★ ★

Dr. Simon seemed like a person whose natural good cheer had been steadily eroded by twenty years or so as an oncologist. He didn't smile much, probably because smiles were in poor taste when you're talking about cancer (and he was always talking about cancer), but an amused inflection still crept into his voice. Chris supposed that natural selection must bring such upbeat types to the specialty—anyone else would have put a gun in their mouth years ago.

One odd by-product of his cancer diagnosis was that it made him feel closer to Tana than at any time since her death. He felt that he had been through all of this before, but from another perspective, that of the sympathetic partner, a role that Sarah seemed to be playing now. Chris felt like an understudy who had been thrust into the lead role, but he hadn't yet mastered the lines or the blocking. And, unfortunately for him, the play was a tragedy. Now he really understood just how brave Tana had been, and how scared.

When Chris entered the exam room, Dr. Simon was smiling. And it wasn't a putting-a-brave-face-on-it smile, or a pitying, sympathetic quarter smile. It was a genuine smile.

"What?" Chris said.

"I have some good news for you," Dr. Simon said. "The medications seem to have worked."

Chris found it hard to get the words out, because he found himself smiling back at Dr. Simon. "Define 'worked.'"

"They've induced remission. The latest biopsy shows no signs of cancer."

"How is that possible?" In his first office visit when he had been diagnosed, Dr. Simon had told him that he had perhaps a 30 percent chance of surviving. In contrast, the cocktail of experimental thyroid cancer drugs that he was taking had a 10 percent chance of succeeding.

"I'm not one to question success," Dr. Simon said. "Congratulations. I'm very happy for you. I don't get to deliver news like this that often."

Chris felt short of breath. With his hands on his hips, he looked down at the square, white linoleum tiles on the floor of the exam room, then up at the fluorescent light, a little like a gasping runner who had just crossed the finish line.

"What are the odds that the cancer will return?"

"We're in uncharted territory now. There's not enough data to predict, but I think you should feel *very* good about this. We'll keep testing, but these results are very, very positive. I'd say you can go back to living your life."

Chris had an overpowering urge to see Sarah and to be outside in the sunshine. That was it—he and Sarah should go for a walk. Beyond that, he wasn't quite sure what to do with all of the new days and years he had just been given, but he was going to give that some thought when his mind stopped happily reeling. He wanted to whoop and jump around like a gleeful idiot, but instead he simply pumped Dr. Simon's hand and thanked him. Blood pounded and roared in his ears. It felt like being swept up in a cheering stadium crowd.

As Chris reached for the door to the waiting room and Sarah, the roaring in his ears subsided.

★ ★ ★

Sarah had a copy of *Newsweek* on her lap and appeared to be just staring at it. When he approached, she looked up as if she had just awakened.

"How did it go?"

"It went well," Chris said, smiling. "Really, really well." He proceeded to tell her everything that Dr. Simon had said. About a quarter of the way through his explanation, Sarah started erupting with little, barking laughs at almost everything he said. About halfway through, she started crying.

Chris gave Sarah a moment to compose herself and, while she did, he studied her face, which had become one of his favorite things to do. She was small, no more than five foot five, with a fair, northern complexion and ears that were too big poking through her shoulder-length brown hair. Sarah grew up in a working-class neighborhood of Boston and, while she didn't have the accent, she had a natural aversion to pretension, which manifested itself in a clear, cool gaze that always seemed to see you for exactly what you were. Chris felt that just standing in her presence and looking into those green eyes had to be more beneficial than any radiation therapy. What was she doing with him? It was a question that he often asked himself, but he wasn't sure he really wanted to know the answer.

An office relationship like this one was supposed to be just a brief interlude of decadent fun. He was supposed to show Sarah a good time for a few months, take her to some nice dinners, plays, a concert or two, and then they would both return to the inevitable trajectories of their lives.

Having cancer, though, had given everything a gravity that it was never supposed to have. When he had first told Sarah about the diagnosis, she had said the right things but then kept her distance for two whole days. She had returned, though, without a word of explanation or apology, and from that point forward she had been there for him through every harrowing, enervating step of the treatment process. He couldn't speak for Sarah, but from that day when she returned, Chris had started looking at their relationship differently.

★ ★ ★

That night, Chris took Sarah to a Steely Dan concert at Masonic Auditorium. She had heard of the band but didn't really know their music. Chris had figured that one of the advantages of being older was that he could introduce her to some of the great things her generation wasn't familiar with, but he wasn't sure the plan was working out.

The seventies rock band was gliding through "Kid Charlemagne," one of his favorite Dan songs. After the morning's miraculous good news, Chris's senses still felt hyperacute. It was as if every nerve ending was hardwired into his heart now. Everything prompted a swell of emotion, even the song's snaking, rising guitar solo. He felt like he was one emotional moment away from making a fool of himself in public.

At the root of this new feeling was the realization that he was going to die—but not today. *I'm going to die.* When you first grasp that concept as a child, it seems like a revelation that is both monumental and entirely irrelevant, like the fact that there are millions of stars like our sun scattered throughout the universe. As you move through your life, you say the words to yourself with varying degrees of conviction. When a car runs a red light and misses you by inches in an intersection, you say it and you mean it for a moment. But Chris now said the words to himself with a bone-deep and lasting certainty that they were true. *I'm going to die.*

And yet he had lived and apparently wouldn't die anytime soon. Forty years wasn't old, but getting that close to death had given him thoughts that most people don't have until they're fifty, or maybe even sixty, if they're lucky. In a typical life, death was like an important new product that was rolled out in the most slow and careful of launches, with viral awareness of the brand building until it was inescapable and the signs were everywhere. He'd had those thoughts sooner than he should have, and they had changed him in ways that he was still discovering.

Once Chris's initial euphoria had worn off, a certain amount of survivor's guilt set in. Why hadn't Tana had his luck?

He remembered the hideously bright red liquid cancer drug Adriamycin that she had taken intravenously. Like her fellow breast cancer patients, Tana had called it "the red devil" because of its terrible side effects. Her treatment had been much more excruciating than his, so it should have worked better. That would have been fair.

Chris's turbulent new feelings were tempered when his thoughts returned to the task that lay ahead of him—tracking down Enigma and Ripley and stopping the threatened cyber-attack. His new lease on life might be short-lived if the hackers had their way. He recalled the image of his faked death certificate and wondered again if it was a prank or a prophecy. *I'm going to die.* That's what someone was telling him.

"So how are you liking the show?" he asked.

"It's good. Good band, really good musicians."

Chris knew faint praise when he heard it. "You're not really into it, are you?"

"Maybe it's just because I didn't grow up on this music. When was the last time these guys were on the charts, like nineteen eighty?"

"Actually, that sounds about right. You don't have to spare me, you know, I can take it. I'm very resilient. After all, *I just beat cancer.*"

"You shouldn't joke about that." She tried to frown, but her pursed lips couldn't hold back a smile.

"No, I want you to be brutally honest with me. Try to forget for a moment that I'm in a weakened state after my bout *with cancer.*"

"Stop it," she said, laughing.

"I just used to think these guys were so cool."

"You thought they were cool?" The note of irony was unmistakable. She looked away, surveying the middle-aged crowd lining up to buy plastic cups of wine and microbrew. "It is nice to see that your musical tastes extend beyond classical and your precious Bach, though. Maybe it's just that I have my mind on other things."

"Like what?"

"Like what we could do to celebrate the good news."

"I've got an idea."

She grinned. "You always have that idea."

"It's a really good idea."

"Are we going back to my place or yours?"

"Mine. It's closer."

They both sipped wine from plastic cups, pretending to watch the concert crowd but really watching each other.

Finally, Sarah said, "You know, I do know what you're thinking."

"Oh, do you?"

"Yeah. I have heard that song 'Hey Nineteen.' How's it go?"

Chris didn't care to admit that she had read his mind. "Oh, right. Something about a guy dating a younger girl. She doesn't appreciate his music and it makes him feel old."

CHAPTER 8

January 9

When Chris saw the message in his inbox the next morning, he found it more shocking than the email containing the faked death certificate. It was from Sarah, and it read simply: "Chris— we're over and I'm moving on. Don't try to follow me. Sarah."

How could the woman who had accompanied him to his oncologist the day before send him that email? And what did she mean by "moving on"? Was she leaving the law firm? Was that what she meant by telling him not to follow?

It wasn't that Chris couldn't handle rejection. In fact, he had always expected Sarah to leave him for a younger man. Just not today, and not after the way she had acted the day before. Although he found it hard to admit, yesterday was probably the first time he had begun to entertain the notion that they might have a future together. Was this some sort of perverse reaction to yesterday's positive prognosis?

Chris immediately went to Sarah's office to see if she was in. Jamie Dahl, a fellow corporate paralegal who had the office next door, started shaking her head when she saw him approaching down the hall.

"She's not in. Resigned today. No notice."

"Did she say why?"

"Not to me. Apparently, she just did it in an email to Don. We've worked together for three years, so I thought I'd at least get a good-bye. I guess you must be feeling the same way . . ." Jamie flinched slightly as soon as she said it, but Chris was already aware that nearly everyone in the office knew about his relationship with Sarah.

"It's okay," he said, already heading for the office of Don Rubinowski, the firm's managing partner.

"Where's the dear leader?" Chris asked Don's secretary.

Don's secretary waved him into the office without any introduction. "He's expecting you. And he doesn't like it when you call him that."

Don was no stranger to the midlife crisis. In a development that even he felt was painfully clichéd, Don had married a woman twenty years his junior who sold Porsches. At the Porsche dealership on Van Ness Boulevard, Don had apparently found one-stop shopping for all of his midlife crisis needs.

Don stood up from behind his desk as Chris entered. He had close-cropped gray hair and a face so taut that some suspected he'd had a lift. Don broke off the call that was on speakerphone, saying, "Sorry, but we'll have to finish this later."

"So is it true?" Chris asked. "Did Sarah actually resign?"

"Yes. I got a terse little email, no explanation. No 'Thank you, I've learned a lot here,' nothing. No sign that she was looking for a recommendation letter, either. It sort of makes me think that the next thing we hear from her is going to be in the form of a pleading."

"I don't think you need to worry about that."

"Oh, I don't? Pardon me if I question how well you know the girl."

"I've been having an affair with her."

"Yes, I've gathered that. Apparently half the office knew before I did. You know, we have a policy about that sort of thing. You were supposed to make an official disclosure to HR."

"I know."

"And it's not that I'm entirely unsympathetic. I understand that you've been going through some tough times. And look who I married. Just not in the office."

"It wasn't something that I planned, believe me."

"Stacy has friends that age, lots of them. She could have set you up if you'd just said something."

"I wasn't just looking for someone younger—"

Don waved a hand to indicate that the relationship counseling session was at an end. It took a lot to get a rise out of Don—his experiences as a veteran litigator and long-time managing partner had rendered him flame-retardant and shock-resistant. "If you do hear from Sarah and figure out what she's thinking, I'd appreciate it if you would share with me, if you're so inclined."

"In all honesty, I have no idea what she's thinking. Just yesterday she really didn't seem like someone who was about to leave."

"You're lucky if you can understand a woman your own age. With someone who's fifteen, twenty years younger than you, you're just never going to get there. You may think you're connecting, but eventually you realize just how much was getting lost in the translation."

"You think we're a couple of fools?"

"Probably. The difference is that I married mine. I really can't tell you if that makes me the smart one between us."

"So what are you going to do?" Chris asked.

"What is there to do? I'm going to accept her resignation. Oh, and I'm also going to hope to God that we don't get sued."

"I think there's something wrong here. It just doesn't seem like her."

"What's wrong is that you've driven off a member of our staff because you couldn't keep it in your pants. Don't compound the problem by trying to find her. You'll just make things worse for all of us."

"Did I say I was going to try to find her?"

"No, but I do have some experience with these sorts of situations." Don stood up from his desk, signaling that the failed interrogation was over. "You need to keep your head in the game. Has BlueCloud engaged you to track down those hackers?"

"Yeah, I even got a personal audience with Dave Silver himself."

"I'm not surprised," Don said. "If BlueCloud takes the hit for a cyberattack, he loses hundreds of millions of dollars the next morning when the market opens."

As Chris rose and turned to leave, Don put his hand on Chris's shoulder. "Take care of yourself."

★ ★ ★

Most people would have simply accepted Sarah's email at face value, but most people didn't have the forensic resources available to them that Chris had. He wasn't necessarily expecting to find anything, but he decided that he was going to glean every bit of information that he could from the email. It was, after all, what he did.

Ed shot Chris a questioning look when he saw him take a seat at a computer in the forensics lab. "Can I help you out with anything there?"

"Thanks, Ed, I'm fine. Personal project."

Ed nodded and returned to his work. He was probably wondering what could be more important than the Lurker virus, but he knew better than to ask directly.

Sarah's email had been sent from her iPhone. Chris examined the routing on the email and noticed something odd. The email had been sent using a local WiFi connection in Barcelona, Spain.

Chris lifted his hands from the keyboard.

The threatening email with the fake death certificate had also originated from Barcelona. This was too unlikely to be a coincidence. Although he had nothing that could be called solid evidence, in that instant Chris knew that Sarah had been abducted by Enigma and Ripley, the hackers who had killed Pietr Middendorf. Perhaps the email that he had received from Sarah had been forced.

Chris knew that the hackers were dangerous, but he had never imagined that they might target Sarah. How could they even know that he was seeing Sarah? Chris felt an anger so intense that it incinerated every thought in his head.

Chris couldn't say exactly how long it took, but he eventually got his emotions under control. He needed to think clearly if he was going to hunt down Sarah's abductors.

Chris logged into his firm email account from a networked computer, opened Sarah's email, and clicked "Reply."

He typed: "Sarah—where are you?"

Chris slumped in his chair. Although Sarah had been gone less than twenty-four hours, he was certain that this was a kidnapping, and that the police needed to be involved.

.

CHAPTER 9

When Chris called the Central Station of the San Francisco Police Department on Vallejo Street, a desk clerk told him that he would need to come down to the station and submit a written report. By one in the afternoon, Chris was sitting in a molded plastic chair in the station's waiting room completing the paperwork.

The Central Station was a gray, concrete complex near the on-ramp to the 101 Freeway. It was a clear, cold, sunny day, and the officers and complainants were all briskly going about their business. From the TV cop shows, Chris thought that you had to wait twenty-four to forty-eight hours before filing a missing persons report, but that was not the case. The missing persons report could be filed immediately as long as you didn't know the whereabouts of the person. Chris suspected, however, that the police would take very little interest in the matter until at least twenty-four hours or so had passed. Because Sarah didn't have any living family, Chris knew that if he didn't file the missing persons report, it was unlikely that anyone else would.

Michael Hazlitt of the FBI had recognized the recurrence of the Barcelona IP address as an interesting coincidence, but he wasn't persuaded that a kidnapping had occurred. Nevertheless, Hazlitt said that they were going to hunt down Enigma and, if he also happened to be a kidnapper, then all the better. Hazlitt politely arranged a meeting for Chris with the unit of the FBI that handled kidnapping cases, but they were similarly unpersuaded, concluding that the matter of real interest was the cyberterrorism case, which was already being pursued.

As Chris completed the report, he described Sarah's appearance, the clothes she was wearing the last time that he saw her (green silk blouse and jeans) and identifying physical characteristics. He described his relationship as "friend." He was struck by how little the contents of the form conveyed about who Sarah really was. For that, he flashed back to the first time she caught his attention.

Bill Ober, an arrogant first-year associate from Harvard, had asked him a peculiar question that sent him in search of a paralegal named Sarah Hotchner. He had seen this sort of sniping before. Paralegals and first-year associates were in some ways natural enemies. The first year's sense of entitlement and salary often rankled the paralegal, who was often considerably older, with more practical knowledge of how the day-to-day aspects of lawyering got done.

Chris peered into her tiny office, where Sarah was collating exhibits for a court filing in an accordion rack. "It's Sarah, right?"

She turned to face him, a small smile already in place. "Right, Sarah Hotchner."

"Chris Bruen. Nice to meet you."

"I know who you are."

"Apparently you do. Did you say something to Bill Ober about me?"

Sarah cocked her head. "What did he say?"

"He said that you told him that I would be driving him over to the courthouse today on a motorcycle—with a sidecar. That he should act like it's no big deal when I ask him to ride in the sidecar."

"Hmm. He said that?"

"He said that."

"And you *don't* have a motorcycle with a sidecar?"

"No, I don't. And I don't think that Bill made that up. He doesn't have that much imagination."

Sarah nodded, giving it some consideration. "Probably right."

"That was nicely done. Just wacky enough to be true. And Bill does need to be taken down a notch or two."

Sarah chose not to comment.

"But while I appreciate the assistance, I've got this one," Chris continued. "Taking down overconfident first years, particularly Harvard Law grads, is something we're pretty good at around here."

"Just trying to help," she said, the half smile still there.

After that exchange, Chris had decided that it might be fun to work with the new paralegal, so he had asked for her when he was assembling his next due diligence team.

He smiled at the memory, then felt the hurt.

When he had completed the missing persons report, Chris was asked to come back to a desk in the squad room that was occupied by an officer in her late thirties with dyed blond hair and a rumpled uniform. She peered over the lipstick-smudged lid of her Styrofoam Carl's Jr. coffee cup at some notes on a yellow legal pad. Her name tag read "Officer Holly Miller."

"Chris Bruen?" As soon as she spoke, he recognized the mildly uninterested tone of the officer that he had spoken with on the phone.

"Yes."

"Okay," Officer Miller said, getting down to business. "So Sarah Hotchner is your coworker?"

"Right. We work at the same law firm."

"But you're here in your individual capacity, right? You aren't here as a representative of your law firm, are you?"

"No, that's right. We're friends."

"Now, I don't mean to pry, but it's my job to understand the situation as best I can before we commit resources to a missing persons case. You can understand that, right?"

"Sure. What would you like to know?"

The officer turned his missing persons report over in her hand. "You seem to know a lot about Ms. Hotchner. You were able to tell us where she lives, the car she drives, family history. Would you say that you had a close relationship?"

"Yes, we were close."

"Pardon me if this seems intrusive, but does that mean you had a romantic relationship with her?"

Chris paused. "Yes."

"Had you and Ms. Hotchner had an argument or anything like that prior to her disappearance?"

"No. There was no problem whatsoever. We'd been to a concert the night before. Earlier that day, she'd gone with me to see my oncologist. Does that sound like someone who's about to leave?"

"I'm sorry to hear that you're seeing an oncologist."

"Thanks, but I'm okay. As of yesterday, in fact, it turns out I'm okay."

"Congratulations. Sounds like you were having a very good day yesterday. Then, the next day, you received an email from her. She breaks off her relationship with you, quits her job, and, as far as you can tell, leaves town."

"Right."

"An outsider looking at those facts might think that she was trying to get away from you and was willing to go to pretty extreme lengths to do it."

"Everything was fine between us."

"Sometimes we think we know someone, but . . . I see it all the time in this job."

"I did a forensic analysis of the email that she sent and found that it was sent from an IP address in Spain. That also happens to be where a criminal hacking scheme that I'm investigating may be based."

"So you're going to have to explain that to me. I'm not much of a techie."

"I think Sarah may have been kidnapped by the same person who sent me a threatening email. Both emails came from Spain."

"Do you have the name of the person who sent the threatening email?"

"No, I don't really have any information about the person. Except for their hacker handle. Enigma."

"Enigma." Officer Miller said it slowly. Chris could almost hear the case file being closed. "So is this Enigma person your archenemy or something?"

"This is not a joke. I really believe that Sarah Hotchner has been kidnapped."

"Sorry, I didn't mean to make light of this. But you should probably think it through before proceeding with the report. It could make things more complicated."

"I don't care how complicated the paperwork is."

"I'm not talking about the paperwork. If it turns out that you're using the police department to locate an ex-lover who's trying to get away from you . . . Well, we don't take that sort of thing very well around here."

"I understand, but I'm telling you the truth."

Chris spent the remainder of the afternoon in the police station, filling out forms, answering questions, and waiting in windowless rooms for people to arrive to ask him more questions. At the end of the day, he felt that the one thing he had truly accomplished was making the SFPD deeply suspicious of him.

He left the police station with no sense that there was going to be an active missing persons investigation and, if that was true, then the whole exercise had been a waste of time. Once more drawing upon his vast store of semi-erroneous knowledge of police procedure gleaned from TV cop shows, he knew that the first forty-eight hours of a kidnapping case was the time when the victim was most likely to be recovered alive. If that was so, then Sarah might not have much more time.

Chris felt the need to move quickly to find her, but he really had nowhere to go. He could fly to Barcelona and hope to find a lead, but he didn't even know with any certainty that she was in Spain. Sarah and her abductors might be in Spain, but they could also be anywhere else in the world.

But Chris did believe that if he found the hackers behind the Lurker virus, then he would find Sarah. It wasn't enough for a police investigation, but it was enough for Chris. As he sat on a concrete bench outside the police station in a chill wind, he admitted to himself for perhaps the first time that he loved Sarah and would do just about anything to bring her back.

CHAPTER 10

When he was done at the police station, Chris returned to the firm's forensic lab to review the results of the Deep Web searches that Ed had conducted for the names Enigma and Ripley. The results appeared to be entirely random and useless, the data-mining equivalent of dragging a net across the bottom of a lake. Surprisingly, there were quite a few hackers using similar handles. The name Ripley alone produced nearly three dozen hits.

Chris culled through the search results, looking for common denominators. There was an Enigma343 in Hamburg, who several years ago had bragged about his exploits hacking a university financial aid database. Further searches for Enigma343 led to the discovery that this Enigma was now an associate professor at the same university that he had once hacked and had a personal website and a blog on cyber law issues. Chris placed Enigma343 in the "unlikely" category, because a university professor didn't fit the profile. Hackers were usually malcontents who held a succession of random jobs—they didn't typically follow a career path. More importantly, a real criminal hacker wouldn't have left such an obvious trail to his true identity.

Eventually, Chris began to see some patterns that suggested he had picked up the trail of the pair. He found several postings in an Internet Relay Chat room from an Enigma that all bore a similar mix of grandiosity and menace. There were also frequent communications from a Ripley on the same message board. Ripley's posts were so laconic that it was difficult get a read on her personality. The postings were all at least six months old and there was nothing that seemed to relate to the January 14 attack, but at least Chris had found one of the places on the Internet that they had frequented, at least at one time.

As Ed had guessed, Ripley did seem to be a woman, judging by the volume of sexual innuendo thrown her way on the message boards. "Seemed" was the operative word because, with so many imposters, as an oft-repeated Internet meme put it, "There are no women on the Internet." In some corners of the Internet, gender and sexuality were fluid concepts. In Chris's experience, the hacker community contained a disproportionately high number of transgender persons. Perhaps engaging in online gender-bending made it easier for some to change who they were in the real world.

Such was the trail of clues that led Chris to be hunched over his home computer at 11:00 p.m., about to log on an IRC channel frequented by Bay Area hackers and techno geeks where Enigma and Ripley had once surfaced. The blinds in his loft were open and he could see the Bay Bridge, its span strung with lights that disappeared into fog.

Chris's plan was to spend some time posing as a hacker on the channel in hopes of tapping into some chatter about Middendorf, Ripley, or Enigma. It took him a while to pick a suitable handle for his posting, but he finally settled on VeraDae, a play on *viridae*, the taxonomic group that includes viruses.

Chris knew better than to start a thread with a direct inquiry about his targets or Sarah. He also couldn't lurk on the message board and then join the conversation at the first mention of one of them. Instead, he needed to establish a presence, so he invented some exploits for his new alter ego.

> VERADAE: Just hacked into the City of San Francisco. I own them.

Chris stared at the screen, waiting for someone to take the bait.

After a few minutes, a response appeared.

> CYNECITTA: Am I supposed to be impressed?
> VERADAE: Yes.
> CYNECITTA: Too easy. The city doesn't pay enough to have decent IT staff. I like more of a challenge.

From the name, Chris guessed that he was communicating with a woman and a movie buff. The name was probably an allusion to Rome's famed Cinecittà movie studio. He was tempted to ask her what sort of a hack might provide a challenge commensurate with her skills, but he didn't want to be too obvious. Instead, he typed:

> VERADAE: So u prefer the private sector?
> CYNECITTA: Correct. Or if ur going to hack a govt system, u might as well man up and take on the feds. Or maybe some mils.

"Mils" was shorthand for military websites using the .mil domain.

VERADAE: Ru calling me a pussy?
CYNECITTA: If the tutu and little velvet dancing shoes
   fit . . .

Chris smiled. Ah, the power of the Internet to turn even the meekest among us into a smartass. The person on the other end of the cursor would probably never say that to his face if they encountered one another in a line at the coffee shop or the grocery store.

VERADAE: Big talk. How do I know ur legit? Who do
   you know?
CYNECITTA: Who do YOU know?

Chris liked where this was heading.

VERADAE: Who don't I know? Fembot, Pwnsauce, Black
   Vector, Xylo . . .

There was a pause long enough to make Chris fear that he had scared her off.

CYNECITTA: GTFO. U knew Black Vector?
VERADAE: Yeah, I knew him a little. I was really sorry to
   hear what happened.
CYNECITTA: I'm going to see the Morning Benders at
   the Bottom of the Hill 2nite. If u want to continue this
   conversation, we can do it there.

VERADAE: How do I know that ur not just messing with me?

CYNECITTA: U don't.

VERADAE: If I do show up, how will I know u?

CYNECITTA: U won't. I'll know u.

CHAPTER 11

The Bottom of the Hill, a rock club on Seventeenth Street in the edgy Mission District, was warm, humid, and redolent of stale beer. As Chris passed the pool tables out front and drew closer to the music, the crowd became increasingly dense, as if the band were exerting a gravitational pull. At the foot of the stage in front of the amps, the throng pressed together, chest to back, with only enough room to bob their heads. He saw no one who seemed likely to be Cynecitta.

Chris had no interest in joining the scrum, so he ordered a beer and stood for a while near the bar, where he would be visible to anyone in the club who might be looking for him. He was wearing jeans, sneakers, and a dress shirt open at the collar. There was no question that he stood out. He examined a wall of the club that was covered with graffiti left by hundreds of bands that had played there. A few of the names were familiar, but most had probably flamed out long ago, victims of creative differences or public indifference. All that remained of most of those bands was an ironic name, a logo drawn in Sharpie, and the alcohol-fuzzed memories of those who had crowded before the tiny stage.

After about fifteen minutes of watching the very young band bash out some decent indie-rock, he began to think she wasn't going to show. He pondered how the band's drummer could be old enough to grow the hipster mountain-man beard that he was sporting.

The bartender, a woman in her midthirties wearing a faded, black Sleater-Kinney T-shirt, reached across the bar and tapped him on the shoulder. "You're not subtle, are you?" she said.

"Is there a problem?" Chris wondered if she had somehow not gotten the tip that he'd left on the bar.

"Yes, there's a problem. We spoke online. You're Chris Bruen."

He winced. While he knew that his undercover identity wasn't going to fool anyone for long, he was a little disappointed that it had proved so transparent. "Cynecitta." She wasn't what he had been expecting. Aside from the T-shirt, Cynecitta looked like she could be one of his colleagues at the firm. She had dark brown, shoulder-length hair and no visible tattoos (which differentiated her from everyone else who worked there). With her quick, dark eyes and an ironic smile that turned her mouth sharply upward on one side, Cynecitta had a face that was made for smart remarks.

"Can I give you a little advice?"

"Sure."

"You should know that most hackers who are any good know you on sight by now." Chris heard what sounded like the trace of a Southern accent, but one with sharp elbows. Chris guessed that she might be from North Carolina. He had learned from his wife, who had been from Birmingham, that every state below the Mason–Dixon line had its own way of torturing vowels.

"You could have just let me drink my beer and go home."

She smiled. "But then I would have missed the opportunity to taunt the famous Chris Bruen."

"You could have waited until I got home and then taunted me by email."

"Not as satisfying." Chris stood corrected. Cynecitta did not have to hide behind the Internet. She was perfectly willing to flame him in person.

"Aside from the taunting," Chris said, "I think there must be something that you want to say to me."

Cynecitta stared at him impassively.

"Can you at least tell me your real name?"

She wiped some beer off the counter with a rag, giving it some thought.

"All I have to do is ask around here," Chris added.

"Zoey Doucet," she said. "Let's sit down over there. I'll get someone to tend bar."

After a brief negotiation with another bartender, Zoey joined him at a table at the back of the bar near the pool tables. Even there, they had to speak a bit loudly to be heard.

"So you knew Pietr Middendorf—I mean Black Vector?" Chris asked.

"I did. Online, anyway. We chatted from time to time."

"What did you think of him?"

"Seemed like a nice guy. And he knew his stuff. He had skills."

"Let me start by saying that I didn't kill him. I had nothing to do with it."

She leaned forward across the table with a confrontational look. "Maybe you didn't kill him, but you were at his apartment when he was killed, weren't you?"

"How do you know that?"

"I'm not going to tell you. But if that's not right, then just say so."

Chris took a sip of his beer. "No, that's right. I was trying to get Pietr to return some source code that he had stolen. But if he had cooperated, he wouldn't have even gone to jail."

"What were you doing trolling on that IRC channel?" she asked.

"Did you know that Pietr was connected to the people who created the virus that caused that midair collision in Albuquerque?"

"I'm not surprised that Pietr was involved with a virus, but he would never hurt innocent people like that."

"Maybe not willingly. He may not have had a choice. Why doesn't it surprise you that Pietr was spreading a virus?"

"Because he wasn't just some script kiddie pulling pranks. He wanted to do some damage—in a good way." "Script kiddie" was a term for a wannabe hacker.

Chris knew what she was going to say, but he asked anyway. "What would you consider good damage?"

"A little disruption is healthy, makes everyone's security stronger. It also lets those big corporations know that not everything is under their control. They can still be brought down—even by people like me." This was a point of view common to the so-called antisecurity or antisec movement.

"Were you working with Black Vector?"

"No, but if he'd asked me, I would have."

Chris believed her, but he wondered if she was merely a hacker apologist or someone capable of doing real harm. "I'm looking for two hackers who go by the names Enigma and Ripley. Do you know them?"

"Why should I tell you, even if I did know something? You obviously know what they're saying about you and Black Vector."

"If you believed that, I doubt that you'd have invited me here."

"You don't know me well enough to say that. Maybe I have a gang of guys outside the club waiting to beat the crap out of you."

"Good point." Chris didn't think that was true, but the remark made him uncomfortable nonetheless.

The music grew louder as the band's set reached its close. They waited to continue their conversation while the crowd cheered for an encore.

"What do you want with Enigma and Ripley?"

"I think they're involved in spreading a very dangerous virus."

"And why is that your concern?"

Chris could have said that he was trying to avert a potential cyberattack, but he sensed that he needed to be more frank than that if he was going to make any headway with Zoey. "The virus would exploit my client's operating system."

"So who's your client?"

"I can't tell you that."

"Okay, and I care about your big corporate client because . . .?"

"Fair enough, but it's also possible that Enigma and Ripley were involved in Pietr Middendorf's death."

"I don't think you're doing this for Pietr."

"You're right. I'm not."

She gave a small nod, seeming to appreciate the honest response. "Look, I will tell you this. You don't want to get too close to those two, Enigma and Ripley."

"Why's that?"

"They're real criminal types. The kind that kill people."

"I think you know something that you're not telling me about Enigma and Ripley. Why not?"

"Because I'm really not interested in helping you protect the integrity of some operating system. In fact, I couldn't care less about that." She paused. "And I don't think you would be careful enough to keep me out of it if you did find those two."

Chris realized that he was going to have to lay his cards on the table if he was going to get more from Zoey. "I think they've kidnapped a woman. Her name is Sarah Hotchner."

Chris drew a deep breath, leaned in close across the table, and told Zoey the entire story, holding little back. Chris knew that if he was going to get Zoey to help him, it would have to be about Sarah, and it certainly couldn't be about BlueCloud.

When he was done, Zoey made a show of studying him. "Well, I wouldn't have taken you for the type."

"And what type is that?"

"The sort of guy who goes batshit in middle age, dates younger women."

"Well, batshit is a little strong."

"And I can understand why the police are skeptical—the evidence for kidnapping sounds pretty thin. But they also probably don't appreciate how unusual it is to have both of those emails originating from Spain."

"Exactly," Chris said. "So do you think they could be kidnappers?"

The amused expression disappeared from Zoey's face. "I think that if Enigma and Ripley, and the people they work with, want to hurt you, then they would be capable of kidnapping—and worse. But I have one question for you."

"Yes?"

"Why would they kidnap Sarah? You're the one they want, right?"

Chris paused, taking another sip of his beer. "That's a good question, and I don't know the answer. But I get the sense that this may be some kind of game that they want me to play. I think they want me to come after her, but I don't know why." The thought hadn't really crystallized until that moment.

Zoey regarded him with an expression that he couldn't quite read. "Is your life always this intense?"

"No, not so much, actually," Chris said. "Look, you talk like you know things about them. I need to know what you know."

Zoey listened to the band for a while, weighing her answer.

Finally, she spoke. "I do know someone who has done business with them. And he's here in the Bay Area."

"Who is it?"

"Eddie Reiser. He's really a slimeball's slimeball. He's some sort of high-tech pornographer, that's all I know—and all I care to know."

"What sort of business does he have with Ripley and Enigma?"

"I have no idea, but I saw his name and website mentioned once in an IRC post by Enigma."

"Where do I find him?"

"His website is PantherSex.com."

"Thank you," Chris said.

"Don't thank me yet. You haven't met Eddie Reiser. Prepare to be slimed."

"I'll wear my parka," Chris said.

CHAPTER 12

To find Eddie Reiser, Chris started with the website, PantherSex. com, which touted itself as an "online spectator brothel." Chris had to hand it to Reiser—he had done the near-impossible— he had discovered what appeared to be a new way to pervert human sexuality online.

Although Chris hated to contribute to Reiser's coffers, he bought an entry-level online subscription for fifty dollars and browsed the website. Apparently, the online spectator brothel experience involved accessing live feeds from webcams from a series of bedrooms that were staged like porno movie sets. One room looked like a Las Vegas honeymoon suite. Another room had a mattress that was in the middle of what looked like a polar bear exhibit at a zoo. Looming over the bed was an enormous stuffed polar bear. Chris could not even begin to imagine who the audience might be for this. He chalked it up to one of the forty-seven Rules of the Internet—if it exists, there is porn of it.

Chris completed an online registration form for those who wanted to be one of the performers in the spectator brothel. He provided a prepaid credit card and fake name that he used for investigating online scams. He would have to provide his credit card information. A half hour later he received an email that read, "Welcome to PantherSex.com!" and provided an 800 number that he was to dial if he was ready for "the wildest action on the Internet."

He called the 800 number and got a breathy, recorded female voice: "Are you ready for some wild action? Please stay on the line and an operator will be with you soon."

After about three minutes of waiting, a sleepy-sounding woman operator picked up the phone. "Welcome to PantherSex. com. What's your name?"

"Sam."

"Hi, Sam. So you've checked out our website and you'd like to be a part of the online spectator brothel experience?"

"That's right. Sounds like fun."

"Are you a police officer or affiliated with law enforcement in any way, Sam?"

"No."

"Sorry, but we have to ask. What's your credit card number?"

Chris provided the information and waited while the operator ran the card and presumably performed some sort of background check on him.

The woman returned. "Okay, when would you like to book your session?"

"What's your earliest availability?"

"Hmm, let's see," she said. "Oh, we had a cancellation for the eight o'clock spot tonight. Does that work for you?"

"That's perfect."

"Are you looking for a male or female partner?"

"Female."

"Any special requests or restrictions that we should know about?"

"No."

"Great. You should arrive at least a half hour early for orientation. Come to 2578 Windward Lane, off Highway 1, just south of Pacifica."

"I'll be there."

"Great." The operator paused. "Oh, I see that you're in luck."

"How's that?" Chris asked, really wanting to know.

"You're in the Polar Bear Suite."

★ ★ ★

As Chris drove south down Highway 1 to Pacifica, the dusk and gauzy fog gave the light a strange gray-green cast. It was impossible to locate the setting sun, and everything was evenly lit as if by fluorescent bulbs. Pacifica was only a twelve-mile drive from San Francisco, but it felt like a very different place. San Francisco is famous for its fog, but Pacifica is the true fog capital of the Bay Area. The community was also known for surfing beaches like Linda Mar and ocean-view apartment buildings that occasionally toppled from crumbling cliffs into the sea.

Chris pulled off onto an unlikely looking private road just outside Pacifica. There wasn't even a mailbox on the street, but there was a security camera mounted on a tree. The narrow, paved road wound up a hillside to a large, well-maintained brick and clapboard ranch house. If the police ever did decide to raid Reiser's establishment, he would have plenty of warning. Chris knew, however, that state and federal authorities did not consider Internet vice to be an enforcement priority, unless it involved child pornography or exploitation.

There were six cars parked in the driveway, so he assumed it was a busy night at the Internet brothel. Chris walked up to the front porch and rang the doorbell. There was a Christmas wreath still on the door and, if he didn't know better, he would have assumed that the place was home to a well-off family that enjoyed its privacy. That impression ended the instant that Eddie Reiser opened the door. Eddie was wearing a Taylor Swift T-shirt, a studded leather vest, and curly, greasy-looking brown hair that was styled in what could only be described as a mullet. He strode quickly up the hallway and opened the door without hesitation.

"I'm Eddie. And you must be . . .?" He consulted a small clipboard. "Sam Cantrell."

"Yeah, that's me."

"You ready to get down, Sam?"

"Well, as a matter of fact, we need to talk about that, Eddie."

"You're lucky. The Polar Bear Suite is usually booked weeks in advance."

Eddie grabbed him by the bicep and hustled him down the hallway into the living room, which was tastefully decorated with traditional furniture. The sofas were covered in plastic slipcovers, probably to make it easier to spray down the area with disinfectant.

"I've got someone who's looking forward to meeting you. And, let me tell you, she's ready to go, if you know what I mean. Have a seat."

"Eddie, we really need to talk."

"Hang on there, stud. I'll be back in a minute and you'll both get a chance to ask your questions."

The slipcover squeaked as Chris sat on the couch. He examined his surroundings, which looked like they might have come straight out of a Thomasville Furniture catalogue, except that the details were wrong. There were hunting prints on the walls, cherry furniture, and tasteful damask fabrics on the sofa and chairs, but the coffee table held a porcelain dish full of condoms rather than mints, alongside DVD cases for porno videos.

Eddie returned with a woman in her early thirties who looked a little like a biker chick, with a hard face that was not unpretty. The woman wore jeans and a faded western shirt with pearl buttons that was open halfway down to her navel. Eddie ushered her over to the couch, and Chris stood to greet her in what he quickly realized was a bit of misplaced chivalry.

"Melinda, Sam. Sam, Melinda."

Melinda met his gaze, and then her eyes traveled the length of his body, all the way down and back up again. She was very businesslike about it.

Chris turned to Eddie. "I need to speak with you in private for a minute."

Melinda turned to glare at Chris. "Oh, give me a break."

"No, no, this has nothing to do with you. I just need to speak with Eddie about something."

Eddie motioned for Chris to join him in the kitchen. "We'll be right back," he said to Melinda. "Don't worry. I haven't lost a man yet."

Once they were in the kitchen, Eddie launched into a practiced spiel. "So you've got cold feet, right? It's a natural reaction. But once you're in the heat of things, you'll completely forget about the audience."

Chris raised his voice a bit to cut through Eddie's patter. "Eddie. Listen to me. I didn't come here to have sex. Signing up was the only way I knew to get your address."

Eddie slammed his palm on a granite counter top. "I knew it! You're a damn vice cop. I'm callin' my lawyer."

"I'm not a cop."

"Then who are you?"

"I'm looking for some people that I believe you've done business with—they go by the online names Enigma and Ripley."

Eddie seemed flustered. Finally, he said, "You didn't answer my question—who the fuck are you? Did they send you here?"

"My name is Chris Bruen. I'm a lawyer investigating a matter for a client."

"Get off my property!" Eddie said. "What, it's not enough that they rip me off, but now they send some dickwad lawyer to intimidate me? Well, I will not be intimidated! Get out, man!"

Eddie reached into a drawer on the kitchen island. After the sound of clattering kitchen utensils, he came up with a pistol and pointed it at Chris's chest. "I said get out!"

"Easy there, Eddie," Chris said, raising open palms. His heart hammered as he imagined a headline in the next morning's *Chronicle* about the law firm partner shot to death by an Internet pornographer after signing up for sex in the Polar Bear Suite. "They didn't send me. I'm not here to cause you trouble. I just want to find those hackers. A friend of mine is in danger and I think they're responsible."

"So are you working for a client or helping a friend?" Eddie said, still agitated but regaining some calm from the gun in his hand. "You've got to work on your story, man."

"How did they rip you off?"

REECE HIRSCH • 99

Eddie paced around the kitchen, apparently deciding whether it was in his interest to talk to Chris. "You really want to get those bastards?"

"Yes, as a matter of fact, that's what I do."

"So you put people like me in jail?"

"Not you personally. Tell me about your problem with Enigma and Ripley. But first, please, Eddie, the gun?"

He slowly lowered the pistol. "Well, I dealt with Enigma. I don't know that other one. He wanted to market some of my videos online to the Asian market. You know, the Japanese love their porn, but they like it cute—all Hello Kitty and shit. He was going to repackage the sex tapes, create a website with a different look and feel. I thought we were going to make some good money off it."

"And what happened?"

"He did what he said he was going to do—up to a point. He created the website, posted the video, and the site was apparently pulling a lot of traffic."

"So what was the problem?"

"The asshole refused to pay me. They kept all of the subscription fees and content that I provided. Told me to go fuck myself."

"So what did you do?"

"Well, I did a little research about who I was doing business with. Sure, I should have done that before. Maybe I'm too trusting."

"Yeah, that's probably it," Chris said.

Eddie shot Chris a look but continued. "I learned pretty quickly that Enigma was part of a bad crew. Everyone who knew them told me to write the thing off as a loss and let it go. Enigma said that if I pushed the issue, they were going to come out here, take my entire business, and bury me in the backyard."

"And you believed him."

"Fuckin' A I believed him. I'm not about violent crime. Some call this 'victimless crime,' but I say, 'how is this even a crime to begin with?' In my business, everyone gets their rocks off, everyone walks away happy."

"Tell me how I can find them."

"I spoke to Enigma a couple of times on the phone."

"Did you ever get an email address or a number?"

"No, he always contacted me. But there was one time when Enigma called me—it must have been last July or August—and I could tell it was an international call from the number on the caller ID."

"I don't suppose you know which country?"

"Nah."

"Never mind," Chris said. "And there's nothing else you can tell me about them? Did you ever talk to a woman? Anyone named Ripley?"

"Nah."

Melinda shouted from the living room, "Eddie! What the hell?"

Eddie looked hopefully at Chris. "As long as you're here and all . . ."

Chris responded with a look that could not have been clearer. "I think I'd better be going now."

"Okay, but listen, you should go out through the kitchen door. I don't think Melinda is the type to respond well to sexual rejection."

"Good idea."

As Chris stepped through the kitchen door onto the back porch, Eddie whispered, "If there's any reward involved, remember that I'm a victim here. They stole my intellectual property."

"Based on what I've seen," Chris said, "there's nothing intellectual about it."

"Listen, man. One more thing. If you do manage to find him, he can't know that I helped you. When he said he'd kill me, I believed him."

Melinda shouted Eddie's name again from the living room, louder and angrier this time.

"Sure, Eddie. Now you'd better get back to your customer."

Chris tiptoed down a gravel path alongside the house, past the living room window where Melinda was still waiting. The curtains were open, so he ducked low to the ground as he passed. While he was willing to pursue a crew of ruthless international cybercriminals, he was not about to tangle with Melinda.

The moon was a dim night-light glowing through the clouds as he pulled his car onto Highway 1 and headed north back to San Francisco, weighing his options. Eddie had not given him much, but Chris was going to run down every available lead. If he was right, Sarah had been abducted more than twenty-four hours ago, and his chances of finding her were dwindling with every hour that passed.

CHAPTER 13

Chris pulled off of Pacific Coast Highway into the parking lot of Pacifica State Beach, better known as Taco Bell Beach. True to its nickname, there was a modern blond wood structure right on the sand that housed a Taco Bell. During the day, the place was frequented by surfers who ate chalupas on the patio in wet board shorts. At night, the clientele consisted mainly of high school kids and the usual assortment of non-calorie-counters.

Even with the windows rolled up, Chris could hear the surf pounding about a hundred yards away. As he dialed his cell phone, he gazed out at the moonlight glinting off the serrated crests of the dark waves.

The phone rang several times, then a gruff voice answered: "The caller ID says Chris Bruen, but that's impossible."

"Been a long time, Charlie," Chris said.

"It's been so long that I just assumed you were dead, and then here you are, calling me on my cell at ten at night. Imagine my surprise. I was just having a beer and watching *Law & Order*—one of the good ones with Vincent D'Onofrio."

"It's good to talk to you again."

Chris could hear Charlie suppress a yawn on the other end of the line. "If it's so good, then we would have done this sooner. I thought you'd forgotten about your old buddies at DOJ now that you're making the big, sweet law-firm dollar. How's private practice treating you?" Charlie McGuane had been a deputy prosecutor in the Computer Crimes Section when Chris had been at the DOJ. During their run together as a team, Chris and Charlie's string of successful convictions was rivaled only by their series of massive bar tabs at The Irish Bank.

"I'm getting along. I heard you're a chief prosecutor now. Congratulations."

"Thanks. Just filling the power vacuum that you left behind. But, I have to ask, buddy, why are you calling after all this time? And why at this hour?"

"I have a favor to ask. I need you to pull some phone records for me. Tonight. And you don't have to say it—I know I'm going to owe you big-time when this is done."

"Would you like to tell me why you want this?"

"I'd rather not. It's important, and it's personal. Someone I care about may be in a lot of danger."

"Have you tried law enforcement? They're sometimes quite effective."

"This is not something that they're particularly interested in. The records belong to an online pornographer named Eddie Reiser, so that might provide some cover if you need it."

"If anyone really looks at this, I'll need more than that to cover my ass."

Chris got to the point, and he didn't try to hide the desperation in his voice. "Can you help me?"

After a moment of silence, Charlie said, "What am I going to do, leave you hanging? The fact that you're calling me like this tells me that you're hard up. Sure, give me the information."

Chris provided Reiser's phone number and asked him to pull all of his phone records for the previous July and August, or at least the numbers for any international phone calls he had received during that period.

"Thanks, Charlie. Did I mention that I owe you big-time?"

"You just start brainstorming how you're going to repay me," Charlie said. "And I'll see what I can do."

Chris pulled back onto Highway 1 and continued north into San Francisco. By the time he was on the 101 overpass with the lights of the city's jagged skyline glimmering before him, he had his answer. Charlie called him back on his cell phone and told him that Reiser had received only one international call during July and August. The call had been on August 8—from a number in Barcelona. Charlie had even looked up the number for him and found that it belonged to a shuttered factory that once manufactured parts for Fiats.

Chris had figured that he was headed for Barcelona, but now he knew where he was going when he got there. But before he could book a flight, he would need to pay another visit to Zoey.

CHAPTER 14

The Bottom of the Hill was open until 2:00 a.m., so Chris figured that he should be able to catch Zoey before her shift at the bar ended.

Chris got his hand stamped with red ink in the outline of a monkey and entered the club, which was crowded, hot, and loud. Another band, more skronky and atonal than the first, was now playing on the small stage. Zoey was working full tilt serving up drinks, so he waited until she took a break. He got a beer from a bartender at the other end of the counter and nursed it while he observed her. He noticed that the largely male crowd tended to congregate at her end of the bar, preferring to be served by Zoey rather than her male counterpart. Zoey didn't seem to solicit that sort of attention and appeared oblivious to the effect that she was having, but Chris was pretty sure that she knew.

As Chris sipped his beer, he planned the trip to Barcelona. An objective outsider, like one of his law firm partners, would probably think he was crazy to embark on this trip to Spain. Chris didn't even know with certainty that Sarah had been abducted. But there was no doubt in his mind that she was in trouble.

When Zoey finally took a break, she came directly over to his table and sat down. He hadn't realized that she had spotted him.

"So, how'd it go?"

"Well, you were right about the slime, but Reiser's information really helped. I found another connection between Enigma, Ripley, and Barcelona: an abandoned Fiat factory in Barcelona. Does that sound familiar?"

"No. So are you going?"

"Yeah. And I want you to come with me."

"Really. Why would I want to do that?"

Chris had been assembling his arguments while he waited. "Because I need someone who knows the hacker community from the inside to help me track this crew. Because my client will pay for you to travel with me to Europe as my assistant. And because, even though you don't know her, you don't want Sarah Hotchner to come to harm."

Zoey watched the band leaning into their instruments onstage like they were summoning a storm. Then she said, "Free trip to Barcelona or tend bar here? That's an easy one. Sure."

Chris didn't believe for a moment that Zoey was as cynical as she let on.

"But I'd need to know who I'm working for," she continued. "No more of this 'my client' stuff. It's BlueCloud, right?"

"Right," Chris said.

Zoey continued, "I get my own room, and I'm not sleeping with you."

"I wouldn't have it any other way. Get your bags packed, because we're leaving tomorrow."

"I have a couple more conditions."

"Yes?"

"Don't call me your assistant."

"How about technical advisor?"

"Okay. And don't ask me to do corporate. I don't do corporate."

"I know. Just be yourself." Chris added, after considering for a moment, "But maybe a slightly toned-down version."

CHAPTER 15

January 10

Chris found air travel tiring under the best of conditions, but since he'd started the cancer medications it had become exhausting. Even though his cancer was in complete remission, it had left him feeling watered down and spread thin. Sitting next to Zoey through the entirety of their cross-country and transatlantic flights wasn't going to enhance the experience.

He usually liked long flights because he felt pleasantly untethered from his work responsibilities. Up in the air was the one place where no client could reach him with a call or an email. It was a relief to be free of the ringing phone, because, in Chris's legal practice, some client somewhere was always experiencing a crisis, such as a hacking incident or the theft of a laptop containing hundreds of thousands of SSNs. Clients expected him to be there for them when that crisis occurred and he understood that, at a rate of $800 per hour, that expectation was not unreasonable.

The one client he was still very much in touch with was BlueCloud. BlueCloud's general counsel, Scott Austin, had, without blinking, authorized his trip to Barcelona and the hiring of Zoey as his assistant. The stakes were so high for the company that they were going to give him just about anything he asked for.

When Chris had disclosed to Austin his belief that Sarah had been kidnapped by Enigma and Ripley, it had clearly troubled him. Austin had immediately arranged a conference call between Chris, Austin, and Silver. While Silver was obviously worried that Chris's personal mission would take precedence, even he was sensitive enough not to state it that bluntly. Since they hadn't pulled the plug on the assignment, he had to assume that Silver and Austin had calculated his kidnapping theory was only going to make him more driven to find the hackers.

Chris knew he might never see Sarah again, and so his mind kept running through the five months they were together, the things they'd done, the things she'd said. Perhaps it was his way of making sure that he remembered everything clearly later, if that was all that he was going to have. It became increasingly obvious that there had been an inflection point in their relationship—the two days after he received his cancer diagnosis when Sarah had disappeared. After her return, there seemed to be an unspoken understanding that there was no going back on their relationship. By pursuing this uncertain trail, Chris felt that he was just living up to the implicit promise that they had made to each other when Sarah returned on that second day. There was no going back for him, either.

The cabin lights dimmed, and he studied the snow-covered Rockies forty thousand feet below. He tried very hard not to think about the computer virus that had sent the two jets crashing to earth outside Albuquerque. On the aisle, with an empty seat between them, Zoey was wearing big headphones and bobbing her head slightly to something thrashy. Chris requested water from the flight attendant and removed a bottle of Zofran from his satchel.

Zoey watched him as he tossed back a couple of pills and lifted one side of her headphones. "If you don't mind my asking, what are those? If they're for sleep, could you spare one?"

"It's called Zofran. For nausea."

"You get airsick?"

"That's right." Chris decided that there was no need to tell her about his cancer, particularly since he was in recovery.

They sat in silence for a while, letting the white noise of the jet engine envelop them. Row after row of passengers watched the in-flight movie, some romantic comedy, each cute reaction shot mirrored in a hundred tiny screens.

★ ★ ★

A couple of hours later, Chris tossed in a restless sleep, dreaming that Tana was sitting in the center seat between him and Zoey.

Tana was reading a paperback, something by Laura Lippman. She liked to spontaneously buy a book in the airport newsstand right before boarding. She said that if she thought about it too long she'd end up buying something that she was supposed to read instead of what she really enjoyed. On some level, Chris knew that it was a dream, so he didn't attempt to speak to her. He didn't want to break the spell. He sat quietly with her, his dream self half dozing while she read, just as he had so often when she was alive. He heard the soft inhale and exhale of her breath, the occasional rustle of a turning page, saw her delicate, pale fingers holding the paperback in the narrow, bright cone of the overhead reading light.

They could have been on a flight to visit her mother in Birmingham. Or on one of the year-end vacations that they took after the law firm had completed its collections and closed its books. On those trips, they would often go someplace outside the country, like London or Cairo.

The thing he missed most about marriage was the quality of the silence. No moment he had spent since Tana's death was as perfectly calm and peaceful as the moments he spent half dozing while she read her paperback crime novels. To an outsider it sounded boring, but it wasn't. He clung to it as long as he could, but the dream receded like a tide until he could no longer pretend that the seat next to him wasn't empty. He motioned to the flight attendant for a drink.

Tana had made him normal in a way that he hadn't really been before or since. Chris had been a geeky computer prodigy as a teenager. Aside from when he was coding or in the computer lab with his friends (dubbed "the Geek Chorus" by one classics major), Chris rarely felt that he was in his element. He'd certainly never been very good with women until Tana.

They had met as undergraduates at Stanford. Chris was a computer science major with his eye on becoming a patent attorney. Tana was a Stegner Fellow in the creative writing program, and a bit of an outsider herself. She was working on a cyberpunk novel in the vein of William Gibson, which wasn't in step with the writing program's august literary fiction traditions. As part of her research on hackers, Tana wanted to interview Chris and some of his friends, who were renowned for pranks, such as doctoring transcripts to give all of the members of the Stanford football team straight As, a stunt that immediately triggered an NCAA investigation.

Chris was instantly attracted to Tana, with her long, reddish-brown hair (which she lost during the chemo) and freckles (which she always hated). Like the Geek Chorus, Tana was a little intense and not all that well socialized herself. She would fire questions at him and then be brought up short with a laugh when he said something that surprised her. He started trying to find ways to elicit that laugh. It became difficult to concentrate on her questions after a while because he couldn't stop thinking about her freckles. He wanted to find out if they covered the rest of her body.

Ordinarily, Chris would have never found a way to talk to a girl as pretty as Tana, but she made things easy. She was always doing the talking, peppering him with questions. It took a while for them to connect, but she was persistent. Pretty soon, Chris was the only member of the Geek Chorus that she was still interviewing—at local bars, restaurants, and, eventually, in bed in Chris's cluttered student apartment.

After Tana's death, Chris had to admit that he had regressed a bit as a person. He wasn't the geeky misfit that he had been as a teenager, but he also wasn't really comfortable in his own skin anymore, either. Where he once threw himself into his coding in Stanford's computer lab, he now threw himself into his work at the firm. He wasn't nearly as shy as he had been back then, but the cool, professional façade that he had developed as an attorney was every bit as difficult to crack. It was his personal firewall, and it was nearly impenetrable.

★ ★ ★

While changing planes in New York, Chris and Zoey had an hour to kill in the food court of the terminal at JFK. It was a cavernous space lined with duty-free stores and shops selling cellophane-wrapped sandwiches.

Chris didn't know Zoey well, but there were things about her that didn't add up for him. This was as good a time as any to ask a few questions.

"You're obviously smart and talented and have certain skills."

"Yes, I agree. But?"

"I just wonder why you're still tending bar."

"You mean why am I still tending bar *at my age?*"

An airline agent blared over the intercom, announcing a boarding flight, forcing a break in the conversation. Chris raised his hands in self-defense, ready to drop the subject.

"No, I'll tell you," Zoey said. "I've tried a few things, but nothing seemed to be a good fit."

"Like what?"

"Well, I worked for an IT consulting firm for a while doing white hat hacking, but I wasn't very good with the clients—especially when they were idiots. I tried writing graphic novels—but I can't draw. I've done word processing. I've temped. I've taught kids computing."

"So you just haven't found something that you really liked?"

"Well, I liked teaching kids, but that didn't pay. And the things that pay tend to be in a more corporate environment and—I guess this is my real problem—I don't do corporate."

"I'm probably the last person who should be saying this, but what about black hat hacking?"

She leaned back and gave him a look of exaggerated shock. "You are full of surprises. Actually, that would be my perfect job. Unstructured working environment. The money's good. I could use my real talents. The only problem there is that I'm not a thief. Believe me, it would be a lot easier for me if I were, but it's just not me."

"So you haven't really told me much about your exploits as a hacker . . ."

Zoey slurped a giant mocha frappuccino. "Are you really the person I should be talking to about that? Don't you have people like me arrested?"

"Now that I've left the DOJ, I just work for my clients. I don't prosecute anyone."

"So how about if I tell you one of my stories and you tell me one of yours?"

"Why not? One professional to another—off the clock."

"You start," Zoey said.

"I'm not much of a storyteller. And most of my best stories are attorney-client privileged. What are you fishing for here?"

"Tell me about when you were a hacker."

A cold look crossed Chris's face.

Zoey grinned. "I knew it! When your name used to come up on the message boards, they always said that you were supposed to have been some kind of brilliant coder as a kid. And what kid who knows how to write code hasn't tried a hack or two?"

"I'm not talking about it."

As Zoey looked at him and assessed his mood, her smile faded. "This really bothers you, doesn't it? I think there's a good story there, but you're not going to tell me today, are you?"

Chris gave her his best impassive, dead-eyed stare.

"Okay," Zoey said. "Let's recap what we've learned today. Chris Bruen was a kid hacker. Something happened and he stares death rays at anyone who brings up the subject." She leaned back in her chair. "I think that's enough progress for now. So do you want me to tell you one of my best hacking stories?"

"Sure," Chris said, welcoming the change of subject.

Zoey hesitated. "How about the story about how I got involved with Enigma and Ripley?"

Chris turned to face her. "You're joking, right?"

From the look of growing discomfort on Zoey's face, he could see that it wasn't a joke.

"Why didn't you tell me this sooner?"

"Do you want to hear the story or not?"

Chris nodded.

"Well, I have a background in website design and, not to be immodest, but I have a special talent. I can replicate any company's website. If you want something that looks exactly like the website of Bank of America, Citibank, Amazon, whatever, I can do that."

"So you were involved in phishing scams?" Chris asked.

"Yeah, but mostly I was using it to play pranks. For example, I'd send out an email posing as Centinela Bank apologizing for its excessive credit card interest rates and charges. If the person receiving the email clicked on a link, they would go to a perfect replica of the Centinela Bank website. It was perfect except for one thing—I gave the bank a new slogan: Lending Money to Those Who Need It Least Since 1904."

"That's a little juvenile, isn't it?"

"Hey, no one has ever accused me of being an adult. As you so delicately pointed out, I'm thirty-five and still tending bar at a club. But at least I didn't steal anyone's money. And I think I had a valid point to make. Enigma and Ripley saw my work on the Centinela Bank prank and asked me to run a phishing scam for them. Well, actually, they didn't really ask."

"But they were more interested in doing a true phishing scam designed to commit fraud."

"Correct. Instead of just making my little satirical, hacktivist point, they wanted recipients of the email to think that they needed to confirm their account information by clicking through to the bank's website."

"But what they were really doing was providing their account numbers and passwords directly to Enigma and Ripley," Chris said.

"Most people know better than to trust an email asking for personal information, but if you send out hundreds of thousands of emails, and you've done a convincing job on the web design, you're still going to find quite a few poor suckers who will just hand over their account info."

"Did you meet them in person?"

"No, it was always by email. Anonymous accounts, of course."

"And what did you say to their proposal?"

"I told them that I wasn't really interested in major crime. They didn't like that answer and insisted that I design a fake Bank of the US webpage. I did it because I was scared of them. They threatened me, showed me that they knew where I lived, the places I went."

"So why aren't you still working for them now?"

"I didn't want to take the money. I didn't like seeing my work used to exploit gullible, regular people. Like I said, I'm not a thief."

"So how was this news received?"

"Not well. But, in the end, they just stopped communicating with me. They kept the money they were going to pay me, and I never heard from them again. Fortunately, I didn't learn anything about their identities, or I don't think they would have let me go."

"Aren't you worried that this will put you back on their radar screen?"

"Sure I am. But you pushed all the right buttons. What am I supposed to do? Pass up an opportunity to get an all-expenses-paid trip to Europe, save the life of your future child bride, and avert a major global cyber crisis? What girl with any sense of drama could pass that up?"

Chris had to wonder whether Zoey was telling the truth. He didn't doubt the part about collaborating with Enigma and Ripley in the phishing scam. But it was less plausible that she would turn down their money. For all he knew, she was still collaborating with the Lurker crew and was alerting them to every step he took.

"I need to ask you again—why didn't you tell me all this sooner?"

"Put yourself in my shoes for a minute," Zoey said. "You're the guy who hunts down hackers for a living. Why would I confess to something right off the bat that you might misinterpret? Anything I did that involved theft was done because they were threatening me. And now you understand how dangerous these people are. What was I supposed to do?" In a sign of agitation, Zoey started punctuating with her hands. "And maybe this is a way for me to even the score with them."

Chris had to admit that Zoey sounded like she was telling the truth now, but he wasn't sure if he would have brought her if he had known this before they boarded the flight. Of course, Zoey knew that.

"I'm here because I want to help you and this Sarah," she concluded, exasperated. "And if you can't see that, well . . ." She pulled the headphones from around her neck and snapped them over her ears.

Throughout the last leg of the flight, Chris and Zoey mostly slept and stared at their TV screens. Chris considered whether he should part ways with Zoey when they touched down in

Spain but decided against it. If she was working with the hackers, then she would probably lead him to them, even if it was by walking him into a trap. If that's what it took to find Sarah while she was still alive, then he was willing.

Chris stole a sideways glance at Zoey as she dozed in the seat beside him, headphones still on. As a former prosecutor, Chris liked to think that he had a good internal lie detector, but he had no idea whether Zoey could be trusted.

The cabin lights dimmed and the plane descended toward Barcelona. Looking out through the oval window, Chris saw the lights of the city glimmering below like phosphorescence on the surface of a dark ocean.

As Zoey sensed the descent, her eyelids fluttered and she asked, "So what do we do when we get there?"

"We go visit that factory and see what happens."

CHAPTER 16

January 11

Jet-lagged and sleep-deprived after sixteen hours of travel, Chris and Zoey blinked and squinted in silence as they waited in front of the baggage carousel in Barcelona's El Prat airport. After picking up their bags, they stepped outside into the bright, cool morning. Chris hailed a cab and used some half-remembered high school Spanish to get them to their hotel.

As they entered the sprawl of the city, Chris noted how many subtle distinctions can mark a place as foreign. Perhaps it was the flat landscape or the makes of the cars. Maybe it was the width of the highway or the style of the billboards. The cumulative effect was that of a place that was both familiar, as any modern Western city would be, and yet markedly unfamiliar.

They checked into the elegant Hotel Casa Fuster, a landmark of *moderniste* architecture (they were on BlueCloud's expense account, after all). The hotel was almost Moorish in style, its white and tan stone façade studded with narrow arched windows and dominated by a turret over the entrance. After stowing their bags with the English-speaking staff, Chris was approached by a tall man with shoulder-length, jet-black hair and fine features. He was holding a package the size of a shoe-box wrapped in brown paper and twine.

"Excuse me, Mr. Bruen."

"Yes?"

"I have a package for you from your benefactor," the man said, handing over the box.

"Oh," Chris said, recognizing that the man had the business-casual-artist look of one of BlueCloud's creative techies. "What is it?"

"You should open it in private." The man turned and walked briskly out of the lobby.

Chris entered the restroom off the lobby and opened the package inside a stall. The box contained a Beretta 92 semiautomatic pistol. Apparently, Dave Silver thought that he needed a weapon. Chris was no marksman, but he did know how to handle a gun. When he worked at DOJ, he was friendly with some FBI agents who liked to frequent one of those cigar lounge/firing ranges that enjoyed a brief vogue. He considered whether carrying a gun was more likely to save his life or get him killed but decided that he was glad to have it. Chris stashed the gun in his computer bag, which he slung over his shoulder.

After Chris rejoined Zoey in the lobby and explained their welcoming gift, she asked, "Don't I get one, too?"

"I think they could probably tell that you're dangerous enough without one," Chris said.

With that, they headed directly for the Fiat factory. As tired as they were, there was no time to rest.

★ ★ ★

The cabbie dropped them in the city's Sants-Montjuïc district, in a desolate industrial park known as Zona Franca. The Fiat factory was a massive redbrick structure going to seed, with the signage out front scrubbed of any corporate allegiance, and assorted broken windows testifying to its disuse. As Chris studied the building's ruined visage for signs of life, a pigeon fluttered out of a smashed window.

The sun shone whitely through a haze, making everything look blanched. They were only a few hundred yards away from the city's port, on the Mediterranean, and the air smelled of petroleum and saltwater. Through some online research, Chris had found that the place had once manufactured entire Fiats, then just side body panels, then nothing at all. He had been unable to tell if the facility was back in use, but now that he saw it, the answer seemed obvious.

Chris knew it would be difficult to get a cab in that deserted part of town, so he attempted to negotiate with the cabbie to wait for them while they were inside the factory. The cabbie, a small, implacable man in a red-and-blue-striped FC Barcelona soccer jersey, shook his head, demanded payment, then sped away, disappearing down the empty street. Aside from a few pigeons, they were now the only living things visible in the urban landscape.

"Well done," Zoey said.

They approached the front door of the plant, which was secured with chains and a padlock.

"Let's go around, see if anything's open," Chris said.

"Do you think they're watching us right now?"

"I doubt it. I don't think they could know that Eddie Reiser had this information, and I also don't think they know that I've spoken to Eddie."

"What if Eddie told them you were coming?"

"Possible, but I doubt it. He seemed genuinely scared."

"Scared enough to have second thoughts about crossing them?"

"All we really know is that they once placed a phone call from this place. Maybe they never came back here again. This is probably going to be a waste of time, but it's all we have to go on right now."

They walked around to the side of the plant, testing a window, a door, and then another door. Chris tried a doorknob and it turned.

"Why would someone lock the front with chains and a padlock and then just leave a back door completely unsecured?" Zoey said.

"Let's see," Chris said.

He pushed open the iron door and peered inside. The windows were boarded up, so they could see very little inside the vast, gloomy industrial space.

"What do you see?" Zoey whispered.

"Not much. But if anyone's in here, I think they'd notice this light coming in."

Chris waited a moment in the doorway while his eyes adjusted to the darkness. Eventually he made out the shapes of a couple of industrial presses used to stamp out car body panels. There were also side panels stacked against the walls.

As Chris stepped inside, Zoey behind him, he saw that there was a single source of light, and it was coming from an office on a catwalk above the factory floor. A soft blue glow, like that of a television set, shone from the open door. Chris removed the Beretta from his computer bag.

Chris pointed at the light. "I'm going to take a look," he said.

"I'm coming with you."

Chris and Zoey crossed the floor to the steps that led up to the catwalk. Chris's foot struck something metal that clattered loudly across the concrete. They froze and waited for a response, but there was none. The factory was so perfectly silent that Chris imagined it was listening to them. They stood motionless for a long moment, watching dust motes spin in a beam of sunlight from a shattered window high above them, then moved on.

They reached the metal steps and climbed them, with Chris taking the lead. When his head cleared the landing, he was able to see into the office from a low angle. The door was open and the room appeared to be empty. The light was coming from a computer monitor that had been left on. Looking up and down the catwalk, Chris saw that there were three other offices up there, but they were all dark. After listening for sounds of movement, Chris stepped up onto the catwalk.

To call the place an office was an overstatement—the room was small and bare, with a single metal desk, no chair, and a computer. Clearly, no one had worked there in a very long time. It made no sense that there was a computer on the desk, and even less that it was plugged in and left on—unless whoever had staged this scene was expecting them.

Chris stepped around the desk to examine the computer monitor. It was blank, but there was a yellow Post-it note stuck to the screen. Scrawled on the note in pen were the words "For Chris + Zoey—Press Play" and an arrow pointing to a file on the computer's desktop.

Zoey peered over Chris's shoulder at the note. "This is not good."

Any sense of control that Chris had vanished in that instant. He wasn't pursuing, he was being led.

After staring at the note for a long moment, Zoey asked, "So, are you going to press Play or what?"

"The computer could be wired to a bomb," he said, leaning down to scrutinize the wiring.

"So what do you want to do?"

"I want you to climb back down and get outside. Just in case. Then I'll press Play."

"I'm not leaving here without you," Zoey said.

"Would you prefer that we call a Spanish bomb squad? Explain to them why we're trespassing in this abandoned factory? Explain to them why we're afraid of a computer that's been left on?"

Zoey nodded. "I see your point. I'll go back down the steps, but I'm really not sure this is a good idea."

Once Zoey was back on the factory floor, Chris walked over to the computer and rested his hand on the mouse. His heart gunned, and he had a momentary loss of nerve, stepping away and pacing about the small room like a prisoner in a cell. But Chris knew that if he didn't do this, he might as well abandon the search for Sarah.

Finally, he placed his hand on the mouse again, bracing himself and turning his face away as he clicked on the desktop icon.

Instead of a bomb detonating, all he heard was the precise click of the mouse.

When he turned around, the computer screen filled with a close-up image of Sarah Hotchner sitting in a high-backed wooden chair. The video was grainy and had probably been shot using a cell phone. Strips of duct tape were wrapped around Sarah's neck and forehead, binding her to the chair so that she was unable to move, trapping her gaze for the camera. Sarah's eyes darted. He couldn't tell what was happening. Chris tried turning up the volume on the computer, but there was no sound with the footage. It was like watching some sort of sick pantomime.

Sarah's eyes were fixed on something before her and out of the frame, with a look of sheer panic. She was speaking faster now, pleading with someone. A man's hand appeared holding a straight razor, turning it slowly as if to catch the blade in the light. The hand with the razor moved slowly downward and out of the picture.

Then Sarah's lips parted and she let out what could only be a violent scream.

Chris noticed Zoey leaning in beside him and staring at the screen with a stricken look.

Sarah screamed and thrashed against the bindings, then finally closed her eyes. She had passed out. Then Sarah's image disappeared and the camera closed in on a sheet of notebook paper. A message was scrawled in block letters with a ballpoint pen: "MEET AT THE PLANE AT TIBIDABO AT 5:00 P.M. IF YOU CONTACT THE POLICE, SARAH DIES."

CHAPTER 17

Michael Hazlitt didn't like the idea of breaking into Chris Bruen's apartment and searching his computer files, but he really didn't have much choice. Earlier that day, an anonymous call had been placed to an FBI hotline alleging that Chris was involved in a major cyberattack targeting a US city on January 14.

While there had been no mainstream press coverage about the possible January 14 attack, the rumor had gone viral on the Internet, at least within the hacker and techno geek subculture. Almost anyone could have placed the anonymous call, and it was most likely false. It was no secret that Chris had plenty of enemies, particularly after the death of Pietr Middendorf in Amsterdam.

Chris wasn't answering his phone, and he wasn't at work. Then Hazlitt ran a trace on Chris's credit cards and discovered that he had purchased two tickets on a flight that had just landed in Barcelona. Hazlitt knew that the threatening email Chris had received was routed through a Spanish IP address, so it was clear Chris was either conducting his own investigation, which Hazlitt had warned him not to do, or he was actually in on the scheme.

Suddenly, the anonymous hotline call became a priority, and Hazlitt and his partner Falacci were standing outside the front door of Chris's apartment with a search warrant. Falacci held an umbrella to keep the cold rain off Hazlitt as he used the lock-picking kit. The umbrella wasn't doing much good, because the wind was whipping the rain at them horizontally. They could have kicked in the door, but Chris would have noticed the damage to the doorjamb.

Finally, the lock clicked and they stepped inside.

"Jesus, it's miserable out there," Falacci said. "You could have been a little faster with that lock."

"Easy to criticize. You had the tough job of holding the umbrella," Hazlitt said.

"Well, at least we know he won't be coming home any-time soon," Falacci said. Peering into the bathroom, Falacci said, "You think he'd notice if I took one of his towels to dry off?"

"Leave it," Hazlitt said, motioning for Falacci to join him at Chris's laptop computer, which was on a desk in the corner of the living room. "If we have to follow him to Spain, then he has a big lead on us already. There's no time to mess around."

The laptop was encrypted, but the FBI, through its collab-oration with the NSA, had a backdoor that permitted access. Once they were past the encryption, Falacci proceeded to examine the laptop's contents, using a write blocker to preserve the forensics.

As Hazlitt looked over his shoulder, Falacci opened up the "Documents" file on the hard drive. They found what they were looking for almost immediately. There was a folder labeled "January 14."

"Would you look at this," Falacci said softly.

Falacci clicked on the folder and scrolled through a list of documents. He opened the most recent one.

It was a copy of an email from Enigma to Bruen dated two days ago that read, "Looking forward to finally meeting you in person in Barcelona. Someday, when the world has forgotten about September 11, they'll still be talking about January 14. Come to the Tibidabo amusement park in Barcelona on January 10 at 5:00 p.m. local time. We'll be at the airplane."

"Are you seeing this?" Falacci said.

"Yeah," Hazlitt said. As an investigator, he was thrilled to uncover evidence that would make his case and convict the suspect when he was apprehended. But he also felt a queasy anxiety, because he understood that a serious threat had just grown much more serious. Although he wouldn't admit it to anyone, even his partner, Hazlitt formed the conviction in that moment that, no matter how relentless their pursuit, more innocent people were probably going to die before this was over.

"He's in on it," Falacci said. "The cocky bastard is one of them. He's a terrorist."

Falacci rapidly clicked through the other documents in the folder. Each one was more incriminating than the last. There were notes on the development of the Lurker virus, more email exchanges between Bruen, Enigma, and Ripley, and materials on the design of the electrical power grids in New York, San Francisco, Chicago, and Atlanta. There were also schematics for a computer system used by Albuquerque air traffic control.

"We've even got him linked to Albuquerque," Falacci said.

Hazlitt leaned in to the screen. "This is all a little incredible, don't you think?"

"It is what it is," Falacci said.

"Maybe. Are any of these emails in Bruen's inbox?"

Falacci clicked over Bruen's inbox. "No, they seem to have been deleted there. He was tucking everything away in this folder."

"Why would he keep all of this incriminating evidence in such an accessible place, even with encryption?"

"Obviously he wasn't expecting us. Maybe he's not as smart as we thought."

Hazlitt stood up and walked around the high-ceilinged living room of the loft. "This could still be a setup, but it certainly doesn't look good."

"What do you mean 'doesn't look good'? We've got him dead to rights."

Hazlitt frowned, his thoughts racing as he worked through the ramifications. "If he's capable of this, then what else has he done? He represents BlueCloud and probably dozens of other Fortune 500 companies. He's the guy that they turn to to protect their most valuable information from hackers. If he's been working for the other side, there's no telling how much damage he could inflict."

Falacci turned his chair around from the computer. "Is it really that surprising that this guy might go off the deep end? Look at what he's had going on in his life. His wife died. Cancer. His girlfriend just dumped him. And he lives alone in this place, which looks like an upscale version of Ted Kaczynski's cabin in the woods. This guy's a classic loner."

"I just don't see a motive for Bruen to do this."

"You know it's not like we're putting together a case for a criminal court judge here. This is terrorism—different rules. And who cares why he did it, anyway? They all have their reasons, and none of them make any sense to me."

"It just doesn't feel right," Hazlitt replied. "But that doesn't change the fact that we're going full bore after Bruen. We'll alert

Quantico and they'll start working with Europol and Spanish authorities."

"So we're going to Spain?"

"We're going to Spain."

"Outside the US. That's the CIA's jurisdiction."

"I'll let the bosses work that out. I've got a feeling everyone's going to want a piece of this investigation—FBI, CIA, DHS, NSA."

"My ex is going to kill me. I was supposed to take the kids to SeaWorld this weekend. You know, we're not going to make it in time for the 5:00 p.m. meet-up. That's just a few hours away."

"That's okay. Quantico will probably get the CIA in on this. They'll be able to get someone there."

"Wish I could be there to see the look on his face when they take him down," Falacci said. "He struck me as smug."

Hazlitt knew what Falacci meant. There was something about Bruen that got under his skin, and he was self-aware enough to know what it was. As a young FBI agent working on computer crimes cases with the DOJ, Hazlitt had looked to Bruen as a bit of a role model. Hazlitt was impressed by Bruen's combination of computer, legal, and investigative skills, which few other agents could match. He also liked the way Bruen didn't entirely dismiss the hackers that he pursued as criminals or nutjobs. He might not agree with their worldview, but he understood that they had one. Hazlitt had actually been a little bit hurt when Bruen hadn't immediately recognized him at the law firm's offices, but it had been quite a few years, and he had been a junior member of the team.

Hazlitt liked to think of himself as first and foremost a public servant protecting unwary citizens from increasingly sophisticated and malicious cybercriminals. He viewed Bruen in his current incarnation as a sellout who served corporations first, and the public only incidentally. But Hazlitt had also felt a bit hypocritical rebuking Bruen when they'd met at his office, because he honestly did not know whether he would take a law firm job if given the chance. After all, equity partners at firms like Reynolds Fincher made a hell of a lot more money than midlevel federal agents, and he was thinking about starting a family and perhaps moving out of his apartment and into a house. Hazlitt liked certainty, and not knowing what he would do if he were offered a law firm job irritated him.

"We shouldn't underestimate him," Hazlitt said. "He's very smart. And he knows our moves because he used to be one of us."

"Yeah, well, the agencies have learned a few new tricks since he was at DOJ."

"And so has he," Hazlitt said.

CHAPTER 18

According to the tourist brochures in the hotel lobby, Tibidabo was one of the world's oldest amusement parks, built in 1889 atop Tibidabo, a mountain overlooking Barcelona. Chris and Zoey saw that the "plane" where they were to meet was Tibidabo's centerpiece ride—Barri de l'Avio, an oversized, red biplane replica suspended by a crane that rotated to give passengers panoramic views of the city.

At 4:00 p.m., one hour early, they took a taxi to the boarding spot for the tram that went halfway up the steep hillside to Tibidabo. The second half of the trip up the mountain would be by funicular.

"If something goes wrong, how would we get out of there?" Zoey asked, squinting in the late-afternoon sun at the park's Ferris wheel high above them.

"I've been studying the maps and I don't see a good way up or down the mountain other than the funicular," Chris said. "You couldn't pick a better place for a trap."

"Should we do this?"

"I don't see what alternative we have if we're going to find Sarah. You could stay down here and wait for me."

"No way," Zoey said, shaking her head. "The message was addressed to both of us. If they don't see both of us there, they might think something's wrong."

Chris and Zoey paid the fare and boarded the blue tram, or Tramvia Blau, a vintage trolley car that was filled with tourists from Sweden who were all carrying the same guidebook like a hymnal. Halfway up the mountain, they changed over to the blue and gold funicular car.

When they reached the peak, the views of the city, which were the park's primary attraction, were obscured by clouds. Nevertheless, they could still see Barcelona stretched out before them to the Mediterranean. The main thoroughfares of the city all ran down to the sea at regular intervals, as if the tines of a giant rake had dug even grooves through the houses and buildings.

The amusement park was nearly empty—the result of winter hours and winter weather. Chris and Zoey left the funicular station and walked the redbrick path that circled the park, searching the crowd for the hackers or Sarah. Chris didn't know what the hackers looked like, but he figured that they should be distinguishable from the tourists. A few of the Swedes stood at the railing, looking out at the city below and eating popcorn. On the crest of the hill just outside the park was The Church of the Sacred Heart, crowned by a towering statute of Jesus with arms outstretched.

After completing the circle of the mountaintop park, Chris said, "I don't think they're here yet. Either that or they've found a place to hide."

"What now?" Zoey asked.

"Let's stake out a place over there," he said, pointing at some iron tables near a concession stand. "There's only one way up the mountain and that's the funicular. If they really aren't here yet, then we can just watch and check out everyone who arrives. We're far enough away that they won't notice us immediately."

They ordered Cokes and *patatas fritas* and sat down at one of the tables. The late-afternoon crowds were so sparse that it was easy to examine each visitor as they disembarked.

The first car held a Japanese couple. "What do you think?" Chris asked. "There's no reason why Enigma and Ripley couldn't be Japanese, right? Eddie Reiser did say they were marketing Japanese porn."

"Too normal-looking," Zoey said.

"Agreed."

They waited for the next funicular car to arrive.

Zoey dropped a fry into the grease-stained cardboard basket as she watched a couple stroll past, a distinguished-looking older man with a much younger woman, a knockout.

"I don't think that's his daughter," Zoey said. "Reminds me of someone I know."

"You just can't let it go, can you?"

"You and Sarah, who's—what?—about fifteen years younger. I'm not saying it's wrong, it just must be—"

"Challenging," Chris said.

"Okay . . . I'll bet," Zoey said. After a pause, she added, "You ever been married?"

"Yes."

"Divorced?"

"No, she died. Breast cancer."

"Oh," she said. "I'm so sorry."

The awkward silence was broken by the rumbling of another funicular car pulling into the station. Two men emerged who appeared to be American tourists. One was wearing a Mets cap, T-shirt, jeans, and a fanny pack. The other was wearing aviator sunglasses with yellow lenses, an untucked western-style shirt, black jeans, and sneakers. Both had muscular builds and short, neatly groomed hair.

"What do you think?" Zoey asked.

"I don't know who they are, but I think they're here for us."

"Are you sure?"

"No, but I'd rather not guess wrong on this one. The one in the Mets cap could have a gun in his fanny pack. The other guy could be wearing his shirt out to get at a gun that's tucked behind his back."

"What should we do?"

"Let's get up slowly and walk around behind this concession stand. Keep your soda. It'll make you look normal."

They watched the two men from around the corner of the concession stand. The pair tried to act nonchalant, but they were clearly surveying the park, and not just to take in the sights.

"Do you think they're Enigma and Ripley?"

"Maybe, but Ripley seemed to be a woman, so I don't think so."

The two men split up, each setting off in a different direction around the park. Sunglasses headed toward Chris and Zoey.

They crouched behind the concession stand and watched him approach. His hand brushed the small of his back as if to confirm that something was in place there.

"Look," Zoey said. "I think that's a gun."

"Probably," Chris said. "They do look like undercover cops, don't they?"

Sunglasses stopped at a souvenir booth selling miniature replicas of Barri de l'Avio and showed a couple of photos to the vendor, who shook his head. He moved on to the next booth, the concession stand where they had purchased their sodas and fries. Once again, the man showed the photos. This time, the teenager behind the counter nodded and pointed to where Chris and Zoey had been sitting moments before.

Suddenly, Chris felt like he had just touched an ungrounded wire—queasy, paralyzed, and with a growing sense that something was very wrong. He was certain now that the two men were agents of some sort and they weren't there looking for Enigma and Ripley—they were looking for him and Zoey.

"Get back," he said, pressing Zoey further behind the concession stand. Chris took Zoey's arm and started moving them quietly away from Sunglasses, down the walking path that ran behind the rides and concession stands and alongside the chain-link fence that bounded the perimeter of the park.

"What's going on?" Zoey asked in an alarmed stage whisper.

"Those two are law enforcement and they're looking for us," Chris said. "Somehow, they knew we were going to be here." They hurried down the path, putting some distance between themselves and Sunglasses.

But then they saw Mets Cap approaching down the main walkway from the opposite direction, completing his circle of the park. He hadn't spotted them yet.

The park was too small to afford them many places to hide. It would only be a matter of minutes before they were captured. They were standing near the entrance to the Ferris wheel and there was no line, so Chris took Zoey by the hand and led her past the attendant into a bright blue bucket with a covering that looked like a giant bottle cap.

"What are you doing?" Zoey said, pulling away.

"I need a few minutes to sort this out," Chris said. "We can't stay where we are."

Zoey stopped resisting and followed Chris's lead. The attendant slammed the door of the car shut. Seconds later, the car lurched forward and upward into space, rocking back and forth until it stabilized.

"If they're agents, how did they know we would be here?" Zoey asked.

"I don't know, but I think I know how I can find out." Chris pulled out his smartphone and dialed Michael Hazlitt.

"Bruen," Hazlitt said, reading the caller ID. He sounded surprised.

"I'd like you to tell me what's going on," Chris said. "I'm not going to lie to you. We're in Barcelona now. But you already knew that, didn't you?"

"Yes."

"There are two men here looking for us. What are they, FBI agents?"

"Probably CIA. They might also be Interpol or Homeland Security. But, whoever they are, you should just turn yourselves in. End this thing."

Chris felt that he and Hazlitt were having two very different conversations. "What thing? End what thing?"

There was a long pause on the other end of the line as Hazlitt seemed to be weighing how much to say. "We found the files on your computer."

"What files?"

Hazlitt snorted. "Play it that way if you like, but the evidence is clear."

"Evidence of what?"

"This is starting to get a little insulting. We know you're collaborating with those hackers."

The Ferris wheel car had reached the apogee of its orbit. A gust of wind hit, and the car tilted back and forth, the entire city of Barcelona lurching and spinning beneath them. Chris had the disorienting sensation that he was hurtling through space.

"I don't know what's in those files, but I didn't put them there," Chris said. "Someone is framing me."

"Okay, then why don't you turn yourself in and you can explain that to us. Don't make us chase you. This will not end well if you make us chase you."

"I have to go," Chris said, hanging up.

Zoey had been listening intently to the conversation. "We're in real trouble, aren't we?"

Chris nodded. "Give me your cell phone," he said.

She handed him her phone. Chris opened up the back and removed the SIM card. Then he wound up and hurled the phone over the park's fence and onto the hillside of Tibidabo.

"Hey, what the hell?"

"They're going to try to track us using the GPS in our phones," Chris said as he followed the same procedure with his own cell phone.

The Ferris wheel was on its way down now. This was the most dangerous part of the ride. When the cars were in the air, it was impossible to see who was inside but as they descended, the agents would be able to spot them if they were looking.

Luckily, the agents were not waiting for them when the ground came into view. The attendant opened the door to the car and they bolted out. Chris looked for a way out of the amusement park that wouldn't be watched by the agents. There was a chain-link fence that marked the park's border. It was only about eight feet tall, with no barbed wire or other impediments on top. Several metal trash cans were lined against the fence.

"Climb up on the cans and go over the fence," Chris said.

Zoey didn't need any encouragement. She hopped on top of an aluminum garbage can. With the can to boost her up, it was an easy climb. Her shirtsleeve caught on the top of fence, and she struggled to pull herself over.

Chris jumped up and shoved Zoey's leg over, sending her toppling to the ground.

Now it was Chris's turn. He climbed onto one of the trash cans, but the lid buckled under his weight, putting him out of reach of the top of the fence. Chris looked back and saw Sunglasses about a hundred yards away, standing in the middle of the main walkway. He didn't seem to have spotted them yet, but it wouldn't be long now.

Chris struggled out of the garbage can, banging his knee hard on the rim. The next trash can did not buckle, and he was quickly over the fence, throwing himself to the other side and landing on his hands and knees. When he looked back through the fence, he saw that the two men were now running toward them, but they were still about fifty yards back. Chris started to reach for the gun in his computer bag but then thought better of it.

Zoey also saw them coming. She helped Chris to his feet and they ran through tall grass and into a forest of ash trees. By the time the two men reached the fence, Chris and Zoey were already far down the slope. The agents now had two choices. They could climb the fence and pursue them down the mountainside on foot, or they could take the funicular halfway down the mountain and try to intercept them. When the agents walked away from the fence, Chris knew they had chosen the latter approach.

Zoey stopped and bent over with her hands on her knees, taking deep breaths.

"We have to keep going," Chris said, gasping himself. They staggered down the hillside as the rocky soil crumbled beneath their feet.

CHAPTER 19

Zoey tripped and scraped her knee. Blood seeped through the rip in her jeans. She was quickly up on her feet again, and she stumbled awkwardly down the steep slope. There was no point in asking her if she needed to stop. There was no stopping.

"Over here," Chris said. "Let's move away from the tracks."

They left the rocky terrain and entered a copse of pale, barren trees. Branches whipped at them. Sweat burned in the cuts and scratches on Chris's face. The setting sun, which had fallen below the clouds, was the color of a blood orange. Zoey was soon pulling ahead of him, and Chris found it difficult to keep up. At first he thought that it was just because she was younger. Then he remembered that he was still weakened from the cancer therapy.

They heard the funicular rumbling behind them. It arrived at the station, which was roughly parallel to them, and about three hundred yards distant. Then it all became a sort of dangerous geometry problem. The two agents climbed over the fence at the funicular station and spotted them in the distance.

One of the agents yelled to them, his American voice coming faintly but clearly across the hillside. "CIA! Stop right there!"

Chris and Zoey hunched lower but kept moving. There wasn't much cover on the rocky ground now. Sunglasses and Mets Cap moved in an awkward gait on the treacherous footing, angling to complete the third side of the isosceles triangle and intercept them before they reached the city streets. The agents would probably prefer to take them alive. But because they were believed to be terrorists planning an attack on a major city, they might also be prepared to shoot to kill if it came to that.

Chris and Zoey stopped for a moment to assess the progress of their pursuers. There was nothing to be said. They were both breathing hard and didn't need to waste the energy. The landscape was quiet, except for the sound of the Tramvia Blau rumbling to the bottom of the hill. Chris and Zoey tried to run down the steep slope and fell repeatedly. Chris's hands were bleeding from using them to break his falls. The bloodstain on the knee of Zoey's torn jeans was spreading down her leg.

Everything was very simple now. There was nothing in Chris's mind but the animal instinct of flight. If they didn't make it to the street before the two agents caught up with them, they would, at best, be imprisoned for a very long time.

Now they were only a half mile from the street. The agents were falling behind. They were trying to make their way through a stand of trees that impeded their progress, while Chris and Zoey were on open ground. A gunshot cracked in the still air. Chris looked back and saw one of the men with a hand raised high.

"Don't stop," Chris said. "They know they can't catch us. We're too far away and we're too close to the street. They don't want to hit bystanders. That was a warning shot."

"I like your certainty," Zoey said.

Chris and Zoey finally reached flat ground and then the bustling sidewalk, with their pursuers still far behind them on the hillside. They crossed a busy intersection and walked quickly through the city streets. They passed a wall plastered with posters for museum exhibits and dance clubs.

Chris hailed a taxi. "Sagrada Familia," Chris said to the driver. He just wanted the taxi to pull away quickly, so he spoke the two words that every cabbie in Barcelona immediately understood. The taxi ride to Barcelona's most famous tourist attraction would buy them a little time to regroup.

"I don't think it's safe to go back to the hotel," he said.

"You know, it's possible that we're the primary targets now," Zoey said, gingerly examining her bleeding knee. "Has it occurred to you that they might think that you and I are Enigma and Ripley?"

"Yeah, I was thinking the same thing," Chris said.

"What do we do now?" Zoey asked. "I mean, it's one thing to run when faced with two guys with guns who aren't dressed like cops. It's another thing to keep running after you know who's after you."

Chris stared out the window of the taxi. "I need to know what we're up against. I want to know what's in those files that were planted on my computer." He paused, and the silence was filled with honking car horns from the street. "They've probably already contacted my law firm. I think we need to reach out to a friend of mine there and see what he knows."

"I hope you can trust him," Zoey said.

CHAPTER 20

Even in their rattled state, when the cab dropped them in front of Sagrada Familia, architect Antoni Gaudí's famous cathedral, the sight was so overwhelming that they spent a few moments just taking it in. Their eyes were drawn to the sky by the cathedral's four soaring, ornately decorated towers. Floodlights blinked on, illuminating the spires in response to the gathering dark.

Gaudí's cathedral was strangely organic and bore so little resemblance to traditional architecture that it looked like the work of an insane man. The structure didn't seem to have been built but rather accreted, like some gargantuan geological deposit. The cathedral was the color of a wasp nest, and it looked like it had the same consistency. Chris thought the word visionary was tossed about far too casually these days (see Dave Silver, CEO of BlueCloud Inc.), but it was the only term to describe Gaudí's masterwork.

Gradually, they became aware that the people on the sidewalk were staring at them. Apparently, Chris and Zoey stood out from the crowd of tourists because they were the only ones who were scratched and bleeding. It was only a matter of time before someone pointed them out to a policeman.

Chris knew they couldn't return to the Hotel Casa Fuster to retrieve their bags. It was a certainty that one or more law enforcement agencies had staked out the hotel. Luckily, they had their passports and all of their currency with them.

They stopped at a convenience store and bought two pre-paid cell phones, which would be untraceable. Then they found an Internet café near Sagrada Familia with weathered wooden tables, threadbare couches, and a handful of students working on laptops. Chris sent Ed de Lamadrid a text that provided a public email address at the café and said simply: "Skype me here. Don't use your work or home computer."

While they waited for Ed, they speculated on what the denizens of the café were working on. Here a novel, there a term paper, there a revolutionary manifesto. Twenty minutes later, they were video-chatting with Ed, who was in a coffee shop.

As soon as they were connected, Ed leaned in close to the speaker and whispered, "Do you have any idea the Category F-5 shit storm that's headed your way?"

"It's already here," Chris said. "Two CIA agents tried to arrest us today. They think we're involved with Enigma and Ripley."

"Jesus," Ed said. "Are you okay?"

"We're fine, but what's going on there?"

"The FBI and Homeland Security were at the office yesterday asking about you. They questioned me for nearly an hour. They think you're involved with the Lurker virus, the January 14 cyberattack, and even the Albuquerque airport hack."

"Did they say what gave them that idea?"

"I snooped around on the system and found a memo that Don Rubinowski wrote for firm management summarizing what the agents told him."

"And?" Zoey interrupted.

"Apparently, DHS received an anonymous phone call about Chris that led them to enter his apartment and check his home computer. I don't know exactly what they found, but they seem to view it as a smoking gun linking you to the Lurker crew. This is a manhunt, not an investigation."

Chris looked at Zoey. "Do they know who Zoey is?"

"They seem to know everything about you two. They've already spoken to the folks at BlueCloud."

"So where does that leave us? What's the firm's position?"

"The firm's position is to run away from you as fast as possible. They realize what would happen to a law firm that's associated with a cyberterrorist. Every corporate client we have would drop us the instant this becomes public. Don says that you're suspended from the partnership pending the outcome of the investigation. They've already called an emergency meeting of the partners to vote on it."

During Chris's tenure at the firm, an emergency partners meeting had been convened only once before to terminate a partner. It had involved a corporate attorney named Will Connelly, who had somehow gotten mixed up with Russian mobsters, insider trading, and a variety of other sordid enterprises. Chris didn't like being in such shady company, but he knew that was the least of his concerns.

"And what about BlueCloud?"

"I think you can consider your assignment—and your expense account—terminated."

"But you believe us, right?"

"Oh, man, how can you even ask me that?" Ed said, genuinely indignant. "Hackers like Enigma are pranksters. This is exactly the kind of thing you would expect them to do. That's what I told those agents."

"I guess when it comes to terrorism, the FBI and DHS don't have a sense of humor."

It had occurred to Chris that the file the FBI had discovered could have been planted on his computer by any one of the many hackers who made a sport of trying to take down his system.

As soon as he spoke the word "terrorism," Chris scanned the café to see if anyone was eavesdropping, but no one was paying attention. They had staked out a spot in the back as far from everyone else as possible.

"What else do you know?" Chris asked.

"Well, those two FBI agents, Hazlitt and Falacci, are apparently coming for you, too. They're the ones who found the files on your home computer."

"You can't do any more for us, Ed," Chris said. "We're toxic now. You probably shouldn't have even done this much. Accessing Don's memo was a dangerous move."

Ed leaned in close to the camera, his broad face swelling to fill the screen. "If I cut you loose now, I wouldn't be much of a friend, now would I?"

Chris knew there was no dissuading Ed, so he simply said, "Thanks."

"I know you'd do the same for me." He rocked back in his chair. "So where do you go from here?"

"I think it's probably best that we turn ourselves in to the FBI. We can share what we know with them and hope they believe us. If we're lucky, they may allow us cooperate in their investigation."

"You really think that's likely?" Ed asked.

"No, I don't." Chris said. Hazlitt and Falacci had been unwilling to work with him even before he became a suspected terrorist. The agents were smart enough to know that it was possible he had been set up, but once he and Zoey were arrested, it would probably take months, if not years, to extricate themselves from the system. Homeland Security's process for detaining and prosecuting suspected terrorists was an enormous, powerful machine that was easy to switch on but nearly impossible to shut down before it had ground its subjects into a fine paste.

"If we turn ourselves in, what's going to happen then?" Zoey asked. "If they think we have information about a terrorist attack, their interrogation techniques are definitely going to be—enhanced." She sounded alarmed, and Chris didn't blame her a bit.

"But if we don't turn ourselves in, we'll be confirming their suspicions."

"It's not going to help that I actually do have a connection to Enigma and Ripley," Zoey said.

"What did she say?" Ed interjected.

"It's okay," Chris said. "I'll explain later."

It was clear that Ed really wanted to hear that explanation, but he let it go for the moment.

"Don't do anything until you hear from us," Chris said. "I don't want you getting yourself into trouble unnecessarily. We should probably cut this off—it's dangerous for you. But first I have two favors to ask."

"Name them."

"I'd like you to send me a copy of the code for the Lurker virus. I want to have the ability to study it here, see if there's anything else that I can learn. Use a secure file-sharing site."

"You got it. What else?"

"You know that hacker Blanksy, right?"

"Yeah. You think he planted those documents on your hard drive when he hacked your computer?"

"No, I scanned afterwards and it was clean. But I would like to talk to him to see if he has any idea who might be targeting me. You know the IRC channel where he hangs out. Tell him that I need to talk to him and give him this new cell number."

"No problem."

A few minutes later, Chris had downloaded a copy of the Lurker virus code and saved it to a flash drive.

"Good luck, you two," Ed said.

"I really appreciate this."

Ed nodded in acknowledgment, then terminated the connection, and the screen went black.

"Do you really think we should turn ourselves in?" Zoey asked.

"It's probably the best option. You didn't sign on for this. If we run—"

"We're already running," Zoey said.

"If we continue to run, now that we know what's happening," Chris continued, "this could get both of us killed."

"Are you doing this for me?"

"No," Chris lied. If Sarah was dead, he held himself accountable, and he resolved that he would not be responsible for Zoey's death as well. "I'm going to call Michael Hazlitt at the FBI and put an end to this." Chris had kept Hazlitt's card, which included his cell number.

Zoey sat next to Chris so that she could hear the conversation.

The phone rang a few times and then he picked up. "Hazlitt. Who's this?"

"Chris Bruen."

There was silence for a moment on the other end of the line.

"You're in some trouble, Chris."

"I realize that. That's why I'm calling."

"Why did you run from those agents?"

"When we started running, we didn't know who they were."

"Okay, so now you know. So why don't you tell me where you are so that we can pick you up? Things will go a lot easier for you that way."

"As a matter of fact—" Chris was interrupted by the buzz of his smartphone signaling an incoming email. He clicked the call with Hazlitt onto speaker and examined his inbox.

"What's going on?" Hazlitt said.

The email's subject line: "HANG UP THE PHONE NOW."

Chris opened the message, which read, "You are under surveillance—we know everything that you're doing. Hang up the call to the FBI NOW or we will kill Sarah. For proof of our seriousness, open the attachment. Your friend, Enigma."

Chris clicked on the attachment to the email while Hazlitt called to him through the tinny cell phone speaker. "Bruen? You there, Bruen?"

The attachment slowly opened. It was a color photo that had probably been shot with a cell phone. The photo showed a severed finger resting on what seemed to be a white washcloth stained with blood. It was a woman's little finger. The nail of the finger was painted in a plum hue that Chris had seen before. He was fairly certain that it was the same color of nail polish that Sarah wore.

Chris felt a wave of nausea. He didn't want to, but he already had the mental image of the event—from the video they'd seen in the abandoned factory. Now he knew what Sarah was staring at with such horror, and why she was screaming.

"Are you there, Chris? It would be a big mistake for you and Zoey to run. We're going to assume the worst then. We'll go after you with everything we've got and we will find you."

Chris disconnected the call.

"What happened?" Zoey asked. "Why did you hang up?" The look on his face seemed to unsettle her.

Chris showed the message and attachment to Zoey, the cell phone screen casting a pale illumination on her face in the dim café.

"Oh god," Zoey said. "Do you think she's still alive?"

"I don't know, but I would assume so. They want leverage with me, and they'll lose it if they can't produce proof that Sarah is still alive."

"How did they know that you were calling Hazlitt?"

"They must have hacked my cell phone."

"They couldn't have had physical access to that phone, you just bought it. So they must be nearby."

Chris and Zoey once again looked around the Internet café, but all eyes were still glued to laptops.

"They must have followed us from Tibidabo and then intercepted the wireless transmissions, gotten the phone number of the burner that way."

"I don't know exactly how they did it, but there'll be time to think about that later. Right now we have to move."

They left the café and surveyed the street, which was dark, with few people on the sidewalk. If the hackers were still tailing them, it wasn't apparent.

"Should we ditch our phones again?" Zoey asked.

"You should, but I don't think I will. The FBI still can't track us using this phone and I'm actually glad that Enigma has the number. I want them to contact me."

"Where to next?"

Chris shook his head. "I don't think we should travel together now. I'm going to keep trying to find Sarah, but we should split up. Law enforcement will probably be focusing most of its attention on me. I'd recommend that you turn yourself in, but I know how terrorism suspects are treated."

"I'm sticking with you," Zoey said.

"No."

"You want to find Sarah, don't you? You need me to do that. This is my world. That's why you brought me in the first place. You stand a better chance of finding Sarah with me than without me."

Chris knew that this was true.

"I have to go with you—how else are we going to save the girl, stop the cyberattack, prove our innocence?"

"Don't be flip about this," Chris said. "This may be the biggest decision of your life."

"You think I don't understand that? My point is that it's really not much of a choice when you think about it."

Chris stared at Zoey and she stared back at him.

Finally, Chris said, "If you want to come with me, I'm not going to stop you, but I hope you know how this is likely to end. They'll probably catch us within the next twenty-four hours—if we're lucky. And it will be much worse than if you had turned yourself in."

"Yeah, yeah," Zoey said, already moving on. "I think we need to do something about the way we look together. Tall, gawky, buttoned-down guy who looks like a lawyer. And me—I don't look like I should be with you."

Chris couldn't help but be a little hurt by the remark.

Zoey read his expression. "I'm just saying that we're going to stand out. Just an observation."

It was true, Chris thought. They were the kind of odd-duck pairing that people remembered.

"If you ask me, you should change your look a bit. In the interest of not getting caught. You could make yourself a little bit—funkier."

"Or you could—"

"I don't do Junior League."

"All right. I'll buy some new clothes."

"Good," Zoey said. "I pick the wardrobe."

CHAPTER 21

Chris and Zoey searched for a clothing store on Las Ramblas, a broad street that ran downhill from Plaça de Catalunya to the port. It was Barcelona's most famous street and busiest thoroughfare At almost any time of day or night, Las Ramblas was as crowded as Times Square and filled with sidewalk merchants and street entertainers. It was early evening and the streets were filling.

They passed a man standing on a soapbox who was dressed like Che Guevara. A couple of American tourists were getting their pictures taken with Che. *Viva la revolución.*

"So, no credit cards," Zoey said.

"Right, no credit cards," Chris said. "We can assume that the agents will be watching for any charges on our accounts. It's a good thing that I cashed out all of my traveler's checks at the hotel."

"You did that? What made you think to do that?"

"I'm a natural paranoid. It comes with my line of work."

They stopped for a moment and listened to a band of buskers, comprised of a violin, washboard, and trash-can drum kit. As they looked on, they saw a very young girl with a boyish haircut lift two wallets off tourists watching the performance. As the girl disappeared into the crowd, Chris caught her exchanging a look with the violin player. The musicians were in on the robberies. Chris turned around quickly and saw that a wolfish-looking boy was stalking him from about two paces back. Chris was glad that he had noticed him in time. His wallet contained everything that he'd gotten from the traveler's checks. If they lost their money, it would be impossible to run.

They were looking for a clothing store where they could purchase Chris something that would allow them to blend in a little better.

"Here, this one," Zoey said, pointing to a little hole-in-the-wall shop with an array of leather jackets in the window. "A coat will do most of the work. We need a cheap leather jacket."

They went inside and found a bored-looking young guy behind the counter. He was in his midtwenties, with long, pointed sideburns, and a hipper-than-thou attitude that registered immediately.

"Can I help you?" he said in English, instantly identifying them as Americans.

"We're going to browse," Zoey said.

Chris absentmindedly ran his hand through a rack of vintage shirts. "I've been thinking about why someone would want to put me in this position," he said.

"They seem to have gone to an awful lot of trouble," Zoey said.

"Right, these hackers didn't just want to stop me from coming after them, they wanted to ruin me."

"So why would someone want to do that?"

"I'd have to say that it was personal somehow, since I've spent most of my adult life catching and prosecuting hackers."

Zoey removed a black leather jacket from a hanger. "Here, try this one on."

Chris slipped it on. "Too many zippers."

"The idea here is not to get what you like," Zoey said. "It's to make you look more like someone who would hang with me."

"That's a lot for one jacket to accomplish."

"How about this one?" Zoey asked, letting the remark pass. She handed him a black leather jacket. "Very Joey Ramone. And let's get this black shirt."

"You're the fashion consultant." It occurred to Chris that the last person who had given him fashion tips in a store had been his wife.

Chris changed into the clothes and paid for them, then carried what he had been wearing out of the store in a bag and tossed it in a dumpster. Chris still looked a little too stiff and professorial to be with Zoey, but now they were not so disparate that it drew immediate attention. They might not quite blend in, but they had definitely become less memorable.

They walked on down Las Ramblas, entering an enormous flower and vegetable market, La Boqueria. Tiny white blossoms tumbled along the street in the breeze like confetti in a ticker tape parade.

"You'd better watch your wallet," Chris said. "Another one of those little urchins is following us."

"Persistent, aren't they?"

"He's been with us for two blocks."

Chris turned abruptly and the boy, who couldn't have been more than thirteen, nearly ran into them. He was dressed in jeans, a Transformers T-shirt, and a denim jacket, and he didn't even try to pretend that he wasn't following them.

"Is there something you want?" Chris said.

The boy didn't say anything, his eyes darting. He seemed so intensely agitated that Chris was afraid he might be about to draw a weapon of some sort. Instead, he reached into his jeans and handed Chris a folded sheet of paper. Chris snatched the paper and read the message that was written with a black marker in block letters:

GO TO THE PÈRE LACHAISE CEMETERY IN PARIS TOMORROW. BE AT THE GRAVE OF GHOLAM-HOSSEIN SA'EDI AT 4:30 P.M. IF YOU'RE THERE, SARAH LIVES. IF YOU'RE NOT, SHE DIES.

At the bottom of the message was what appeared to be a phone number. When Chris looked up from the note, the boy had already turned away and was disappearing into the throng.

Chris leapt forward to grab him, but he missed as the boy ducked past a swarm of advancing pedestrians like a minnow darting in the shallows. The boy was in his element, and they were not. When he wasn't delivering messages, he was undoubtedly a professional pickpocket who made his living navigating the cobbled alleyways that radiated from Las Ramblas.

Chris lowered his shoulder and barreled through a middle-aged couple. They began cursing him in Catalan from a prone position on the sidewalk. Zoey was quicker and got out in front of Chris, dancing through the pedestrians like a halfback, working her way around, rather than through, them. Extending her hand to make a grab for the tail of the boy's denim jacket, she just missed. She staggered against the brick wall of a shop as he ran off down the street. Finally, he stopped running and disappeared around a corner, but not before giving her a cocky little salute.

Now the Catalan couple were on their feet. They were a heavyset pair who seemed to have a real talent for cursing, judging solely by the intonation, speed, and vigor of their invective. They were clearly just warming up and, now that they had regrouped, the decibel level was rising fast. Chris walked away quickly, grabbing Zoey by the arm and bringing her with him. It wouldn't be long before a policeman became interested in the disturbance.

As they walked away, Chris stared at the scrap of paper in his hand and felt a surge of hopelessness. The hackers were playing a game with Sarah's life and it was a game that was completely stacked against him. He had no choice but to continue to follow the path that had been laid for him, but he felt increasingly certain that he would find Sarah's lifeless body at the end of it. He needed to find a way to start making them react to him, instead of the other way around.

Chris struggled to calm his thoughts. He would not give in to hopelessness. He had to believe that Sarah was still alive. Chris forced himself to concentrate on the problem at hand—how to cross the border into France while on Europol's most-wanted list.

CHAPTER 22

As soon as they had put a safe distance between themselves and the angry couple on Las Ramblas, Zoey asked, "Who is Gholam-Hossein Sa'edi?"

"I have no idea," Chris said. "But we're going to find out."

They wound through the labyrinthine, cobbled streets of the Barri Gòtic, one of the city's oldest neighborhoods. The narrow streets were closed to cars, except for taxis. The ancient buildings leaned in so close over the narrow streets that you could feel their musty, old man's breath on your face as you passed. When one of the warren-like streets opened into another small square, Chris felt like he was coming up for air. He pulled out his cell phone and dialed the number provided in the note, which presumably belonged to a burner phone that Enigma was using. No response.

They walked for a while until they found a library with Internet access, the Biblioteca Jaume Fuster, a modern structure that resembled artfully crumpled sheets of aluminum—sort of a Frank Gehry knockoff. Chris sat down at a computer in the library's airy main room and Googled the name Gholam-Hossein Sa'edi. He read from a Wikipedia entry.

"Sa'edi was a noted Iranian novelist and playwright." Chris skimmed through the entry, reading the highlights. "In 1966 he joined a group of Iranian intellectuals in protesting a government policy requiring all publishers to seek state permission to print literature. He pushed for democracy in Iran as part of a leftist coalition that opposed Ayatollah Khomeini's right-wing Islamist movement. After Khomeini assumed control, Sa'edi fled to Pakistan and then France."

"How did he end up in Père Lachaise?"

Chris read to the end of the entry. "Exile doesn't seem to have agreed with him. Sa'edi suffered from depression and alcoholism during his time in Paris. He was diagnosed with cirrhosis, died soon afterward in 1985, and was buried at Père Lachaise."

"What does this have to do with us? Or with Enigma?"

"I'm not seeing a connection either," Chris said.

Chris printed out what information he could find about Sa'edi online. "There's no time to sit here studying this. We can do that while we're on the road. We have nineteen hours to get to Paris, which is a drive of more than six hundred miles."

"Even if we drive, how are we going to cross the border into France?" Zoey asked. "Border guards on both sides will probably be looking for us."

"Ever since the Schengen Agreement in the eighties, papers haven't been required to cross borders between most EU countries," Chris said. "But since Europol is involved and this is viewed as a major threat, I'll bet they're doing border checks."

"The Schengen Agreement," Zoey said. "Sometimes I think you make this stuff up."

"We're going to need someone to drive us," Chris said. "Someone with a valid passport and a car. Someone who's not afraid to break the law."

"Even if we find that someone, how do you propose we get into France?"

"They probably won't be searching vehicles. There's usually too much traffic for that. If we hid in the trunk, we'd have a fairly good chance of getting across the border without being detected."

"You're assuming a lot."

"The plan isn't perfect," Chris conceded. "But it's the best I've got so far. Do you have anything better?"

Zoey shook her head. "But I may know where we could find someone to drive us."

"Another of your criminal friends?"

"You're going to have to adjust that attitude if you want to hear this proposal."

Chris sighed. "I'm not going to like this, will I?"

"I'm going to take that as a yes," Zoey said. "I know some people who might be willing to take the risk of driving us. There's this group of hackers based in Barcelona. They call themselves the Hive."

"I've heard of them. How bad are they?"

"They're not like Enigma and Ripley. Not violent. On the other hand, they're not as harmless as I was."

"So they steal information," Chris said.

"Among other things."

"And will they know who I am?"

"Oh, they know who you are. And they don't like you very much, either."

"So why would one of them risk jail by driving us into France?"

"Because they *do* like me," Zoey said. "In some circles, my Centinela Bank prank was a big hit."

"So where can this Hive be found?"

"They occupy vacant office space where they can tap into phone lines and Internet connections. They're part of a much larger group, and most of them wouldn't be caught dead meeting in person and revealing their identities, but this bunch in Barcelona are sort of the social butterflies. They actually like hanging out together, but they don't stay in one place for long. I know a chat board they use. I can make contact."

Chris rose from the computer and let Zoey take a seat. Within fifteen minutes, she had established a connection with a member of the Hive called Soma. Ten minutes later, they received a text with the address of an abandoned office building that the group was using as its temporary headquarters.

The Hive had set up shop in a three-story brown-brick office building in the Barri Gòtic. The building's façade was charred by fire. The damage had been enough to render the property temporarily uninhabitable, but apparently the phone and Internet connections were still intact.

Chris ducked under a red plastic warning tape and pushed open the front door, covering his hands with soot in the process. Inside, it looked like hell's reception area—everything was charred but still discernible. A crumbling front desk stood guard over the entryway. The lacquered surface of a coffee table was black and covered with glistening bubbles. A rack was festooned with the scorched spines of magazines. The only thing missing was a scorched, skeletal receptionist. There was a powerful smell of smoke and burnt plastic. He could taste it in his mouth and could almost feel it soaking into his clothes and hair.

"Mmm, carcinogens," Zoey said, pinching her nose.

"What floor are they on?" Chris asked. His throat was scratchy and he felt like coughing.

"Third floor," Zoey said. "We can take the stairs."

They entered the stairwell, which was untouched by the fire, all pristine white concrete and iron railings.

When they opened the metal security door and stepped out onto the third floor, they were greeted by a small olive-skinned man with prematurely gray, close-cropped hair. He was wearing black jeans, a bright red T-shirt, and an ironic smile.

"Soma?" Zoey asked.

"Cynecitta!" Soma said in lightly accented English. "I had no idea that you were such a spicy little dish. Now I wish we'd met in person years ago." Zoey had informed Chris that Soma was an Oxford-educated heir to a Spanish manufacturing fortune who had decided to go in a very different direction with his life.

Chris could understand why the Hive had settled on this space. It was an expansive, open room with big windows. The floor appeared to have been untouched by the fire, and the smell of smoke was faint. Outside was a gorgeous view of La Seu cathedral, with its three towering Gothic spires. There were only a couple of desks, so most of the hackers were sitting on the floor in lotus positions with their laptops on their knees. It looked like an even looser version of an Internet start-up, with everyone permitted to maintain their idiosyncratic work habits as long as they kept coding. The difference was that if the Hive was dedicated to producing anything, it was probably disorder.

Zoey wandered around like a fangirl at Comic-Con, delightedly looking in on what the various hackers were up to. When Chris caught up with her, she was leaning over the shoulder of a heavily tattooed young man wearing a gray knit cap.

"What's this?" she asked.

"This is Officer Raymond Eagleton, Atlanta Police Department. He has *so* been doxed." Doxing was the practice of trolling online for the most sensitive and personal information about a person and posting it publicly, usually as some sort of retribution.

"What did Officer Raymond do?"

"You probably saw the video. He pepper-sprayed Occupy protesters right in the face. They weren't violent, just passively blocking a building."

"Did you find some good stuff on him?" Zoey asked.

"Oh, you have no idea," the hacker said.

Zoey's forehead furrowed as she leaned in closer to examine the photo on the monitor. Officer Eagleton was attired in full bondage regalia, with skintight latex and many, many zippers. "There's a zipper for everything, isn't there?"

The largest group of hackers was gathered around a large monitor where a scrawny teenage boy with jet-black-dyed hair was playing a video game with a fresh-faced young girl in her early twenties. Chris and Zoey watched round two of the game from over their shoulders. It was a combat game set in what appeared to be a postapocalyptic New York City. The characters were carrying automatic weapons in Times Square, but all of the giant neon and video billboards were flat black.

Disconcertingly, the two Uzi-toting characters in the video game bore exactly the same facial features as the pair playing the game. Zoey looked at the boy, who squinted as his fingers flew over the game console. On the screen, and in nearly the same instant, the boy's avatar squinted as he stepped over a pile of concrete rubble, Uzi at the ready.

"What game is this?" Zoey asked. "Digital motion capture is one thing but . . ."

"I know," Soma said, beaming "It's *First-Person Shooter—Avatar Edition*. Same technology that the animation studios use, but it works with a webcam. It's next year's biggest video game release. They're going to spend tens of millions of dollars marketing it—but we'll be offering it for free download next week—worldwide, baby."

"How did you get this?" Chris asked.

Soma looked suspiciously at Chris. "You said he was off-duty, right?"

Zoey nodded. "Busting you is the last thing on his mind."

Chris looked at Soma. "Aren't you worried that someone is going to take the trouble to hunt you down if you interfere with a revenue stream as big as this one?"

"The Hive knows no fear," Soma said. "We strike like lightning and disappear like smoke."

"Well, I think you'd better disappear like smoke when you make this download available," Chris said.

"Information wants to be free and the Hive is an army of liberation," Soma said, looking like he was warming up for a speech.

"Yes, I get it," said Chris, who had heard this sort of manifesto before.

Zoey saw trouble brewing and attempted to steer the conversation in a less contentious direction. "So what else have you been up to? Anything entertaining?"

"Just stockpiling vulns." "Vulns" was short for website vulnerabilities, which the hackers identified through a process of automated scanning, or crawling. A reasonably competent group of hackers had more vulns than they knew what to do with, and often they were sold to others to exploit. Then Soma smiled. "But have you seen our latest YouTube video?"

"We've been a little preoccupied lately," Zoey said.

"Best lulz ever." "Lulz" was a variation of the term "lol"—laugh out loud—and had come to mean entertainment at someone else's expense.

Soma sat down at a nearby laptop, opened a YouTube video, and maximized it to fill the screen. The camera shook violently. It looked like footage from the thick of some sort of riot. Then the camera steadied and details came into focus. An enormous stuffed giraffe loomed over a central escalator. It was the giant FAO Schwarz toy store in New York City. And the rioters were boys and girls who looked to range from ages eight to thirteen. The shelves were being ransacked and kids were engaging in fierce tug-of-war battles in the aisles over games and dolls. A tiny, blond-haired girl, who seemed to be about seven, wearing a flower print dress and a steely expression, won a struggle for a stuffed panda. The panda flew backward into the camera, and the footage came to an abrupt end.

"What was that?" Zoey asked.

"An FAO Schwarz employee was pissed off because he was getting laid off after the Christmas rush so he gave us the passcode to the store's intercom system. We hacked in and broadcast to the entire store that, as part of a very special promotion, all items in the store were free for the next fifteen minutes."

"You didn't."

"It was preteen Thunderdome, baby."

"It's all very impressive," Chris said, "but we need to talk about whether you can help us."

"*I* really need your help," Zoey added.

"I'm flattered," Soma said, not exactly committing himself. "What is it that you need?"

"Someone to drive us to Paris."

"Why don't you just rent a car?"

"Because we're currently wanted by Europol and just about every other law enforcement agency that you can imagine."

Soma brightened. "So baby did a bad, bad thing."

"We haven't done anything," Zoey said. "Someone is framing us for a cyberattack that's supposed to happen in the US."

"That's poetic justice, isn't it, Chris?"

Chris grimaced but held his tongue.

"You're talking about the January 14 thing, right?" Soma added.

"You've heard about that?" Chris asked.

"There's been talk on the chans that something was coming, but I didn't really believe it."

"Believe it," Chris said.

While they had been talking, word of Chris's identity had spread among the group. Hackers encircled them, each one glaring at Chris. They were all a little too scrawny and anemic-looking to pose much of a physical threat, but they were definitely radiating animosity. Chris hoped that he hadn't had a hand in getting any of them arrested.

"You're expecting border checks?" Soma said.

Chris nodded.

"So how do you propose to get across?"

"In the trunk. They probably won't be searching the cars."

"But if they do, everyone goes to jail."

"Worse than jail, because it would be a terrorism charge." Chris figured that there was no point in sugar coating the situation. Anyone who went with them should know what they might be getting themselves into.

"Why do you need to get into France so badly?"

"That's our business," Chris said.

"I wouldn't do this for him, you know?" Soma said, nodding at Chris.

"I know, but I really need your help."

"Since this is for you, I'll drive you myself. For a fee, of course," Soma said. "Five thousand US."

Chris had already anticipated pricing. "I can pay you two thousand now. There's another three thousand at a locker here in Barcelona. I'll give you the key and the location when you've gotten us to Paris."

"Usually, I'm not this trusting," Soma said. "But since it's you two—you have a deal."

"Thanks, Soma," Zoey said. "You're a sweetheart."

Soma waved off the compliment, then turned to Chris. "Do you know how talented our Zoey is? She's famous around here for the Centinela Bank exploit." He smiled. "I hope I didn't say something that I shouldn't have."

"He already knows," Zoey said. "I told him about CB."

Soma raised his gray eyebrows at Chris. "And that doesn't bother you? What's happened to you, man? I thought you tracked down people like us."

"Call it a temporary truce."

"You vouch for him?" Soma asked.

"I do."

Soma considered for only a moment. "Okay, when do we leave?"

"Right away," Chris said. "We want to cross the French border tomorrow morning when the traffic will be heavy and they'll be less likely to search trunks."

"I have one more favor to ask," Zoey said.

Soma looked like his patience was being tested. "More than this? What is it?"

"We need a clean, fast laptop with wireless. Whenever we've needed access, we've had to go to libraries and Internet cafés."

"I was afraid you were going to ask for something difficult," Soma said. "Let me see what I've got."

Soma went to the other side of the office and returned with a new MacBook and handed it to Zoey. "There you go. There's an account that's been set up using a stolen identity. No way to trace it to you." Soma turned to Chris. "I hope this doesn't pose a moral dilemma for you," he said.

"That's perfect," Zoey said, not waiting for Chris to respond. "Thank you."

Soma left them to get his car keys. As soon as he was out of earshot, Chris said, "I don't trust him."

"Do you know anyone else who will risk arrest to drive us into France?"

"No."

"Okay then," Zoey said.

CHAPTER 23

As they drove through the empty streets of Barcelona at 4:00 a.m. in Soma's Audi, Zoey was sitting up front in the passenger seat, where Soma seemed to be trying to talk her into using her web design skills for one of the Hive's illicit schemes. Zoey appeared impervious to his advances.

Chris had misgivings about traveling with Soma, but he could think of no other alternative that would get them into France in time. For all he knew, Soma might be in league with the Lurker crew. For that matter, Zoey might also be working with them. But even if both statements were true, what did it really matter? The hackers somehow seemed to be tracking their every move, anyway. And Enigma already knew exactly where Chris was headed—to the rendezvous in Paris at Père Lachaise. All that really mattered was that he was probably getting closer by the minute to Sarah. She was deceptively tough, and he knew that, wherever she was, she was holding on.

Soon they were on a highway headed out of the city and north through the Costa Brava, where beach towns clung like barnacles to the rugged coastline that extended to the French border. They drove slowly by necessity along the road that snaked beside the Mediterranean. Chris figured that any police would be more likely to be hunting for them on the main highway, which was inland. They passed through the sleepy beach towns of Blanes, Lloret de Mar, and now Tossa de Mar.

There are few things as desolate as a beach town at night in winter. The dun sands of the beach at Tossa de Mar were presided over by Vila Vella enceinte, a fortified medieval town that occupied the hill above. The fortress, with its stone walls studded with turrets and towers with parapets, seemed incongruous so near to a popular beach. Several small fishing boats were pulled up on the sand. Unlike Barcelona, where the locals seemed to stay out all night, Tossa de Mar was shuttered and vacant.

Chris struggled to stay awake. The last sleep he had gotten had been on the plane to Barcelona, and that had been fitful. But he didn't want to waste any time, so he opened up his laptop and tried to concentrate once more on the coding of the Lurker virus. The yellow streetlights strobed in reflection on his computer screen as they sped along the coastal road.

A particular segment of the coding mystified him. Something seemed out of place. Lurker was designed to expire six months after activation. At that point, the virus would effectively disappear from the hard drives that it had infected and cease to spread to other computers. Chris could not understand why a black hat hacker like Enigma, whose intent seemed to be to cause as much destruction possible, would put that sort of failsafe mechanism into a virus.

REECE HIRSCH • 179

Despite his best effort, Chris fell into a deep, exhausted sleep, still mulling over the riddle as he drifted off.

He was awakened by the thrumming of his prepaid cell phone. For a long, groggy moment, Chris tried to pull apart the tangled threads of reality and dream. The dream consisted of an image of his unlined sixteen-year-old hands drifting down to a black plastic computer keyboard in underwater slow-motion. With the index finger of his right hand, he reached out to press the Enter key. Something bad was about to happen. He didn't want to hit the key, but his hands were not under his control, scuttling across the keyboard like two pale spiders. It was a familiar, recurring dream and the phone was not part of it. His eyes focused on his phone's screen and he was suddenly fully alert. It was a text from Enigma, and it read:

ENIGMA: Hola, Chris.

Chris stared at the screen, still getting his wits about him, then he hurriedly typed out a response, his fingers fumbling over the keys.

CHRIS: Is Sarah alive?

ENIGMA: She's just missing her little finger. Mickey Mouse gets along just fine with four and so will she.

CHRIS: What do you want? If you want something from me, just release Sarah. I'll do it.

ENIGMA: I wish it were that simple, Chris. I really do.

CHRIS: Then what do you want?

ENIGMA: Just wanted to make sure that you're still on schedule to make it to Paris.

CHRIS: We'll be there. But I'm surprised you need to ask. I thought you knew our every move.

ENIGMA: Actually, I do. Hope you don't have any trouble at the border checkpoint. If someone placed an anonymous call telling them to watch for a blue Audi . . .

CHRIS: We wouldn't make it to Paris then, would we?

ENIGMA: You just keep running the maze, little rat.

CHRIS: What's in Paris?

There was no reply, and he received no further texts from Enigma. He had to assume that Enigma was simply jerking his chain. They really only had two choices: proceed on to Paris or give up any hope of finding Sarah alive.

When Chris looked out the window, he saw that they were driving through Girona, the capital of the Costa Brava region, which lay inland, away from the beach towns. Girona seemed to be two cities, one on top of the other. First, there was a modern and fairly nondescript metropolis that wrapped around the Onyar River. But when you raised your eyes, there was a medieval fortress and cathedral lit for effect and glowing palely atop the hill overlooking the city. One city for the living, one city for the dead (or, at any rate, for the tourists).

Zoey was asleep up front, her head resting against the car window, her lips parted slightly and her breath fogging the glass.

"You awake?" Soma whispered.

"Yes," Chris said, not anxious to start a conversation.

"If you don't mind me asking, what are you working on back there?"

"I think you should stick to driving."

"Just making conversation. You called this a cyberattack, yes?" Soma said. "Are we talking some kind of weaponized virus?"

Chris remained silent as they wound their way through the city, trying to get back on the highway.

"All right. Have it your way," Soma said. "Your loss. I might have helped you out of sheer boredom."

Now that Chris was awake, his attention turned again to a seemingly random series of numbers, letters, and symbols that were buried in the coding of the Lurker virus to no functional purpose. The sequence read:

```
b:\9y7c6ykh0y6yd\\M3:R-I-II-III:RS:MCK:R:AAA:P:
FP,MD,WE,XO,ZS,JV,AH,BC,QK,RT:G8U9O3M3G0R
3O5M2N1Z\\%phgopaigihgiaog22590808ad\src\objfre_
w2k_x86\i386\guava.pd.
```

In extraneous segments of code like this one, hackers sometimes buried a calling card, something that they could use to claim credit, at least among their friends. Chris felt certain that there was some significance to the sequence, but no matter how long he stared at it or how many code-breaking techniques he tried, it refused to render up its meaning.

Chris wasn't having any luck with the fragment of code, but another component of the virus was suddenly beginning to make sense. He thought that maybe he knew why the Lurker virus had a six-month expiration date built into it. The virus was designed for a demonstration. Like the Los Alamos test, as Enigma had mentioned to Middendorf. The impending attack was not intended to cause unlimited collateral damage, and the expiration date ensured that.

While the Lurker virus had clearly been designed for a very particular purpose, Chris had not yet been able to identify the segment of code that revealed the virus's target. Maybe Ed or the team at BlueCloud was having better luck with that. But there could be little doubt that, no matter what the specific target was, Lurker was intended to be a weapon of cyberterrorism.

What would happen if Enigma and his band of hackers turned such a powerful virus loose on a major US city? It was a deeply disturbing prospect.

The intercepted message board chat between Enigma and Middendorf had been full of ominous pontificating about a new era of cyberwarfare. Thus far, cyberwar had been a term bandied about occasionally in the press, but there was little evidence that it had actually been waged. One of the first publicized incidents occurred in 2008, when Russian troops invaded the South Ossetia region of Georgia. During that military action, it appeared that the Russian government had also conducted a multipronged cyber campaign to cripple the Georgian government. As Russian troops poured across the border, the Georgian government had difficulty responding, due to crashed websites and disruption of the VoIP phone system. It was a relatively crude effort, but effective.

More recently, the Obama administration had considered, but ultimately rejected, the use of cyberwarfare tactics against Libya to disable the Qaddafi government's air-defense system. The administration again declined to use a more targeted cyberattack that would have knocked out Pakistani radar so that they wouldn't detect the helicopters carrying Navy Seal commandos in the raid that killed Osama bin Laden. Reportedly, Defense Department officials didn't want to be the first ones to "break the glass" on a dangerous new form of warfare.

The adversary had no such qualms. Enigma and Middendorf had spoken of a "cyber Hiroshima." Chris wondered how the world would have reacted if the first atomic bomb had not been detonated by the United States in 1945, but rather by a terrorist group. In 1945 everyone knew instantly that the world had changed irrevocably, but some comfort could be taken from the fact that the United States was the only nation that held the secret of the atomic bomb. What if Lurker was the cyberwar equivalent of Hiroshima's Fat Man bomb? And what if such a terrible new weapon was unveiled not by an accountable government, but by a nameless, faceless group of hacker terrorists? Chris realized that the worldwide panic that would ensue could be nearly as destructive as the attack itself.

When the first atomic bomb was detonated in the New Mexico desert, Robert Oppenheimer said that he thought of a line from the Bhagavad Gita: "Now, I am become death, the destroyer of worlds." What if the next Oppenheimer felt the same sentiment, but without the horror and remorse? Chris stared out the window of the car, absorbed in these terrible thoughts, as the first shades of dawn began to appear over the rust-colored hills of Catalonia.

CHAPTER 24

Ed de Lamadrid had hardly left the firm's computer forensic lab in the past thirty-six hours and his thought processes were getting a little glitchy. An early winter dusk had just faded from ember to cinder, and the office was emptying out, but Ed was determined to keep working for as long as he could keep his eyes open with coffee and energy drinks. When he was on a tear like this, Ed liked to keep the lights down so that the lab was lit mainly by the glow of computer monitors, giving the room an unearthly luminescence. He thought of it as Spaceship Ed.

He was feverishly analyzing the Lurker virus to understand its target and how it worked. Ed hoped that when he found the answers to those questions, they would help exonerate his friend Chris. As his hands moved over the keyboard, Bach's *Goldberg Variations* played softly in the background. Ed had hated classical music until Chris introduced him to Bach, but now it was an indispensable part of his work process when he required deep concentration.

Ed had noticed that the attorneys and staff were starting to cast not-so-subtle glances at him as they passed the doorway. Everyone knew how close he was to Chris. Most of them probably assumed that he had either collaborated with him in the terrorist plot or provided assistance to him now that he was on the run. If there had been even a shred of evidence implicating him, Ed would have been suspended from work.

"When was the last time you slept?"

Ed spun around in his chair, startled by the quiet voice so close behind him. Managing partner Don Rubinowski stood in the doorway, immaculate and unflappable in a bold striped shirt, pinstriped suit pants, and suspenders. Ed distrusted lawyers—they were a little too adept at tailoring themselves to their situation. And Don Rubinowski was exactly the type that made Ed most uncomfortable. Talking to Don always felt like playing chess with a computer, with each of his responses eliciting a subtle recalibration. Ed's data security peers were the exact opposite in temperament—they tended to be obstinate, opinionated, unfiltered, certain that something either worked or it didn't. The only lawyer that Ed trusted was Chris, who was less like an attorney and more like a member of his own geeky tribe.

"I don't know, it's been a while," Ed said. "That Lurker virus is a bear."

"Well, we all appreciate the effort you're putting in. Even with Chris gone, BlueCloud is still an important firm client." After a brief, calculated pause, Don added, "Oh, and speaking of Chris, have you heard from him?"

"No, but if I did, I would certainly let you know."

"Of course you would," Don said. "It's a shock, isn't it? I was his friend, too, you know. I didn't want to believe any of it."

"So you really think Chris is responsible for killing those people on that plane in Albuquerque?"

Don stepped out of the doorway and into the lab. He strolled around a bank of computers, causing Ed to swivel in his chair to follow him.

"At this point," Don said, "It doesn't really matter what we believe. What matters now is what the FBI and Homeland Security believe."

"I guess that's right," Ed said. He wasn't about to give Don anything.

"And assuming that the FBI is right about Chris, then it means that Chris was never the person we thought he was. He was somebody else all along."

Don approached a whiteboard covered with a scribbled sequence of code. "So this makes sense to you?"

Ed shrugged in acknowledgment.

Don shook his head. "Might as well be Sanskrit as far as I'm concerned. More of a right-brain type myself."

"Most lawyers are."

"In light of everything that's happening, you're probably wondering about your position here at the firm now that Chris is gone."

"I wasn't really thinking about that," Ed said.

"Well, you will, and I want you to know that your job is secure here. The firm wants to maintain a presence in this data security practice area, and we want to keep a computer forensic lab. When the dust settles, we'll recruit a new partner to fill Chris's spot."

"Maybe Chris will return to fill his old spot himself. Innocent until proven guilty, right?"

"Maybe, maybe. But that seems pretty unlikely right now." Don looked Ed in the eyes with his best closing argument gaze. "The point is that we want you to know that you have a home here at Reynolds Fincher—and it would be a shame if you were to jeopardize that out of some misplaced loyalty to someone who looks pretty damn guilty."

So there it was—the transaction. The firm wanted him to sell out his friend Chris and, in exchange, he could keep his job.

"I appreciate the vote of confidence." That was what Ed said, but what he was thinking was very different.

CHAPTER 25

January 12

To loosely paraphrase Samuel Johnson, the prospect of being locked in the trunk of a car focuses the mind. And when Chris's mind was thus focused, his first realization was that any plan that involved being locked in a car trunk probably was not a very good one.

Two miles from the French border, they pulled off the road and prepared for the border guards. Soma turned the Audi off onto a rutted trail that cut across a field and into a stand of pine trees. They didn't want passing motorists to see Chris and Zoey climbing into the trunk. Chris arranged some blankets and tried to figure out how he was going to fit inside. The sun was over the horizon now and a light breeze rippled the field of chest-high grass.

"You're tall, so we'd better get you in there first," Zoey said.

Chris crawled inside, curling himself with his back against the wall of the trunk.

Zoey sized up the remaining space, which was not that big. "Okay, I'm going to try this spoon-style." She put one foot delicately into the trunk like she was stepping into a swimming pool. Then, not so delicately, she tumbled forward, knocking the wind out of Chris.

"Are you okay? Sorry," she said.

"Fine," Chris said when he had recovered his breath. Zoey settled in with her back to him.

Soma placed his hands on the lid of the trunk. "Don't do anything I wouldn't do," he said with a smirk. Soma was one of those people who always seemed to be speaking in ironic quotation marks. Chris really hated that.

The trunk slammed shut and they were cast into darkness, except for a few dusty shafts of light that seeped in through the lock and around the seams of the lid. The ignition turned and the car began to move. The shock absorbers were shot, and he felt every bump and pothole as Soma drove back over the trail that crossed the field.

"Hands," Zoey said. "Hands."

Chris realized that he had placed a hand on Zoey's hip to steady himself as they were shaken about. "Sorry."

Things went smoother once they were back on the highway, but the trunk grew warm under the midmorning sun. The car's air-conditioning didn't ventilate the trunk. Chris could feel the rise and fall of every breath that Zoey took. She didn't wear perfume, but she smelled nice nonetheless.

"Do you think Soma's still taking us to the border?" he asked. "I don't like trusting him like this."

"I think he'll come through," Zoey said. "He likes me."

"Yeah, but he really doesn't like me."

"True, but he doesn't get the rest of his fee until we hand over the locker key."

Chris tried to gauge if the Audi was slowing or speeding up. The hiss of the tires on the pavement seemed very close at hand, reminding him of a streaming water faucet.

After about ten minutes, the car slowed to an idle. Chris had been right. Border checkpoints had been put in place, regardless of the Schengen Agreement. They were probably in a line of cars advancing toward a team of agents.

The car inched forward. The temperature in the trunk inched upward. Chris and Zoey were both sweating. Chris reached up to wipe perspiration from his forehead before it rolled down into his eyes. There was no talking now. If they were discovered in the trunk, they would be in the custody of Europol and/or Homeland Security within the hour. Chris wondered what sorts of interrogation techniques DHS was using these days, but he quickly decided that was not a helpful exercise. And it meant nothing to him compared with what he imagined Sarah must be experiencing.

The car advanced a bit and they could hear the sound of French being spoken in an authoritative tone. They were at the checkpoint. The car didn't move for one minute, two minutes, perhaps even five minutes. Chris couldn't lift his arm to check his watch, but it wouldn't have mattered, anyway. For all practical purposes, time had stopped.

Chris could feel Zoey's body tense beside his. This was taking too long. Perhaps there was something wrong with Soma's passport. He was the sort of person who would use false credentials. What if he had the audacity to use a fake passport, jeopardizing their lives in the process?

The voices speaking French grew louder and seemed to be coming from all directions. The border guards were circling the car. He tried to remain absolutely motionless. Zoey must have been holding her breath, because he no longer heard the rustling of her inhale and exhale.

Then the trunk echoed with a loud bang. Chris thought for a moment that someone had fired a gunshot. He hoped that he hadn't reflexively kicked the wall of the trunk. He really couldn't be sure. He stared at the roof of the trunk, expecting it to pop open at any moment, but it remained shut.

The Audi rolled forward again, slowly at first, then accelerating. Chris realized that the sound had probably been a border guard slapping the trunk, urging Soma on his way. Chris and Zoey had both jumped at the sound, and now their pulses and heart rates were slowly ticking down to normal. Chris didn't have to ask Zoey if she was okay. They were so closely entwined that he knew without asking.

"You think he's ever going to pull over and let us out of here?" Zoey asked.

"Yeah, when he stops finding this amusing."

When Soma finally opened up the trunk, a smirk was still lacquered on his face.

"Gauloises?" he asked, offering his pack of cigarettes.

Chris and Zoey shook the numbness from their legs and arms, walking around in another field of tall grass identical to the one in Spain. The same cool breeze rippled the tall grass here, but Chris appreciated it much more after over a half hour in the trunk of a car. He checked his watch: 8:45. They had eight hours to make it to Paris for the meet-up at Père Lachaise. Rain clouds the color of fresh bruises hung over the northeast horizon where they were headed.

CHAPTER 26

Soma drove quickly through the French countryside south of Toulouse. It was an overcast day that deepened the color of the winter wheat fields. Off in the distance, in a crook in the rolling hills, the red-tiled roof of a farmhouse stood out like a drop of blood on a tablecloth.

On another day, Chris would have appreciated the landscape and the ancient villages with their crumbling stone walls. But not today. Chris watched for police cars at every bend in the road and kept Soma in line whenever he crept over the speed limit. He didn't want to make Europol's job easier by getting pulled for a speeding ticket. The CIA and a host of other law enforcement agencies were probably still looking for them in Spain, assuming that they wouldn't be able to cross the border.

As they made their way toward Paris and Père Lachaise Cemetery, Chris continued to puzzle over why they were instructed to meet at the grave of Gholam-Hossein Sa'edi. He unfolded the printouts on Sa'edi, reviewing what he knew about the author.

When Chris looked up, they were driving over the historic Pont Neuf into Toulouse under a sky full of clouds that seemed to be lit from within by a pale sun. The seventeenth-century bridge was suspended over the Garonne River by asymmetrical arches of stone and the city's trademark pink brick. The arches were reflected in reverse in the waters of the Garonne, forming a series of ellipses.

The defining characteristic of Sa'edi's life seemed to be his struggle for political and intellectual freedom in Iran, which went hand in hand with his opposition to Ayatollah Khomeini and the Islamists. Maybe Enigma was a zealot who was aligned with anti-Islamist groups. Or perhaps he intended to offer the Lurker virus to one of those factions so that they could use it against Iran or another Islamic fundamentalist state. So far, Enigma hadn't sounded particularly ideological about anything except the disruptive potential of cyberwarfare, but Chris still knew very little about him. Chris sensed that he had the information to solve the mystery of the virus and its creator, but it wasn't coming together.

Despite Enigma's assurances, Chris wondered if Sarah was still alive. The image of her severed finger stayed in his head. Most kidnap victims were dead three days after the abduction, but this was not a typical kidnapping. There was no indication that Enigma was a sexual predator, and it wasn't about ransom. Somehow, this was about him.

The hours passed in a daze. He eventually nodded off. When he awoke, the rustic villages had given way to billboards and nondescript office parks. They were reaching the suburbs of Paris. The lowering sky finally delivered on its threat and the rain started to fall in fat, dirty gray drops.

It was time to part ways with Soma. Chris still didn't trust him, and the sooner that he and Zoey could be on their own again, the better. They had never told Soma the exact location of their meeting. Two hours remained until the rendezvous at Père Lachaise, which was on the eastern edge of Paris in the 20th arrondissement. Chris thought they could use the time to make contact with Ed and see if he had learned anything new about the virus.

Chris had Soma stop in the 20th arrondissement in front of a WiFi-friendly looking café. Soma turned around to face him from the front seat.

"So that's it, is it?" he asked.

"That's it," Chris said, handing over an envelope containing a key and the location of a bus station locker in Barcelona.

"Things were just getting interesting," Soma said. "And you'll need a ride to get around Paris, won't you?"

"Thanks, but we'll take the metro," Chris said. "You already took a big risk to get us here. I don't know why you'd want to press your luck."

"She knows why," Soma said then, nodding at Zoey, "even if you don't. I live for this."

"And what is this?" Chris asked.

"The things that nobody wants you to know. It's what we do. And I've got a feeling that you two are on the verge of learning some very big and very bad secrets."

"I get it," Zoey said. "But you have to remember that this will probably end with Chris and me in some supermax prison for life. They have our names, so we don't have a choice. You do."

Soma smiled. "You care about me after all, don't you?"

"We're going to have to insist," Chris said, "but we appreciate what you've done."

"Okay," Soma said. "If that's how it has to be."

Chris and Zoey climbed out of the car and onto the noisy, bustling streets of Belleville. If Belleville were a French wine, its bouquet would have exhibited notes of fried garlic noodles, wet pavement, and car exhaust. Belleville was a working-class neighborhood in which Greek, Armenian, and North African communities existed side by side, along with Paris's second largest Chinatown. The tan stucco of the storefronts was worn away in spots, exposing ancient red brick. Across the street was the Marché Belleville, an open sidewalk market where vendors hawked vegetables, meats, and flowers in a dozen languages. The Indian fabric stand was a riot of color, and the Babel of voices from across the street sounded like a bad day at the UN.

They entered a café frequented by denizens of the nearby music clubs. Chris sat down at a computer and attempted to connect with Ed in San Francisco. After waiting a half hour for Ed to respond to a text, they established a Skype connection. Ed's hair was tousled and his face looked puffy. It was 8:00 a.m. in San Francisco, and they had clearly woken him up. Ed liked to work late, so he tended to start his day at the computer lab at 11:00 a.m. He was in his slobby bachelor's apartment in lively North Beach, a French poster for *Blade Runner* mounted with thumb tacks on the wall behind him.

"Look at you two, a couple of outlaws," Ed said. "You look different, Chris."

"It's the jacket," Chris said. "She picked it out."

"I would have guessed that," he said.

"Is this a safe connection for you?" Chris asked.

"Yeah, it's clean. It's a borrowed computer and an ISP account that no one would connect to me."

"I think I've figured out a few things about the virus," Chris said.

"Me, too," Ed said. "I've been talking to the forensic team at BlueCloud. I learned some things from them, some I figured out on my own. Let's hear what you've got first."

Chris explained what he had learned about the Lurker virus's expiration date and his theory that Enigma might be linked to anti-Islamist groups. Chris asked Ed to search for connections between Enigma and anti-Islamist factions. As Chris continued, Ed began nodding excitedly.

"That's all consistent with what I've got," Ed said. "For example, when the virus attacks a computer, guess what's the first thing it does?"

"What?"

"It checks the computer's keyboard. If the keyboard has the Ukrainian alphabet, it deactivates."

"That neatly avoids the problem of blowback if you're a Ukrainian hacker who's concerned about having your virus take out your own systems," Zoey said.

"Exactly, and wait till you hear this," Ed said, clearly pleased with himself. "I know what the virus was targeting—programmable logic controllers manufactured by Sonnen."

"What are those?" Zoey asked.

"PLCs are tiny digital computers used to control automated processes," Chris said. "They were first developed to operate the machinery on factory assembly lines. Now you can find them almost everywhere—they run traffic lights, hospital equipment, most of the power grid." Chris turned back to Ed on the monitor. "Is the virus aimed at all PLCs or just specific types?"

"You saw that there are two different styles of coding in the payload of the virus," Ed said. "One is very sophisticated. Elegantly coded, disciplined, highly labor intensive—the sort of thing a team of top corporate programmers might have written. The second is an effective but fairly crude edit."

"Which would be the work of Enigma and his crew," Zoey said.

"Probably," Ed said.

"What was the purpose of the edit?" Chris asked.

"I haven't figured that out yet, but I'm working on it. But I can tell that the previous target was deleted."

"So what replaced it?" Zoey asked.

Ed shook his head in grudging admiration. "It's pretty insidious. When the virus infects a computer, the first thing it does is spread itself to every other computer on that system. Then it looks for where Sonnen software is running. Once it finds Sonnen software, then it checks for connections to Sonnen PLCs."

Chris leaned in closer to the monitor. "Then what?"

"That's where I hit a dead end. The coding is clearly directed at PLCs with specific functions, but I can't make out which ones. If there are no Sonnen PLCs connected to a system, then the virus becomes dormant and inactive. But if the virus finds Sonnen PLCs, it seems to be checking for those that are operating in a particular environment under specific conditions. To identify the target, it's not enough to just understand the virus. You have to identify the system environment that has the characteristics that the virus is searching for."

"What happens when it finds what it's looking for?" Chris asked.

"It injects some kind of rogue code intended to disable the targeted equipment."

"Have you researched the types of functions that are performed by Sonnen PLCs?" Chris asked.

"Yeah, but that doesn't help narrow things down. Their PLCs perform pretty much every automated process that you could imagine, and quite a few that you couldn't. Sonnen's the PLC market leader in just about every industry, everywhere."

Zoey interjected. "Most viruses that I'm familiar with hit a target by giving the hacker remote control of a system—root control. Then the hacker basically acts as the guidance system. But this virus is like a self-directed stealth missile. It's finding very specific targets entirely on its own. Whoever created this is scary good."

"Or scary bad," Chris said.

"Of course. Right," Zoey said, pivoting from her customary prohacker orientation. "But once Lurker has found its targets, it doesn't immediately take them out, does it? Otherwise, Enigma wouldn't be announcing a specific date for the cyberattack."

"Exactly," Ed said. "There's a remote activation feature. When he's ready, Enigma can take out the infected equipment with a keystroke."

"Back up for a second," Chris said. "If you have information about the function of the virus, then you must have determined the point of entry, so that you could watch it operate. That means it might be possible to create a security patch and limit the damage, right?"

"Maybe if we knew the equipment that was being targeted, we could . . ." Ed stopped in midsentence as a mechanical, clacking sound came through the speakers.

Ed's face contorted in a frozen rictus, teeth clenched. Then they saw the two small dart-like electrodes attached to filament wires that protruded from his shoulder. He had been incapacitated by a Taser. Ed's mouth worked for a moment like he was trying to say something, but no sounds came out. Then he slumped over his keyboard, looming into the camera frame.

"We can see you!" Chris shouted. "We're calling the police!" But, in fact, all they could see of the assailant was a pair of black pants, a blue-striped dress shirt, and a pair of black leather gloves.

They heard the attacker moving about the apartment, out of view. Then the attacker's hand reappeared in frame, now holding a hypodermic. He jammed the needle into Ed's neck and injected a full chamber of a milky solution. Ed's hands continued to twitch for an endless, stomach-churning moment, but then he stopped moving.

They heard movement in the apartment for another minute or two, then the attacker returned and picked up Ed's wrist, checking for a pulse. Seeming to find none, he let Ed's wrist drop limply beside the keyboard. The attacker rolled Ed aside in the desk chair. He approached the computer.

Chris and Zoey watched for a glimpse of the killer's face, but their view of the murder scene was cut off as the screen went black. The last thing they saw was two black-leather-gloved hands closing the laptop.

CHAPTER 27

Chris felt like a swimmer caught in a riptide, dragged downward into the depths with no light, no sound, and no oxygen, carelessly smashed on the ocean floor, sustaining injuries that couldn't yet be inventoried in the rushing moment. Gradually, the buzz of voices and clinking of glasses and silverware returned, and he found himself still staring at the laptop where he had witnessed Ed's death.

And as soon as Chris managed to gain a degree of control over his shock at what he'd seen, the guilt hit. He was responsible for Ed's death. He had allowed him to become involved as an accomplice in their flight. Chris was not by nature a violent person and, as an attorney, he believed in the legal system, but when he finally caught up with the person who was responsible for Sarah's kidnapping, and now Ed's murder, legal remedies would not be good enough.

202 • THE ADVERSARY

Chris could see that Zoey's cheeks were wet with tears. He reached across the table and put his hand over hers. They sat like that for a while.

Eventually, he recognized that it was dangerous for them to stay so long in a public place. "We need to get out of here," he said. "And there's a call I have to make."

Zoey nodded as Chris took her arm and they walked out of the café into the streets of Belleville. The sidewalks were more crowded now, as the clubs were filling for the evening. Chinese characters glowed in neon reds and greens on a row of shop signs. The lurid colors seemed to match his agitated state of mind.

As they walked, Zoey pulled herself together enough to start asking questions. "Who do you think killed him?"

"It could have been Enigma or one of his crew. Maybe they knew Ed was making progress in figuring out how to stop the virus."

They stepped into a narrow alley that felt as dank and claustrophobic as a cavern. Chris dialed an international call to the San Francisco Police Department hotline using his burner phone and left an anonymous message that Eduardo de Lamadrid had been murdered in his apartment at 230 Folsom Street. Chris also told the officer that he needed to alert FBI agent Michael Hazlitt so that they could search Ed's apartment and computer for evidence of his work in unpacking the Lurker virus. The officer sounded understandably confused, but he let Chris talk, and the call was being recorded. Chris was fairly certain that Ed's attacker would have found and removed all of Ed's work product, but there was a chance that the agents would find information that could be used to develop a security patch. At least the work being done on the virus by BlueCloud's security team had not been lost.

When the officer on the line asked whom he was speaking to, Chris hung up.

"I couldn't just leave him there in his apartment. It might have taken days for someone to find him."

"I understand," Zoey said.

Chris had considered calling Hazlitt directly and explaining everything that he had learned about Lurker in the hopes that it might convince him that they weren't terrorists. But he couldn't bring himself to do it. Chris feared that Enigma might somehow intercept his call to the FBI as he had the last one. His first offense had cost Sarah a finger. He didn't want to learn the penalty for a second offense.

They walked the streets in silence for a while until Chris's thoughts returned to the task at hand. He checked his watch. The meeting at Père Lachaise was only forty-five minutes away. They headed down Rue de Belleville and then Boulevard de Ménilmontant toward the cemetery. The neighborhood's cultural hodgepodge was evident in the shops they passed, from an Algerian restaurant to a Greek grocery to a Chinese bookstore.

Finally, the imposing white marble gates of Père Lachaise Cemetery came into view. It was the most exclusive address in Paris, home to the wealthy and famous, but no one was in a hurry to take up residence. Chris had bought a map of the cemetery at a tourist shop, and now they wound their way in a misting rain through the impressive mausoleums and markers toward Sa'edi's grave.

"You know that this is another trap, don't you?" Zoey said.

"Yeah, but I don't see what choice we have but to walk into it with our eyes open," Chris said.

Père Lachaise Cemetery on a rainy day in January was a study in shades of gray. Gray marble headstones, gray paving-stone path, charcoal clouds heavy with rain, rows of bare, ashen trees lining the path, and pearly gray light to dimly illu-minate it all. They passed the graves of Jim Morrison, Chopin, Oscar Wilde, and Edith Piaf as they followed the maze-like cobbled paths through the cemetery. A stone angel atop a mau-soleum spread its wings above them, drops of rain beading on her face like tears.

Chris pulled out the map and examined it. "It's grave num-ber 35. I think it should be around this corner."

Zoey checked her watch. "We only have five minutes." The rain was only a mist, but Zoey's hair now hung in a mass of dark curls around her face.

Chris led the way, steps clicking on the paving stones.

After rounding a corner, Chris stopped in the middle of the path and turned in a circle. "This should be it," he said.

Zoey took one side and Chris took the other, examining the gravestones.

"Over here," she said at last.

Chris stepped up behind her next to a low, black iron railing and saw a small headstone that read:

Gholam-Hossein Sa'edi
January 4, 1936–November 23, 1985

"So, what now?" Zoey asked.

"We look closer," Chris said. But first he scanned the cem-etery for someone approaching to meet them. The walkways were empty. The light rain was enough to keep the tourists away.

He stepped over the railing and inspected the grave. There was a six-foot-long gray marble slab with a matching headstone flanked by two urns. Chris examined the grass around the grave and looked behind the headstone. Nothing.

Chris tried to lift the lid of one of the urns, but it was a solid piece of sculpture and did not move. Next, Chris rolled the heavy marble urn on one side to see what was underneath. Again, nothing.

"Do you think they really intended to make contact with us?" Zoey asked. "Maybe this was all a waste of time."

"I don't think so," Chris said. "They're probably watching us right now. They wanted us to be at this place for a reason. Maybe because it suggests that we're sympathetic to some anti-Islamist movement. Maybe Enigma is trying to create a backstory for us that will make it easier for the government to turn us into scapegoats later."

Chris noticed a scuff mark on the marble around the second urn, the kind of mark that suggested that it had been recently moved. He turned the base of the sculpture on one edge and rolled it. Zoey saw the white letter-sized envelope first and picked it up. She tore it open and held it out to Chris so that they could read it together. The message was written in black marker and read:

EXIT THE CEMETERY BY THE MAIN GATE. GO TO 33 BOULEVARD DE MÉNILMONTANT, SUITE 225. THE DOOR WILL BE UNLOCKED. YOU HAVE FIFTEEN MINUTES—THE CLOCK STARTS NOW.

Once more, Chris scanned the cemetery but he could not spot whoever was observing them. Then he turned to Zoey and asked, "Do you remember the path we took to get here?"

"You're the one with the map," Zoey said. "Everything here looks the same to me."

Zoey was right. The cobbled path lined with funeral statuary looked like every other route they had taken since they entered the sprawling necropolis.

"Let's start this way," Chris said, pointing back the way they had come.

He knew that if they made one wrong turn on the way out, they would miss the kidnappers' deadline. If that happened, Sarah might die.

They retraced their path through Père Lachaise without a word, with Chris leading the way.

After a few minutes, they reached a fork in the path. Chris studied the cheap tourist map but didn't see any markers or landmarks that he recognized. Zoey stared at him. She knew that he was guessing and she knew the stakes. This was Chris's decision to make. Chris pointed to the left down one of the identical paths just as a pellet-like rain began to fall.

As they set out again, Zoey said, "I would have chosen that one, too."

In a matter of minutes, they could hear the sounds of the street and knew that Chris had guessed correctly. They emerged from the hushed spell of the cemetery and were back among the car horns and street noise of Belleville.

Thirty-three Boulevard de Ménilmontant was a narrow, inauspicious office building that was an exemplar of a badly dated seventies-modern style. It looked like the sort of place where failed French accounting firms went to die. They climbed the stairs to the second floor, where Chris noted one video camera in the lobby, another in the stairwell. There would be a record of their visit.

There were three offices off of a short hallway with worn, mottled chocolate-brown carpeting. The last door on the right displayed a small brass plaque that read "225." Chris checked his watch. They had made it in almost exactly fifteen minutes.

Before he could try the doorknob, Zoey asked, "Are you sure this is a good idea?"

"Not at all," Chris replied.

CHAPTER 28

Chris drew his gun and tested the door of Suite 225. As the note had indicated, it was unlocked.

He turned the knob and the door slowly swung open to reveal a small, dingy but fully operational office. The fluorescent lights were on overhead. The computers were running. Some screen savers bounced images of a generic corporate logo. On other monitors, the screen savers hadn't even activated yet. The office must have been occupied only minutes before.

There was a smell of burnt coffee from a simmering coffee pot. A tinny radio somewhere in the rear of the office was playing "Lisztomania," a bouncy, upbeat song by the French pop band Phoenix. But there was no one in the office. It was as if everyone had just gotten up from their desks and walked out. It occurred to Chris that Enigma might have cleared the office with a bomb threat—or an actual bomb.

Chris stepped inside. He couldn't tell what sort of business was conducted there, and his French wasn't good enough to read the papers strewn across the desks.

"It's kind of like a ghost ship," said Zoey, who was right behind him. "A really boring and corporate ghost ship."

Chris walked among the desks and back to a small kitchen in the rear of the office. He found the radio there and turned it off.

Zoey called to him from the other room. "Chris, come here. I found it."

There was a large, blue Post-it note on the screen of a desktop computer that read: "CHRIS AND ZOEY—PRESS PLAY." On the screen was a gray command box with no text.

"This looks like some kind of custom programming," Chris said. "Otherwise, the command box would include some explanation of its function."

"So what now?"

Chris was down on his knees examining the computer and its wiring, checking for explosives. There was nothing out of the ordinary.

He stood up. "I'm going to click it. But you should step outside into the hallway. Just because there was no bomb the last time we did this—"

"I don't need to be persuaded," Zoey said. Although she deflected, Chris could see the anxiety in her face. She stepped into the hallway and peered around the corner.

Chris sat down at the desk. His hand hovered over the mouse. He knew that following this series of electronic clues from Enigma was like playing Russian roulette with a keyboard. Sooner or later, he would press a key or click a mouse and be blown to bits. The question was, was this the time?

He extended his fingers in front of him and noticed them trembling. But if he walked away, what would happen to Sarah?

Chris rested his right hand lightly upon the mouse. Then, in the silent office, it was possible to hear a distinct click as Chris pressed Play. The gray command box disappeared from the screen.

And then—nothing.

"What happened?" Zoey asked from the doorway.

"Nothing that I can see."

Chris's prepaid cell phone rang. He examined the display, which showed "UNKNOWN CALLER," then answered.

"Chris." It was Enigma.

"We met your deadline. We did what you wanted. What now?" Chris asked.

"You just sent an email to the office of the Mayor of New York City announcing that there will be a catastrophic cyberattack on the city on the night of January 14."

After a stunned moment to absorb that statement, Chris said, "No one's going to believe that."

"I think they will. The security cameras will show you and Zoey entering the office. Don't bother trying to destroy them. The images are already stored with the security company. When you clicked that button, it sent an email through an account that was set up using your personal information. You may have been viewed as a significant national security threat before, but I'd like to be the first to congratulate you on hitting the top of the most wanted list."

Chris tamped down his anger. "Is Sarah still alive?"

"Yes, she's fine. But you don't have much time to talk."

"And why is that?"

At that moment, Chris and Zoey heard distant sirens. It sounded like an entire battalion of gendarmes. The sirens were in stereo, coming from the streets outside and, faintly, through the phone's speaker. Enigma was in Paris, and apparently not that far away.

"You called the police," Chris said flatly.

"Yes."

"I'm going to find you."

"Maybe. It doesn't look too promising right now, though. Personally, I'm kind of hoping you escape. I'm going to miss this when it's over."

Chris hung up the phone. "That's for us," he said to Zoey, waving a finger in the air to indicate the sirens. "We need to leave now."

The building was modern enough that it didn't have windows that opened or a fire escape. The sirens were much louder now below. He looked out the window and saw the white-and-blue hatchback patrol cars pulling up in front of the building.

Chris and Zoey dashed out of the office and, in the hallway near the elevators, found stairs. After dashing up three flights, they faced a metal door. Luckily, it wasn't locked. It made Chris wonder for a moment whether someone wanted them to follow this escape route, but there was no time for second-guessing. They stepped out onto the black tar-paper roof of the building, which looked out on a panorama of dingy apartment buildings. A light rain was still falling, and the wind was gustier than it had been at street level. The 20th arrondissement was filled with tightly packed structures. It was only a jump of four feet across and six feet down to the roof of the neighboring building. The four-foot gap seemed much larger, though, if you looked down to the pavement five stories below. The sense of vertigo hit him even stronger as his eye followed the raindrops down and he imagined his clawing, plummeting body doing the same.

"If I go first, I can catch you," Chris said.

He didn't wait for an answer, jumping across to the next building and tumbling awkwardly as he landed on the neighboring roof.

"Are you okay?" Zoey asked.

"Fine. Come on," Chris said, wincing. "Don't think about it."

But Chris could see she was thinking about it. Then, after one last glance back at the entrance to the roof, Zoey took a couple of quick steps and pushed off, her feet spinning beneath her in black Converse All Stars.

She didn't get quite enough distance on her jump—she was going to hit the ledge rather than land cleanly on the rooftop. Chris locked his arms around Zoey as she came down and threw himself backwards, pulling her away from the ledge. She landed heavily on top of him, and they both lay gasping for a moment.

Chris eyed the ledge of the building above them, expecting to see the police appear at any moment. He slipped his hands under Zoey's arms and supported her as they made their way around a corner, getting out of view of the police. Fortunately, it was an easy jump onto the next adjoining rooftop. From there, they entered a stairwell and descended to the street. Emerging onto Boulevard de Ménilmontant, they were about a hundred yards away from the building they had entered. Down the street, there were now nearly a dozen patrol cars with lights strobing and sirens bleating in alternating tones.

"Walk on the other side of the street," Chris said. "We need to split up. They're looking for a couple. Let's meet at the gate of Père Lachaise in a few minutes."

Zoey turned a corner to the right and Chris turned left as they took roundabout routes back to Père Lachaise. Chris walked to the cemetery in the rain, trying not to hurry. He knew that he couldn't continue to jump through every hoop that Enigma presented to him. It wasn't bringing him any closer to finding Sarah, and it was getting them deeper and deeper into a mess from which they might never extricate themselves.

There was so much evidence now branding them as terrorists that, even if they could disprove it, they might spend the rest of their lives doing it. Worse yet, Chris knew that terrorism suspects were effectively presumed guilty and often given little opportunity to prove their innocence. More than ever, Chris regretted that he'd gotten Zoey involved. She was someone who had clearly been looking for a direction in life and he had certainly given her one. He would never forgive himself if he was responsible for getting her killed or locked away in prison.

A police car passed, no doubt headed to join the growing manhunt that was rapidly expanding outward from 33 Boulevard de Ménilmontant. A moment later, he discreetly glanced back.

It was then that he saw Soma duck into a doorway.

CHAPTER 29

Though Soma might be a talented hacker, he was an amateur when it came to surveillance. It wasn't hard for Chris to spot Soma following him through the streets of Belleville, ducking into storefronts and trying to keep a handful of pedestrians between them.

Chris considered losing him by disappearing through one of the Chinatown shops selling foo dogs and cheap ceramics, but he settled on a better idea. When he reached the gates of Père Lachaise, Zoey was already there waiting for him.

Chris walked up to her and said, "I'm going to tell you something, but I don't want you to react. And don't look around."

"Poker face. Got it."

"We're being watched. From the coffee shop."

Zoey drew a breath. "Who?"

"Soma."

"What is that little creep doing following us?"

"I don't know, but I'm guessing that he sold us out to Enigma. That would explain how they knew exactly where we were at each point along the way to Paris."

"What do you propose that we do about him?"

"If he's working with Enigma, then maybe he will lead us to him . . . and to Sarah."

"Okay, but I don't think he's going to do that voluntarily."

Chris reached into his jacket pocket and removed the flash drive. "I'm going to make a show of giving this to you, but I'm going to palm it and keep it. Then we'll split up again."

"He's going to have to choose which one of us to follow."

"Right. I think he'll want to go with you if he thinks you have the flash drive. While he's following you, I'll be tailing him."

"But if he's working with Enigma, wouldn't he already have access to the code?"

"Not necessarily," Chris said. "He seemed awfully curious about it when we were on the road. And, if you were Enigma, would you trust Soma with that sort of information?"

"Good point," Zoey said. "But what if he decides to follow you instead?"

"Then I'll lose him and we'll meet at the Hotel Pleiades. You remember, we passed it earlier. Even if he's following you, you should go there and check in."

In a well-executed bit of theatrical stage blocking, Chris made a show of handing over the flash drive and Zoey made just as big a show of placing the drive in her pocket, with the sight lines just right so that Soma could observe almost everything from the coffee shop across the street. Then Chris and Zoey walked briskly away in opposite directions. While looking back from a crosswalk as if to check for oncoming cars, Chris saw Soma saunter out of the coffee shop and set out after Zoey.

Chris walked on and then, as soon as he was out of Soma's view, he doubled back and began following him.

Night was falling quickly on the overcast day and the street-lights came on. The wet streets gathered up the garish neon of the shop signs into iridescent pools. Chris wished that it was still raining, which would have made it harder for Soma to detect him. He followed from about a hundred yards back.

The Hotel Pleiades wasn't as elegant as its name suggested—it seemed about one worn, uneven step above a youth hostel. Soma watched from a doorway as Zoey checked in. French hotels were required to obtain a passport or ID from guests, which would bring the authorities down upon them in short order. As they had discussed earlier, Zoey came prepared to pay cash and plead a stolen purse and passport. Chris watched the desk clerk's resolve waiver as Zoey placed note after note on the counter until he handed over the key. Apparently, they had judged correctly that Hotel Pleiades was just seedy enough to flout the law. Chris had to give her credit. Zoey never once glanced through the lobby's windows to see if Soma was out-side.

Soma watched from the sidewalk as Zoey climbed the stairs to her room, but he didn't go inside. If he had, then Chris would have had to stop him and there would have been no chance of finding Enigma and Sarah. Instead, Soma bought a cup of cof-fee and sat on a bench at a bus stop for an hour, watching the front door of the hotel to make sure that Zoey didn't leave. He spent much of the time talking on his cell phone, most likely to Enigma or one of his crew.

Chris observed Soma from a café down the street over cups of espresso, forcing himself into a stillness that didn't match how he felt. He wanted to walk over to Soma, pull him up off the bench, and pound him until he gave up Sarah's location. Chris had never been in a real fight in his entire life. As a kid he had managed to stay out of the usual childhood scraps because he was both an extreme nerd and about a foot taller than most of his peers. He made a mental note of just how far he had ventured outside his geek comfort zone. Chris resisted the urge to confront Soma only because he doubted that the approach would work. Like Eddie Reiser, Soma would never be as scared of Chris as he was of Enigma.

Chris's thoughts turned again to whether he could trust Zoey. The fact that she had brought him to Soma was a definite strike against her. Add to that her history of working with Enigma on phishing schemes and he knew there was really no compelling reason why he should trust her. On the other hand, she had been up front about her connection to Enigma, which wouldn't have served her interests if she was trying to win his trust. Given the world that Zoey inhabited, Chris should have expected that anyone she knew had the potential to betray him. And when they had approached the Hive, they had no other viable options that would get them across the border into France.

Soma tossed his coffee cup in a trash can and started walking. Chris rose and left some crumpled notes on the table.

As he walked, Chris dialed Zoey on her burner phone. She picked up on the first ring. "Are you okay?"

"I'm fine," Zoey said. "Where are you?"

"Following Soma. You need to check out of that hotel now and move to the other one. Soma could have sent someone there." They had agreed in advance that, if necessary, she would move to Hotel du Moulin, another dumpy hotel a few blocks away.

"I will. Come back, okay?"

"I've gotta go. I'm going into a metro station." He paused before hanging up. "And I will."

Soma descended the steps of the Couronnes Métro station. Chris followed and lingered in the stairway. The train entered the tubular, white-tiled station with a whoosh of cool, dank air. Soma stepped across the narrow platform and onto a train headed into the city. Chris quickly boarded the adjoining car. Chris took a seat where he could see into the next car and keep an eye on Soma. They rode the train for a few stops before Soma stood. He was exiting at the Saint-Michel station in the Latin Quarter. He waited until the last possible moment before stepping onto the platform after Soma. Chris followed him up the stairs and under the art nouveau "Métropolitain" sign onto the bustling sidewalk of Boulevard Saint-Michel.

They proceeded through Place Saint-Michel, with its baroque fountain crowned with a statue of Saint Michel slaying some sort of demon. Soma hurried along into the teeming, narrow, brick-paved side streets of the Quarter. It wasn't easy for Chris to stay close enough to track of Soma in the throng and remain concealed.

On Rue Saint-Séverin, gargoyles loomed high overhead from the parapets of the elaborately gothic Saint-Séverin cathedral, which mirrored the architecture of the nearby Notre Dame. The area was commercial and touristy, lined with Greek restaurants, cafés, used-book stores, and souvenir shops. But in the street's stonework, you could still see evidence of the medieval sewer system. Chris was concentrating so intently on his pursuit that he was momentarily startled at a burst of flame close at hand. To his relief, it was immediately followed by a round of applause for a fire-eater street entertainer.

Soma eventually turned from Rue Saint-Séverin onto a side street and left the tourists behind. The streets became steadily less crowded as they moved into a low-rent residential district, causing Chris to drop further and further back to avoid detection. He assumed that they must be getting close to the destination, because Soma started looking back with increasing frequency. Chris dodged behind a tree. When he looked out, the sidewalks were empty and Soma was gone.

When Chris reached the spot on Rue du Sommerard where he had last seen Soma, he found a redbrick walk-up with a small brass plaque beside the doorbell that read, "La Conception Web Perturbatrice," which he translated as "Disruptive Web Design." The shop seemed to be open for business. Golden light gleamed from the windows. Slowly climbing the steps, Chris peered in the window next to the door. It was a townhouse that had been converted into office space. What was once the foyer was now the lobby of the web design business. The reception area was empty except for a young girl with short black hair and blue highlights who was resolutely focused on the monitor at her desk, fingers tapping. There was something unusual about the girl's motions, an extra flutter in the movement of her hands.

Then Chris saw it. The girl was hobbled in her typing because there was a bandage on the stubby little finger of her left hand. There was a spot of blood that had seeped through the gauze, so the injury seemed fresh.

The receptionist was missing the little finger of her left hand.

CHAPTER 30

Chris was relieved that the finger in the photo had not been Sarah's, but he didn't know yet what that meant. Maybe she hadn't been tortured at all. There were other possibilities, too, but Chris dismissed them for the moment.

He took up a position on the steps of an apartment building across the street, where he could watch the office. He could see into the brightly lit lobby, but there was a parked car in between that would make it difficult for them to spot him, particularly at night. The view through the front window was so brilliantly lit against the surrounding darkness that Chris felt like he was watching a play, with the stage lights blinding the actors to the audience.

It was ten o'clock, but there was still a great deal of activity inside. He saw several figures pass through the lobby but was unable to make out any faces. A man in his early twenties in a black windbreaker exited the building and walked off toward the Latin Quarter. Chris considered following him but decided that it would be better to stay put and see who else emerged. There was a chance that Sarah was inside, but he tried to keep his hopes in check.

A new group entered the lobby, three men and a woman. A tall man in a fleece jacket stepped to one side, allowing him a view of the woman's face.

It was Sarah.

She looked unharmed and was dressed casually in jeans and a blue silk blouse. Chris felt a surge of adrenaline. He wanted to charge across the street and take her out of there. He had a gun, but they were probably armed, too, and he still didn't know whom he was dealing with or how many were in the office. Sarah was speaking to the group, and she seemed strangely at ease.

The three men started taking half steps toward the door, preparing to leave. She shook hands with one of the men, clasping his hand in both of hers and saying something. This was not the way a hostage spoke to her captors. At first, Chris thought that maybe his vision was playing tricks on him in the dark. But after a moment to process, he knew that wasn't the case. The suspicions that he had been pushing to the back of his mind were now impossible to ignore. Everything fell into place so quickly that he felt like an idiot for not seeing it sooner. Sarah had set out to betray him from the start.

There was no doubt in his mind now that Sarah had applied for the paralegal job at Reynolds Fincher expressly for the purpose of getting close to him. And, in his loneliness and isolation, he had made it awfully easy for her.

The stages of their brief relationship flashed before him. The sidecar prank that Sarah played on Bill Ober had been a way to draw his attention, and it had worked. The meeting in the bar at the Four Seasons also had not been a coincidence.

Sarah had probably followed him before and knew that was the place he went after work to unwind. She had accompanied him to his appointment with his oncologist knowing he was vulnerable and it would seal the deal, winning his trust completely.

Chris sat in the darkness, waiting for her to leave the office. There would be time enough later to conduct a full inventory of their five-month relationship. Every encounter. Every lie. The more Chris thought about it, the angrier he became. Angry at himself, angry at his need. But what he didn't understand was why Sarah had done it. He realized that she must have been working with Enigma from the beginning. But why had they gone to such elaborate lengths to lead him across Europe and into this trap?

Chris turned this question over and over as he crouched in the darkness, waiting for Sarah to appear, but the answer didn't come. Forty-five minutes later, the door across the street finally opened and Sarah stepped outside. Chris waited until she was nearly a block away from the office. Then he strode up behind Sarah, grabbed her by the shoulders and spun her around. He felt her jump when he put his hands on her shoulders. And when she saw who it was, she was even more startled.

"Why don't you start telling me the truth now?" Chris asked. He took a step back, removed the gun from his bag, and leveled it at her.

It didn't take her long to compose herself. "It's too soon for that. When it's over, you'll know."

"Who put you up to this? Enigma? Ripley?"

Sarah gave a grim half smile.

"You took the job at Reynolds just to get at me."

"It was the only way. You don't have much of a life outside that place."

"That's a lot of trouble to go to. Why me? This is personal somehow, isn't it?"

"It's very personal, but not to me."

"Was Enigma the one who decided to go after me?"

"Yes."

"Why?"

"I can't answer that question just yet. Like I said, you'll know when it's over."

"After the January 14 attack."

"That's right. After Zero Day."

Chris paused. "So this is a Zero Day event?"

Sarah didn't respond.

Zero Day was the term for the first day that a virus was activated to exploit a previously undiscovered vulnerability in a computer program. On Zero Day, a virus can spread like wildfire, causing unchecked damage because there is no security patch or remedy. On Zero Day, computer security experts around the world spring into crisis mode, attempting to identify and fix a vulnerability that they didn't even know existed the day before.

"The vulnerability is in BlueCloud's Aspira system," Chris said, seeking confirmation.

"I don't think I'm really giving anything away by saying that much," Sarah said. There were millions of lines of code in the operating system, so this didn't bring him any closer to identifying the specific vulnerability. Ed had found it but hadn't lived long enough to tell him what it was.

"Are you really prepared to be responsible for the loss of hundreds or thousands of lives if New York City goes dark on January 14? You won't be just watching anonymously from the sidelines like you were when those planes went down in

Albuquerque. You're going to be in federal custody when this happens, and they are going to make you pay."

"I knew what I was getting into," Sarah said, but Chris could see she was anxious.

He tried another angle. "Who is Enigma? Do I know him? Did I put him in jail when I was at the DOJ?"

Sarah shrugged.

"Why are you doing this? If it was for money, there won't be any of that for you now."

"This is not about money. This is about making the government pay for what it's done. Even if I live the rest of my life in prison, I'll be remembered in a way that you never will. People are eventually going to understand why I did this, and some are going to agree with it."

Chris was struck by how drastically Sarah's demeanor had changed. There had always been a flintiness to her, but that had made her interesting. Now he saw that the hardness was what was real and the warmth was an act.

"An ideology that involves killing innocent people isn't much of an ideology," he said.

"Don't kid yourself. All ideologies worth anything require someone to die for them."

Chris could tell that he wasn't going to get much more out of Sarah. He grabbed her arm. "We're going back to the office."

Chris turned Sarah around so that she faced away from him and ran his hands over her, searching for weapons.

"I wish I'd brought a gun," she said. "I didn't realize that you were so close."

He shoved Sarah in front of him along the sidewalk. Returning to the office was worth the risk because, if it was the crew's headquarters, it was likely to hold some clue to the virus.

Sarah had been removed from the equation, but Chris's mission was no less urgent and the stakes no less great.

When they arrived at the offices of Disruptive Web Design, Chris walked around to the back of the building with Sarah.

"Make a sound and I'll have to hurt you," Chris said.

Chris peered into a couple of windows but the lights were off and the office appeared vacant.

After circling the building, Chris climbed the front steps. He saw no movement through the front window. "Use your key."

Sarah pulled a key chain from her jeans pocket. A tiny, grinning devil's head dangled from the chain, metal showing through the red paint where it was worn like bone showing through skin. It was the same image that had been pasted to the flash drive that he had recovered in Middendorf's apartment.

"Let me see that," Chris said, taking the key chain. It was in that moment that the realization dawned on Chris.

"You're Ripley."

"I was wondering how long that would take," Sarah said.

Chris gave the keys back to Sarah. She opened the door and they stepped into the lobby. The computer at the front desk was off—a good sign.

To the casual observer, Disruptive Web Design appeared to be a legitimate business, or at least a legitimate front operation for Enigma's fraud and hacking schemes. The rear of the townhouse was a large room filled with cubicles and computers. The walls were adorned with framed screen shots of client websites.

Before he could search the place, he needed to secure Sarah. She might know where a weapon was hidden or destroy evidence, so he couldn't afford to have her wandering about. He looked around for some rope. Chris settled on some long extension cords that were lying twisted in a corner.

"Have a seat," Chris said, motioning Sarah to a desk chair.

Chris tied her wrists to the arms of the chair. The chair had rollers, so he used another cord to tie the undercarriage of the chair to a leg of the desk. Then he used four more cords to bind Sarah into the chair until she couldn't move.

"I think you've got it," Sarah said. "You want to leave me a little circulation?"

Next, Chris went from desk to desk, looking for something out of place. All he saw were customer order sheets and graphic design books.

He paused in his search. "You helped them track us. You had access. But the tracking device wasn't in my cell phone, because even after I ditched it, Enigma knew where we were each step of the way."

Sarah remained impassive, the good soldier.

"What else would you have access to? Something that I always have with me." Chris removed his watch, opening up the back panel to examine the workings. Nothing.

Chris sat down at a desk and emptied the contents of his wallet, every bill, every credit card, every BART ticket. Then he shook the empty wallet until a couple of bits of dark lint fell out—along with a tiny, round tracking device that resembled a watch battery, smaller than the nail of his little finger. Chris walked over to Sarah and placed the tracking device on the desk next to her.

She shrugged. "Better late than never."

Chris returned to his search of the office, pausing when a familiar logo caught his eye. Picking up the papers, he saw that they were printed pages from the website for the DefCon hacker conference. A schedule of conference events included panels on topics such as "Julian Assange: Hero or God?" and "The Future of Hacktivism." Chris saw his own name on a panel about governmental and private enforcement, listed as "Invited." He was perplexed for a moment, then remembered that Blanksy had elicited a grudging "maybe" from him after hijacking his computer. Chris was certain that the presence of his name in the program drew snickers in certain circles. No one expected him to actually show his face at DefCon.

The front page of the conference brochure, which was covered with biohazard symbols, showed that DefCon was going to be held in Brooklyn on January 13 to 15. *Of course.* The cyberattack was scheduled to strike New York City during the world's largest hacker convention, which would be going on right across the East River in Brooklyn. It was far enough away to escape the worst of the disruption, but close enough for a ringside seat.

Enigma and his crew had to be attending DefCon. What better place to take a victory lap in the wake of their mayhem? And what better place to proclaim whatever half-baked manifesto they were espousing? The conference was still three days away, but for all he knew Enigma and his crew had already abandoned the office to travel to New York.

"They're going to DefCon, aren't they?"

Sarah shrugged and said nothing, which Chris took as a confirmation. Chris pulled out his untraceable cell phone and dialed Agent Hazlitt.

"Bruen," Hazlitt said. "You ready to turn yourself in yet?"

"No," Chris said, "but I am turning someone in."

★ ★ ★

As Chris left the office, he glanced back at Sarah, bound to the desk chair in the dark. "I have one more question for you," he said. "What happened during those two days after I was diagnosed with cancer? You disappeared."

Sarah shifted in the chair, trying to get comfortable in the bindings. "After you were diagnosed, I actually suggested to Enigma that we call it off—at least the part that involves you. Call it a moment of weakness."

"But he wasn't having it."

"No. He won't stop. You should know that about him. But can I give you a bit of advice?"

"That's not something I'm really looking for from you, but go ahead."

"You need to get over your wife's death. It makes you weak."

"You're probably right, but there are worse things to be."

He heard the sound of sirens in the distance, drawing nearer.

"Sounds like your ride's here," Chris said as he closed the door on Sarah.

CHAPTER 31

Agents Michael Hazlitt and Sam Falacci were having dinner in a Barcelona café, trying to figure out how they might pick up the ever-colder trail of Bruen and Doucet. The walls of the café were plastered with yellowing bullfight posters, despite the fact that the blood sport was now banned in Catalonia. Outside, headlights spun ceaselessly around Plaça de Catalunya like a crazed carousel. The restaurant was nearly empty except for some tourists. For the natives, 8:00 p.m. was far too early for dinner.

Their hunt for Bruen and his hacker friend was getting nowhere and Hazlitt felt that his forensic skills could have been put to better use studying the Lurker virus back at Quantico. However, his boss had noticed that he seemed to have unusually sharp recollections of Bruen from their days working together. Over Hazlitt's protestations, he'd been ordered to stick to his assignment in the hopes that those insights, such as they were, might give him some advantage in the pursuit.

"I'm getting tired of all of these little plates," Falacci said, picking at his bacalao, a fritter of rice and salt cod. "A great people do not live on appetizers."

There were days when Hazlitt felt that conversing with Falacci was like driving an eighteen-wheeler—he had to throw all of his weight into wrestling the conversation back onto the road.

"Those hackers at the Hive knew something they weren't telling us," Hazlitt said.

"Like your Social Security number?"

Earlier that morning, they had shown up unannounced at the Hive's base of operations in a burnt-out office building. They figured that Bruen and Doucet might reach out to the group for assistance. But once the hackers figured out that, despite their best threats, the agents were out of their jurisdiction and not serious about prosecuting them, a profound and hostile silence descended.

Hazlitt's phone rang. It was the phone number that Bruen had used in his last call, the one where he had signed off so abruptly.

"Bruen," Hazlitt said. "You ready to turn yourself in yet?"

"No," Bruen said, "but I am turning someone in."

Hazlitt mouthed "Bruen" to Falacci. After his last call, the FBI's Operational Technology unit in Quantico had attempted to trace the number and confirmed that, as expected, it was a prepaid burner phone.

"Okay, I'm intrigued. So what, or who, do you have for us?"

"In Paris, in the offices of Disruptive Web Design on Rue du Sommerard, you'll find Sarah Hotchner, also known as the hacker Ripley."

"Sarah Hotchner is Ripley," Hazlitt said slowly. "That's a twist. Is she alive?"

"She's fine, but you'd better get someone over there soon before she works her way out of her ties."

"Are you in Paris right now?"

"Don't tell me you're still in Barcelona?"

Hazlitt chuckled.

"You're definitely not going to catch up with me today," Bruen said.

"But we will eventually. You know that, right?" Hazlitt was surprised that Bruen and Doucet had managed to cross the border into France, but there would be time to ponder that later. "So Sarah's been working with Enigma."

"Correct."

"Just like you, right?"

"You've been misinformed. Enigma and his crew are setting me up."

"Now why would they want to do that?"

"I wish I knew. But I think you know that I'm not exactly popular among hackers."

Hazlitt changed the subject. He wasn't interested in giving Bruen any indication that he might be buying his story. "We could tell that was you calling in Eduardo de Lamadrid's murder to the San Francisco police. How did you know?"

"We were speaking with Ed by Skype when it happened. But we never saw the killer's face."

"Or maybe you were responsible for his death," Hazlitt said.

"He was my friend. I'd like to know how he died. What was in that syringe?"

"Potassium cyanide. It was quick."

They were silent for a moment.

"I appreciate how forthcoming you're being," Hazlitt said. "Is there anything else you want to tell us?"

"Yeah," Bruen said. "As a matter of fact, thanks to Ed, I have quite a bit of information about the virus." Bruen proceeded to describe how the Lurker virus targeted Sonnen programmable logic controllers.

"Some of this I've already heard from our forensic team, but some of it is new," Hazlitt said.

"Ed also found the vulnerability in the Aspira system that Lurker was designed to exploit, but he died before he could tell us. You should search his apartment for any notes he might have kept."

"Oh, believe me, we've been over that apartment. But, look, Chris, if you really want to be helpful, why don't you just stop running and we can get this thing sorted out?"

"I can't do that."

"Why not?"

"Because if I turned myself in to you, I don't think your bosses would be able to keep an open mind about me. You know what happens to a person once they've been labeled a terrorist. I'd be hustled off to Eastern Europe for a year or two of secret interrogation before I could even ask for a lawyer. And I'd certainly be taken out of the game when it comes to pursuing Enigma."

"Running from those agents at Tibidabo didn't help matters," Hazlitt said. "Why'd you do that?"

"I thought Enigma and his crew were holding someone that I cared about—used to care about."

"I know. We saw the missing persons report on Sarah that you filed with the San Francisco PD." Hazlitt paused, trying to decide which of his many questions to pursue next. He sensed that he couldn't keep Bruen on the line for much longer. "So if that situation has changed, why keep running?"

"I have something to do before I turn myself in."

"What's that?"

"Find Enigma and stop the January 14 cyberattack on New York City. It's the only way we're going to get out from under this."

"You know we think that you're trying to cause that attack, not prevent it?"

"I realize that, but then why would I be doing so much to help your investigation?"

"Maybe you want to send us down a dead end. Maybe it's just arrogance. Everyone at the DOJ always thought you were arrogant as hell. But let's assume for a moment that you're telling the truth. If that's the case, then I'm just a little insulted by your attitude. Don't you think we're capable of tracking down Enigma ourselves?"

"No offense, but no," Bruen said.

"You always thought highly of your skills."

"For what it's worth, I don't really care who gets there first. In fact, I've got something else that will improve your odds. I just figured out that Enigma is going to be at DefCon in Brooklyn. The January 14 date is right in the middle of the conference."

"That makes sense," Hazlitt said. "In fact, I can't believe that didn't occur to me sooner, but I guess I never have taken those DefCon geeks seriously. But why should I believe you?"

"Because I think by now you know that we're on the same side in this."

The line went dead. Bruen had hung up on him.

Hazlitt had to admit, at least to himself, that Bruen sounded like an innocent man. And if his information proved out, then it offered their best chance yet of catching Enigma. But none of this was going to cause him to ease up a bit in his pursuit of Bruen and Doucet. He could never persuade his bosses to call off an international manhunt based on a gut instinct. Those sorts of decisions were reserved for higher-ups, such as the Oz-like Louis Vogel at NSA, who was receiving all of their reports.

"Well, what did you learn?" Falacci asked.

"That we're going to Paris, and then Brooklyn."

Falacci brightened. "Brooklyn," he said. "I'm going to take you to a pizza place there that will blow your freakin' mind."

Hazlitt shrugged in resignation.

CHAPTER 32

Chris hurried out of the office of Disruptive Web Design and onto the treelined street, the branches overhead like hands with interlaced fingers drawing the darkness near. He headed in the direction of the lights and noise. The police cars started arriving with strobing sirens just as he merged with the throngs of the Latin Quarter.

For a while, Chris allowed himself to drift with the current of pedestrians, stumbling occasionally on the cobblestone streets. He had no idea what the next move was and he feared that he had reached the end of his run. Maybe it was finally time for them to just turn themselves in. Chris had no idea how long he wandered the ancient, narrow streets like that, but after a while he realized that he was exhausted and needed to return to the hotel.

Chris arrived at the shabby two-star Hotel du Moulin at 2:00 a.m. As he climbed the stairs to Zoey's room, a crippling weariness settled over him. Maybe it was the tension of waiting in the dark for a glimpse of Enigma's crew or the fact that he had barely slept in days. Or perhaps it was sadness at discovering that, after allowing himself to feel something for the first time in years, he had been duped.

As soon as Zoey opened the door, hair tousled, and blinking at the bright hallway lights, she seemed to see that Chris was at a low point. She was wearing a long nightshirt emblazoned with the disembodied face of Peter Criss of Kiss in full makeup.

"What happened to you?" she asked.

Chris pulled up a chair and recounted the events of the night. Zoey listened from the bed, nodding and occasionally punctuating the narrative with a murmured "No way," or "What a bitch."

When he was finished, she asked, "What now?"

"I have no idea how we would get to Brooklyn. We're on every international watch list. There's no way they'd let us get on a plane."

She shook her head. "No, I mean tonight."

"Oh," he said. "I'll get a room and I guess we'll figure it out in the morning. I can't think straight right now."

"You don't have to do that," she said.

"Do what?"

"Get another room."

She grabbed handfuls of his shirt and pulled him toward the bed. They struggled out of their clothes, which was easier for her than him. When they were lying in bed together, the feeling was strangely familiar. Then he realized that he remembered the contours of Zoey's body from when they had hidden together in the car trunk crossing the French border. Now he realized just how much he had enjoyed that sensation the first time. Chris wasn't certain that this was a good idea, but he also didn't want to stop. He had more reasons to distrust Zoey than he'd ever had with Sarah, and look at how that relationship had turned out.

Somewhere outside, a street entertainer was beating an African drum. He wondered why no one stopped him at this late hour. The sound played tricks on Chris's ears as it echoed across the Latin Quarter. When you listened to the drumming closely, it seemed to speed up, sort of like his pulse as he pulled Zoey beneath him and started kissing her.

CHAPTER 33

January 13

Chris awoke to the smell of coffee. The curtains were open and the air was fresh and cool. From the height of the sun, Chris calculated that it must be nearly noon. There was a cardboard cup on the night table next to him, which Zoey must have set there. She was sitting at the desk across the room, concentrating intently on something.

He peered at her for a while through half-open eyes He liked the way her brows furrowed as she studied her work. She reached up occasionally to thread an unruly strand of her hair over her ear. Despite everything they had been through together in the past few days, he still wasn't sure if Zoey could be trusted. After all, she had admitted to having worked with Enigma. With what he knew now about Sarah, it occurred to him that Zoey and Sarah/Ripley might have crossed paths. But all of this troubling information had not stopped him from sleeping with her.

Zoey turned around at the sound of his stirring. "I was wondering when you were going to wake up. How are you feeling?"

He ran a hand through his hair, thinking about it. "Not bad, actually." He had been so tired last night that his entire body ached. "Are we okay?"

"We're okay," Zoey said. "Being the rebound girl is kind of an area of specialization for me. I think I've pulled down more rebounds than Charles Barkley."

Chris sat up in bed. The bright sunlight made the cheap hotel room look more pleasant than it had any right to. "What are you up to over there?"

"Seeing if I can turn our passports into something that will actually get us past customs. It won't be easy. We'd need to buy blank passport books on the black market and I'd have to hack the security chip that's inside the back cover."

There was a white paper bag on the night table next to the coffee. "What's in there?"

"Chocolate croissants," she said. "They're amazing. And I think they might still be warm."

He pulled a croissant from the bag and devoured it. They were still warm, and Zoey was right. As Chris slid out of bed, he realized that he felt better physically than he had in weeks, maybe years. Perhaps it was just the fading half-life of the cancer medications. He wasn't in any less trouble, and every time he thought of Ed's death he felt sick, but he was no longer as hopeless as he had been the night before. He wasn't ready to turn himself in to the FBI just yet.

Chris stepped over to the window, dressed in nothing but his boxers, and put his hand on Zoey's shoulder. Outside, the lone percussionist from the night before had multiplied into an entire drum circle, complete with trash can lids, timbales, and steel drums.

"I'm glad that last night happened," Chris said, "but—"

Zoey raised her hand to silence him. "You don't have to say it," she said. "You did just break up with your last girlfriend, who was, like . . . evil."

"Look at it this way," Chris said. "As long as you're not trying to kill me or frame me for a terrorist attack, you would have to be considered an upgrade."

"Setting the bar pretty low for me there," Zoey said. "I like that. I thrive on low expectations." Chris watched over her shoulder as she returned to working on the passports, delicately prying at the corner of her passport photo with an X-Acto knife. In the photo, Zoey looked about five years younger and was beaming a wide, wicked smile.

"I wish I could remove that smartass smile," she said. "It's the kind of thing that stands out. But there are limits to what I can do here."

Chris leaned in closer, studying the subtle whorls and dyes of the passport.

"For example, you have to stay away from the digital watermark," she said, indicating with the knife. "Some things you can tweak, some things you have to work around."

This got Chris thinking, and he took a step back into the middle of the room.

After a few seconds, Zoey noted his silence and turned around. "What?"

"I think I was wrong about the expiration date," he said.

"What expiration date?"

"The Lurker virus. It had an expiration date so that it would vanish from all the infected computers after a few weeks. I thought it was Enigma's way of conducting a controlled test of the virus, a way to limit the collateral damage."

"And it's not?"

"No, it was something that *he* needed to work around. I don't think Enigma is that sensitive to consequences. Lurker must have been an adaptation of another virus. The expiration date was something that was already there in the original coding that he had to work around."

Zoey turned her chair around to face him. Chris could tell that she already recognized where this was leading them.

"So who would put all of those resources into developing a supersophisticated computer virus and then rein it in like that?" She said it like she already knew the answer.

"A government," Chris said. "An ethical government—"

"You're an optimist, aren't you?" Zoey interjected.

Chris continued. "The government that created Lurker probably developed it for a specific purpose, to take out a target. A target that they felt was justified."

"And after hitting that target, they wanted to make sure the virus stopped spreading," Zoey said. "They weren't looking to show off or do damage for its own sake—unlike Enigma."

"But he somehow got his hands on a copy of the virus before it disappeared and adapted it for his own purposes."

They were both silent for a moment, working it through to the conclusion.

Finally, Zoey asked, "So what do you think this government-developed virus was intended to do?"

"Maybe Enigma gave us the answer when he sent us to Sa'edi's grave at Père Lachaise."

"Of course," Zoey said, shaking her head. "Iran. I never really liked the theory that Enigma had ties to anti-Islamist groups. Lurker must be an adaptation of Stuxnet."

REECE HIRSCH • 245

"Exactly."

In 2010 it was widely suspected that either the United States or Israel had launched a virus much like Lurker known as Stuxnet, which was specifically designed to destroy the centrifuges Iran was using to produce enriched uranium for its nuclear program. Stuxnet took control of the centrifuges, spinning the rotors too fast or putting the brakes on too hard. The Iranian nuclear program was set back for months or perhaps years when the Natanz centrifuges began to mysteriously blow apart like so many expensive shrapnel bombs. In June 2012 a leak from the Obama administration effectively confirmed that the NSA, in collaboration with Unit 8200, its Israeli counterpart, had developed Stuxnet as part of a larger cyber espionage program dubbed "Olympic Games."

"If Lurker is a version of Stuxnet, then why do you think Enigma sent us to Sa'edi's grave?"

"Maybe it was a way of tweaking the feds. The NSA would be very embarrassed if it became known that it had helped create such a powerful cyberweapon only to have it turned back against the US. Maybe he sent photos of us at that grave as a way of reminding the feds that he had something on them."

"So now we know that the NSA would go to great lengths to keep this information secret," Zoey said. "How does that makes our situation any better?"

"I guess it doesn't," Chris said. If the new theory was correct, then they were in even more trouble than he had previously imagined.

Zoey returned to her work on the passports and they were both quiet for a while, absorbing the new information. Chris lay on the bed with his back against the headboard, sipping the strong, black coffee. He reflected on the events of the previous night and Sarah's betrayal. And that led him to consider once again the identity of Enigma. Who from his past could hate him enough to go to that much trouble to hurt him? Clearly, it was someone for whom killing him was not enough. Killing someone isn't that hard, really, once you've made up your mind to do it. Look at what they had done to Ed. For some reason, Enigma was saving him for a different fate. Enigma wanted to destroy him, humiliate him, negate everything that his life and career had stood for.

Chris's cell phone rang and he grabbed it off the night table, but the number wasn't one that he recognized.

"Hello?"

"You raised the Bat Signal, so here I am."

"Blanksy." Chris had almost forgotten that he had asked Ed to reach out to him.

"Are you okay, dude? This is not like you. Usually, I have to get your attention."

"True," Chris said. "But I'm in some trouble."

"What's up?"

"There are some people who think I'm involved in cyber-terrorism."

"That makes no sense. And who are 'some people'?"

"Pretty much every law enforcement agency in the US and European Union."

"So you're on the run?"

"Yes."

"I always knew you were an outlaw, man."

"I want to know about a hacker who goes by the name Enigma."

There was silence on the other end of the line.

"Are you still there?"

"Why are you asking about him?"

"He's behind a planned attack on New York and, for some reason, he's framing me for it."

Another silence. "I've heard the name, but I don't actually know him. I wasn't even sure he really existed."

"What have you heard?"

"They say he's a black hat. The blackest."

"More specific."

"Everything I know is just gossip, stuff that gets kicked around on the message boards and at DefCon when people have had too many beers. They say he's a brilliant coder who is also a genuine bad dude. You know how it is—in our world, you have people who have hands-on-the-keyboard skills and you have criminals who want to use them. You don't often see someone who combines the two."

"What's he into?"

"If the stories are true, everything. Asian porn sites. Phishing schemes. Big-time identity theft. You remember the Winslow's department store security breach? It was an SQL injection. Two million Social Security numbers, two hundred million dollars in fraudulent charges?"

"Sure." The use of Structured Query Language or "SQL" was a common technique for extracting data from a company's databases. SQL injection involved finding a weak point of entry and "injecting" commands into a server hosting a website. Instead of reading the entries as text, the website processed them as commands to be executed, giving the hackers control over the database.

"That was him." Blanksy paused. "I even heard that he killed a guy who wanted to back out of working with him. I never believed most of the stories, though."

"Do you have his real name?"

"Nah. The dude's a phantom. And you're going head-to-head with him?"

"Very much so."

"Sounds epic."

"I wouldn't put it that way."

"You'd better watch yourself. You're dealing with a real killer there."

"But I thought that I was—what was it?—a legendary badass."

"See, sometimes I think you aren't listening, and then you go and surprise me like that. That's why I love you, dude."

Chris smiled despite himself. "Is there anything else that you can tell me that might help?"

"That's all I've got. But I'll ask around."

"If you do, be careful."

"I really feel like our relationship is evolving here."

"Good-bye, Blanksy."

Chris picked up the cell phone and sent a text message to Enigma. He reflected on how odd it was that technology allowed him to reach out and communicate with the hacker whenever he wanted to without bringing him any closer to actually locating him. But that was how Chris made his living, closing that gap.

CHRIS: Who are you?

ENIGMA: The direct approach. Refreshing.

CHRIS: You went to a lot of trouble to get at me.

ENIGMA: It was worth it. And I'm just getting started. C U on 0day.

CHAPTER 34

The streets of the Latin Quarter were still wet from the rain under a flat blue, cloudless sky. Chris and Zoey were in search of an art supply store so Zoey could continue to experiment with falsifying their passports. Chris figured that if they walked in the direction of the Sorbonne, the city's prestigious university, they were bound to run across one.

As they drew near Place de la Sorbonne, the crowds grew younger as the buildings grew older. The district had always been defined by its student population—it was called the Latin Quarter because Latin was the language spoken by students during the Middle Ages. At the end of the gray paving-stone street lined with cafés sat the imposing Sorbonne Chapel, built by Cardinal Richelieu.

"Over there," Zoey said, pointing at a large art supply store with a row of easels in the window. "That one looks promising."

Before they could cross the street, a black Mercedes limousine with dark tinted windows pulled up in front of them, blocking their way.

The door to the limo that faced the sidewalk was already opening as it rolled to a stop. A tall man stepped out of the limo directly in front of Zoey and Chris.

"Get inside," he said in French-inflected English. He opened his jacket to reveal a gun in a shoulder holster. "But first, hand over the computer bag. I'll need the gun."

A jolt of panic seized Chris. If he got into the limo, he would lose any degree of control over the situation. Chris looked up the street to see if there were police in sight, or anyone who might intervene. No one was close enough to see what was happening.

When he looked back at the man, he was leaning in close. "We are not going to hurt you—unless we have to. Hand me the bag and then get inside—please."

Not seeing any other option, he complied.

Chris and Zoey stepped into the limo and the door slammed shut behind them.

★ ★ ★

They had an opportunity to study their abductors as they sat in the back of the limo facing them. The tall man had short hair that was salt-and-peppered at the temples, a long, thin nose, and the faint outline of a skiing goggle tan line around his eyes. He was wearing a tan crepe Armani suit and seemed a little too dapper to be a thug. His vaguely exasperated expression seemed to indicate that he considered this task beneath him.

Next to him sat a smaller man, a little older, a little pudgier, maybe midforties, wearing a black cashmere pullover that unflatteringly highlighted his volleyball-sized gut. Like his companion, he didn't look like a hit man or an assassin, and he didn't appear to be carrying a gun. Chris thought they looked like they belonged at an investor conference.

"Where are you taking us?" Chris asked.

"We'll be there soon," the smaller man said, shutting down all further conversation with a stony look.

After a short drive, the limo pulled into the underground parking garage of a green-glass office tower. The garage was completely empty, and Chris wondered if the building was vacant. He had seen no corporate logo or other identifiers outside. A good deserted spot for an execution.

The limo stopped. The small man climbed out and opened the doors, still holding the gun. Chris and Zoey were hustled across the vacant garage, their footsteps echoing hollowly on the concrete.

"Get inside," the tall man said when they reached the garage elevator.

Once in the building's lobby, a vast expanse of tan marble dominated by an abstract black sculpture, they boarded another elevator. The tall man punched the button for the thirty-eighth floor. Breezy French Muzak piped incongruously in the elevator. Chris glanced over at Zoey, who was watching the floor numbers tick upward on the display. If she was scared, she didn't show it.

The doors opened to the lobby of an office that occupied the entire floor. The conference rooms ahead of them looked out on the stunted Paris skyline, which was dominated by the Eiffel Tower and, to a lesser extent, the unsightly Tour Montparnasse. Most of the buildings in Paris did not exceed five or six stories, but the Paris City Council had lifted that restriction in recent years for the 13th arrondissement in the southeast quadrant of

252 • THE ADVERSARY

the city. The two gunmen motioned them into the largest conference room.

If the floor was unoccupied, it might be weeks before their
bodies were found, Chris thought. His eyes darted around the
room as he looked for a possible weapon or escape route. Inside,
there was a long, oval, mahogany conference table, and Chris's
gaze traveled down it to a large videoconference screen on the
wall.

And there on the screen was BlueCloud Inc. CEO Dave
Silver, eating what appeared to be a chicken Caesar salad.

"Don't look so surprised," Silver said around a forkful. "I
said I had your back, didn't I?" Chris recognized the backdrop,
which was a conference room in BlueCloud's inner corporate
sanctum in San Mateo.

"Are you going to turn us in?" Chris asked.

"No, I'm going to help you."

"Why would you help us?"

"Enlightened self-interest. You've done more to get to the
bottom of this thing than a whole army of federal agents. For
example, I hear you think that the hackers behind the cyberattack will be at DefCon."

"So what do you want us to do?" Chris asked.

"I want you to finish the job that I hired you to do." Silver
wiped his mouth with a black linen napkin. "I always thought
you were the best team to stop those hackers and salvage the
reputation of my company—and I still do."

"Why?"

"Well, while I don't discount your skills as an investigator,
you bring something more to the table, don't you?"

"I'm not sure what you mean."

"Oh, I think you do. In some way, this whole thing is about
you, isn't it?"

"I wouldn't go that far. But, yes, I think there's some truth to that."

"So it's in my interest to see that you two stay in play. If you're on the sidelines, then we lose our best source of information. This Enigma person communicates directly with you."

There was a moment of silence, which Zoey wasted no time filling. "If you want to salvage the reputation of your company, then tighten up the coding of your operating system. It's full of holes."

"And you must be Zoey," Silver said. "It's a pleasure to finally meet you. And we're working on it."

"At this point I'm surprised you're willing to be associated with us," Chris said.

"Oh, I don't intend to be associated with you. That's why we're meeting in this unfinished office building and I'm on videoconference. And don't worry about these two gentlemen. I have complete confidence in their discretion."

The two henchmen looked at each other and brightened perceptibly, like two dogs who have just received a "Good boy" from their master.

"You can put the guns away," Silver told them. "There's really no need for that."

"You said you want us to finish the job," Chris said, "but the only way we can do that is by getting to New York. We'd never make it past airport security."

"I've given that some thought," Silver said. "I considered flying you into Teterboro on my jet, but someone could link you to me if I did that. Instead, I'm going to help you make it onto a commercial flight."

"And how does that work?" Zoey asked.

"I think you'll appreciate this, given your skill set," Silver said.

"You know my work," Zoey said, looking surprised and pleased.

"Isn't it riskier for us to use fake passports?" Chris asked. "There's probably a higher chance of getting caught than if we flew private air."

"I won't deny that," Silver said. "But it's safer for me, and that's the deal I'm offering."

Chris looked at Zoey, who nodded. "We'll take it."

"Good. Claude, give him back his bag—but keep the gun." To Chris, he added, "You won't be able to take it with you, anyway. When you reach JFK, I'll have someone meet you to provide another one."

"Don't you think I should get one, too?" Zoey asked.

After a pause, Silver said, "Okay. Two guns."

"Even with fake passports, won't they still spot us on sight at the airport?" Chris asked.

"Not when we're done here. I've arranged for the services of a couple of specialists."

The elevator doors in the lobby opened and out stepped a tall woman of indeterminate age with magenta hair and a long face. She wore a loose black blouse with black pants and had a large khaki messenger bag slung over one shoulder.

The magenta-haired woman was accompanied by a lanky young man in his early twenties. He wore wire-rimmed glasses and was dressed in a retro fifties button-down shirt and jeans.

The woman walked directly over to the conference room and pushed open the glass door with both hands. "So," she said in heavily French-accented English, casting an appraising glance at Chris and Zoey, "these are the fugitives?"

"Meet Sandrine," Silver said. "She's going to give you new appearances. Sandrine was a top hair and makeup artist for the film industry there. She did Deneuve."

"In what sense?" Zoey asked.

Sandrine turned to Zoey without cracking a smile. "In every sense," she said.

"And this is Tomas," Silver continued. "He'll be doctoring your passports and taking new photos." Tomas gazed out the windows at the Paris skyline.

"I'll leave you in their capable hands," Silver said. "Good luck." The videoconferencing screen went black.

The pair began setting up without saying another word. Sandrine pulled a makeup kit from her messenger bag and arranged a chair from the conference room table in a well-lit corner of the room. Then she removed a tray of eyeglasses from her bag.

Tomas unpacked an aluminum case that contained a camera, tripod, and lighting. He tacked a blue screen to the conference room wall as a backdrop for the photos. When he was done constructing his makeshift photo studio, he asked for their passports. Then he set up a kit at one end of the conference room, where he arranged his forgery tools—an X-Acto knife, a tube of glue, an assortment of pens and bottles of pigment, and that rarest of commodities, blank American passport books.

Chris and Zoey sat at the conference room table watching the pair go about their business. Chris always found it comforting to watch true professionals at work. Before you saw the end result, you could usually tell that someone knew what they were doing just by watching how they handled the tools of their trade. Sandrine and Tomas murmured to each other in French, studied Chris and Zoey, then conferred some more. Finally, they seemed to settle on an approach and began to work in earnest.

★ ★ ★

When Chris and Zoey stepped out of the lobby of the office tower and onto a sidewalk in the 13th arrondissement, they weren't new people—more like bizarro versions of themselves. Zoey was wearing an elegant maroon dress with a wide black belt. She was in full makeup and her hair was blown out, styled, and glossy. In stark contrast, Chris's unruly black hair was cut severely short and dyed blond, and he was wearing blue contact lenses, angular wire-framed glasses, and a sleek black leather jacket. He looked like the kind of person who might own an edgy Berlin art gallery.

They were indeed in the 13th arrondissement near the massive construction site of the Rive Gauche project. Nearby was the Bibliothèque Nationale de France, with its four modern towers designed to resemble open books. Before them were the dark, sluggish waters of the Seine and, on the opposite bank, the Quai François-Mauriac with its floating nightclubs and cafes, known as *péniches*. They spent a moment checking each other out in their new personas.

"You look nice," Chris said.

"I haven't worn this much makeup since I was fifteen," Zoey said. "They sized us up pretty well, don't you think?"

"How so?"

"They figured out what we're like and then they went in the opposite direction. Look at me. They've turned me into an anchorwoman!"

"And me, I'm some sort of Teutonic fashion victim hipster."

"I do miss your hair," Zoey added. "Almost everything about your old appearance said 'buttoned-down lawyer.' But your hair always said to me 'mad scientist.'"

"Good to know," Chris said. "Not the message I was trying to send." Chris pulled a thick stack of dollars and euros that

Silver had provided and performed a rough count. "Shall we get a taxi to the airport and see how good a job they did?"

It felt good to be back in the hunt.

CHAPTER 35

They managed to check their bags on the Air France flight at Charles de Gaulle without incident, but as the queue of travelers slowly advanced toward the security station, Chris grew anxious. Zoey was two spots behind him in line. They weren't standing together because, in their new guises, they were an unlikely pair that might attract suspicion.

The security clerk, a tired-looking woman in a blue uniform, extended her hand. Chris gave the clerk his passport and boarding pass and tried not to watch her as she examined them. He didn't like that she actually seemed to be attentive to her work. The clerk's eyes darted to the passport, then to Chris's face, then back to the passport. After a moment, she pulled out a green marker and made a cryptic symbol on the boarding pass.

When Chris reached the X-ray screener, he wasn't pulled out of the line, so apparently the mark merely signified the clerk's review. Chris glanced back to check on Zoey's progress. He was alarmed to see that she was being escorted from the line to undergo enhanced screening. Zoey was led over to an area next to the X-ray machine by a woman security clerk. Zoey walked slowly to the area where more thorough inspections were conducted. From the other side of the security zone, he watched as Zoey was frisked. There was nothing that he could do to help her. He could only hope that it was just a random screening and that she hadn't been identified from the watch list.

Zoey sat in a plastic chair, and the woman security clerk removed her shoes and wiped them with cotton swabs. The swabs were then tested for bomb residue. The woman clerk was speaking to Zoey—another bad sign. Then he saw Zoey laugh and make a gesture toward her shoes as she put them back on. They were talking about Zoey's shoes, a strappy pair with high heels that she never would have worn otherwise. She was going to make it through security.

A few minutes later, Chris and Zoey were gliding on an escalator through a clear plastic tube suspended over a sunlit atrium. Charles de Gaulle Airport had a Jetsons retro-futuristic look. Jet packs and shiny silver jumpsuits would not have seemed out of place. Chris started to relax a bit. Unless they were pulled off the plane at the last minute, it appeared they would make it to New York.

★ ★ ★

As they flew over the Atlantic, Zoey leaned in close to Chris and said, "Now that we know each other a little better, will you tell me what happened to make you stop hacking as a teenager?"

"It's not very interesting," Chris said.

"Oh, I think it probably is," she said. "Come on, I told you my story."

Exactly, and that's why I still don't entirely trust you.

"It's a long flight, and you know how persistent I can be," she said, drawing in closer.

"I got arrested, okay? And I never hacked again."

"From that day forward, you used your superpowers for good, not evil."

"Something like that."

"But that still doesn't explain why you're so sensitive about it," Zoey said, fiddling with the headphones that hung around her neck. "Someone got hurt, didn't they?"

★ ★ ★

There are moments when life becomes very binary. For Chris, there was life before he clicked that Enter key in the summer of 1987, and there was life after. But his memory of that pivot point was actually very different from the gauzy, slo-mo car crash version that was his recurring dream. It had all happened so much faster at the time.

Chris was sixteen years old and sitting at the computer in the bedroom of his best friend, Josh Woodrell, also sixteen. It was late afternoon, but the curtains were drawn to cut the glare on the screen, and the room was lit only by the techno moonglow of the monitor. The junior member of their little computing club was fourteen-year-old Dylan Nunn, who sat cross-legged on the floor in front of an interrupted game of Risk, the fate of the free world teetering in the balance. The three friends had spent the past six hours downing Mountain Dew and Skittles while toggling between Risk and desultory attempts at hacking on Josh's computer.

Dylan was a genuine math and computer prodigy and already the most brilliant coder of their group. But he was still two years younger than Chris and Josh, which allowed them to treat him like he was their dim-witted assistant. Dylan was a hyperactive Ritalin kid with an intense bug-eyed stare. He accepted their juvenile abuse because he was just glad to be hanging out with the older, cooler kids. Since Dylan was probably the only person in a fifty-mile radius who would have considered Chris and Josh cool, their little social pecking order worked. Dylan looked up to Josh in particular, which meant that when matters were put to a vote within their triumvirate, Chris was usually in the minority.

When Chris clicked that key, his green monitor screen filled with an imposing seal warning him that he was about to view classified Department of Defense data. As he scrolled through directories with headings like "X-13 Helicopter" and "Graywolf Missile," Chris slowly lifted his hands from the keyboard as if they had just become weaponized.

"Holy crap," he said. Chris was thrilled to claim the bragging rights that went with accessing the database, but he was also frightened. And the more he examined the data, the more frightened he became. These were state secrets and probably critical to national defense. From a less forgiving, adult point of view, what he was doing might be called treason.

"What is it?" Josh asked. He was sprawled faceup on his bed, stretching his back after hours hunched over the keyboard.

"You know that Department of Defense system that you were trying to crack?"

"Yeah."

"Well, I'm in."

Josh shot up in bed. "Awesome! So what did you find?"

"Very Tom Clancy–looking stuff. Like here," he said, pointing at the screen. "This looks like the specs for some kind of stealth helicopter."

"Let me see," Josh said. After examining the screen for a moment, he added, "Anybody have friends at the Russian embassy?"

"Don't even, man," Chris said. "Don't even."

Dylan was bouncing on his toes and peering over Chris's shoulder. "This is so, so cool," he said. "So very cool." Dylan always seemed to walk a fairly fine line between geek enthusiasm and mania. Josh and Chris sometimes worried about him.

"We need to log off now," Chris said. "I never thought we'd actually get in. You realize what this means, don't you?"

"That we are ninja cyber warrior gods?" Dylan offered.

"No," Chris said. "This is not like the high school's system, or that department store's. This is the Department of Defense. They probably have a sniffer program running. They're going to know that we've been here. Maybe they know already."

Josh sobered up fast. "And they're going to trace this to my IP address."

"As long as we're in, can't we just look around a little?" Dylan pleaded. "Give me something to decrypt." Dylan was the best of three at encryption, so he was always looking for an opportunity to show off.

Chris immediately logged off and hit the power switch on the computer. The three of them sat in Josh's dark, silent bedroom for a few minutes, half expecting to hear sirens pulling up in the driveway.

"I think I'd better get home," Dylan said. "Mom's making a special dinner."

Josh turned to Chris. "You'd better get out of here, too. There's no point in sticking around."

"We're all in this together," Chris said.

"Hey, they'll probably never know we breached their fire-wall," Josh said. "And we're damn sure not going back."

Chris raced home on his bike, trying to imagine how his parents would react if the FBI showed up at his front door. When he arrived, Chris went straight to his bedroom and threw himself on the bed. He stared at his posters for the Replacements and the Pixies, waiting for his pulse to slow. When you're sixteen, every slight or triumph seems life changing, but Chris knew that this was more than an adolescent fever dream. If their hack was detected by the DOD, then his life truly would be changed forever. All he could do now was wait to see if the knock at the door came.

That moment in Josh's room was the culmination of a long, hot summer that had started out deadly boring but grew steadily more interesting as it went along. Chris's family lived on a cul de sac among horse farms near the entrance to Mount Diablo State Park. His father, Frank, was an accountant for one of the Big Six accounting firms (back then there were six). Frank was a sort of throwback to the gray flannel corporate men of the fifties—genial, confident, and with an unhealthy respect for authority. His mother was a modestly successful photographer, who had turned one of the bedrooms into a studio and showed her work at local street fairs. Gazing out his bedroom window, Chris would watch as a parade of horseback riders and bicyclists headed into the state park. Up to that point, his childhood had been fairly uneventful, maybe even idyllic, but you only recognize that in retrospect—after something has happened to break the spell.

At sixteen, Chris was pimply faced and gawky. He was already over six feet tall, and skinny as a mantis. He didn't have a summer job, his junior year of high school was still weeks away, and he spent most of the long days in front of his computer—playing games and coding. U2's "The Joshua Tree" was on the radio constantly, but Crowded House's yearning "Don't Dream It's Over" was the song that he most associated with that summer.

Chris met Josh Woodrell when he moved into the house three doors down. Chris had seen him riding his ten-speed around the neighborhood for a week or two before they finally spoke. Chris's father had ordered him to mow the yard to get him away from the computer. Josh stopped his bike in the driveway and waited for Chris to shut off the phlegmy roar of the lawnmower.

After some introductory remarks mumbled gruffly at one another, Josh asked, "So what are you into?"

"Computers mostly," Chris offered, not expecting much of a reaction. His sweaty forehead was plastered with tiny green shards, and the smell of grass cuttings rising from the lawnmower's bag was humid and yeasty.

"Do you have one?"

"Yeah, a Commodore Amiga 500."

Josh held his nose and grimaced.

"So you've got something better?" Josh paused for dramatic effect. "An Apple Macintosh SE. Eight megahertz, 68000 processor, one megabyte of RAM."

"What, are your folks rich or something?"

"Nah, not really. My teachers told them that school wasn't challenging me intellectually, so I was able to guilt them into springing for it."

"Nice move. I'll have to try that," Chris said.

"You ever done any hacking?"

"A little bit." Even this modest statement was an exaggeration.

"You ever gotten into the school's system?"

"No, you could get busted for that."

"Yeah, I know. That's sort of the point."

Chris left the lawnmower in the middle of the yard and spent the rest of the afternoon in front of Josh's Mac. They passed most of July and August that way, their early summer tans fading. Josh brought Dylan into their circle a few weeks later, saying, "This twerp is a genius, but we must never tell him that, okay?"

Josh Woodrell had lank, dark brown hair and electric blue eyes that seemed to be fueled by a more volatile power source than everyone else was using. Josh and Chris became instant friends, not because they were particularly similar in temperament, but because they were the smartest people that they knew. Josh, in particular, was learning at a sprinter's pace that summer. He never just bought one book, he bought ten at a time, mostly science fiction, but also history, science, biology, and chess manuals. And he always seemed to be restocking.

Because they were, after all, teenage boys, there was a competitive element to the hacking. Josh led Chris to take greater risks in the virtual world, goading him into attacking ever more secure systems, targeting more sensitive and valuable information. But Chris found it difficult to express reservations, because Josh was always willing to take the leap himself, and Chris did not want to be left behind.

It took two days for the FBI agents to call on Josh, and the dreaded knock on Chris's front door finally came the day after that. It was 6:30 p.m. on a Wednesday night and everyone was just sitting down to dinner, all of them sluggish from the long, hot day—with the exception of Chris. Chris was an enervated wreck because he had called Josh's house the day before and been tersely informed by Josh's mother that Josh could not speak with him. He thought he knew what that meant. All day long he had agonized over whether he should come clean to his parents, but he still clung to the desperate, deluded hope that the knock at the door wouldn't come.

His father was the one who opened the door. It was his face that Chris saw first when he entered the dining room, trailed by two FBI agents. They were big men who looked like they knew how to use the pistols they wore in pointedly visible shoulder holsters.

Chris would never forget the look of hurt and disappointment on his father's face, but he would always be grateful for the reaction that followed. Frank took one look in Chris's eyes and immediately told the agents, "He's not saying anything to you without a lawyer present." It was the one time that Chris could recall his father standing up to authority.

Once the legal process began, Chris wasn't permitted to speak with Josh. Chris's parents hired a good lawyer and supported him through the process. The lawyer was a grim former federal prosecutor who specialized in scared-straight stories about the prosecutions of first-generation hackers like Kevin Mitnick. Chris was charged with violations of the federal Electronic Communications Privacy Act. He got off with probation and a sealed juvenile record because he was a minor, he did what the lawyer told him to do, and, most of all, because Josh never implicated his two friends.

Dylan wasn't even charged. It was clear that he was merely a follower of the two older kids. Three months later, Dylan's father, who was a store manager for a department store chain, was transferred to Sacramento and Chris never heard from him again. Chris wrote Dylan one guilt-filled letter, but he never responded.

Josh must have figured that there was no escaping for him, because it was his computer that had been used in the hacking. Chris and Dylan could still walk away if he stuck to his story. As far as Chris was concerned, Josh had given him his life. But, for Josh, things went less well. Because he was unwilling to point fingers at Chris and Dylan, Josh ended up sentenced to two years in the John A. Davis Juvenile Hall in Martinez.

Chris visited Josh regularly at the facility, but it was soon apparent that he had begun using drugs. Those eyes, once so electric, were now dull and unfocused. There was still a light there, but it was the wild, sparking light of a downed power line, there for a moment and then gone. Chris knew that Josh was in real trouble when he stopped asking Chris to bring him books.

On his last visit to the correctional facility, he and Josh fell out as only two boys who have been best friends as teenagers can. Chris couldn't remember everything that was said, but every resentment that had been festering since the arrest came to the surface. What Chris did remember, he deeply regretted. Josh called Chris a coward. Chris called Josh a screw-up.

A guard came over at the sound of raised voices and told them that the visit was over. As Chris walked out of the antiseptic visiting room, he knew that he would never see Josh again.

Stories about Josh occasionally drifted back to him through mutual friends and former classmates. Josh served out the remainder of his two-year sentence and emerged with a fullblown drug habit. Chris heard that he took a part-time job at a computer repair shop but turned to dealing meth in order to better support his habit. About a year after Josh was released, Chris lost track of him entirely and the stories stopped. None of his old friends knew what had happened to him.

Chris guessed that Josh had either died of an overdose or gone back to jail, this time to an adult facility. He would always feel responsible for Josh's downward spiral and wondered what would have happened if they had shared the blame for the DOD hack. Chris never extinguished his hope of finding Josh. If he was alive, then there was still a chance to atone for what he had done at age sixteen. Every year, Chris asked an investigator that he worked with to run a trace on Josh, but it was as if he had been purged from the world.

Chris had resolved that he was going to spend the rest of his life trying to correct the mistake. It was a promise that he renewed every morning that he went to work at the Department of Justice and, later, Reynolds, Fincher & McComb.

All of these memories of the summer of 1987 flashed through Chris's mind in an instant. They were easy to access, like webpages that had been cached from frequent viewing. When Chris refocused, he realized that Zoey was still there in the seat next to him, waiting for an answer to her question.

"Yes," Chris said, "someone got hurt."

CHAPTER 36

January 14

Chris awoke somewhere over the middle of the Atlantic to the white noise of the jet engines. The lights were down in the plane's cabin and almost all of the other passengers were asleep. He checked his watch—12:30 a.m. If the fake death certificate that he'd received from Enigma was to be believed, this was the day he was going to die.

Opening his laptop, he pored over the code of the Lurker virus yet again, hoping to find some previously undiscovered clue to the malware's purpose or creator. He already knew that there were different styles of coding present in the virus. The injector portion of the virus, which breaks into computers to deliver the payload, displayed extremely sophisticated, labor-intensive coding. Those were the parts that were probably taken from Stuxnet, the virus created by the US and Israeli intelligence agencies. The coding in those segments was clean, without extraneous characters.

The payload, which accomplished the virus's purpose, was more handcrafted and quirky, the work of a talented but more idiosyncratic coder. It was in this section that Chris had identified a seemingly random series of numbers and letters that he believed might hold the hacker's calling card. No virtuoso artist wants to go entirely uncredited for a masterwork, an impulse that had been the downfall of many art forgers and hackers.

The sequence read:

b:\9y7c6ykh0y6yd\\M3:R-I-II-III:RS:MCK:R:AAA:P: FP,MD,WE,XO,ZS,JV,AH,BC,QK,RT:G8U9O3M3G0R 3O5M2N1Z\\%phgopaigihgiaog22590808ad\src\objfre_ w2k_x86\i386\guava.pd.

He scanned the virus's thousands of lines of code over and over again until the characters and symbols blurred, but he kept returning to that one anomalous sequence. He nodded off bathed in the light from his laptop screen.

Chris awoke with a start. It might have been an hour later or only fifteen minutes, but it was still pitch-black outside the oval window. His subconscious must have been working overtime, though, because he now had an idea.

The coded message alternated between numbers and letters, and there was something hidden in the numbers that had struck him. Chris paged down to the segment of the coding to make sure that he hadn't imagined it, but there it was in every other digit of the code following "RT"—Chris's Social Security number.

Why had Enigma placed Chris's Social Security number into the code? If he simply wanted to lead authorities to believe that Chris had created the virus, then he would have been more obvious and wouldn't have bothered to mask the SSN, however transparently. As a means of pointing the finger at Chris, this was a clumsy and not very effective tactic. But as a means of sending a coded message for the sole benefit of Chris, it was pretty clever. Anyone else would assume that the nine digits of the Social Security number were just part of the coded message—only Chris would recognize them for what they were.

Chris tried dropping out the nine digits of his Social Security number to see what was left after the introductory section: GUOMGROMNZ. Just a random string of letters, but a short one that would probably translate into no more than two words.

He stared at the letters, waiting for a pattern to emerge, but nothing came. He rubbed his eyes and gazed out the window at an undifferentiated black expanse of ocean and sky.

And then it dawned on him. A hacker taking the name of Enigma would have to be a cryptography enthusiast—Enigma was the name of the machine used to encode Nazi military communiqués during World War II. The British recovered an Enigma machine and code book from a capsizing German submarine and installed it at Bletchley Park, a country house outside London, where a team of military cryptographers decrypted a series of intercepted Nazi messages, helping turn the tide of the war. Chris was now convinced that Enigma had encrypted the message using the Enigma code. But to decrypt a message encrypted using that code seemed impossible without one of the antique Enigma machines, which were preserved in military history museums.

Chris formulated a plan, but he would have to wait until the plane was on the ground to test it.

He considered waking Zoey to tell her what he had learned, but she was sleeping in the seat next to him like someone who

274 • THE ADVERSARY

might not get the chance again for a while. He let her sleep. After all, he didn't know yet if he was right.

When the wheels of the plane finally bumped down and they felt the g-force of deceleration, Chris immediately accessed the Internet on his smartphone. He searched the Internet for the term "Enigma machine simulator."

And there it was, just as he remembered it, a website offering a downloadable mobile app that replicated four different editions of the Enigma machine. It was a labor-of-love project created by an English cryptography expert for fellow crypto geeks.

The first segment of the code key was "M3." A quick review of the website proved that he had guessed correctly—one variety of Enigma machine used by the Wehrmacht and Luftwaffe was designated as the M3. There was no single Enigma machine used by the Germans—it evolved through the war years as the Nazis tried to stay ahead of the Allies' code breakers.

Chris downloaded the Enigma machine simulator app onto his smartphone and was soon looking at a photo of the M3 device, a big black box with metal rotors, a keyboard, and a plugboard of raised buttons. The Enigma machine scrambled letters through its three rotatable wheels, which had twenty-six electrical contacts on each side. A letter of a message entered on one side of a wheel was encrypted through a random electrical contact to a letter on the other side of the wheel, the first of numerous scrambling procedures built into the system. As he typed in the encrypted text on the touch screen image of the Enigma machine, the app produced a loud clacking sound like a heavy-duty manual typewriter.

The rest of the code key fell into place, reflecting the options that could be selected when using the M3 Enigma machine. "R: I-II-III" signified that he should select the option of using all three of the machine's rotors. "RS:MCK" meant "Rotor Start" at setting "MCK." The next portions of the code told him where to set the Enigma machine's three metal rings and the keys that should be pressed on the plugboard on the front of the machine. Using his smartphone, Chris entered each of these options into the app.

All that remained was to input the encrypted text.

Chris hit the ENTER key and a moment later the decrypted text appeared: DARBYCRASH.

Darby Crash, lead singer of the Germs.

Blanksy's hero.

Blanksy, the seemingly harmless prankster who had pestered him to speak at DefCon, was Enigma.

CHAPTER 37

What did he know about Blanksy? Not much, really. But they had spoken often enough over the years for Chris to feel betrayed. Blanksy had provided information that had been useful in several investigations, and Chris had begun to trust him. At the very least, he had believed that he was the immature, pop culture–obsessed fanboy that he made himself out to be. Blanksy had always seemed so jokey and harmless that Chris suspected Enigma might have enlisted him as an unwilling collaborator, as Chris had with Zoey.

He thought he knew the hacker's name—Jay Hartigan—but he now doubted that was his real identity. Chris knew that Blanksy liked seventies LA punk bands like the Germs, so maybe he was from California. He knew that Blanksy was active in organizing the DefCon hacker conference because he had tried to get Chris to speak there. Blanksy had to have friends at DefCon and some of them would likely know how to find him. Although the discovery of Blanksy's involvement was significant, it remained to be seen whether it brought them any closer to actually stopping the cyberattack on New York City.

As they taxied on the runway at JFK and waited for the ping that would send everyone scrambling for the overhead bins, Zoey's eyelids fluttered. She had been half-asleep and half observing him as he decoded the message from Enigma/Blanksy. The clacking sound from his mobile phone as he entered the encrypted text had roused her.

"That sound," she said, yawning. "What were you doing?"

Chris told Zoey what he had discovered. She had heard of Blanksy but had never encountered him directly.

"So who is this guy and why does he hate you enough to go to all that trouble?" Zoey asked.

"I just don't know. Maybe if I saw him, or saw what he looked like, I'd recognize him."

"Do you think he'll be at DefCon?"

"I'm almost certain of it. He tried to persuade me to speak there by hijacking my home computer."

Zoey laughed. "I'd love to see you in front of a DefCon crowd."

"He timed the attack to occur during the conference, probably so he could show off in front of his peers."

"So all of Blanksy's little geek buddies will be there at DefCon," Zoey said. "There's bound to be someone there who knows where he is."

"If they'll talk to us." Chris checked his watch. "And we only have about seven hours until the event. Seven hours to find Blanksy."

Chris and Zoey disembarked from the plane and walked quickly, but not too quickly, through the terminal. They stopped only to purchase two new prepaid cell phones from a shop

along the concourse and discard the phones that they had purchased in Europe.

They had checked bags in Paris because they thought it
would attract suspicion to board an international flight without
luggage. They weren't going to stop to collect them now at
baggage claim. Chris didn't want to spend a moment more than
necessary in the airport, which was clearly under heightened
security.

Chris and Zoey were walking down a long terminal hallway lined with airline gates, newsstands, and fast-food restaurants. Ahead of them, Chris counted about ten airport security
personnel, and those were just the ones that he could see.

Zoey leaned over to him, "Have you ever seen so much
security at an airport?"

"Not since right after 9/11 . . . or in Tel Aviv," Chris said.

"If they really expect the attack to happen, why don't they
do something to alert people?"

"What are they going to do?" Chris said. "Evacuate New
York City?"

As they passed through the baggage claim area and neared
the exit to the taxi zone, Chris noticed an airport security guard
who seemed to be staring at them from across the terminal.

Zoey followed Chris's gaze. "Do you think he knows who
we are?"

She got her answer when the security guard began walking
toward them, slowly at first and then breaking into a jog.

"Let's go," Chris said.

As they exited the terminal into the bright, cold day, a chill
wind hit them. Chris's heart sank when he saw the long line at
the taxi stand.

"Follow me," Chris said, walking briskly toward the unoccupied taxi at the front of the line.

Chris opened the door and climbed in, with Zoey right behind him. He heard disgruntled exclamations from the taxi line but did not look back. Cutting a New York City taxi line was a good way to get yourself killed, but Chris knew that if you were going to try it, you must show no weakness, no hesitation. The attendant in charge of the taxi stand was gesturing wildly at Chris through the closed window of the taxi.

The driver turned around, his pale, hangdog face filling the opening in the Plexiglas partition that separated the front and back seats. "That's not the way it works. You gotta wait your turn."

Chris pulled a roll of bills from his pocket, peeled off five twenties, and passed them forward to the driver.

"I'm sorry, pal, but there are rules."

Chris peeled off another wad of bills. The taxi driver didn't refuse the offering. The taxi stand attendant was knocking insistently on the window now, but the driver was examining the bills and seemed to be wavering.

The security guard who had spotted them was pushing his way through the crowd, much closer now. Chris shoved an entire roll of crumpled twenties through the partition.

The driver rolled down his electric window on the passenger side an inch and yelled to the taxi stand attendant, "Hey, Carl, I'm sorry, but I gotta take this one. I owe you one." As an afterthought, he added, "Medical emergency!"

The taxi pulled into a stream of cars leaving the terminal.

"Where to?" asked the driver over the smooth jazz on the car radio.

"Where's the closest place that we can get another cab quickly?"

"You sure?" the driver asked. "You paid me four hundred bucks already."

Zoey whispered to Chris, "They're going to call his dispatcher. He's going to be getting a call about us soon."

Chris nodded.

The cabbie was wearing a Bluetooth headset and nodding to someone on the phone. They couldn't hear what he was saying over the burbling, smooth jazz. Maybe he already knew who they were.

"Just take us where we can get another cab," Chris said. "And if anyone asks, tell them you dropped us at a different hotel. That's what the four hundred dollars is for."

"Okay. The airport Hilton is a good bet. Always a bunch of taxis there at this time of day."

At the Hilton, they quickly caught another cab.

Once inside, Chris said, "I think we missed our meet-up with Silver's guy, the one who was going to give us the guns."

"He probably saw us run out of there."

"I guess we just have to hope he catches up with us."

As they hummed along the Brooklyn–Queens Expressway, Chris took the opportunity to check his home voice mail. It was comforting somehow to listen to the messages. They were signs that his old life still existed, even if it was only in the minds of a couple of curious and worried friends who wondered why he had suddenly dropped off the face of the earth. Absentmindedly, he programmed the number for his home voice mail into a speed-dial button on the prepaid phone. It made him feel like he was still connected, however tenuously, to his former life.

It wouldn't be easy for the agents to follow them now. Someone at the Hilton would have to remember seeing them get into a cab and remember the cab company. Chris knew, however, that they hadn't really lost their pursuers. After all, they knew their destination—DefCon.

★ ★ ★

Michael Hazlitt and Sam Falacci arrived at the Air France customer service desk at JFK about an hour after Chris and Zoey had escaped in a cab. An airport security agent had reported his suspected sighting of Chris and Zoey, and the FBI agents were trying to confirm it.

A burly, uniformed baggage clerk with a heavy Bronx accent led them to a stack of unclaimed luggage from the Paris flight. Hazlitt didn't know what he was looking for, but he felt fairly certain that he would know it when he saw it.

There were five bags in the stack. The third bag was nearly empty, containing only a stack of *Le Monde* newspapers. The bag had no name tag on it, but there was a plastic routing band with the name of the passenger who had checked it.

Michael Falacci.

"Hey, Falacci, look at this," Hazlitt said to Falacci, motioning him over. "He's just messing with us now."

"So he must have gotten a fake passport," Falacci said. "He must think he's pretty smart."

"We're going to want to see the security camera film of the passengers coming off of that flight," Hazlitt said. "They've probably changed their appearances."

The clerk opened the two remaining bags and Falacci examined one, tossing back the lid of the black case. The bag was empty except for some French magazines. "This must be Doucet's."

"What's the name on the tag?"

Falacci leaned down and frowned as he read: "Samantha Hazlitt." He shook his head. "In the NFL, they would call a taunting penalty for this kind of behavior."

"Oh, they're going to be penalized," Hazlitt said.

CHAPTER 38

Chris and Zoey climbed out of their taxi in front of the venue for DefCon, the world's largest and oldest hacker conference. The conference took its name from the military shorthand for "defense condition," the term used to grade the worldwide alert posture, from one (war) to five (peace). Changes in DEFCON status had driven the plot of *War Games*, a movie that occupied a special place in the hearts of many first-generation hackers.

During its twenty-year history, DefCon had usually been held in Las Vegas at one of the casino hotels, but this year it was at Skylight One Hanson in Brooklyn, a magnificent Art Deco building topped with a clock tower. Nearby was the giant, collapsing chocolate soufflé that was The Barclays Center, home to the Brooklyn Nets. There were rumors that the CEO of one of the tech giants had bankrolled the elegant venue as a form of peace offering, and bribe, to the hacker community.

They entered the main hall under a black "DefCon 20" banner bearing a logo that was a combination of a skull and bones and a smiley face. That was a fitting symbol for the conference, which was viewed by the mainstream media as a gathering of high-tech pirates but was in actuality a fairly harmless collection of malcontents coming together to let their geek flags fly.

The main hall was a vaulted, ornate space with soaring pillars of sand-colored marble and rows of old-fashioned, mahogany-framed teller windows. The teller windows were decorated with literal-minded carvings of images of thrift, like beehives, squirrels storing nuts, and a seated lion with its paws protectively draped over the bank's lockbox. To give the place a more of-the-moment feel, it was dimly lit and highlighted with spotlights in cool blues, reds, and oranges.

As they purchased their passes, Chris and Zoey gave their assumed names. The twentysomething guy with shoulder-length, brown hair working the registration desk took a long look at him, and Chris wondered if he'd been already been recognized, despite the disguise.

"Okay," Chris said as they strode through the main hall. "We start by looking for someone we know who might also know Blanksy."

Chris saw no familiar faces in the throng, so he took a moment to examine his unusual conference badge, which was an aluminum rectangle. The front of the badge bore the DefCon 20 logo and a small LCD display. The back of the badge was studded with microchips, wires, and a mini-USB-connector. "What does this stuff do?" Chris asked.

"That depends on you," Zoey replied. "It's a DefCon tradition—the hackable conference badge."

"Interesting," Chris said, examining the badge and starting to think through what it could be turned into with some tweaks to its firmware.

"Focus, Chris," Zoey said with a slight smile. "Have you ever actually been to DefCon?"

"No," Chris conceded, "but I've arrested quite a few of the attendees."

"You should know the social etiquette. You're going to have enough trouble making friends as it is."

"So how should I conduct myself?"

"First, don't ask anyone what they do or where they work. Everyone here is paranoid about being identified as a hacker and losing their day job."

"Got it. What else?"

"No photos without getting the permission of everyone in the frame, and that includes your smartphone. Everyone thinks that law enforcement agencies are keeping files on the attendees."

"Their paranoia is justified."

It was an eclectic crowd. Some of the hackers sported tattoos and piercings, but others were in khakis and polo shirts. They passed a booth that was offering mohawk haircuts for fifteen bucks.

"Maybe it's time to change your appearance again?" Zoey offered, deadpan.

"I think I'd rather go to prison," Chris said.

They entered a large ballroom where one of DefCon's main attractions was being held—the Capture the Flag contest. "If I were Blanksy, this is where I'd be," Zoey said. "This is the main event."

Capture the Flag was a hacking contest that involved twelve computers elaborately configured to repel intrusion attempts. Teams of hackers were given forty-eight hours to penetrate as many of the computers as possible, with points assigned for each successful hack. Competitive teams had strong skills and the right equipment, such as a good site cracker, reliable laptops, a farm of computers back home that were prepped to compare and exploit code, and mirrors of several full-disclosure sites— hacker-generated sites that publicly display lists of vulnerable websites. The team with the most points at the end of the marathon session was the winner.

The ballroom was decorated in a minimalist style, with low-slung chairs grouped around the tables that held the computers. Conference attendees strolled past, encouraging and taunting the various teams. Chris and Zoey looked in on the nearest team of hackers. Cans of Mountain Dew Code Red littered the table, and a vintage boom box blasted the Clash's "The Magnificent Seven." The team was called "Trotsky" and wore matching red T-shirts emblazoned with the image of the bespectacled Marxist. Each team member had his or her eyes locked on a laptop screen, furiously coding.

"I competed here once with a bunch of guys from San Francisco," Zoey said.

"How'd you do?" Chris asked.

"Finished third," Zoey said. "Around the thirty-six-hour mark the team got punchy and started squabbling. We never recovered."

It wasn't much of a spectator sport, but the event still drew an avid crowd, watching to see how the teams were bearing up under the stress of more than twenty-eight hours of nonstop coding.

"You see any familiar faces?" Chris asked.

"No one who would be able to help us," Zoey said.

They moved on to another conference room off the main hall where a crowd was gathering. The area was plastered with posters that read:

WARNING!! Cell phone calls may be intercepted or disrupted in this area from 4 to 5 p.m. today. This is due to a practical demonstration of the insecurity of GSM cell phones at the DefCon security conference. If you do not consent to having your cell phone hacked, please do not use it in this area between 4 and 5 p.m. PLEASE BE WARNED THAT WE DO INTEND TO ACCESS THE CONTENT OF THE INTERCEPTED CALLS.

Chris and Zoey stood in the back of the room as the presenter explained that, using a laptop, a transmitter broadcasting over a ham radio frequency, and two antennas, he had created a GSM base station that would intercept the calls of mobile phones in the vicinity by fooling them into thinking that they were linking to an AT&T cell tower.

Copies of a flyer were being passed back through the crowd. Chris took one—it was a list of cell phone numbers that were now under the control of the fake GSM base station. The number of Chris's new prepaid cell phone was on the list.

Chris pointed the number out to Zoey. "Any calls I make to Blanksy or the feds are going to be intercepted during this demonstration."

"Then you'd better stay off your phone," Zoey said.

"If this guy intercepts one of my calls, then some federal agency is probably going to get those records sooner or later," Chris said. "Probably sooner."

"You think he'll be arrested?" asked a teenager with bleached blond hair standing in front of them.

For a moment, Chris was puzzled by the question. Did he know that Chris was a former DOJ cybercrimes prosecutor? "Why would you say that?" Chris asked.

The kid's face was shadowed with acne and the anxious look that comes with adolescent social anxiety. He looked like he could still be in high school. "Hacking phones is, like, a crime. Some people think the FCC is going to arrest him during the presentation."

"No, I doubt that's going to happen," Chris said.

"You're probably right," the kid said. "That would be some extreme cyberdouchery, even for the federal government. He's just trying to make a point, right?"

"Yeah, right," Chris said.

Chris glanced over at Zoey and, as expected, caught her grinning.

"Did I just hear you acknowledge that hacking can serve a social purpose?" Zoey asked.

"You said I should try to blend in," Chris said.

Chris surveyed the large crowd gathered for the demonstration, many of them talking into their cell phones despite the knowledge that they were being hacked.

Chris had a brainwave. "We need to talk to that guy when the demonstration is over," he said, pointing at the figure at the podium explaining the cell phone hacking experiment. Chris saw in the conference program that his name was David Yoshitake, and he resembled a young, Japanese Jerry Garcia, with a peach-fuzz soul patch and a large belly distending a black *Reservoir Dogs* T-shirt.

As soon as the demonstration concluded, Chris pushed his way onto the podium.

"I need to speak with you in private—right now," Chris said.

A cloud passed over Yoshitake's placid stoner's face. "You're not—"

"No, I'm not with the FCC, but I am someone you need to speak to."

Yoshitake studied him for a minute. "Step into my office," he said, leading them into an adjoining conference room, then motioning for them to step behind a mountain of pizza boxes. To anyone who opened the doors of the conference room to look for them, the room would appear empty.

Chris and Zoey sat down in plastic chairs on either side of the computer. The close, marinara-scented space caused Chris to flash on a childhood memory of building a fortress out of blankets and a card table. As he took a seat at the computer, Yoshitake pointed at the walls of Fort Domino's. "My friends' idea of a joke," he said.

"Interesting demonstration you gave in there," Chris said.

"I just think people need to know that their cell phones are not secure. If I can do it, then other people can, too." Yoshitake spoke in halting bursts like a webpage downloading over a dial-up connection.

"I can vouch for that," Chris said.

"So who are you people? You don't look like DefCon types. No offense."

"None taken. We're trying to track down a hacker who's here at DefCon and is about to do something very, very bad. Something that's going to hurt a lot of people."

"So are you cops or what?"

"No. I'm an attorney, but right now we're—unaffiliated."

"What is it that you want?"

"Your notice said that you were recording the content of the intercepted cell calls. Is that right?"

"Right. I'm creating a transcript using voice-recognition software. I'm going to use it in a later session to call some people out from the audience, have a little fun with them."

"We need to search that transcript. It may help us find the person that we're looking for. I think there's a decent chance that he was within reach of your base station."

Yoshitake rubbed his thumb over his wispy soul patch. "How do I know that you're the good guys? Maybe you just want to get the cell numbers of a bunch of hackers so you can harass them."

"He's telling the truth," Zoey said.

"And who are you?"

"I've been coming to this conference for years. There are people who know me, you can ask around. My name is Zoey Doucet, but I go by Cynecitta."

"The Centinela Bank exploit? Why didn't you say that in the first place?" Yoshitake said, opening up his laptop and getting to work.

Zoey waved a hand at Chris as if to say, *See, you should have let me handle this.*

A few minutes later, Yoshitake had the database of hacked cell phone call transcripts up on his computer. "Okay, what's our search term?"

"Blanksy. B–l–a–n–k–s–y."

Yoshitake frowned. "I've heard of him."

"What do you know?"

"Not much, just that he controls a huge botnet." A botnet is a network of computers that are all infected with, and controlled by, a virus—the bot. A botnet could be used to launch massive volumes of email, either as a delivery system for spam in a phishing scheme or to crash a website through a distributed denial-of-service attack.

Yoshitake typed in the name, but before pressing the key to search, he said, "After I do this, we're done, okay? I'm working toward a PhD in mathematics at MIT. I need to keep this stuff separate from my real life."

"No one is going to know," Chris said. "We just need to find this guy."

Yoshitake seemed assuaged. A few seconds later, he was skimming through the search results.

"Got one," Yoshitake said, pointing at this entry as Chris and Zoey leaned in to read the screen:

CALLER 1: AFTER I ACTIVATE AT 6, I'LL COME INTO THE CITY AND MEET YOU AT THE HOTEL.
CALLER 2: IT'S GOING TO BE SOMETHING TO SEE NEW YORK GO DARK. I HOPE YOU CAN GET HERE BEFORE IT KICKS IN.
CALLER 1: WHAT SHOULD I BE CALLING YOU THESE DAYS, ANYWAY, BLANKSY OR ENIGMA?
CALLER 2: CALL ME BLANKSY. AFTER TONIGHT, I THINK ENIGMA'S GOING TO HAVE TO GO AWAY FOR A WHILE.

"Do you have phone numbers for these two people?" Chris asked.

"Only the first person, the one who's here at DefCon, not the person he's speaking to."

"That will have to do," Chris said, checking his watch. It was 5:45. If the caller was right, the Lurker virus would be activated in fifteen minutes.

CHAPTER 39

The podium was now empty where the phone hack demonstration had been conducted. Chris and Zoey stood at the back of the room, waiting as the attendees found their seats for the next presentation, titled "The New Face of Social Engineering."

The auditorium was nearly full, it was five minutes until the start time, and the next speaker wasn't yet at the podium—time to get started.

"Wait for my signal, then call the number Yoshitake gave us," Chris said. "Get as many people in here as possible, and I'll talk for a couple of minutes to keep their attention."

"What are you going to say to them?"

"The truth," Chris said. "I mean, why not?"

He strode up the aisle, climbed the steps to the stage, and stood at the lectern. The audience didn't immediately notice him.

Chris tapped the microphone, and it let out a startled shriek of feedback.

Now everyone was staring at him. Chris was not at all sure how this was going to go. He wiped his damp palms on his pants and gripped the sides of the lectern. He felt like someone about to knock down a hornet's nest with a broom handle.

Clearing his throat, he said, "My name is Chris Bruen." This was greeted by scattered boos. "I guess some of you know who I am."

Now the boos rose from the audience in a chorus.

Chris looked out upon a sea of unfriendly faces. The crowd was mostly young, mostly male, mostly wearing jeans and T-shirts, and mostly muttering epithets.

Zoey was standing at the foot of the stage and wincing at the hostile reception.

"I have something to say and I really hope you'll listen," Chris said. "Over the years, I've gotten to know many of you when I was a cybercrimes prosecutor at the DOJ and now in private practice. And, yes, I may have put some of your friends in jail."

"Get off!" someone shouted from the back of the auditorium.

Chris pressed on. "Some of you have heard the rumors about a possible cyberattack on New York City tonight. It's an extremely sophisticated virus and it's capable of doing a great deal of harm."

There were scattered nods of acknowledgment from the crowd. Clearly, the word was out.

"I have reason to believe that the person behind that virus is here at DefCon, and I need your help finding him before the attack can be carried out," Chris said. "If it's successful, people will die—probably a lot of people."

The auditorium was silent.

"Okay," Chris said. "I know that I'm not the most popular person here, but something bad is going to happen tonight. If one of you has the power to prevent that, I'm hoping that you will step up. Now."

Maybe he was deluding himself, but he sensed that the crowd was listening.

"I believe that the hacker behind the attack is known as Blanksy. He also goes by the name Enigma. His real name might be Jay Hartigan, but I'm not certain. I know that he has some connection to DefCon, because he asked me to speak here. Can someone here help me find him?"

People began to pour into the back of the auditorium. Chris gazed out at the crowd and they stared back at him. There was some conversation going on in the audience. It was likely that some audience members at least knew who Blanksy was. Despite the chatter, no one stood up to volunteer information. That was to be expected. It would have taken a lot of nerve to stand up in that crowd and publicly identify a hacker for criminal prosecution.

"Okay, I tried," Chris said. "But if you know Blanksy or know where to find him and you say nothing, you're going to have blood on your hands if the attack happens."

The audience of hackers didn't disperse immediately. Most were still in their seats debating what they had just heard and waiting to see if there was more.

Chris figured that he had the largest crowd that he was going to get and that people were going to start drifting away soon. He nodded to Zoey. Zoey dialed her cell phone, punching in the number that they had obtained from the intercepted cell call. Chris and Zoey both intently scanned the audience. And then a lone cell phone sounded loudly with the jarring ring tone of an old rotary dial.

Thank you, Yoshitake.

At the back of the auditorium, Chris saw a tall man in a leather jacket remove a ringing cell phone from his pocket and glance at the screen. He quickly silenced the phone without answering and disappeared into the hallway.

The microphone let out another squeal of feedback as Chris dropped it on the lectern and jumped down from the podium to pursue Blanksy's accomplice. Zoey was already ahead of him, sprinting down the aisle.

CHAPTER 40

The man in the leather jacket shoved his way through the throng in the main conference hall, a computer bag slung over his shoulder and bouncing heavily against his back. Chris and Zoey were about thirty yards behind, slowed by the disgruntled hackers that he was leaving in his wake.

Chris knew he might be armed, but there was no time left to wait for Hazlitt and Falacci or any other assistance. If they didn't stop him immediately, he was probably going to activate the virus. The crowd thinned as they reached a section of the conference center that was not in use. Now it was a footrace, and their steps clattered on the polished marble floor of the old bank building. The man in the leather jacket turned a corner ahead of them, and when Chris and Zoey rounded the corner, they were met with a long, empty hallway and two corridors branching off to the right and left. Each corridor was lined with closed doors.

"Which way?" Zoey asked.

Chris raised a finger for quiet. They listened for any sounds of movement, but there was only the faint buzz of conversation from the conference crowd they had left behind.

"If I had to guess," Zoey said, "I'd bet he went right or left. He'd be too easy to spot if he went straight down this long hallway."

"Agreed." Picking at random, Chris set off down the right hallway with Zoey.

They opened the first door and found a small, empty conference room with a PowerPoint projector and rows of folding chairs. They tried three more doors and found more of the same—the rooms were empty.

"What happens if we find him?" Zoey asked.

Zoey was right. Even if they caught up with the man, what would they do without a gun? Chris considered what might work as a makeshift weapon, then pulled his laptop bag off his shoulder and swung it back and forth, gauging its heft. They entered another conference room that was slightly larger than the last. Behind the podium was a plastic accordion-like partition that cut the room in half. Chris and Zoey stood perfectly still and listened. Chris heard a familiar skittering sound that at first reminded him of a rodent inside a wall. Then he recognized it—the sound of fingers flying over a keyboard. Chris nodded to Zoey and motioned for her to wait.

The sound was coming from behind the partition, so Chris slowly stepped closer, his footsteps muffled by the carpeting. Judging by the persistent pattering of the keyboard, whoever was on the other side was probably too engrossed in their work to notice his advance. Heart throbbing in his rib cage, Chris was having trouble catching his breath. He tightened his two-handed grip on the strap of the laptop bag and felt the vinyl bite into his palms.

Chris let out a slow breath and then pulled back the partition. And there he was—the man in the leather jacket sitting cross-legged on the floor furiously working on his laptop. At the sight of Chris, he dropped his hands to his sides, like a concert pianist who has just completed a brilliant recital.

"Step away from the laptop," Chris said.

"You are too late," he said with what sounded like the ghost of a Russian accent. The man smiled, revealing a mouth full of small, yellow teeth. It was a smile that had the same effect on Chris as when he turned over a rotten log to find a host of tiny, pale creatures.

The man started reaching into his inside jacket pocket. Expecting the move, Chris quickly stepped forward, swinging the laptop bag in a broad arc. Just before the blow landed, Chris saw a look of surprise on the man's face. The bag connected with his temple with a loud, metallic thump and he crumpled to the floor, bleeding from an ugly gash on his forehead. Chris and Zoey stared down at the unconscious man for a moment.

"That worked better than I thought it would," Zoey said.

Chris bent down and opened the man's jacket. There was no gun, but there was a Taser, the kind with electrodes on filament wires that could be fired like a gun. Chris took the Taser and put it in his laptop bag.

"This was the same kind of Taser that was used by Ed's killer," Chris said.

"Steady there, Chris. You don't know that he did it."

Zoey was already sitting in front of the laptop, trying to tell if the virus had been activated, and whether there was anything to be done. Chris gazed at the prone man for a long moment, wrestling with the impulse to take his laptop bag and finish what he had started. For an instant, he glimpsed something dark inside himself that wanted to claw its way out. The anger didn't disappear, but the moment when he might have allowed it to blind him passed. Although he hadn't been sure what he would do in this situation, Chris discovered that, fundamentally, he believed in the law. He was going to let the law deal with this.

"Chris?"

"What have you got?" Chris asked, snapping back into focus.

"The virus might have been activated, but there's nothing here for me to work with."

Chris needed to do something with Blanksy's accomplice. He looked out in the hallway and saw a janitor's trash can on wheels in front of a utility closet. Zoey and Chris lifted the man so that he was seated in the full trash bin with his head and legs dangling over the sides. They rolled him into the utility closet and when they got there, Chris reached inside the man's jacket and removed his cell phone. He was just beginning to regain consciousness when they pitched him inside and locked him in by wedging a chair under the doorknob.

Chris showed the cell phone to Zoey. "The last call he made was probably to Blanksy."

Chris turned on the phone and checked the recent calls. "Here's a 212 number from ten minutes ago."

"Okay, so what are you waiting for?" Zoey asked.

Chris dialed the number.

A cheerily professional male voice answered. "W Hotel Times Square."

Chris asked the front desk clerk if a Mr. Hartigan was staying there. Or a Mr. Crash. Or a Mr. Blanksy. No luck.

"So you think he's there?" Zoey asked.

"Yes, but we're going to have to go there and find him ourselves."

CHAPTER 41

Chris and Zoey entered the main hall of the DefCon conference, hoping to find a taxi out front that would take them into Manhattan to the W Hotel. After Chris's controversial performance, they were attracting plenty of hostile stares from the crowd of hackers.

Chris froze and clutched Zoey's arm. On the other side of the vaulted lobby, a man and woman in suits were at the registration desk, questioning the long-haired kid who dispensed the conference badges. They had to be FBI agents. Given Chris's current level of notoriety in the room, someone was going to point him out to the agents any second.

"FBI," Chris said, turning sharply and walking quickly away.

Returning to the unused wing of the event center, they hit the first emergency exit they could find. It brought them to a hallway that led to a loading dock. The agents were probably calling in reinforcements for a manhunt.

Chris and Zoey hurried through the empty loading dock and onto a residential street with rows of brownstones fronted by barren trees. There were no taxis in sight, but Chris knew that if they didn't put some distance between themselves and the conference site, they'd be picked up within minutes. They walked quickly and in silence past the handsome Fort Greene brownstones.

Chris contemplated the virus attack that was probably only hours away now. He reviewed what he knew, or thought he knew, about the Lurker virus. It was designed to exploit BlueCloud's Aspira operating system. That didn't help to narrow down the possible point of attack, though, because Aspira was used by nearly every business and government agency in the country. It was clearly a virus that could be activated remotely but, once activated, it required some time to find its mark. It wasn't like flipping a switch.

If the Lurker virus was intended to shut down New York City, then there were a few obvious targets that the FBI was undoubtedly monitoring—the New York Power Authority, Con Edison, MTA, New York City Transit, major hospitals like Mount Sinai, Beth Israel, and New York-Presbyterian, and JFK and LaGuardia airports. The key, though, was being able to spot the often subtle indicators that a virus was present. Ed had given the virus its name because it had the capacity to burrow into systems and cover its tracks, lurking on computer hard drives, waiting for activation like a sleeper cell.

Chris and Zoey made their way out of the residential neighborhood and reached Flatbush Avenue, Brooklyn's main thoroughfare. They felt exposed standing on a street corner trying to hail a cab, but they managed to catch one. They needed a place near the subway where Chris could spend a few minutes on the phone sending a warning before they caught a train into the city. After a conversation with the cabbie, they settled on Fort Greene Park.

The park was deserted except for a couple of dog walkers and a mother with a stroller. The trees were mostly bare and there were patches of snow on the ground. Chris and Zoey sat down on a bench near a child's playground where they couldn't be seen from the street.

"Before we head into the city, I need to talk to Hazlitt again," Chris said. "I want to make sure that they know what they're dealing with."

Chris dialed Hazlitt on his prepaid cell. He picked up on the first ring.

"You shouldn't have run," Hazlitt said.

"So you keep saying," Chris said.

"I didn't catch your little speech, but I heard about what you said. So Jay Hartigan, aka Blanksy, is who we're looking for?"

"It seems so. Your colleagues will find one of his accomplices in a utility closet in the east wing of One Hanson. He's wearing a leather jacket and has some sort of Eastern European accent, possibly Russian. I'm pretty sure he killed Eduardo de Lamadrid."

"You know you're making our job too easy."

"Well, someone has to do it. What you need to know is that I'm pretty sure he activated the Lurker virus before we could stop him."

There was a silence on the other end of the line, then Hazlitt asked, "How long do you think we have?"

"Whatever that virus is designed to do, it's probably going to start doing it soon. It could take hours or minutes, I don't know."

"So, since you seem to have all the answers, do you know where Blanksy is?"

"I'm pretty sure that he's staying in the W Hotel in Times Square," Chris said. "It faces right out on Times Square. Probably a good place for a ringside seat to watch as all hell breaks loose."

"Do you know what name he's under?"

"No."

Zoey whispered something to Chris, who nodded. "There's something else that you should know."

"Yeah?"

"I'm sure you're watching for the virus at all of the key points in the city's infrastructure—the power grid, the airports, hospitals."

"Yeah, right. So?"

"There's something you should probably be looking for. A way Blanksy's crew might disguise what they're doing."

"What are you talking about?"

"A virus as potentially disruptive as this one will usually leave some clues that it's infected the host. Little glitches in the system, crashes, the kind of thing that shows up in additional calls to the help desk."

"You're not telling me anything I don't know," Hazlitt said, sounding impatient.

"I'm getting there. You're probably checking with the help desk at power companies like Con Edison, correct?"

"Maybe."

"Because if their system was infected, they would most likely be getting a higher than normal volume of calls."

"Yes, of course. What's your point?"

"What if the calls aren't going to the company's help desk?"

There was silence on the other end of the line for a moment. Then, this time with far less attitude, Hazlitt said, "You're saying that Blanksy's crew might hack into the help desk line and take the calls themselves?"

"I've seen it happen before."

"Really. Huh," Hazlitt said, frankly amazed at the ingenuity of the technique.

"The fake help desk employees would try to ameliorate the situation, get the employees back to work, keep them happy, just like a real help desk would. They might even do a better job than a regular help desk, because they would be highly motivated."

"Because if the company doesn't see any of the warning signs of the virus, they'll never know what hit them."

"Exactly," Chris said.

"Why haven't I heard of this tactic before?"

"Working in the private sector, I guess I see a lot of hacks that never reach the attention of the feds."

"I want you to stay on the line," Hazlitt said. "I'm actually at Con Ed headquarters right now. I can speak with their privacy officer. It shouldn't be hard to test this theory."

The line went quiet for a while, but Chris could hear Hazlitt and Falacci talking in muffled tones.

"Hang on," Hazlitt said. "This should only take a few minutes. Con Edison is sending an email to all employees asking them to respond if they've filed a help desk call today. We'll see if the numbers that we get back match up with what the help desk is reporting."

Chris held on the phone for perhaps ten minutes, watching a couple of small, barrel-chested dogs chase each other around the park. The sky was low and hazy. It looked like there might be more snow.

Finally, Hazlitt came back on the line. "Well, Con Edison is infected. The emails are pouring in and they've already far exceeded the number of calls the help desk is reporting—the fake help desk. We'll see if we can trace them."

"You won't find them," Chris said. "They'll be ready for that. They knew you'd figure it out eventually."

"At this point, our only option is to hunt them down. The virus has already been activated, and we still don't have a security patch. We haven't even isolated a particular vulnerability in the operating system."

"What do you mean 'our' only chance?" Chris said with a slight smile. "Are you acknowledging that we might be on the same side?"

"What I think really doesn't matter," Hazlitt said. "But okay, yeah, I'll admit it. But that's just my personal opinion and it doesn't change my orders. We're still coming for you."

"I wouldn't expect anything less," Chris said. "And I won't be turning myself in just yet."

"I wouldn't expect anything less, either," Hazlitt said. "And I'm warning you to stay away from the W Hotel, okay? We'll bring him in."

Chris hung up on the FBI agent.

CHAPTER 42

As dusk settled in, Chris watched the throngs pushing through the turnstiles at the Jay Street subway station, faces slack, heading home, the forced smiles of the workplace gone.

"They have no idea what's about to happen, do they?" Zoey said.

"There's probably been some kind of statement about a threat warning, but I doubt that many details have been provided," Chris said. "No one wants to create a panic."

"I don't know why panic gets such a bad rap," Zoey said before descending the steps to the platform. "There are some situations where the only appropriate response is batshit panic. I don't like to eliminate it as an option, you know? In the email that went to the New York Mayor's Office, Blanksy said that the virus was going to be activated tonight . . . and it's nearly dark. I'm not sure how I feel about boarding this subway train. Do you think the virus could shut down the MTA?"

A dirty sirocco swirled through the tunnel as a train pulled into the station.

"It's possible," Chris admitted. "But there are good people combating this sort of threat. US Cyber Command in Fort Meade, Maryland, is dedicated to protecting the infrastructure."

"Yeah, I know," Zoey said. "But are they good enough to stop this?"

"Well, they say that you have to be right five hundred times out of five hundred in defending attacks. The adversary only has to be right once."

"Not helping," Zoey said. "I'd hate for this train to stop when we're under the East River. I've always had a thing about that."

"Believe me, I thought about taking a cab into the city," Chris said. "But it's rush hour and it would take forever. If we're going to catch up with Blanksy, I think our best shot is to get into Manhattan as quickly as possible on the subway before any sort of shutdown occurs."

They found a couple of seats on the train, and the doors gasped shut. With a lurch, the train began moving. Everyone observed the etiquette of the subway, eyes fixed on the middle distance or closed in nodding half sleep, faces buried in laptops, smartphones, e-readers, and tablet computers, earbuds on. The train was silent, with no one talking and no sound but the rattling of the car over the tracks, which wavered in pitch from a low rumble to a high whine.

Chris knew it was quite possible that the MTA would be one of the targets of the cyberattack if it was carried out. He reflected on how much of daily life was governed by the tiny programmable logic controllers that were Lurker's target. The switches told the trains when to stop and go, which tracks to follow . . . and how to avoid collisions. PLCs also controlled

New York City's traffic lights, the flow of water through the sewer system, the operation of nuclear reactors, and the allocation of electricity throughout the grid to avoid blackouts. If the city were a human body, PLCs would be the nervous system, regulating a million tiny transactions and adjustments that allowed the organism to function.

The train leaned to one side as it passed over a curved bit of track and everyone reflexively leaned in the opposite direction to compensate. Then the train pulled out of the York Street station and went under the East River. Chris frequently rode San Francisco's BART trains, which traveled back and forth under the San Francisco Bay on the lines that linked the city with the East Bay. Chris understood Zoey's phobia. He always tried to forget about the millions of gallons of water overhead as the BART train hurtled through the tunnels. The New York subway trains were narrower than BART's, which only heightened his claustrophobia.

Chris tried to push those thoughts out of his mind. They weren't productive. They didn't help solve the problem.

After they had passed under the river and were several stops into the city, the lights in the subway car suddenly blinked off. Then the lights sputtered back on, only to . . .

Blink off again in a way that somehow seemed final.

As Chris and Zoey sat next to each other in the sudden darkness, Chris felt the car decelerating. The high-pitched whine of the subway car rocketing down the rails descended an octave or two as the train slowed and, finally, stopped.

Power was out on the MTA and Chris knew that it wasn't going to be coming back any time soon. What he didn't know was how massive the attack was and what they would be faced with when they reached the surface.

Zoey whispered to him in the dark, "It's starting, isn't it?"

CHAPTER 43

When the lights went out in the subway car, MTA etiquette went out the window. Suddenly, everyone was talking. At first, it sounded like the typically jaded gripes of New Yorkers.

"Jesus, I'm already late for dinner."

"This city's going to hell under this mayor."

"So this is what I pay taxes for?"

Everyone stayed seated, assuming that the lights would come back up in a few minutes and the train would continue on its course. Every subway rider had experienced brief shutdowns like this at one time or another. But about five minutes in, an anxious tone crept into the voices in the darkness. Some passengers were starting to talk about getting out onto the tracks.

Chris spoke up. "Why doesn't everyone turn on their smartphones, laptops, whatever you've got. The screens will give us some light."

Devices clicked on around the car, together casting a faint glow like a night-light.

"Is anyone getting Internet access?" Chris asked.

A few voices chimed in from around the car. "Nah, I don't see nothing."

"Listen, I have an emergency," Chris said. "I need to open the doors of this car and walk out of here. Anybody want to help me with that?"

There were some dissenting opinions voiced, but a couple of big guys were with him, and that was enough. His allies were a burly guy in his thirties who was dressed in jeans and work boots and a tall, wiry man in his forties wearing a dark pinstripe suit. Chris would guess that they were a construction worker and an investment banker, blue collar and white collar momentarily united by their shared impatience at being delayed on the way home to their families.

"What's your hurry? You know there's a third rail out there," the burly guy said.

Chris groped for a story. "My wife just went into surgery. I have to get out of here."

The three men pried their fingers between the doors and pulled. As designed, the doors popped open with the application of a little force. Chris stepped down into the tunnel, followed by the two men.

He looked up and down the tracks, but the darkness was impenetrable. There were no other cars visible, no safety lights on the walls. He looked for a ladder to the surface but didn't see one. Chris stuck his head into the car and called out to Zoey, who climbed down onto the tracks.

"Which way?" Zoey asked.

"Well, Times Square is this way," Chris said.

Chris and Zoey set off down the tracks, barely able to see three feet in front of them. Once they realized that there wasn't an easy exit to the surface, the two men who had helped open the doors decided to wait a while longer to see if the trains started.

They stepped carefully to avoid tripping over the rails, steadying themselves by running their fingers along the mildewed brick wall. "Don't hurry," Chris said. "The third rail might still be electrified. If it is, you hit it and you're toast."

They heard a skittering sound on the tracks ahead.

"Those are rats, aren't they?" Zoey asked.

"It's too dark to tell," Chris said.

"You're a bad liar, but I appreciate the effort," she said.

The faint, cool breeze that blew through the tunnel seemed to be growing stronger as they advanced, along with the smell of urine, which might mean that they were approaching an exit.

"Is there a square inch of New York City that hasn't been pissed on?" Zoey asked.

They approached the empty platform of the 42nd Street-Bryant Park station. The lights were out but, now that his eyes were adjusted to the darkness, Chris thought he could detect a faint brightening up ahead that might originate from the surface.

Then they heard a faint rumbling ahead of them, growing steadily louder. It was a subway train barreling down the tracks. Apparently, some of the MTA lines still had power.

"We need to get to the platform," Chris said. "Run."

"What about the third rail?" Zoey asked.

"Just run."

They loped awkwardly over the uneven tracks. Chris held Zoey up when she tripped and Zoey did the same for him. By the time they were fifty yards from the platform, the rumbling was much louder. The train was closing in, but the tunnel remained dark. The car was running with its lights out.

Chris gave Zoey a boost onto the platform and she crawled up.

"C'mon!" Zoey said, extending a hand. "Those trains are going to hit!"

He glanced back and saw that it was true, the oncoming train was switching tracks with a high, grinding sound and heading straight for the car that they had just left behind. The virus must have disrupted the MTA's routing system. Chris struggled to pull himself up, his elbows on the platform and his feet kicking beneath him in space. Zoey grasped his hand but he was too heavy and he fell back onto the tracks. He didn't have to look. The noise told him how close the train was. Chris leaped upward at the platform and got his chest over the ledge. Zoey grabbed his arm and threw her full weight into it. With Zoey's help, he wriggled up onto the subway platform.

Chris made sure that his feet weren't dangling over the edge of the platform, then they both scrambled away on their knees, trying to get as far away from the tracks as possible before the impact. With their backs against the wall of the station, they watched as the out-of-control train hurtled past. The lights were out inside the car, but Chris could still make out the panicked faces of passengers through the windows.

A moment later, the subway cars collided with a horrendous dying-beast sound of rending metal. As soon as the noise stopped, Chris hurried back to the edge of the platform and jumped down onto the tracks, with Zoey right behind him. Chris and Zoey quickly retraced their steps to see if there was anything that they could do to help the passengers. They were confronted with a mass of metal that filled the tunnel from wall to wall, as if the cars had been paper bags squashed in a trash compactor. They could hear pneumatic hisses, the sizzle and pop of misfiring electrical connections—and screams.

Chris tried the door on the rear of the car, but the metal was so twisted that it wouldn't open. Through the window, he could see figures inside, some moving, some not. There was no other point of entry without heavy equipment.

Chris stepped down off the back of the car. He didn't want Zoey to see what he had just seen.

"C'mon," Chris said, turning her back, "there's nothing we can do here but get help."

Stunned into silence, they returned to the platform, slid over the turnstiles, and climbed a frozen escalator. Although the subway station was entirely dark, Chris was relieved to see a lit streetlight on above them as they emerged at Bryant Park.

"I've never been so glad to see a streetlamp," Zoey said. "We need to find a cop or something."

Chris had spotted a policeman a half block away and was already running to him.

"We just came out of the subway," he gasped. "Two cars just collided down there. It's bad. Just happened."

"We know," the young cop said, eyes wide, looking like a soldier who was seeing his first combat. "Fire Department's already on the way."

"They're going to need equipment to get in there."

"Thanks. We got this." The cop looked over Chris's shoulder and saw Zoey watching them. "Go find someplace safe and get off the streets."

Chris went back to get Zoey. Behind her was Bryant Park, the empty ice-skating rink and the monumental white marble temple that is the New York Public Library.

If they were going to catch Blanksy, they needed to move quickly. Without a word, they began walking.

"Do you think . . .?" Zoey began, but she stopped in mid-sentence as she followed Chris's gaze up Sixth Avenue, down a corridor of skyscrapers. Far down the avenue, it seemed as if someone was taking a giant eraser to the city. Before he even realized what he was seeing, Chris's eye was drawn to the skyline by a surreal sense that things were vanishing.

Upon closer inspection, it was clear what was happening. The city's power was going out. Chris could see the darkness rolling across the city like a tidal wave. At the far end of the avenue, one massive building after another went black. The blackout moved quickly toward Chris and Zoey as they stood motionless on the sidewalk, just watching it come.

Chris found himself bracing for the impact as if it were an actual wall of water racing at him.

And then it was upon them. Chris gripped Zoey's arm.

"Times Square is this way, isn't it?"

"Yeah," Zoey said. "Should be about eight blocks."

"We'd better hurry," Chris said. "It will probably take a while for the virus to fully install. Things are likely to get worse."

The city was lit only by the headlights of cars as Chris and Zoey walked along the Midtown sidewalk. New York was such a city of lights that it was unnerving to see it almost entirely dark.

Zoey looked up at the strip of sky visible between the skyscrapers. "Look at that," she said.

"What?"

"The stars."

"What about them?"

"You can actually see them. I don't think I've ever seen stars in New York City. It's like we're in a field in the middle of Nebraska or something."

Chris walked for a moment with his face to the sky like a marveling seven-year-old. "I think we'd better keep our eyes on what's ahead."

CHAPTER 44

As they hurried up Broadway toward Times Square, Chris knew that they were witnessing something new in the world—a city under full-on cyberattack. But, no matter what lay before them, he was not going to stop until they had found Blanksy, the architect of the destruction.

When he glanced back at Zoey, she was still staring up at the night sky as she walked.

"C'mon, Zoey. Focus."

"You don't understand," she said. "Look."

Chris saw that now there were more than stars filling the night sky. There were an unusual number of planes circling overhead—passenger planes. The flickering white and red navigation lights were clustered more tightly than he had ever seen before.

"I hope that doesn't mean what I think it does," Zoey said.

"Lurker must have knocked out the air traffic control systems at JFK and LaGuardia—just like Albuquerque."

"I hope they can divert them to another airport like Newark before there's a collision."

"If Newark is operational," Chris said. "Why don't you get CNN up on your smartphone? Maybe we can get a sense of what's happening."

They passed a bank ATM with a few people clustered in front of it. As they passed, Chris heard someone say, "It's not working at all."

"The virus has probably taken down the banks and financial institutions," Chris said to Zoey.

Zoey was concentrating on her phone. "Here. I've got a story. It's not just the banks. Wall Street has been hit, too. The New York Stock Exchange's systems have failed and it looks like the market won't open tomorrow."

"That could cause a crash in the global markets," Chris said. "Do they understand what's happening yet?"

"There's speculation that it's a cyberattack, but no one has confirmed it."

"There's more," she said. "The city's water filtration system is malfunctioning, so people are being advised to boil water until it comes back. Three train accidents—one in Grand Central Station. And there's a chemical plant in Jersey that's leaking toxic chlorine gas."

Chris picked up the pace. He and Zoey were nearly running now.

Everyone they saw on the street was also rushing, looking for a safe place. They seemed dazed. They didn't understand why the city had gone dark, but it wasn't hard to guess what every New Yorker was thinking in that moment as the news reports of the damage spread—this was the next September 11. For most residents of the city, there was a dark compartment of their subconscious where they kept the knowledge that it would happen again, and that it would probably be worse—if that was possible.

When they were still three blocks away from Times Square, they heard an explosion and saw a bright flash over lower Manhattan. There was no smoke or flames but a searing white light that faded and then erupted again, not to return.

"That was a transformer blowing out," Chris said.

"All of Manhattan must be dark now."

"Things are going to be down for a while," he said. "Transformers contain a lot of one-off equipment. It takes time to replace them."

Chris had read Department of Defense studies on the threat of cyberattacks and he knew that this was what their worst-case scenarios looked like. He also knew that each system failure would lead to a cascading chain of consequences. For example, a widespread and long-term power failure would disrupt the shipping and transportation systems that fueled New York. Modern inventory control systems were based on the ability to deliver goods just in time before they were needed. The gas and food shortages would begin very soon after the grid went down.

Chris recognized that there was one element from the DOD worst-case playbook that wasn't present yet, at least as far as he knew. He didn't mention it to Zoey. In fact, he didn't even want to allow himself to think about it.

CHAPTER 45

The Con Edison control room in Midtown Manhattan regulated the electrical power grid for nine million people over nearly seven hundred square miles. The place looked a little like the NASA Space Center, with a room full of technicians at computer monitors, all facing a giant display that consumed an entire wall. Even to Michael Hazlitt's untrained eye, it was apparent at a glance that Houston was having a problem. Every computer was manned, and supervisors were hovering over the shoulders of the technicians and moving from one station to next. It was like the controlled agitation of a jostled beehive.

Like everyone else in the room, Hazlitt and his partner kept glancing up at the "Big Board," which displayed a floor-to-ceiling grid of all of the transmission lines currently in service on the island of Manhattan. If one were to fail, then a red light would flash. Thankfully, there was no red showing on the board so far.

As soon as they received Bruen's call, Hazlitt and Falacci had wanted to set out for the W Hotel in pursuit of Blanksy. They were the agents closest to Times Square, but their bosses at Quantico had instructed them to stay at Con Edison to see if they could do anything more to help avert the impending crisis. Hazlitt had already received considerable credit for unveiling the hackers' fake help desk ploy, even though he had been clear that the idea had come from Bruen and Doucet.

Con Edison's data security team, working closely with the FBI's techies, was finally catching up with what Ed de Lamadrid must have uncovered on his own days earlier—the vulnerability in the Aspira system that Lurker had exploited. Lurker targeted Port 583, a "listening" point in the Aspira system that performed a function called Remote Procedure Call (RPC), enabling file sharing with other computers. Lurker would make contact with a potential host system and deliver a series of instructions that would cause the system to place the additional requests in a temporary stack known as a buffer. When the buffer overflowed after being bombarded with requests, Lurker was able to redirect the functioning of Port 583, giving Lurker access to the heart of the operating system, the "kernel." Once a hacker like Blanksy had remote control of a computer's kernel, he owned it.

This information was being shared with the agents by Ian McIlwane, Con Edison's IT director, who was clearly having the worst day of his professional life.

"We can see how the virus is installing now, but there's nothing that we can do to stop it, short of pulling the plug on the entire control system."

"Is that a viable option?" Hazlitt asked.

"No, it would be as certain to crash the grid as anything the virus could do," McIlwane said. "Even under normal circumstances, the grid can be fragile. Remember the 2003 Northeast blackout? It started with a tree falling on a sagging power line and it cascaded from there across eight states. And that tree—it was in Ohio."

McIlwane was a wiry, red-faced man whose default facial expression was a scowl. Under the pressure of the crisis, that scowl was screwed on so tightly that he looked like he was about to pull a muscle in his jaw. In a career-meltdown moment, Hazlitt knew that some men retreat into themselves. They stop working the problem and start spinning the postmortem. McIlwane still seemed to be working the problem, and that was something.

"Now that you know how the virus works, can't you develop a patch?" Falacci asked.

"We could develop a patch, but not in time to stop what's already in process," McIlwane said. "The entire control system is infected."

"So what's the plan for tonight?" Falacci asked. "There is a plan, right?"

Hazlitt knew the answer before it arrived. McIlwane shot his hands into his pockets and removed them just as quickly, a nervous tic. "We're experimenting with some quick fixes," he said. "It may be too late, but we're still pitching."

"What does that mean, exactly?" Hazlitt asked.

"It means that, realistically, our best shot at this point is that the virus just doesn't work as intended. And if it does work, then we'll just have to remediate the situation as best we can."

"That sounds pretty lame," Falacci said.

"Well, it's the best we can do," McIlwane said, his frustration showing.

"Any progress on the fake call center scam?" Hazlitt asked.

McIlwane shook his head. "No, they've pulled out. We have some IP addresses, but they're all dead ends, as expected. Your FBI team is working that."

Hazlitt, Falacci, and McIlwane were standing at the back of the control center when they heard the sound, and all three of them looked up simultaneously. It was a murmur rising from the technicians around the control room—the sound of bad news. When Hazlitt looked up at the Big Board, it was clear that what they had feared most was happening. Red lights flashed, starting on the right-hand side, which represented Harlem, and spreading quickly to the Upper East Side. There were scattered curses and exclamations from the Con Edison team, but nobody was at their keyboards anymore. Everyone was just standing and watching the disaster unfold.

Next, the red lights appeared on the left side of the board—lower Manhattan. It took no more than three minutes for the fields of red to converge on Midtown, and when the red wave passed over the location of the Con Ed headquarters, there was a queasy buzz and flicker as the lights went down for an instant before the backup generator kicked in. Although there were no windows in the control center, everyone in the room knew that outside, the entire island of Manhattan, from Battery Park to Harlem, had just been cast into complete and total darkness.

"It's a total blackout," McIlwane said, seemingly to himself.

"What now?" Hazlitt asked.

"We try to reinstall the operating system on all of the computers, but that's going to take a while."

"How long before the power's up again?"

"It could be hours, it could be days. It's impossible to know at this point. It depends on the extent of the damage to the infrastructure."

"How does that happen?"

Hazlitt's question was answered by a video feed that appeared in one corner of the Big Board. It was a crisp video image shot on a smartphone. It began with a shaky close-up of a young Con Edison field worker in a hard hat, holding out his camera at arm's length.

"This is Reynaldo Cruz and I'm at East Forty-Third and First. Power is down everywhere I can see—and there's a major fire here in Tudor City."

The image took a vertiginous swoop as Cruz turned his camera on what was before him. The screen filled with the historic Tudor City apartment buildings, home to more than five thousand residents and topped by the landmark "Tudor City" sign looking down on East Forty-Second Street. The entire area around the base of the towers was engulfed in flames. The Chrysler Building glinted in the background like a fifties fantasy of a rocket ship.

"It started in the shops here, but it's spreading to the apartment buildings," Cruz shouted. "There's a downed power line that caused it. If a fire crew doesn't get here soon, the whole block could go. The residents are being evacuated."

Hazlitt and Falacci were mere bystanders now as the Con Ed team sprang into frantic action. Most of the technicians were on cell phones, coordinating with crews in the field, NYPD, NYFD, and reports from observers around the city. Some video screens on the Big Board were tuned to CNN and local news stations, which were already beginning to report the story, first from anchor desks and soon from reporters in the street.

After a couple of tries, Hazlitt managed to get a call through to US Cyber Command headquarters, which was operated by the Defense Department and charged with cyberspace defense. The director that he had spoken with had a broader view of the scope of the event, and he sounded shaken. All of Manhattan and a good portion of New Jersey were completely without power. Workers were stranded in high-rise buildings. Electric-powered gas pumps at gas stations weren't operating. There were massive traffic jams and traffic accidents everywhere. The air traffic control systems at JFK and LaGuardia were down. Midair collisions had been avoided thus far, but just barely. A chemical plant in Newark had been compromised and was emitting a toxic cloud of chlorine gas that was leading to evacuations. Fortunately, the winds had not sent the cloud across the river into Manhattan yet.

Most distressing of all, the officer on the other end of the line said something about "unidentified complications" at the Indian Point nuclear power plant, which was on the Hudson River just south of Peekskill, thirty-eight miles north of Manhattan.

"What sort of complications?" Hazlitt asked.

"It may still be nothing, and you don't need to know, anyway. You are not to repeat that to anyone, you understand? We don't want to create a panic."

"Got it." Hazlitt had more questions for Cyber Command, but he didn't have a chance to ask them—the line went dead.

"What are we supposed to do now? Just stand around and watch as everything goes to hell?" Falacci asked.

Falacci was right. Now that the blackout had descended, they no longer served a useful purpose at Con Edison. Hazlitt didn't want to disobey a standing order from Quantico, but if Blanksy was at the W Hotel in Times Square, he couldn't let the opportunity go. After an attack like this, if he had any sense, the hacker would go to ground, and it could be months or years before they had another opportunity like this one.

Hazlitt checked his watch. The call that Bruen had placed from Brooklyn had come in only twenty minutes ago. Bruen and Doucet most likely hadn't reached the hotel yet. Other agents were undoubtedly on their way to Times Square, but with all of the chaos of that night, who knew when they would arrive? Hazlitt and his partner were still probably the agents closest to the hotel, and their window of opportunity to catch the hacker was probably closing fast.

"C'mon, we're getting out of here," Hazlitt said. "We're going to Times Square. And if they ask you about this later, and they will, just tell them that I never told you that we were ordered to stay here. This one's on me."

CHAPTER 46

Chris had visited Times Square innumerable times but, as they walked up Broadway past West Forty-Second Street, he had never seen it like this.

Instead of being visually assaulted by walls of shimmering LCD screens, Times Square was in near darkness. The primary source of light was a van that was on fire in the middle of Broadway. The flames flickered in the plate glass windows of the stores. A few cars had their headlights on, but most had been abandoned in the streets. There was an orange glow on the horizon to the east in the direction of the neighborhood known as Tudor City. Chris knew that if the fire was that visible from Times Square, it must be enormous.

It seemed that the city had been returned to the natural world. Times Square was like a long, dark canyon bounded by the sheer faces of the surrounding towers, which deepened the shadows. An NYPD helicopter hovered overhead and strafed a spotlight over the thinning crowd in the square. The streets were no longer streaming with cars and taxis. When the traffic lights went out, collisions had clogged the intersections. Drivers had abandoned their cars in the middle of the street rather than attempt to drive in the chaos, bringing traffic to a complete standstill.

Chris and Zoey walked toward the center of Times Square and the red bleachers that adjoined the TKTS booth. A beer bottle shattered on the sidewalk nearby, thrown by some people who were sitting and drinking on the bleachers. Chris tried to make them out in the gloom, but it appeared that the bottle hadn't been directed at them. An Indian cabbie sat in a yellow cab watching them pass, apparently unwilling to abandon his car and his livelihood to vandals. A policeman strode across Broadway, heading east. Chris wondered why there wasn't more of a police presence on the streets, but then he realized that all available resources were probably being dedicated to combating the blaze in Tudor City or assisting the injured passengers from the subway car crash.

Four figures emerged from the darkness before them covered in makeup and faux animal skins. The mutant band consisted of a woman costumed as a cheetah and three men who were attired as a gibbon, and the head and tail, respectively, of a giraffe. Apparently, the cast of *The Lion King* had fled their darkened theater.

Chris and Zoey hurried onward to the W Hotel. The hotel's restaurant, Blue Fin, was located on the ground floor with big windows looking out on Times Square.

The burning van was in the middle of Broadway directly in front of the hotel, the flames still crackling, casting flickering reflections on the windows. If someone was watching from inside the restaurant, it was impossible to see them.

Chris and Zoey observed the entrance to the restaurant for a while from behind a parked car.

"Do you think he's in there?" Zoey asked.

"Probably. And if he is in there, he'll probably have a gun."

"What's the plan?"

"Well, from this vantage point we can watch the door of the restaurant and the hotel entrance on Forty-Seventh. I don't think he could leave without us spotting him. I'm going to call Hazlitt and Falacci, see how long it's going to take them to get over here. We know *they* have guns."

"Oh, they have guns all right," Zoey said. "And they'll probably use them to shoot at us."

Chris dialed Hazlitt, but the line was busy, or maybe the cell towers were down. He tried sending a text: "We're outside the W watching for Blanksy. Can you get here?"

He watched his phone's display, but there was no response. With the city in the state that it was in, there was no telling where the FBI agents were, or when they might be able to make it to Times Square.

"Have you ever seen anything like this?" Zoey asked.

"All of Manhattan must be down."

They heard a footstep and turned.

The first thing Chris saw was the TEC-9 semiautomatic pistol pointed at them. It was in the hands of a man in his late thirties with a short, neatly trimmed beard, mustache, receding hairline, and close-cropped brown hair. In his other hand, he carried a green nylon Nike gym bag. The man was wearing a brown leather jacket over a burnt orange T-shirt, and he was smiling at Chris and Zoey like he knew them. The smile seemed to say that they should know him, too.

"Nice night, isn't it?" The voice was high and slightly adenoidal, and Chris felt certain that he had heard it somewhere before.

Chris inched his hand toward the computer bag that held the Taser.

"I wouldn't do that. TEC-9 beats Taser every time."

Chris suddenly knew where he had heard the voice—on the other side of the door of Pietr Middendorf's apartment in Amsterdam and in a series of phone calls. "Blanksy," he said.

CHAPTER 47

"I was wondering how long it would take you to recognize me," Blanksy said. "When I spoke to you as Enigma, I used a filter to disguise my voice."

Chris concentrated on how Blanksy held the gun, looking for an opportunity.

"C'mon, toss that bag over," Blanksy said. "Don't make me shoot you here."

Chris slowly slid the computer bag to Blanksy.

Blanksy smiled. "Zoey. Nice to finally put a face to the name."

"You've moved down in the world," Zoey said. "Last time we met, you were just a thief. Now you're a mass murderer."

He wasn't as young as Chris had imagined from their phone conversations, and he could see now that the Blanksy he had known had been a complete fabrication. Blanksy didn't look like a killer or even a vandal. He looked like the office IT guy or any thirtysomething NYU graduate student you would find in a coffee shop on Bleecker Street. If he was walking on the street in the middle of this turmoil, he probably wouldn't draw a second glance from the police. However, graduate students didn't usually look so comfortable carrying automatic weapons.

"Turn around," Blanksy said. "Both of you."

"Can't look us in the eye?" Chris said.

"I'm not going to shoot you, at least not yet," Blanksy said. Still holding the gun in his right hand, Blanksy patted them down with his left. He wasn't able to do a very thorough job, and Chris was glad that he missed the thin cell phone in the inside pocket of his jacket.

"Is there anyone with you?" Blanksy asked.

"No, we came alone," Chris said.

"Maybe so, but I have to assume that others will follow, including those two FBI agents." He pointed with the gun toward the hotel, "Let's go. This way."

Blanksy marched Chris and Zoey into the restaurant. As they passed the burning van, Chris felt the heat on his face and smelled the gasoline. He looked around to see if anyone was observing them enter the building, but no one was.

It took a minute to make things out in the gloom, because the blazing car fire outside had dazzled his eyes. As his vision adjusted, he could see that the restaurant was a large, high-ceilinged room with modern, dark wood tables and booths on either side. To the right was an open kitchen.

"How did you know to find me here?" Blanksy asked.

"Your friend with the Russian accent. We found the hotel's number on his cell phone."

Blanksy nodded. "With a plan this big, you know that something is going to go wrong, but you just never know what."

"But it only takes the one thing, doesn't it?" Chris said.

Blanksy directed them through the restaurant to the hotel lobby, an expansive room with modern furniture in neon colors that were muted in the gloom. The lobbies of W Hotels were always dimly lit, so all the place was missing was some well-placed halogen spotlights and a few black-clad staff and it could have been business as usual.

There were still a handful of lost-looking guests wandering through the lobby, trying to find missing friends or a safe place to wait out the blackout. A member of the hotel staff was ushering the last of the stragglers out of the hotel, urging them to take refuge in one of several impromptu shelters that had been established until the power returned.

Blanksy leaned in close and shoved the muzzle of the gun into Chris's spine. "If you want these people to die, just try calling out to them."

They entered a stairwell near the elevators and climbed the stairs to the second floor. Blanksy held a flashlight in one hand and the gun in the other.

Chris thought he knew what Blanksy was thinking. He probably wasn't certain whether they had alerted law enforcement to the location, but he had to assume that they had. He had probably considered taking them elsewhere, but that was risky. The agents wouldn't know what Blanksy looked like, but they would certainly know Chris and Zoey. If he walked them through Times Square, it would be like wearing a sign. His safest bet was to keep them out of view and take them someplace where they wouldn't be immediately discovered, like a room upstairs. Then, after he killed them, he could stroll out into the night like he was just another hotel guest.

"Room 217," Blanksy said. They walked slowly down the dark hallway and stopped in front of the door.

Blanksy produced a plastic card key and tossed it at Zoey's feet. "Open it."

Zoey leaned down and picked up the key, then she let it dangle at her side, rubbing it against her pants pocket. It was an unnatural movement, and Chris noticed it. *Smart girl*, he thought. *She's trying to demagnetize the key.*

Blanksy had also missed Zoey's cell phone, which was inside the pocket. Zoey inserted the key in the electronic lock and the tiny LED flashed red. The door locks were powered by internal batteries, so they were still functioning.

"No go," Zoey said. "You want to try it?"

"No, that won't be necessary," Blanksy said. "I have another copy." Blanksy extended his hand. "Give me the phone."

Zoey handed it over, then Blanksy gave her another key. "If you demagnetize this one," Blanksy said, "I'll make sure you regret it."

Zoey nodded, neither admitting nor denying. She tried the other key. The LED flashed green and the lock clicked.

They stepped inside the room, followed by Blanksy. "Sit," he said, motioning to two chairs by the window.

On the other side of the room, Blanksy turned his back on them for a moment to rummage through the nylon gym bag. While Blanksy was digging through the contents of the bag, Chris reached into his jacket pocket, removed his cell phone, and clicked two buttons. The first button speed-dialed Chris's home answering machine. The second button activated the phone's speaker. Chris quickly slid the phone back into his jacket pocket.

When Blanksy turned around, he had four plastic zip ties in his hand, which he used to bind their hands and feet. Then Blanksy took a seat on the bed across from them, the gun resting across his knees and the flashlight propped beside him so that it pointed at them.

Fear and adrenaline clouded Chris's thoughts, as powerful and toxic as chemo. But he wouldn't show that. He couldn't show that.

"I think I know what the virus is," Chris said, figuring that the longer he talked, the longer they stayed alive. He hadn't had a chance to check to see if the phone had connected to the answering machine, so he had no idea if their conversation was recording. With the power outage, the nearest cell tower could be down. Or maybe the speaker wouldn't pick up their voices through his jacket. But most of all, Chris hoped that the phone didn't give him away with a squawk of feedback or dial tone.

"So this is where you try to keep me talking and I tell you all about my plans, is that it?"

"I've followed you to Europe and back," Chris said. "I think I'm entitled to at least a little explanation."

"Entitled? No. But I am curious to see how much you've managed to figure out," Blanksy said. He probably assumed that anything that Chris knew had been shared with the FBI. Blanksy wanted to know how close the FBI was to catching him, or at least understanding what he was up to. "All right, I'll play. Tell me what you know," he said.

Chris spoke slowly. "The virus—we're calling it Lurker— exploits a vulnerability in the Aspira operating system."

"Obvious," Blanksy said. "Am I wasting my time here?"

Chris wasn't going to tell Blanksy everything he knew, but he needed to keep him talking. "The coding of the virus reflects more than one team of programmers. Some of it looks like the work of an individual, like you or one of your crew. But other segments are very sophisticated and labor-intensive, the sort of thing that probably could only have been produced by a large team of coders working under rigorous protocols—a government-sponsored team."

Blanksy gave a slight nod, encouraging him to continue.

"The virus was programmed to erase itself seventy-two hours after activation, apparently to ensure that it didn't cause too much collateral damage. This was intended to take down a specific target, but it wasn't meant to cause unlimited destruction. It was a controlled burn."

"And what do you gather from that?"

"That the virus was developed by not just any government, but by a nation that views itself as a good actor on the world stage, one that would have trouble justifying unleashing a destructive virus on a global scale."

"And which government might that be?"

"I'm thinking the US, perhaps Israel. And since you dragged us to the grave of an Iranian dissident, I have to think that Lurker is an adaptation of the Stuxnet virus."

"Ding, ding, ding. We have a winner," Blanksy said. "Our virus is a variation on Stuxnet. Stuxnet was designed to stick to the systems used by Iran's nuclear program and delete after three weeks—but that part didn't work quite as designed. The virus malfunctioned and started spreading through the Internet, and I happened to acquire a copy. From there, it just took a little clever coding to repurpose the virus, give it a new payload. Now the NSA can see how they like being the target of cyberwarfare. They should have known better."

"How so?"

"You fire a missile at someone and the bomb is destroyed on impact. But you use a virus to wage cyberwarfare, like the US did against Iran, and the weapon, and its code, is out there in the world for the taking. And we took it. It wasn't that hard to anticipate that this would be the next move."

"You know, some of us used to have a drinking game," Zoey said. "Every time you used the term cyberwarfare in one of your posts, we took a shot."

Blanksy gave a tight, humorless smile. "I would think you would get this."

"Why's that?"

"Because hacktivism is a pathetic joke," Blanksy said.

"I happen to like jokes," Zoey said.

"Making some satirical jab at Centinela Bank may impress your little band of geek friends, but it's a pointless exercise. It changes nothing. What's happened tonight changes everything."

"Maybe so," Zoey said, "but with my work, no one gets killed, either."

Blanksy shrugged. "In a day or two, we'll see how many people actually died tonight. Even in a worst case, it'll be nothing compared to Hiroshima or Nagasaki—and the US government had no real qualms about that. It was the only way to convey that particular message—it's the same with the message that we're delivering tonight."

"Guys like you always think they have a message but, and I hate to break it to you, the only message you're sending is that you're a coward and a murderer."

"You're lucky to be here at all, Zoey."

"How do you figure?"

"We really should have burned you after you had outlived your usefulness with those phishing schemes. You've been on borrowed time for quite a while now."

Then, in an aside to Chris, he added, "You do know she's worked with us, don't you?"

"She told me all about it," Chris said.

"A relationship based on trust," Blanksy said. "I must say I'm oddly touched."

"You killed Ed de Lamadrid, didn't you?" Chris leaned forward in his chair.

"Well, I didn't do it personally, if that's what you mean," Blanksy said. "But I didn't expect you to have a computer forensic lab working with you while you were on the run. I needed to make sure that you stayed a step or two behind. You were friends?"

"Yeah, we were friends," Chris said. "And I'm going to make sure that you pay for what you've done."

"That's bold talk for someone in your position," Blanksy said. "Look at you, maintaining your game face even when it's clear that it's all over."

"So what do you get out of this attack?" Zoey asked. "It has to be about money. Despite all the talk, it was always that way with you."

Blanksy paused, deciding whether or not to share. "Sure, I'm going to make money from this. But there's also a larger principle at work. Highly targeted, destructive viruses are now in the hands of a few of the more technologically sophisticated nations. The Stuxnet and Flame viruses are proof of that. We're going to level that playing field. My crew has simply adapted one of those viruses and repurposed it. The result is something new in the world—a weapon of mass destruction that can be launched anonymously. Tonight's attack is the unveiling of a new product, and it's going to be like the iPad of terrorism—every radical fringe group is going to wake up tomorrow and want one."

"If they pay your price," Chris said.

"Like the iPad, prices will come down over time, but for now you're going to have to pay a premium to be the first kid on your block. The bidding opens next week. I've already met with one of the interested parties earlier this evening. When they saw what the virus could do, they wanted to make a payment of earnest money to go to the front of the line." Blanksy nodded at the gym bag at his feet.

"So how much money is in the bag?"

"Five hundred thousand. Just a down payment. The final bid is going to be much higher. And then there are the add-on services."

"You need to find the vulnerabilities for them," Zoey said.

"Exactly," Blanksy said. "As sophisticated as the virus is, you can't just flip a switch and launch an attack. You need to set the table, find the vulnerabilities in the target systems that it will exploit, make tweaks in the programming to ensure maximum impact."

"Black hat IT consulting," Chris said. "I suppose you'd consider it naïve to worry about the innocent people who could be harmed?"

"I sort of take the opposite view," Blanksy said.

Chris smiled grimly. "What a surprise."

"I think these new weapons are . . . democratic. Force is still pretty much the only way to make your voice heard in this world. The biggest, richest nations, like the US and China, have the greatest force and are able to impose their will upon everyone else. How does a smaller nation or political cause have that big a voice? One way is by developing a nuclear weapons capability, but that's labor-intensive, expensive, and difficult to accomplish in secret. These superviruses present a much lower barrier to entry."

"And that barrier to entry is you," Chris said.

"For now, yes," Blanksy said. "You pay my price and you get that strike capability. I have no illusions that I will have this market cornered forever, but I do now, and I think I should be able to do very well for myself."

"Terrorism is not a first amendment issue," Chris said. "The people who will want to buy this from you are going to be irresponsible killers, not idealists."

"Who am I to make those moral distinctions?" Blanksy said.

"Exactly," Zoey said.

"I think we'd better wrap this up now," Blanksy said, raising his gun and pointing it at Chris. "Do they know that I'm behind the attack?" he asked.

"Who's they?" Chris responded.

Blanksy fired a shot into the chair cushion that Chris was sitting on. "I think I've been very patient so far. But please."

"They have the name Blanksy," Chris said. "And they have the name that you gave me before—Jay Hartigan. But that's not really you, is it?"

"No, it isn't."

"Then who are you?"

"I think what you really mean is 'Why you?'"

Chris nodded.

"I guess I should tell you now," Blanksy said. "This is all going to be over soon and if I'm the only one who knows, it won't be very satisfying for either of us, now will it?"

CHAPTER 48

Michael Hazlitt and Sam Falacci entered Times Square on foot after their taxi was stranded in a massive traffic jam on Park Avenue. Hazlitt observed that the city sounded different that night. The white noise of cars hissing by in the streets was noticeable in its absence. Sirens wailed urgently from all corners of the city in response to fires and assorted mayhem. This is what blacked-out London must have been like during the Blitz after the bombs had fallen.

Hazlitt's phone buzzed and a text message appeared: "We're outside the W right now watching for Blanksy. Can you get here?"

Hazlitt typed out a response. "We'll be there in ten minutes. DON'T DO ANYTHING." There was no reply text, and Hazlitt wondered whether the message had been received. During a major power outage like this one, cell towers usually have enough backup battery power to last for a few hours. But it was also possible that the Lurker virus had directly attacked cell towers, taking them completely out of service.

"You still think they're responsible for the attack?" Falacci asked.

"Not my call," Hazlitt replied.

"Let's just hope that we aren't left with the pointy end of the stick when the dust settles," Falacci said.

Hazlitt chose not to comment on the mixed metaphors. "How do you figure that?"

"Well, it was our job to catch Enigma—or Blanksy—or whatever the hell you want to call him," Falacci said. "The heads of the Bureau, DOD, and DHS will all be looking for a scapegoat. You know that someone's going to take the fall for this, and I'll bet there are bosses at the Bureau who are already liking us for that role."

"Not if we catch him tonight."

A helicopter passed so low overhead that he felt the breeze from its rotors. Probably headed to the Tudor City fire.

Hazlitt had been convinced for some time that Bruen had nothing to do with the cyberattack, but he couldn't prove it, and he certainly wasn't about to stake his career on a hunch. The physical evidence linking Bruen to the attack remained overwhelming. Bruen's assistance in the hunt for Blanksy didn't fit the narrative, but that might be dismissed as evidence of a conflicted mind rather than an innocent man.

Dodging among stalled cars, they searched for Bruen and Doucet in Times Square, but they were not to be found. Either they had moved on or, more likely, they were inside. Hazlitt hoped they weren't trying to capture Blanksy on their own, which was a sure way to get themselves killed and send Blanksy running.

Moving single file with guns drawn, Hazlitt in the lead, they approached the entrance to the restaurant, sticking close to the wall. He glanced quickly inside. Falacci raised his eyebrows in query.

"Too dark to see anything," Hazlitt said.

"Are we going in?"

Hazlitt tested the door to the restaurant, which was unlocked. "Yeah."

Hazlitt stepped into the entryway and surveyed the room, but the place was empty.

Falacci joined him in front of the reservation desk and took a handful of mints from a tray. "What now?"

"There are hundreds of rooms and more than fifty stories. It would take forever to search this place. Maybe the guest register will tell us something."

Most of the hotel staff were gone but a single desk clerk remained, escorting a family out of the hotel to one of the designated shelters with a backup generator. The clerk, a rail-thin kid with artfully disheveled hair, made some noises about protecting privacy but showed the agents a hard-copy printout of the guest list after they flashed their badges. Hazlitt and Falacci split the list in half and scanned the guest logs.

After about five minutes of poring over the records, Hazlitt said, "I think I've got it. Look who's registered to Room 216—A. Turing, like the British mathematician and cryptographer Alan Turing. As in Bletchley Park. As in the Enigma machine."

"That seems pretty obvious, doesn't it?" Falacci said. "He must think we're idiots."

"Maybe, or maybe he's expecting us."

At that moment, they heard a single gunshot from somewhere in the building.

"Hard to tell, but that didn't sound too far away," Hazlitt said.

Hazlitt led the way to the stairwell and they climbed the first flight. It was pitch-black on the stairs and he wished that they'd brought a flashlight.

There was a brief hiss and a flicker, followed by the pungent smell of sulfur. Hazlitt turned around to see Falacci lighting a couple of matches from a matchbook bearing the restaurant's name and a stylized blue fish logo.

Falacci reached in his pocket and produced a handful of matchbooks. "Here, help yourself," he said. "I just wish I had the cigarettes to go with them."

They pushed through the security door and emerged on the second floor. By the light of a few more matches, they saw that the long corridor was empty. Falacci's matchbook burned down until he threw it to the floor with a soft curse. When they were returned to darkness, Hazlitt saw a glimmer ahead in the hallway from under the door of a room. There was definitely a light on inside.

Hazlitt tapped his partner on the shoulder and motioned for silence, indicating the light. Falacci nodded. They advanced quietly down the carpeted hallway until they were at the door of the room that was casting the pale glow.

Room 216.

CHAPTER 49

"So this is personal, isn't it?" Chris asked, squinting into the flashlight beam. He and Zoey were sitting in Room 217 in a pair of blue velour chairs. Blanksy stood in the middle of the room a few feet away with the automatic pistol trained on them.

"Of course it is," Blanksy said. "If it wasn't personal, I would have just killed you a long time ago."

"So are you going to tell him, or is this part of the torture?" Zoey asked.

Chris knew he would have to make a lunge for the gun at some point. But the opportunity wasn't presenting itself and, if he timed it wrong, they would be dead before he could get to his feet.

Blanksy paused and rubbed his neatly groomed beard. He'd clearly waited a long time to have this conversation, but he didn't seem satisfied with how it was going. Revenge is a dish that never tastes quite as good you thought when you ordered it, no matter how it's served. Undeterred, Blanksy forged ahead.

"More than twenty years have passed, and I know I look different now, but I somehow thought you would know me on sight."

"Sorry to disappoint you." Twenty years. Chris must have known Blanksy when he was still just a kid.

On some level, Chris knew instantly what was coming next, but he couldn't, or wouldn't, formulate the thought. He felt like a swimmer who had a premonition of the shark rising beneath his dog-paddling feet.

"Maybe this will help," Blanksy said, opening up his wallet and removing a tattered square of lined notebook paper. Blanksy unfolded the document, which was coming apart at each fold, and handed it to Chris. Chris accepted the thing, which was as fragile as a paper doll.

When Chris recognized the careful, childish cursive writing of his sixteen-year-old self, still tracking the curlicues and whorls of school handwriting exercises, he knew without a doubt who was standing before him. He had existed for so long in Chris's memory that he had almost forgotten that he was an actual person.

"Dylan," Chris said.

Chris looked at Blanksy/Dylan with new eyes, struggling to reconcile the slightly bug-eyed, hyperactive fourteen-year-old that he had played Risk and Tetris with, and the twisted middle-aged man that stood before him.

"You remember that letter, don't you?"

"Sure I do—Dylan."

Chris had written the letter to Dylan after he had already moved to Sacramento, pouring out his guilt over the fact that Josh Woodrell was in a juvenile detention facility and they were both free to carry on with their lives. When he was an emotional sixteen-year-old, Chris had still been capable of sharing all his darkest, most personal thoughts with another person. Chris's parents, and his lawyer, would never have allowed him to write such an incriminating letter, but they didn't know it existed. When Dylan didn't respond, Chris wondered if the letter had even reached its destination.

"It reads like a confession, doesn't it?"

"I still think about Josh every day."

Dylan's features contorted. "That's a very easy thing to say, but you should have been there in jail with him. It would have made it easier on him, and it probably would have reduced his sentence."

"It was the biggest mistake of my life."

"A mistake you never paid for."

"The same could be said for you. You could have come forward."

Dylan's anger flared and he brandished the gun at Chris. "I was fourteen years old!" he shouted, and Chris suddenly recognized in the man the petulant boy that he had known. "I worshipped you two—especially Josh. I would have followed you into anything. When it came to hacking that DOD database, I was just tagging along. And after we were caught, I looked to you. They would have gone easier on me because I was only fourteen. I probably would have gotten probation, at most. But I couldn't bring myself to put you behind bars. Not if you weren't willing to do it yourself. Over the years, though, my attitude changed."

"Even at fourteen you knew what we were doing."

"You really want to pursue this avenue, Chris? Do you?"

"What do you want from me? I wish I could change what happened back then. I really do." Chris felt an odd kinship with Dylan because they had both spent most of their lives cauterizing the same wound. He saw that Dylan was a pitiable figure, but he couldn't afford to feel pity—not for someone who had killed so many people and was capable of killing so many more.

"I've followed your career. First, you prosecute cybercrimes for the DOJ, then in private practice you hunt down hackers on behalf of big corporations. Your life has been dedicated to punishing kids who are exactly like we were back in '87. It's an affront to Josh's memory."

"You talk about Josh like you know what happened to him."

"He died eight months ago. And you killed him. That's what brought me here."

"What are you talking about?"

"Josh and I hacked together for more than ten years. He contacted me when he got out of juvie and I helped him get clean, got him into rehab. With his record, he couldn't find a decent job, even after he was straight, so we started hacking for real. No more kid stuff, we were doing it for the money, and we did very well. It sure beat repairing crappy old desktops. Josh was his old self again. You remember what he was like."

"Yeah, I do. But why do you say that I killed him?"

"It's almost as if you killed him twice. The second time was about a year ago. You were investigating a fraudulent tax return scheme in San Diego for your client Firefly."

Chris remembered the incident well. A client's employees had sold thousands of Social Security numbers and other personal information to fraudsters who used it to file $5 million worth of falsified tax returns. The criminals collected tax refunds before the real taxpayers had an opportunity to claim them. The IRS made it all too easy for the identity thieves, because refunds can be mailed out as gift cards upon request. All the thieves had to do was submit fake returns and change-of-address forms for the taxpayers and wait for the funds to arrive in the form of highly fungible gift cards. Chris had led the client's investigation of the incident, sharing the findings with the IRS and an assistant US attorney, who had prosecuted and convicted three members of the ring.

"So you and Josh had something to do with that?"

"It was one of our operations. Josh was one of the three convicted."

That statement stopped Chris for a moment. "But I saw the information that we turned over to the AUSA. His name wasn't in that file."

"He created a new identity when we got serious about hacking. Just another firewall to protect himself. The feds eventually saw through it, but by that time you'd moved on. You never did go back to read the transcripts of the case, did you?"

"No, I'm not a prosecutor anymore. My job ends when I've helped the client deal with the threat." He paused. "So what happened to Josh in prison?"

"Well, he was a stand-up guy to the end. He could have cut a deal and turned on me, but he didn't. But he started using again almost immediately. He said that he'd gotten a big dose of reality, so he needed an equally big dose of his reality suppressant. Three weeks into his sentence he overdosed in his cell."

"I didn't even know it was him," Chris said.

"You put him behind bars twice, and the second time it killed him. I couldn't just let you walk away from that, could I?"

"If it hadn't been me, it would have been someone else. You two were stealing from innocent people. You were bound to get caught."

"Sure, it could have been someone else," Dylan said. "But it wasn't someone else, it was you. We were all friends once, and you don't turn on your friends. I knew then that you had to pay for your sins."

Chris wanted to keep Dylan talking. "One thing I don't understand. Why would Sarah do this? And why wouldn't she just cut a deal now that she's been caught?"

"Sarah has her own reasons. She lost a brother in Afghanistan. An Afghan soldier that he was training turned a gun on him. They were close and she took it very, very hard. She blamed her brother's death on wrongheaded US foreign policy. She thought it would be poetic justice to take a weapon of US intervention like Stuxnet and turn it back against its makers, sort of like what happened to her brother. Sarah is a zealot, maybe even more so than I am. She'll never crack."

"You went to an awful lot of trouble," Chris said, leaning forward in his chair. "Planting Sarah at the firm. Framing me for the cyberattacks. Leading me to Europe and back. Was it really worth it?"

"After Josh died, I spent a lot of time thinking about what should happen to you. I figured that the worst thing I could do to you is ruin your precious reputation. You like to think you're fighting crime, but that's not really what you're about. You get paid by giant companies like BlueCloud to do their dirty work."

"No one likes to have their property stolen," Chris said.

"I think I once told you the same thing," Zoey added.

"The point," Dylan said, nearly taking the bait, "is that if I let you live, you're going to spend the rest of your life in a federal prison as a convicted terrorist. Even if I kill you right now, you'll always be known as a terrorist."

"The truth will eventually come out. It usually does," Chris said.

"The truth?" Dylan said, nearly shouting. "You're still talking about the truth like it belongs to *you*?"

Even in the gloom, Chris thought he saw Dylan's face redden as he ran a hand through his hair. Dylan was growing increasingly agitated. He was working up to shooting them.

"I think you completely missed the point of my story," Dylan said, squeezing the trigger.

The air in the room seemed to explode and Chris felt a searing pain in his thigh as he fell forward, landing hard on the carpeted floor, still bound at the hands and feet. He felt blood spreading warmly down his leg.

"I want you to tell me that you understand that you were responsible for Josh Woodrell's death," Dylan said, more calmly now. "Hey, that's a lot of blood. I think I may have hit an artery."

Zoey struggled violently against her ties, leaving red welts on her wrists. "Tell him what he wants," she said to Chris.

"I understand," Chris said through clenched teeth.

"What do you understand?"

"That I was responsible for Josh Woodrell's death."

"*Thank* you," Dylan said with a touch of mock exasperation. "Now I have to get ready for our guests."

Dylan helped Chris to his feet and pushed him back into the chair, a move that only highlighted their physical disparity. Chris was bigger and at least six inches taller than Dylan, but with a bullet in his leg and his hands and feet bound, he had little opportunity to use that physical advantage. He nearly passed out when he put just a little bit of weight on the injured leg.

Dylan backed away from Chris and Zoey, the gun and the flashlight still pointed at them. He entered the hallway, then produced a plastic card key and opened the door to Room 216 across the hall. Dylan set the lit flashlight down on the floor in Room 216, then returned to the hallway and shut the door. The flashlight was the only artificial light around and it cast a very visible glow through the gap beneath the door of Room 216.

Back in Room 217, Dylan went to the bathroom and returned with two white washcloths. He shoved the washcloths into the mouths of Chris and Zoey. Without the flashlight, the room was in absolute darkness, so Dylan opened the curtains and let a little pale winter moonlight into the room. As Chris's eyes adjusted, he saw that Dylan was sitting on the bed in the center of the room, with the TEC-9 on his lap. From that position, he could target either them or the door.

The hotel was absolutely silent, with none of the sounds of a building that has electricity—no thrumming aircondi-tioners, rumbling elevators, or chattering television sets. That made it easier to hear the low whispering of two male voices approaching in the hallway. Chris thought he heard a muffled curse.

The whispering stopped, but the footsteps continued. It had to be Hazlitt and Falacci. Chris could visualize them approaching the light emanating from under the door, both assuming that Blanksy was holding them hostage inside Room 216, when they were actually across the hall in 217.

Dylan stood up and approached the closed door. An auto-matic like the TEC-9 could blast right through the flimsy hotel room door. He raised his eyebrows at them in a way that seemed to say, *This is exciting, isn't it?* He leaned in close to the door, listening intently for something, maybe the sound of a hand on the doorknob of Room 216.

As Dylan raised the gun to fire through the door, Chris swung his elbow and knocked a ceramic lamp off the table that sat next to his chair. To Chris, who had been straining to hear any sound in the silence, it was as loud as a grenade.

Dylan started to pivot toward Chris and Zoey, but then he thought better of it and began firing into the hallway. The sound was deafening as the TEC-9 punched inch-wide holes in the door of Room 217, sending a spray of splinters into the air like a wood chipper.

CHAPTER 50

Hazlitt lightly tested the door but, as expected, it wouldn't turn. He knew the electric door locks would still be working, but he had to try. He could try kicking down the door after a few bullets in the doorframe, but there was no element of surprise there, and that wasn't as easy as it appeared in the TV cop shows.

Hazlitt motioned for Falacci to get ready. But before he could make a move, there was a crashing sound from the room across the hall. Hazlitt spun around and ducked reflexively. An instant later, deafening noise in the hallway. Six or seven shots in rapid succession. Behind him, close at hand. *Had they gone to the wrong room?*

He saw Falacci put a hand to the wall, as if he had just been running and needed to take a breather. Then his partner collapsed in the hallway.

Hazlitt wasn't thinking clearly. It was that feeling you get when you've just been in a car accident. Your neck has whipped forward with the collision and you are suddenly brought up short by how fragile you are.

He saw a small stain on the front of his shirt at the left shoulder and wondered if he had spilled something earlier. He touched it and felt a spreading wetness.

Then his knees gave way and he went down.

The side of his face was flattened into the hallway carpeting and he found himself staring at his partner's right pants leg, which was directly in front of him. Falacci was not moving.

Hazlitt had been shot once before, in a convenience store parking lot in Portland, Oregon, five years ago. The simple thought that formed in his mind was the same one that came to him then as he blacked out, like a last air bubble escaping the lips of a drowning man: *So this is how it ends.*

CHAPTER 51

Dylan fired two more rounds and listened for any sounds of movement in the hallway. Then he picked up the gym bag, opened what was left of the door, and looked out to assess the damage.

Chris could see one body lying facedown in the hallway. His stomach turned when he saw it was Falacci. Chris couldn't tell if he was dead or just badly wounded.

Dylan glanced about with quick, jerky movements, looking for the second body. Apparently, there wasn't one.

A shot rang out in the hallway. Then another. Chris had a clear image in his mind of what he thought was happening. Hazlitt had probably taken cover at the end of the hallway after the hail of automatic weapon fire and was now advancing on Dylan, taking aim and steadily firing as he came. Framed by the doorway, Dylan was trying to fire back but his gun was jammed. Dylan only had a moment to decide what to do, and he decided to run. More gunshots.

Chris and Zoey had crouched down next to the bed to avoid stray bullets and stared at the empty, shattered doorway, not sure if it would reveal Dylan, returning with his TEC-9 blazing, or Hazlitt. Or maybe they were both dead.

After a long moment, it was Hazlitt who lurched into the doorway. The agent's shirt was covered in blood and he gripped the doorframe with one hand like it was his primary structural support. Hazlitt looked into the room and saw that they were okay. He nodded and slipped down to the floor.

Chris was too badly injured to move in his bindings.

"I've got this," Zoey said, managing to stand with her feet tied together. She hobbled over to the minibar and got her hands on a corkscrew, using it to cut the hard plastic zip tie. Soon she and Chris were free.

Chris and Zoey grabbed Hazlitt under the arms and dragged him into the room. Chris returned to the hallway to retrieve Hazlitt's gun, alert in case Dylan returned.

"Where were you hit?" Chris asked. His shirt was so soaked in blood that it was hard to tell.

Hazlitt pointed weakly at his left shoulder, his left thigh, and his right hand. Chris opened up Hazlitt's shirt and rolled up the left pants leg to examine the wounds. He was losing a lot of blood but he might live—if he got immediate medical attention. That was a big if on that particular night in New York City.

Zoey kneeled down next to Falacci and checked his wrist for a pulse. "It's there, but it's very weak," she said.

Hazlitt lifted his head with what seemed like a great deal of effort. "He's getting away," he said.

Sensing Chris's next question, Zoey said, "I can try to get medical help for them and treat their wounds. I can handle that."

Chris didn't want to leave Zoey alone to care for the agents, but he also didn't want to let Dylan escape. Now that he had savored the chaos he had caused, Dylan probably had an exit strategy that would get him out of the country. If he had any sense, he would go to ground and not show himself in public again for months, if not years. He would be replacing Chris and Zoey at the top of every most-wanted list.

"Okay," Chris said. "I'll try to send help back here, but you'd better also make your own arrangements." He knew there was a decent chance that he wouldn't be coming back, and he didn't want Hazlitt and Falacci to bleed out while they waited for him.

"But before you go, drop your pants," Zoey said.

Zoey tied two pillow cases together then secured them tightly around Chris's thigh where he had taken the bullet.

"Can you walk on that?" Zoey asked.

Chris put his weight on the leg to test it and still felt a stab of pain, but not so acute as before. "That'll work. Thanks."

Zoey reached out and touched his shoulder.

Chris retraced their steps down the dark hallway and descended through the stairwell to the hotel lobby. He gripped the railing with one hand and held Hazlitt's gun in the other. He wasn't sure how good a shot he would be if he caught up with Dylan. He doubted that Dylan was a good shot either, but you didn't have to be with that sort of automatic weapon, which could empty an entire clip in seconds.

The hotel lobby was quiet and dark. The evacuation that had been proceeding earlier seemed to be complete. Chris needed to move quickly to catch up with Dylan, but he couldn't move too quickly, in case he was lying in wait. Chris advanced through the lobby with his gun raised and entered the restaurant. He knocked over a chair in the dark and it clattered, badly startling him. He paused to listen for a responsive sound. If Dylan was

362 • THE ADVERSARY

waiting for him, then he'd lost any element of surprise. But the room was silent except for the faint crackling of the car fire outside, and Chris decided that he was alone.

Chris emerged through the smashed front door of the restaurant into Times Square. There were only a few people milling about. By now, most ordinary citizens had found a safe place where they could wait for the power to come back. Those who remained didn't look like the usual tourists. They looked like natives and they were walking with a sense of purpose.

Chris scanned the square for a sign of Dylan. He didn't have that big of a lead on Chris, but he could have taken off in any direction and disappeared down one of the many avenues that converged at Times Square. He wanted to get the police involved in tracking down Dylan, but, surprisingly, there were none visible on the street.

Chris hid the gun in his jacket pocket and walked around the hotel to the main entrance, where two doorman were still on duty out front. They watched him advance, smoking cigarettes to keep warm.

"I've got two injured people who need immediate medical attention," Chris said. "They're law enforcement officers—FBI agents."

A beefy, red-faced doorman tossed down his cigarette and stubbed it out with his shoe. "Where are they?"

"Room 217."

"What sort of injuries?"

"Multiple gunshot wounds. Both are hurt pretty bad."

"How'd that happen?"

"I don't know."

"Okay," the man said with a slight tilt of an eyebrow to show that he wasn't an idiot and he recognized the evasion.

"I think we've got a doctor and a couple of nurses across the street in the ballroom of the Marriott. We can see if we can get someone over here."

The other doorman exchanged a look with his red-faced partner, nodding at the blood that was seeping through Chris's pants leg. "Carl," he said.

"You look like you could use some help yourself," Carl said.

"I'm fine," Chris said, "but do you know where I can find the police?"

"No, I think every available resource is being directed at the fire," Carl said, nodding toward the glowing horizon. "Tudor City is burning."

"Why don't you come inside and someone can take a look at that. And if you need the police, we can try to call them."

"Thanks, but I've got something I need to do."

There was a burst of automatic weapon fire from somewhere in the distance and all three men flinched. Chris was no ballistics expert, but he thought he recognized the same quick burst that he had heard in the hotel hallway. It could have been a TEC-9.

When Chris had collected himself, he realized that upon hearing the gunshots, his right hand had flown to the pocket that held his gun. This was not lost on the two doormen, and their hands were hovering near the pockets of their parkas.

Carl was now studying him very closely. "I'm going to assume that you're one of the good guys—unless you prove me wrong."

"I appreciate that," Chris said. "And now I'm going to move along." He withdrew his hand from his pocket and started backing away. "Remember, Room 217."

Carl lit a new cigarette as he watched Chris walk into Times Square and up Seventh Avenue in the direction of the shots. His partner had disappeared, hopefully to find a doctor.

Chris stood in the middle of the normally busy intersection of Seventh and Forty-Seventh and turned in a circle. A half a block away, Chris saw a figure in a leather jacket carrying a green nylon gym bag. Dylan was walking away from him toward Sixth Avenue, also known as the Avenue of the Americas, but natives usually didn't waste that many syllables.

Chris got out of the middle of the street, where he could be easily spotted, and began following Dylan, sticking close to the buildings. It was the Diamond District, so the street was lined with jewelers and not a single plate glass window was intact. After hearing the gunshots, Chris was half expecting to find a body, but Dylan had probably just fired a round to chase away a band of looters who had mistaken him for an easy victim.

He was feeling lightheaded from blood loss and his movements felt awkward and out of sync like he was a poorly tethered balloon in the Macy's parade. As Chris stalked Dylan through the nearly empty urban landscape, his feet crunching on broken glass from the shop windows, he was reminded of the postapocalyptic New York of the video game that he had seen when he visited the Hive in Barcelona. *First-Person Shooter.*

This is the ultimate first-person-shooter experience. If only it were a game.

The city was like a video game that night in more ways than one. Each block seemed like a new level, with distinct properties and obstacles. One block teemed with people and the next was nearly deserted. This particular stretch of Sixth Avenue was eerily quiet, with few people in sight. Chris recognized that the seemingly abrupt transitions might be a sign that blood loss was clouding his perceptions.

Chris put one foot mechanically in front of the other and drew inexorably closer to Dylan like he was on a conveyor belt. He would have said that it felt dreamlike, except that dreams didn't involve such excruciating pain.

Dylan reached the corner of Sixth Avenue. Chris ducked into a doorway, anticipating that he would look back from the corner to see if anyone was following, which he did. Chris didn't think he had been spotted, so when Dylan turned onto Sixth, he limped forward as best he could on his numb leg. He didn't see Dylan ahead of him on the sidewalk, nor anywhere else. He gazed up the long, dark alley of skyscrapers that ran all the way to Central Park. Chris slowed his pace as he moved up Sixth, nearing Rockefeller Center.

He was scanning the opposite sidewalk, so he didn't immediately notice when Dylan stepped out of a doorway twenty yards ahead of him. When Chris finally saw him, Dylan was standing in the middle of the sidewalk with the TEC-9 leveled at his chest.

"You shouldn't have followed me," Dylan said. "You could have gotten out of this alive."

Chris's hand hovered near his jacket pocket and he thought about reaching for his gun.

"I wouldn't try that. I may not be a great shot, but this bad boy makes it easy," Dylan said.

"Is it getting easier—killing people, I mean?"

"I'm not a killer, Chris," Dylan said. "You should know by now that's not what I'm about. Now, lift the gun out of your pocket with two fingers."

Chris removed the gun as instructed and held it away from him.

"Now put it down on the sidewalk—slowly."

Chris laid the gun down on the sidewalk.

"Now kick it into the street," Dylan said.

Chris kicked the gun and it skittered across the pavement of Sixth Avenue, giving off a couple of tiny sparks and coming to rest under a Mercedes that had been left parked in the street. Dylan smiled and started walking toward him slowly.

Chris heard footsteps behind him. He looked back to see a band of about twelve men, all armed, all with heavy backpacks that were undoubtedly loaded with stolen goods. The apparent leader of the crew was wearing a blue hooded sweatshirt under a black leather bomber jacket.

Chris was amazed at how quickly things had deteriorated in the hours since the blackout. He had seen a few isolated looters early on, but now they had given way to more sophisticated criminal enterprises like the group that was now advancing on Chris. They were clearly well armed, organized, and determined to steal as much as possible before the city's lights came back up.

The gang's leader, who had short, curly, black hair and heavy-lidded eyes, clocked Chris as a harmless civilian and they ignored him, flowing around him on the sidewalk—until they saw Dylan and his TEC-9. That brought them all to a dead stop, with their guns raised.

"I'm not looking for trouble," Dylan said, lowering the muzzle of his gun. He knew he was outnumbered and outgunned.

"Neither are we, so why don't you drop your gun?" the leader said. "What is that, a TEC-9?"

"Yeah," Dylan said, backing up toward the corner. "I'm just going to get out of your way here."

While the gang leader clearly coveted the TEC-9, he didn't seem to want it badly enough to pursue Dylan. It wasn't worth a firefight, especially not on this night when everything else came so easily. Chris was alarmed to see that the standoff was quickly resolving itself. Unless he did something, the gang was going to proceed on its way and Dylan was going to finish what he started.

Chris spoke up, his voice hoarse and strange-sounding to him. "He's got half a million dollars in that gym bag."

The man in the black leather jacket stopped again and so did his crew. He nodded and his companions kept their guns trained on Dylan, then he turned to face Chris.

"What did you say?"

"I said that he has half a million dollars in that gym bag."

"And you know this how?"

"Because I saw it." This was not quite true, but Dylan had said that the money was in the bag when they were at the hotel.

The man addressed Dylan now. "Is what he says true?"

While they were speaking, Dylan had continued to slowly back away, putting more distance between himself and the gang. He was probably trying to figure out at what point he could make a run for it without getting instantly gunned down.

"No, he's a liar. He's playing you."

"Now why would he do that?"

"Because I was about to kill him," Dylan said, shrugging it off like he was confessing a traffic violation. He sensed that, at least with respect to a matter like that, he could confide in these gentlemen.

The gang leader rubbed his hands together for warmth, taking a moment to evaluate the situation. His breath condensed in tiny white clouds. Chris knew that his life hung in the balance.

Finally, he spoke to Dylan. "I could ask you why you want to kill this guy, but I don't really give a shit. Open the bag."

"Why would you believe him over me?" Dylan asked.

"Just open the bag."

Before he could ask again, Dylan made a run for it, dashing around the corner and into the main concourse of Rockefeller Center, which dead-ended in the gray tower of 30 Rock. The gang set out after Dylan, their shoes clattering on the sidewalk as they disappeared around the corner.

Two members of the crew stayed behind with Chris, urging him forward at a walking pace, which was the best that he could manage, anyway. The pair didn't have much to say to him or each other. They were tall, sinewy city kids who looked like they had mastered petty larceny and B&E and were ready to graduate to the next level.

Somewhere up ahead, Chris heard bursts of automatic weapon fire, with replies from several handguns. The gunfire continued as Chris limped down the main concourse of Rockefeller Center past the shops, his escorts right behind him. They finally arrived at the railing that looked down on the sunken plaza with the ice-skating rink, glowing white in the moonlight and casting its own pale illumination. They took a set of stairs down to the rink and stood at a low railing next to the ice.

The last shots seemed to have come from the offices that adjoined the opposite end of the skating rink—a series of single reports with no response from the TEC-9. Chris wondered if the firefight was over.

The two men stood at the railing, waiting to see who would emerge.

Chris said to them, "I'm going to have to sit . . ." Before he could finish the sentence, a lightheadedness came over him and he crumpled to the sidewalk at their feet. If his life was a movie, then he had just experienced a jump cut. One moment he was standing, the next he was on the sidewalk concentrating on trying to hoist his eyelids.

"Should we get him up?"

"Not until we have to go. He doesn't look like he's going anywhere."

Chris stared up at the two thugs looming over him. He wondered if he was dying, considering the question with a surprising degree of detachment.

A burst of automatic weapon fire ruptured the silence. Chris waited for his two captors to return fire, but instead they simply collapsed. The bodies of the two men lay crumpled on either side of him.

I need to get up. Whoever shot them is probably coming over here to make sure everyone is dead.

Chris tried to lift his head, but either his skull had grown very heavy or his neck had grown very weak. Either way, it seemed to be a nonstarter.

The handgun of one of the men lay beside Chris. It was within reach, and he got his hand around the stippled grip.

I need to get on my feet.

Chris managed to sit up and, with the bit of strength he had left, pushed himself up off the sidewalk. As he rose, there was a moment when his eyes swam and he might have blacked out, but he didn't. He grabbed the railing next to the ice rink with one hand for support.

When Chris looked out on the ice, he saw Dylan awkwardly trudging toward him, the TEC-9 in one hand and the green gym bag in the other. He had apparently been cornered and saw the ice as his only escape route. His pursuers were not yet in sight. Maybe they were dead.

Dylan was wearing sneakers on the ice and he seemed to be on the verge of slipping with every step, waddling in a comical wide-legged stance for balance. When Dylan saw Chris appear before him at the railing, he smiled like someone who had just gotten lucky. Dylan started to raise his gun to take aim at Chris.

"Hey, asshat!" Dylan spun around to see Zoey standing above them at the railing looking down into the rink. As he turned, Dylan pulled the trigger and sent a spray of bullets in her direction. An instant later, Zoey was no longer standing at the railing.

Dylan turned back to Chris, bringing the barrel of the TEC-9 around. But, slow and groggy as he was, Chris had now managed to lift his gun and take aim at Dylan. Chris pulled the trigger and the shot boomed in the partial enclosure of the skating rink.

When Chris regained his bearings from the recoil, he saw Dylan staring at him from the center of the ice. Chris didn't see a wound and wondered if he had missed. Then Dylan coughed and a spot of blood appeared on his chin. A surprised, anxious look flashed across his face before he fell. Chris had seen that expression before—on the face of fourteen-year-old Dylan at Josh Woodrell's house in the summer of 1987.

Chris didn't wait to see what happened next. Somehow, he struggled up the steps to the upper railing to find Zoey. When Chris reached ground level, he saw Zoey sprawled and motion-less on the sidewalk, and his heart sank. He dropped to his knees beside her and saw that her eyes were open. They opened wider when he came into view and she saw that he was still alive.

"I heard the gunshot and . . ." She was unable to finish the sentence.

"It's okay. I'm okay."

"I'm cold," she said, visibly shivering.

"You just keep your eyes open. You're going to be okay. Where were you hit?"

"I don't mean I'm cold as in 'I'm dying.' I mean that it's freaking cold lying on this pavement. I haven't been shot. I tripped and banged my head."

Chris managed a smile. "What are you doing here, anyway?"

"A doctor got there pretty fast for the agents, so I followed you. The doormen sent me this way."

"Very ill-advised, but thank you."

Chris and Zoey descended the steps to the ice rink to see if Dylan was still alive. Zoey put Chris's arm on her shoulder so that he could brace himself as they made their way across the ice. Chris leaned down over Dylan's body.

Dylan's eyes opened.

He spoke with effort through teeth smeared with blood. "It's not over. Not even close."

"What do you mean?"

"I activated a second strain of the virus just a little while ago. The target is the Indian Point nuclear power plant." He coughed. "Guess I win after all, huh?" With that, Dylan's eyes closed.

Chris felt for a pulse, but Dylan was gone.

He looked up to see the gang leader and his men advancing carefully across the ice.

"He dead?" the leader asked.

Chris nodded.

The man zipped open the gym bag and lifted out a laptop, setting it down on the ice. He plunged his hand into the bag again, and drew out a couple of fat stacks of banded hundreds. Performing a rough tally of the money in the bag, he seemed satisfied with the contents.

Before he could put the laptop back in the bag, Chris asked, "Could I have that laptop . . . as a finder's fee? I could use a new one."

The man considered for a moment, then said, "Sure, take it. You earned it."

The man and his crew crossed the rink and walked briskly away into the night like last-minute shoppers looking to check the last items off their Christmas lists before the shelves were bare.

"Indian Point," said Zoey. "That nuclear plant's only like— what?—thirty-five miles from Manhattan."

"If a virus caused a nuclear disaster there, then the radioactivity would reach the city."

"And you can't evacuate New York."

The scenarios were unthinkable. The Chernobyl nuclear disaster had left the town of Pripyat in Belarus a radioactive ghost town, uninhabitable nearly thirty years later. The Fukushima Daiichi event had done the same thing to the Japanese town of Okuma. But both of those meltdowns had occurred far from a major population center. Chris couldn't even begin to contemplate the consequences if a nuclear disaster at Indian Point sent a radioactive cloud over Manhattan and the nation's most densely populated areas.

Zoey stared at Dylan's laptop like it was a live grenade. "You think he launched the new virus from that?"

"I do," Chris said. He picked up the laptop and carried it over to the steps next to the rink. "I'm going to work on this," he said, sitting down on the steps. "You get on your phone and see if you can get through to someone at Indian Point."

Chris opened the laptop and saw that it was password-protected. Since he hadn't known Dylan for the past thirty years, the chances that he could guess his password were slim, but he was going to try.

Chris typed in "Lothar," the German Shepherd that Dylan had loved when he was fourteen. "ACCESS DENIED." Even hackers could be careless enough to use a pet's name as a password.

He tried several variations on Josh Woodrell's name—"Josh-Woodrell," "JWoodrell," "WoodrellJ." "ACCESS DENIED."

Chris keyed in "Enigma," "Ripley," and "Blanksy." "ACCESS DENIED."

A different approach occurred to Chris and he carefully entered the numbers "81687." "ACCESS DENIED."

He was growing desperate, running out of ideas. He tried a variation on the last attempt—"081687"—not expecting much, just unwilling to give up. And a moment later, he was staring at the desktop of Dylan's laptop.

"I'm in," Chris said to Zoey. 081687. August 16, 1987. The date that Chris, Josh, and Dylan had accessed the DOD database and altered the course of their lives. "How's it going over there?"

"I've reached someone and told them we had information about the cyberattack. They put me on hold. I think he's trying to find his boss."

"This laptop is encrypted," Chris said. "I've gotten past the password protection, but now I'm stuck."

"Let's trade places," Zoey said. "I've got this."

Chris took the phone. Zoey sat down at the laptop and her fingers began flying over the keys.

"Who am I speaking with?" It was a woman's voice on the phone. In the background, he could hear agitated voices and a strident alarm sounding.

"This is Chris Bruen. I'm a lawyer and I've been tracking a hacker who just told me that he launched a computer virus attack on Indian Point."

"You're with the FBI? Homeland Security?" Chris noted that she didn't react with surprise to the talk of a computer virus. She already knew what was happening.

"No. Who am I speaking with?"

"This is Althea Winfield, nuclear facilities manager. I need you to tell me why I should be listening to you. Because I have other things I should be doing right now."

"I am—was—a partner in the San Francisco office of the law firm Reynolds, Fincher & McComb. I'm also a former Department of Justice cyber crimes prosecutor. I've spent my entire career tracking down hackers. When you check me out, you're going to find out that there are plenty of reasons for you not to trust me. The FBI has been pursuing me. They think I caused this attack."

"But you say you didn't."

"Right."

There was silence on the other end of the line. "So why should I believe anything that you have to say?"

"Because the person who launched the virus that is attacking your plant just died and I have his laptop. There's a chance—maybe—that we can stop the virus."

"Who's we?"

"I'm working with someone. She's the one who spoke to your colleague. Right now she's trying to decrypt the laptop."

"Okay, I'm listening," Winfield said. "I'm not saying I trust you or believe you, but I'm listening."

"What's happening at the plant? How bad is it?"

"I'm not going to tell you any more than what the press already has. We seem to have a malfunction in the cooling system for the spent fuel pool. The water in the pool is boiling away and if the spent fuel rods are exposed to the air, then there's the potential for a release of radioactive gas."

"So there would be a meltdown?"

"I didn't use that term," Winfield said. "Now start talking."

"Does your cooling system use Sonnen programmable logic controllers?"

"Yeah. Why?"

"Because this virus attacks those PLCs."

"Hmm. What am I supposed to do with that information? The cooling system is already shut down."

"Got it!" Zoey shouted.

"We've just cracked the encryption, so we have access to the laptop now. Hang on. I'll be back."

Chris looked over Zoey's shoulder at what appeared to be a dashboard of controls. "Would you look at this," Zoey said. "When he called this the iPad of terrorism, he wasn't kidding. This thing is very user-friendly."

It was true. The dashboard that controlled the virus looked a lot like iTunes, with clear labels and buttons. Zoey pointed to the banner over the dashboard that read "Arrowhead Virus."

"Arrowhead. Indian Point. I get it," Chris said.

"I think it must be this button here," Zoey said. "It says 'ACTIVATE/DEACTIVATE.'"

"But how is this going to work? The nuclear plant's systems would have to be connected to the Internet to receive a deactivation signal. They're going to be air-gapped."

In order to guard against computer viruses and hackers, most highly sensitive computer assets, like nuclear reactor systems, are "air-gapped," meaning that they are entirely freestanding systems that are not connected to the Internet or other computer systems. Somehow, Dylan's crew had managed to install the virus on Indian Point's systems, overcoming the air gap.

Chris returned to the phone. "I think we may have a way to deactivate the virus."

"Then do it," Winfield said.

"I'm going to need your help. You'll have to connect your systems to the Internet. We need to get past the air gap."

"There is no way I am going to do that!" Winfield said, nearly shouting.

"I think we can send a deactivation signal to stop the virus, but we can't do that if we can't connect."

"Look, Bruen, for all I know this is all just an elaborate social engineering tactic. Do you really expect me to connect you to our systems and put you in a position where you could do even more damage? That *is not* going to happen. Do you hear me?"

Chris recognized that he was going to have to try another angle. "Is the NSA involved yet?"

Winfield cooled down quickly. "Yes, they know what's happening."

"Are you dealing with a man named Louis Vogel?"

"I don't know who that is."

"But you're speaking with an NSA agent?"

"Yes."

"Tell him what I just told you. Tell him to contact Vogel and ask for approval to connect your systems to the Internet. He knows who I am." Chris knew that Vogel was probably getting detailed reports on the manhunt from Hazlitt and Falacci. He strongly suspected that Hazlitt knew he was being framed but didn't have the authority to act on that suspicion. Louis Vogel, the NSA official so high-ranking that he didn't have a title, would have that authority.

"The Nuclear Regulatory Commission operates this plant, not the NSA . . ." Winfield stopped, recognizing that this was no time for jurisdictional pissing contests. "Okay, I'll talk to the NSA guy."

Chris waited on the line for several minutes. When Winfield returned, she said, "Okay, we've confirmed your identity with voice-recognition software. It looks like you are who you say you are. And Mr. Vogel says to do what you say. Personally, I don't get it, but I guess he knows some things that I don't."

Winfield was off the line again for a few minutes. When she returned, she said, "We're in the process of connecting the system to the Internet. Just hang on. Shouldn't be long."

Chris heard a bang like a door slamming and a loud male voice in the background. "What the hell do you think you're doing? Why don't you just put up a sign that says 'Hackers Welcome'?"

"Excuse me for a minute," Winfield said to Chris.

Chris heard Winfield addressing the man, who had apparently just stormed into her office. "Listen, Harvey, you think I don't understand your point? I understand the importance of the air gap. But you're going to have to trust me that this is our best chance of shutting this thing down."

"My family lives just five miles from here and—"

"This is my community, too, Harvey. I live in Peekskill with my eight-year-old daughter. You think I don't get it?" Her voice rose several decibels as she added, "We're doing this and you need to get back to your work station *now.*"

Chris wasn't able to hear Harvey's response, but Winfield returned to the phone a minute later.

"We're connected," she said, giving him a URL so that the deactivation code could be transmitted directly into the nuclear plant's cooling system.

Chris stood behind Zoey as she placed her finger over the Enter key of the laptop. "Chris, this could be another trap."

"I know, but we're going to have to take that risk."

Zoey pressed the key.

"The deactivation signal has been sent," Chris said to Winfield.

Silence on the other end of the line. "Nothing's happening," she said.

"Where do things stand?"

"The spent fuel pool is forty feet deep. The fuel rods are stored in the bottom fourteen feet, and if the water level goes down to eight feet—then we have a problem."

"What's the water level at right now?"

"Twelve feet." A warning siren was still droning insistently in the background.

More silence as Winfield watched the monitors.

"Wait a second," she said. "The cooling system is starting to work. It's working."

"Is it over?"

"We're not out of the woods yet. The water level is still dropping. I don't know if the cooling system can kick in fast enough to stop it from boiling off and exposing the rods."

"So we're just waiting?"

"We're waiting."

"What's the level at now?"

"Ten feet."

Winfield continued the countdown. "Nine point six feet."

"Nine point two feet."

"Eight point eight feet."

Zoey had left the laptop and was standing with Chris now, both of them just staring at the phone, which was on speaker.

"Eight point four feet."

A long pause, then "Eight point four feet."

Another pause.

"Still at eight point four feet. We're stabilized. The event is contained."

Chris and Zoey heard a cheer go up in the background at the plant over the tinny phone speaker.

"Chris," Winfield said. "Are you a drinking man?"

"Yes, I am, Althea."

"Then I am going to buy you a drink when we meet."

★ ★ ★

Zoey helped Chris climb back up the steps to the concourse. He had lost a great deal of blood and was in need of immediate medical attention. Chris needed to rest for a moment at the railing and they both looked down into the ice-skating rink.

A pool of bright red blood seeped from beneath Dylan and extended a tendril across the ice. Overhead, the gilded, bronze statue of Prometheus bringing fire to mankind looked down. On the granite wall behind the statute was the inscription "Prometheus, teacher in every art, brought the fire that hath proved to mortals a means to mighty ends."

CHAPTER 52

When Chris first returned to his job at Reynolds, Fincher & McComb, his leg ached so badly that he took a taxi to work, even though he lived only six blocks from the office. Now, after two weeks back, he was walking to the office again, taking a long route to strengthen his muscles, looping down by AT&T Park and then up the Embarcadero. Chris slipped in earbuds to listen to Glenn Gould's bravura 1955 recording of Bach's *Goldberg Variations*. This was the virtuoso performance that revolutionized the way Bach was played, so different from Gould's somber 1981 recording of the same piece.

It was a crisp, sunny March day and the city seemed to be just as he had left it. The Bay Bridge towered directly overhead and the cranes of the Oakland waterfront were in view across the Bay. Chris always thought they resembled giant rocking horses. A breeze was blowing and every ripple on the Bay was catching the sunlight. Gazing at the scene, Chris understood

Van Gogh's frame of mind when he painted those landscapes where every blade of grass seemed to be pulsing and trembling.

He felt a stab of pain, though, remembering that his friend Ed would have no more days like this one. During the mad dash across continents to hunt down Dylan Nunn, he didn't have time to properly mourn the death of his colleague and friend, but in the past few weeks the full force of it had hit him. Chris felt responsible for involving Ed in his investigation of the Lurker virus after his suspension from the firm. But Chris also knew that it would have been impossible to dissuade Ed from aiding his friend. He carried Ed's loss with him like the dull ache in his leg, but he knew that, unlike the leg, the wound would never fully heal.

He stopped to watch four fishing boats that had come in close to shore following a school of sardines dipping their nets in and hauling them up flowing with gleaming liquid silver. The gulls had also taken note of the school and were diving into the water to catch the fish that fell from the nets.

Chris still couldn't quite believe that he had been allowed to return to his old life and job. Just a couple of months ago, he thought he would spend the rest of his days in a federal prison—if he was lucky. The fact that Chris was a free man was due in part to his answering machine, which *had* recorded the conversation between Dylan, Chris, and Zoey in the W Hotel. Dylan's words had been a bit muffled and Chris had been afraid that he wouldn't have the evidence to exonerate himself. With a little bit of digital enhancement from the FBI's audio experts, however, Dylan's words came into sharp focus. Chris figured that Dylan couldn't help himself—revenge just isn't revenge unless the person knows why you did it.

But Chris didn't have to rely entirely on the answering machine recording for his exoneration. After all, he had stopped Dylan and averted the cyberattack on the Indian Point nuclear plant. He had been interrogated for weeks by agents from the FBI, CIA, NSA, and Department of Homeland Security, but no extreme tactics were used. From the outset of the interviews, it had been clear that the agencies recognized how instrumental he had been in understanding Lurker and tracking down Dylan. He was not treated as one of Dylan's accomplices, but that didn't mean that the process hadn't been arduous. Call it a very, very thorough debriefing.

Some at the agencies apparently believed that Chris should have been criminally prosecuted for running from the authorities and impeding a federal investigation. But he had it on good authority that Louis Vogel at NSA had intervened on his behalf. It also didn't hurt that Dave Silver's company BlueCloud happened to be the largest IT vendor to the federal government and had some influence with the agencies. Chris had grown to appreciate that being friends with Silver was like having a super-rich, influence-peddling, high-tech demigod in your corner. To call Silver a Master of the Universe would have been a slight.

In the end, Chris was allowed to walk, so long as he signed the scariest nondisclosure agreement that he had ever seen. Vogel probably recognized that if they locked Chris up and the press ever figured out why he was in prison, Chris would be portrayed as a martyred hero. Hunting down Dylan had been a big win for the FBI and several other agencies, and no one wanted Chris stealing even a sliver of the spotlight.

It also helped that Dylan's story checked out. The FBI unsealed the records of Chris's juvenile offense and reviewed the Firefly tax return fraud case—the connections between Dylan, Josh, and Chris were all substantiated. The file's mug shots showed Josh's shockingly sallow, sunken face. Meth seemed to have accelerated his aging process by about twenty years. Josh glared into the police camera with a crazed grin that seemed to be saying, *Go ahead, hit me again.*

As Chris walked farther north along the Embarcadero, he arrived at one of his favorite dives, Red's Java House, a white clapboard shack that had been precariously perched on Pier 30 for decades. With its weathered wooden floorboards, red vinyl stools, dull Formica countertops, and framed photos of San Francisco luminaries like Bill Graham and Patty Hearst, Red's was the anti-Starbucks, and Chris liked it for exactly that reason. He took his first sip of coffee of the morning, warming his hands on the white cardboard cup. As he was leaving, a couple of pigeons, two more regulars, fluttered inside to scavenge their breakfast from the floor.

During one of the interrogations, an FBI agent had been kind enough to provide an update on the condition of the two agents that had saved his life. Hazlitt and Falacci had survived their gunshot wounds at the W Hotel. Falacci's injuries were severe enough that he had been placed on disability. He would probably be taking an early retirement.

New York, a city that knows how to take a punch, had also survived that night in January. Power and heat were restored in all neighborhoods of the city within six days of the attack. Within two weeks, the city was back to its old furious, hurtling self. The attack had resulted in 184 fatalities. Twenty-six people died in the subway car collision. Five more died from inhaling chlorine gas from the breached chemical plant. Several died in car accidents due to failed traffic lights. A few of the elderly died from the cold when their heat went out. Still others perished because they failed to get needed medical care during the blackout.

Even though BlueCloud promptly issued a security patch to fix the Port 583 vulnerability, that didn't stop its stock price from plummeting when the press reported that a weakness in its system had led to the cyberattack on New York. But the feds had acknowledged BlueCloud's cooperation in their investigation and it helped that the primary culprit had been stopped. BlueCloud's aura of invincibility had been severely dented, but the public still seemed to love their products. It appeared that BlueCloud would continue to be the world's leading computer company. Dave Silver, who fully realized just how bad things could have been for his company without Chris's efforts, now referred to Chris as his "wartime consigliere."

The Lurker attack did accomplish some of what Dylan intended. It put the world on notice that a new era of cyberterrorism had begun. The event also focused attention on the need to better secure the nation's critical infrastructure against cyber threats. The proliferation of smart grid devices, such as the smart meters installed in homes, had made the electricity infrastructure more interconnected, but that connectivity had also made the system more vulnerable to attack. A bill had already been introduced in the Senate that would appropriate funds for a comprehensive upgrade of cyber defenses for key power grids, public transportation systems, and chemical and nuclear plants.

A Congressional investigation of the cyberattack also revealed how Dylan and his crew had gotten past the air-gapped systems at Indian Point nuclear power plant using a decidedly low-tech approach. A few flash drives containing the virus had been dropped in the facility's parking lot, marked to indicate that they contained documents relating to plant operations. As soon as a curious employee picked up the flash drive and plugged it into his work station, Lurker had found its mark.

As the press investigated the origins of the Lurker virus, questions were raised as to whether it was derived from the US-developed Stuxnet virus. The National Security Agency made a statement in which it acknowledged that the Lurker virus represented a new level of sophistication for computer viruses and pledged to combat acts of "cyber aggression." The NSA never responded, though, to the charge that the government had created the Stuxnet cyberweapon only to have it turned against its own citizens in the form of Lurker. Governments don't just come right out and admit their mistakes—that was what the press was for, and it was digging.

Chris sipped his black coffee as he continued up the Embarcadero toward the fog-colored column of the Ferry Building, where the clock in the tower read 8:40. People were moving with a sense of purpose to make it to their desks by 9:00. As a partner in a law firm, he had no boss to glower at him if he showed up at 10:00 or even 11:00. But, in the end, it was a moot point, because the press of client demands kept him coming in well before 9:00 on most days.

He crossed the Embarcadero and the open concrete expanse of Justin Herman Plaza, passed the Vaillancourt Fountain, which resembled a bunch of giant, corroded ventilation ducts, and entered the lobby of 4 Embarcadero Center.

Chris emerged from the elevator into the firm's thirty-eighth-floor reception area, which was bright with sunlight from the floor-to-ceiling windows. He saw managing partner Don Rubinowski standing and talking with a cluster of the attorneys, their suits punching black holes in the bright panorama of the Bay that was spread out behind them.

Don nodded at Chris as he passed by. Things had been a little awkward since he had returned to the firm. Everyone thought that he must hold a grudge over the way they had summarily suspended him when the FBI declared him a suspect in the threatened attack. Chris understood completely—it was just business. What corporate client would want to retain a law firm that had a potential terrorist among its partners? Chris knew that Don considered him a friend, but he couldn't jeopardize the livelihood of the other partners by backing him, especially when all appearances indicated that he was guilty as hell. Chris didn't hold a grudge, because he knew that being a partner in a big law firm is a little like swimming in a school of sharks—even though they seem to be working together, one shark does not sacrifice itself for another. Chris just acted as if nothing had happened and waited for everyone to start behaving normally.

Chris was pretty sure that Don would always hold him at least partly responsible for the trouble that he had gotten himself into. After all, as Don had so pointedly noted, he had no business sleeping with one of the firm's paralegals to begin with.

Being back in the office brought frequent reminders of Sarah. He had learned that Sarah had been using her real name at the firm. She had moved to Sacramento from Boston, and she and Dylan had dated for a time. The romantic relationship had faded but their partnership as the hackers Ripley and Enigma lasted more than twenty years, with Josh Woodrell joining the criminal enterprise later. Dylan's story about the death of Sarah's brother in Afghanistan checked out. Jim Hotchner had been shot and killed by an Afghan police officer, along with three other American special forces soldiers, at a base outside Kabul.

As far as the firm was concerned, Sarah had simply moved on to a new job somewhere and never provided a forwarding address. His partners never learned that they had hired a hacker and terrorist. Chris knew that Sarah had to be in federal

388 • THE ADVERSARY

custody, but his inquiries about her status were stonewalled. The facility that housed Sarah probably did not, at least in any officially recognized capacity, exist.

In the wake of the cyberattack on New York, Homeland Security and a host of other agencies had dedicated themselves to hunting down Dylan's cohorts with a zeal previously reserved for al-Qaeda. Most of the hacker crew, including Soma, had already been apprehended in a series of arrests from Amsterdam to the Ukraine to Barcelona. The identities of most of the remaining hackers in the crew were known, and they were running for their lives.

Chris arrived at the door to the computer forensic lab and was visited once again by memories of Ed de Lamadrid. As he entered the lab, Chris half expected to see Ed gliding around from one monitor to another in his favorite black leather desk chair. Instead, he was greeted by the lab's new director. She was wearing a Bikini Kill T-shirt under a gray cardigan, jeans, and black Converse All Stars—Zoey. She swiveled around from her three-monitor setup and smiled her crooked smile.

"You don't even have to say it," she said.

"Did I say anything?" Chris asked.

"You were radiating disapproval."

"Has Don seen what you're wearing today?"

"Oh, yeah, he saw it."

"Did he say anything?"

"He just got that sort of tight-faced look he gets. I think he needs to dial down the Botox."

Chris put a fist to his forehead in mock hopelessness. Zoey laughed. "Hey, you know what I told you going in . . ."

"Yeah, right," Chris said. "You don't do corporate."

Zoey nodded and returned to scrutinizing her monitors. Chris could tell that Zoey was beginning to enjoy her work at the firm, in no small part because her presence irritated so many members of firm management. Although a few misgivings were expressed about Zoey's attitude and hacker past, Chris was allowed to bring her in as Ed's replacement because he had leverage with the firm after they wrongly suspended him. His partners knew that Zoey and Chris had collaborated on the investigation of the Lurker virus and, if they weren't going to hold the episode against Chris, then they couldn't really hold it against Zoey, either.

Zoey had drifted through her twenties and half of her thirties without focus, unable to find anything that matched her very unique skill set and temperament. Chris knew just how grateful she was for the opportunity, even though it would take months, maybe even years, before she fully copped to it. He could wait.

Chris was glad she took the job. Ed's presence still seemed to haunt the forensics lab, but at least now he felt like a friendly ghost. He was pretty sure Ed would have approved of his successor.

Most people of Chris's age trailed a few ghosts with them through life—the people lost along the way. For Chris, however, they took the form of a nightly CNN panel show. After Tana's death, he had taken to tuning the television to CNN while he slept. He found the drone of the murmuring voices comforting. Over time, though, the cast of talking heads had melded with his dreams, morphing into a panel of commentators comprised of his dead friends, family members, and acquaintances.

The undead pundits mostly offered point-counterpoint commentary on his day's events. The panel included his mother and father—there was love there, but the relationships were not without complexity. Ed was there, too, benignly giving him shit as usual.

But his dead wife, Tana, was the one true fixture on the panel. When the topic of Zoey came up, as it often did recently, Tana followed the discussion with a smile. Occasionally, in an aside to the television audience, she rolled her eyes at him in one of her signature mannerisms. Chris suspected that she liked the way that Zoey kept him off-balance, just like she used to. She didn't want him to be alone anymore, and she certainly didn't want him to feel guilty for having lived through cancer.

"Still watching for signs of the Lurker virus, but it hasn't returned," Zoey said. "I also just got off the phone with Sirius Security Consulting in Berlin and they haven't seen anything, either."

"I'm hoping that it died with Dylan, but you never know," Chris said. "He clearly had a large team working with him."

"But then again, he also had trust issues," Zoey said. "After all, Pietr Middendorf had already betrayed him and he felt the need to stage that scene in Amsterdam to send a message to the rest of the crew. You don't send that kind of message to people you trust."

"Maybe without Dylan the auction of the Lurker virus never took place," Chris said. "If so, there are a lot of disappointed terrorist organizations out there."

"I feel their pain," Zoey said.

"But the precedent's been set. Weaponized viruses are a reality now and the whole world knows it. Every fringe group on earth wants one."

"Yep. Like Dylan said—the iPad of terrorism."

They worked in silence for a while. Chris reviewed a report on their investigation of an employee's theft of a database of more than three hundred and fifty thousand Social Security numbers from a client. Thanks to Zoey's forensic work on the employee's laptop, they would be able to demonstrate what was stolen and how with a certainty that would stand up in court. At the other end of the lab, Zoey was hunched over her monitors with her bulky silver headphones on, head bobbing slightly.

Zoey slid the headphones down around her neck. "Come over here. You should see this."

Chris walked over and stood behind Zoey, looking at the screen, his hands on the back of her chair in a familiar gesture. "What am I looking at?"

"Something new," Zoey said. "This malware has shown up in all of our honey traps in the last twenty-four hours." The honey traps were dummy servers maintained by the lab to troll for the latest viruses.

"And?"

"Look," Zoey said, nodding at the screen. Characters and numbers were cascading across the three monitors.

"How many antivirus programs have you run?"

"Twenty-three so far."

"Hmm," Chris said. He knew that there were only about thirty-two serious AV programs. If this bit of malware wasn't recognized by any of them, then they were looking at something new in the world—and new viruses were far and away the most dangerous. A new virus exploiting a previously undiscovered operating system vulnerability was what created a Zero Day event like the Lurker attack on New York.

Chris and Zoey sat down and simply watched in silence as the rest of the programs ran, streaming characters and numbers. This didn't happen very often and, when it did, it meant that something bad was on the way.

Finally, the programs stopped running. At the bottom of each screen was the message "UNKNOWN MALWARE."

Zoey slumped back in her chair. "You think this is Lurker 2.0?"

Chris frowned. "I knew this day was coming, but I just didn't expect it so soon. It's Zero Day again."

ACKNOWLEDGMENTS

I'd like to thank my agent and wartime consiglieri, David Hale Smith, for his belief in this book—and for finding me a new home at Thomas & Mercer. I'm grateful to the entire team at Thomas & Mercer—my editors, Courtney Miller and Alison Dasho, along with Jacque Ben-Zekry, Amara Holstein, Shannon Mitchell, and Marcus Trower, for providing the most author-friendly, collaborative, transparent, and enjoyable path to publication imaginable. I'm looking forward to working with them on the further adventures of Chris Bruen.

Ed Stackler provided his usual astute editorial insights after reading the first draft. Winston Krone, of Kivu Consulting, helped me get the data security details right (and any remaining errors are definitely on me). Jay Hershey and my law-firm partner, Ron Dreben, generously took the time to read early drafts, and their clear-eyed edits and input made this a much better book. Cyber warrior Shane McGee provided a reality check of the early chapters.

I owe a debt to several books that provided invaluable background on hackers, computer viruses, and Stuxnet, including *Confront and Conceal: Obama's Secret Wars and Surprising Use of American Power*, by David E. Sanger; *Worm: The First Digital World War*, by Mark Bowden; *We Are Anonymous: Inside the Hacker World of LulzSec, Anonymous and the Global Cyber Insurgency*, by Parmy Olson; and *The Art of Intrusion*, by Kevin D. Mitnick and William L. Simon.

As in most good things in my life, none of this would have been possible without the grace, patience, humor, and brilliance of my wife, Kathy. Especially the patience.

ABOUT THE AUTHOR

Reece Hirsch's first book, *The Insider*, was a finalist for the 2011 International Thriller Writers Award for Best First Novel. Like *The Adversary*, that book draws upon his experiences as an attorney—although his legal work is a lot less exciting and hazardous than that of his character Chris Bruen. Hirsch is a partner in the San Francisco office of an international law firm, specializing in privacy and data security law. He is also a member of the board of directors of 826 National (www.826National.org). Hirsch lives in the Bay Area with his wife and a small, unruly dog. www.reecehirsch.com

Printed in Great Britain
by Amazon